TAKING LIBERTIES

A RICHARD KASAK BOOK

TAKING LIBERTIES:

Gay Men's Essays on Politics, Culture, and Sex

EDITED BY MICHAEL BRONSKI

CREDITS

"Dumbed Down and Played Out" copyright © Bill Andriette, 1995. An earlier version of this essay appeared in *Steam: A Quarterly Journal for Men*. (Vol.2, No.1)

"from A Reluctant Journal" copyright © by the estate of Allen Barnett, 1995.

"Notes on Stonewall" copyright © Bruce Bawer, 1994. This essay originally appeared in *The New Republic*, June 13, 1994.

"Love with the Light On" copyright © Ron Caldwell, 1995.

"Silence, Language and Masculinity" copyright © Lawrence Chua, 1995. An earlier version of this essay was given at the OutWrite conference, The Park Plaza Hotel, Boston, Massachusetts, October 20, 1994.

Continued on page 469.

Taking Liberties: Gay Men's Essays on Politics, Culture, and Sex
Copyright © 1996 Michael Bronski

First Richard Kasak Book Edition 1996
First Printing October 1996

ISBN 1-56333-456-9

Manufactured in the United States of America
Published by Masquerade Books, Inc.
801 Second Avenue
New York, N.Y. 10017

Library of Congress Cataloging-in-Publication Data
Taking liberties: gay men's essays on politics, culture, and sex / edited by Michael
    Bronski. -- 1st Richard Kasak book ed.
        p.   cm.
    "A Richard Kasak book."
    Includes bibliographical references.
    ISBN 1-56333-456-9
    1. Gay men--United States--Attitudes. 2. Homosexuality, Male--United States. 3.
Gay rights--United States. 4. Gay men's writings. I. Bronski, Michael.
HQ76.2.U5T35 1996
305.38'9664--dc20
                                                                            96-28071
                                                                                CIP

Allen Barnett 1955—1991
Craig G. Harris 1957—1991
John Preston 1947—1994

TAKING LIBERTIES

Introduction by Michael Bronski   1

POLITICS   7

Notes on Stonewall   11
Bruce Bawer

The Politics of Homosexuality   23
Andrew Sullivan

A Socialism of the Skin (Liberation, Honey!)   49
Tony Kushner

Blight and Fruit   61
Scott Tucker

Speaking Parts   85
Lawrence Chua

SEX   95

Naming the Addiction   101
Vestal McIntyre

The Men From the Boys   109
Jesse Green

Dumbed Down and Played Out   145
Bill Andriette

What You Learn After Thirty Years of S/M   175
John Preston

Making Sex Public   187
Michael Lassell

Deliverance   201
Craig Hickman

LITERATURE   205

on pretentiousness   207
Tony Kushner

What We Write About When We Write About Porn   229
Christopher J. Hogan

Five Houses of Gay Fiction   247
Reed Woodhouse

How to Write a Short Story   275
Mitzel

AIDS   287

These Things   291
Jesse Green

Love With the Light On   297
Ron Caldwell

The Reluctant Journal   323
Allen Barnett

Rage, Rage   329
John Weir

IDENTITY   335

Malcolm X's Wild Side   339
Charley Shively

Danny   353
Rondo Mieczkowski

You're the First Person I've Ever Told   369
Larry Gross

Musical Closets   387
Lawrence D. Mass

I'm Going Out Like a Fucking Meteor   441
Craig G. Harris

Saying Kaddish for Peter   455
Michael Lowenthal

acknowledgments

Once again I find myself thanking all of those people who helped this book to move from piles of paper on my bed to what you are holding in your hand. That many of the names are repeated from my acknowledgments in *Flashpoint: Gay Male Sexual Writing* is a testament to the strength and durability of those friendships. Once again Michael Lowenthal came through with unconditional support, superb editing, and endless good advice. Chris Hogan provided friendship and a sharp sense of reality ("Why would you want to publish *that*?"), Tom Cole was there at all the right moments. Wickie Stamps was available whenever I needed to talk something through. Bill Andriette and my brother, Jeffrey Bronski, taught me more about computers than I ever wanted to learn; and what I didn't learn they did for me.

As before, Richard Kasak, Jennifer Reut, and Michele Karlsberg of Masquerade Books supplied generous deadlines and advice.

And, once again, even after the fact, to Walta Borawski for twenty years of love and support.

Introduction

In recent years—as issues of gay culture and politics have become more a staple of the mainstream press—it is fashionable to declare the existence of a single, cohesive, and unified gay viewpoint. It is not unusual to read in, say *The New York Times*, or *Newsweek*, phrases like "most people in the gay community think..." or "....is generally believed to have the support of the gay community." Such extravagantly staked claims are patently false. Anyone who has identified with and participated in the "gay community" knows that the very concept of a single-minded and consolidated community is so far from reality as to be, depending upon one's frame of mind, either a myth or a joke. In recent years the phrase "lesbian and gay communities" is in vogue. This describes not so much a gendered split but rather an attempt to reflect the very real divisions that exist in the shifting configurations of people and groups and identities that compose the "gay community."

Taking Liberties: Gay Men's Essays on Politics, Culture, and Sex makes no pretense to being a comprehensive survey of gay male thought on the current state of politics and culture. It is neither comprehensive nor encyclopedic, but simply a sampling of what some gay men have been writing—or speaking or performing; *Taking Liberties* has expanded the notion of "the essay" to include speeches and performance art—about an array of topics. There is no single point of view here. How could there be? The opinions of gay men are as varied and as idiosyncratic as their lives and experiences. And as often as not the writers here voice opinions that are seriously and contentiously opposed to one another. Sometimes the pieces in *Taking Liberties* construct a dialogue among themselves, sometimes a fight.

Spirited dialogues and fights occur not only when people disagree, but when their opinions are firmly held. Reading through these essays, readers will be struck not only by how far ranging the topics are—from how we think and talk about pornography, to the lingering after-shocks of Jeffrey Dahmer on the gay male imagination; from the impact of gay characters in soap operas on the lives of gay and lesbian teenagers, to the pedagogical and affirmational effects of sado-masochism on the life of the mind—but how passionately each of these ideas is argued.

Gay and lesbian spokespeople—"spokespeople" being defined as those who have access to mainstream press coverage—routinely decry the divisions within gay and lesbian political and cultural circles. "If we could only all agree…" goes the standard plea. Well, the reality is that we don't all agree. As lesbian activist and sociologist Margaret Cerullo has noted, "the minute we all agree on a politic, or a position, or a policy, I feel we are stuck. Discussion stops, people become entrenched in their old thinking, and the movement—however you define that—simply does not move forward."

Taking Liberties is profoundly committed to the idea of disagreement as a means of moving forward. There are essays here with which any number of readers may seriously—even violently—

disagree. This is not a bad thing. Honest and open disagreement leads not to derision or destructive dissension, but to discussion. In the end *Taking Liberties* is about community—not a community in stasis but a community in constant evolution and flux, even upheaval.

Although, in its subtitle, *Taking Liberties* differentiates among "culture," "politics," and "sex," these easy distinctions are admittedly misleading. We are constantly being told—by the media, politicians, and conservative social thinkers—that "culture," "politics," and "sex" have very little to do with one another, that they are all separate entities, easily isolated from one another. This is a lie. Culture, politics, and sex are all intimately connected—in sometimes obvious, but often very surprising, even alarming ways—in our emotional and psychological lives, in our creative endeavors and our political work.

One of the most exciting aspects—and effects—of gay male culture is that it has worked hard to break down these bogus categories: sex is political, culture is sexual, politics is about culture, and vice versa. When you look at the most recent political and culture battles surrounding gay and lesbian issues—NEA funding of openly gay and sexually explicit artists, the military ban on openly gay people in the armed services, the rainbow curriculum fights and the inclusion of gay-themed children's books in classrooms, the presence of gay men and lesbians in local St. Patrick's Day parades—all involve a combination of the sexual, the political, and the cultural.

Homosexuality in our culture is more tolerated when it is kept quiet, private. The language of this enforced silence is everywhere: "I don't care what they do, I just don't want to see it"; "Don't ask, don't tell"; "Why do they have to march in that parade every year"; "I don't mind the quiet ones, it's the screamers that I hate." And these sentiments are echoed in the gay world as well—controversies about whether drag queens and leather folk should participate in gay pride marches are still rampant; the North American Man-Boy Love Association (NAMBLA) has been forbidden to participate in local and national demonstrations; issues of public cruising and public sex are sources of embarrassment to mainstream gay and lesbian organizations. In each of these instances we are being told that our sexuality is a private matter and that we would gain acceptance and tolerance if only we agreed with this lie. The essays in *Taking Liberties* each in its own way contest the idea that any progress can be made by denying the connections among sexuality, politics, and culture, or by denying the importance of sexuality in our lives.

PART ONE:
Politics • Sex • Literature

POLITICS

Although lesbians and gay men have been engaged in explicit—and argumentative—discussions about political tactics since the founding of the Mattachine Society in 1949, the enormous changes brought on by the Stonewall riots and the emergence of the gay liberation and gay rights movements have completely transformed the scope of these discussions. While early homophile groups understood the need for political leverage, they had neither the organizational power nor the social position to realize this goal. In was only in the late 1960s—in the context of the second wave of feminism, the anti-war movement, the Black Power movement, youth culture, the sexual revolution—that the very idea of gay liberation was able to come into being and flourish.

The Stonewall riots were both an expression of rage and a manifestation of newly found power. The resulting political movements began the heady, and confusing, process of discovering just how this power worked. As gay political groups began to form, two distinct positions were articulated: gay liberation, which saw itself as part of a broader progressive movement, and gay rights, which focused on a single issue. Urvashi Vaid in the opening chapter of her book, *Virtual Equality*, neatly delineated these differing approaches:

> Are we as a movement aimed at mainstreaming gay and lesbian people (legitimation), or do we seek radical change out of the process of our integration (liberation)? For some gay and lesbian people, mainstream integration is the paramount concern for our political movement. For others, the transformation of mainstream culture holds the key to genuine gay and lesbian equality. Some of us believe that our political movement exists solely to fight anti-gay and anti-lesbian prejudice. Others believe that the elimination of homophobic prejudice is intimately related to the end of gender inequality, the end of racial prejudice, and the institution of a moral economic system.

This tension between a liberationist and an assimilationist philosophy is the defining marker of contemporary gay politics: a core conflict, as unresolvable as it is contentious. The first three essays in this section not only articulate the dimensions of the arguments but push the parameters and the scope of each position.

Bruce Bawer's "Notes on Stonewall" argues that it is time for the gay movement to move beyond the "Stonewall myth"—the idea that gay and lesbian concerns are essentially different from the concerns of heterosexuals, and that setting up a combative, pro-gay agenda does a disservice to both gay and straight people. Bawer takes on the popular history and ideology of Stonewall and its ramifications in an attempt to construct what he sees as a more useful and effective political agenda. "The Stonewall Myth" is as much about the importance of reinterpreting and reimagining history as it is about setting a course for the future.

Bawer's concerns are mirrored in Andrew Sullivan's "The Politics of Homosexuality," which formed the basis for his book, *Virtually Normal*. Like Bawer, Sullivan is concerned that gay and lesbian people not remove themselves from mainstream political discourse, and in both the article and book Sullivan attempts nothing less then a new ordering of how we conceptualize the "politics of homosexuality." Sullivan's aim is the revamping of the gay movement's political priorities and a revision of how we might obtain them. In his critique of anti-gay discrimination laws, as well as his strong moral defense of gay marriage, Sullivan pushes the traditional arguments for legitimization further than they have been pushed before.

"A Socialism of the Skin (Liberation, Honey!)" by Tony Kushner is a direct answer to the arguments of both Bawer and Sullivan. While he refers specifically to "Notes on Stonewall" and "The Politics of Homosexuality," Kushner (as do Bawer and Sullivan) pushes the boundaries of the "assimilationist vs liberationist" debate. In a political climate in which the word "liberal" has become a taunt, and in which even progressives, in hope of being more accessible, have been known to tone down their language and vision, Kushner is unafraid to declare himself a socialist and a utopian. Perhaps most bravely he forthrightly discusses the centrality of sexuality in gay and lesbian life and culture.

If "Notes on Stonewall," "The Politics of Homosexuality" and "A Socialism of the Skin (Liberation, Honey!)" form a three-way dialogue on the merits of differing political philosophies, Scott Tucker's "Blight and Fruit: Some Thoughts on Sex, Death, and Censorship" brings to these more theoretical arguments a passionate personal perspective. Tucker speaks of the pervasive power of censorship—how it has affected his ability to write about his own life-experiences, in particular his internment in a "mental ward" and his sporadic career as a hustler—and the many ways that our culture silences lesbian and gay voices. He also discusses how, ironically, after being diagnosed, he "felt freer to speak [his] mind and speak it loud as never before." His breakdown, he writes, was "a period of heightened clarity, and therefore of rage and grief." Tucker tacitly implies that even madness may be a reasonable—and healthy—reaction to a world so fraught with anti-gay hatred. While Bawer, Sullivan, and Kushner speak of how gay men and lesbians might change the world, Tucker reminds us of the harsh realities that shape those struggles.

In "Speaking Parts: Unraveling silence, language, and masculinity," Lawrence Chua takes up some of Scott Tucker's themes and investigates the ways in which gay male identity—and, by extension, gay male politics and culture—are shaped by our ability to articulate our lives as well as by our decisions to be silent: "Silence is the place where speech is made." For Chua, a great deal of gay male power and speech is located in our sexuality and sexual imaginations and he deftly delineates both the junctions and intersections of gay male identity, race, ethnicity, and masculinity.

Notes on Stonewall
BRUCE BAWER

Twenty-five years ago, in the early morning hours of June 28, 1969, several patrons at the Stonewall bar in Greenwich Village, many of them flamboyant drag queens and prostitutes, refused to go quietly when police carried out a routine raid on the place. Their refusal escalated into five days of rioting by hundreds of people. Though it wasn't the first time anyone had contested the right of the state to punish citizens just for being gay, that rioting marked a pivotal moment because news of it spread in every direction and sparked the imaginations of countless gay men and lesbians around the world. It made them examine, and reject, the silence, shame, and reflexive compliance with prejudice to which most of them had simply never conceived a realistic alternative.

There is something wondrous about Stonewall, and it is this: that a mere handful of late-night bar patrons, many of them confused, lonely individuals living at the margins of society, started something that made a lot of lesbians and gay men do some very serious thinking of a sort they had never quite done before—thinking that led to action and to a movement. It was the beginning of a revolution in attitudes toward homosexuality. How odd it is to think that those changes could all be traced back to a drunken riot at a Greenwich Village bar on a June night in 1969. But they can. And that's why Stonewall deserves to be commemorated.

Today, however, Stonewall is not only commemorated but mythologized. Many gay men and lesbians routinely speak of it as if it were a sacred event that lies beyond the reach of objective discourse. They talk as if there had been no gay rights activism at all before Stonewall, or else they mock pre-Stonewall activists as Uncle Toms. They recite the name "Stonewall" itself with the same reverence that American politicians reserve for the names of Washington and Lincoln. And indeed the word is perfectly suited to the myth, conjuring as it does an image of a huge, solid barrier separating the dark ages prior to the day that Judy Garland died, from the out-loud-and-proud present. Every year, on what has long since become an all-purpose gay holiday—a combination of Independence Day, May Day, Mardi Gras and, since the advent of HIV, Memorial Day as well—millions ritualistically revisit the raucous, defiant marginality of Stonewall in marches around the world. This year in New York, on the twenty-fifth anniversary, the ritual will reach a climax. For many, Stonewall has already become a Platonic model of gay activism—and, indeed, a touchstone of gay identity.

A few weeks ago, in a sermon about an entirely different subject, the rector of the Episcopal church I belong to in New York used the phrase "the politics of nostalgia." The phrase has stuck in my mind, for it seems to me that both sides of the gay rights struggle are trapped in what may well be characterized as a politics of nostalgia. Many of those who resist acceptance of homosexuality and reject equal rights for gay men and lesbians know on some level that they are wrong, but they cling to old thinking because a change, however just, seems to them a drastic departure from the comfortable world of "don't ask, don't tell." Some gay people, likewise, cling to what might be called the Stonewall sensibility, reacting defensively and violently, as if to some horrendous blasphemy or betrayal, even to the hint that perhaps the time has come to move in some way beyond that sensibility. Such people often declare proudly that they have been "in the trenches" for twenty-five years, which is to say that in a way they have been reliving Stonewall every day since June 1969.

Yet every day can't be Stonewall—or shouldn't. And in fact the time has come to move beyond the Stonewall sensibility. For, thanks largely to developments that can trace their inspiration to that barroom raid, some things have changed since 1969. Levels of tolerance have risen; gay rights laws have been passed; in the last quarter-century, and especially recently, gay Americans have come out of the closet in increasing numbers. As a result, it has become clear to more and more heterosexuals that gay America is as diverse as straight America—that many of the people who were at the Stonewall bar on that night twenty-five years ago represent an anachronistic politics that largely has ceased to have salience for gay America today. To say this is not to condemn people who consider themselves members of that fringe or to read them out of the gay community. It is simply to say that for gay America to continue to be defined largely by its fringe is a lie, and that this lie, like all lies about homosexuality, needs to be countered vigorously. The Stonewall sensibility—like the Stonewall myth—has to be abandoned.

On May 6 *The New York Times* described the arguments among gay leaders about the planning of Stonewall 25, the forthcoming New York event that will culminate in a march on the United Nations. Some of these leaders worried that Stonewall 25 wouldn't focus enough on the fact that many of the Stonewall heroes were transvestite and transsexual hustlers. One woman wanted, in her words, to "radicalize" Stonewall 25. "Stonewall," she told the

Times, "was a rebellion of transgender people, and this event has the potential to reduce our whole culture to an Ikea ad."

It is strange to read the words of those who speak, on the one hand, as if Stonewall, in and of itself, achieved something once and for all time that gay Americans are now free to celebrate, and, on the other, as if the kind of growing acceptance that is represented by the depiction of a middle-class gay couple in a furniture commercial on network TV is bad news, a threat to a Stonewall-born concept of gay identity as forever marginal. It would almost seem as if those leaders don't realize that Stonewall was only part of a long, complex process that is still proceeding, and that the best way to honor it is to build upon it by directing that process as wisely and responsibly as we can.

In the May 3 issue of the gay magazine *The Advocate*, activist Torie Osborn wrote that thirty-nine gay leaders, whom she described as "our community's best and brightest," had gathered recently to discuss the state of the movement and "retool [it] to match the changing times." The group, she wrote, "had a collective 750 years of experience in gay rights or other political work." But even as she wrote of seeking "common ground" and "common vision" among the gay leaders, Osborn reaffirmed the linking of gay rights to "other progressive movements with which many of us identify."

In other words, she embraced the standard post-Stonewall practice of indiscriminately linking the movement for gay equal rights with any left-wing cause to which any gay leader might happen to have a personal allegiance. That practice dates back to 1969, when radical activists, gay and straight, were quick to use the gay rights movement as a way to prosecute their own unrelated revolutionary agendas. Such linkages have been a disaster for the gay rights movement: not only do they falsely imply that most gay people sympathize with those so-called progressive movements, but they also serve to reinforce the idea of homosexuality itself as a "progressive" phenomenon, as something that is essentially political in nature. Osborn wrote further that she and the other gay leaders at the summit "talked about separating strategic thinking into two discrete areas: our short-term political fights and the long-term cultural war against systematic homophobia." And she added that "we have virtually no helpful objective data or clear strategy on the long-term war, which grapples with deep-seated sexphobia as well as heterosexism." Her conclusion (my emphasis): "We need to start working on this problem."

With all due respect to Osborn and her fellow gay leaders, it seems to me more than a bit astonishing that in spite of their collective 750 years of experience, at least some of them only now have begun to realize that homosexuals should be giving thought to something other than short-term political conflicts. At the same time, those leaders still can't quite understand the long-term challenge as anything other than, in Osborn's words, a "war." Nor can they see that achieving real and lasting equality is a matter not of changing right-wingers into left-wingers, or of emancipating Americans from "sexphobia," but of liberating people from their discomfort with homosexuality, their automatic tendency to think of homosexuals in terms of sex and their often bizarre notions of who gay people are, what gay people value, and how gay people live.

Perhaps, at the threshold of the second generation of the post-Stonewall gay rights movement, it behooves us to recall that, as I've noted, there was at least some species of gay activism prior to Stonewall. Years before those patrons at the Stonewall bar hurled garbage, beer bottles, feces, and four-letter words at the policemen who had come to arrest them, a few small groups of men in business suits and women in dresses staged sober, orderly marches at which they carried signs that announced their own homosexuality and that respectfully demanded an end to anti-homosexual prejudice. Those people were even more radical than the rioters at Stonewall, and—dare I say it?—perhaps even more brave, given how few they were, how premeditated their protests, and how much some of them had to lose by publicly identifying themselves as gay. They were heroes, too; they won a few legal battles, and they might have won more. Sure, Stonewall was, without question, an important step—indeed, the biggest single step the gay rights movement has taken. But that's all it was: a step, the first big one in a long, difficult journey. It was a reaction to intolerance, and it set us on the road to tolerance. The next road leads to acceptance—acceptance not only of gay people by straight people, but an easier acceptance by young gay people of their own sexuality. It's a different road—and, in a way, a harder one.

First-generation post-Stonewall gay activists saw themselves as street combatants in a political war. Second generation activists would better see themselves as participants in an educational program of which the expressly political work is only a part. Getting America to accept homosexuality will first be a matter of education. The job is not to shout at straight Americans, "We're here, we're queer, get used to it." The job is to do the hard, painstaking work of getting straight Americans used to it. This isn't dramatic work; nor is it work that provides a quick emotional release. Rather, it requires discipline, commitment, responsibility.

In some sense, of course, most straight Americans are used to the idea of people being gay. The first generation of the post-Stonewall gay rights movement has accomplished that. At the same time, it has brought us to a place where many straight Americans are sick and tired of the very word "gay." They've heard it a million times, yet they don't understand it nearly well enough. They still feel uncomfortable, confused, threatened. They feel that the private lives of homosexuals have been pushed "in their faces," but they don't really know about those private lives.

And why should they be expected to? Yes, at Gay Pride Day marches, some gay men and lesbians, like the Stonewall rioters, have exposed America to images of raw sexuality—images that variously amuse, titillate, shock and offend while revealing nothing important about who most of those people really are. Why, then, do some people do such things? Perhaps because they've been conditioned to think that on that gay high holy day, the definitively gay thing to do is to be as defiant as those heroes twenty-five years ago. Perhaps they do it because they can more easily grasp the concept of enjoying one day per year of delicious anarchy than of devoting 365 days per year to a somewhat more disciplined and strategically sensible demonstration designed to advance the causes of respect, dignity, and equality.

And perhaps they do it because, frankly, it is relatively easy to do. Just as standing up at a White House press conference and yelling at the president can take less courage than coming out to your parents or neighbors or employers, so taking off your pants or your bra for a Gay Pride Day march in the company of hundreds of thousands of known allies can be easier than taking down your defenses for a frank conversation with a group of colleagues at an office lunch about how it feels to grow up gay. For an insecure gay man or lesbian, moreover, explaining can feel awfully close to apologizing, and can open one up to charges of collaboration with the enemy by those who join the author Paul Monette in seeing America as the "Christian Reich" and themselves as members of the queer equivalent of the French resistance.

As a friend said to me recently, building acceptance of homosexuals is like teaching a language. When gays speak about themselves, they are speaking one language; when most straight people speak about gays, they are speaking another. Most heterosexuals look at gay lives the way I look at a page of German. I may be able to pick out a few familiar words, but I feel awkward when I use them, and if I try to put together a sentence I'm likely to find myself saying something I don't mean at all, perhaps even something offensive or hurtful. There's only one way to get past that feeling of confusion: tireless, meticulous dedication to study. You can't

learn a foreign language overnight, and you can't teach it by screaming it at people. You teach it word by word until, bit by bit, they feel
comfortable speaking it and can find their way around the country where it's spoken. That's the job of the second generation of
post-Stonewall gay activism: to teach those who don't accept us the
language of who gay people are and where gay people live. Indeed,
to the extent that professional homophobes have stalled progress
in the movement toward legal and social parity for gay men and
lesbians, it is not because those homophobes are so crafty, and
certainly not because they are right. It is because they have spoken
to straight America in its own language and addressed its concerns,
whereas gay Americans, more often than not, out of an understandable fear and defensive self-righteousness, haven't.

Some reviewers in the gay press read the title of my book, *A Place
at the Table: The Gay Individual in American Society*, as a sign that I,
personally, long to sit at a dinner table with people like Pat
Buchanan and Jerry Falwell—that this book is my attempt to indicate to them that I'm a nice, well-mannered gay man and that I,
along with the other nice, well-mannered gay men, should be
allowed at the table, while the "bad," ill-mannered gays are
excluded. Some other gay press reviewers have understood that I
don't mean that at all, and that I feel everyone should be welcome
at the American table, but they have angrily rejected the idea:
"Why," one critic wrote, "should I want to sit at that table?" A
writer for the gay magazine *Out* dismissed the book in one line:
"Bruce Bawer has written a book about the gay individual in
American society entitled *A Place at the Table*. Some will prefer
take-out." What these reactions signify to me is a powerful tendency
among some homosexuals to recoil reflexively from the vision of
an America where gays live as full and open members of society,
with all the rights, responsibilities, and opportunities of heterosexuals. Many gay people, indeed, have a deep, unarticulated fear
of that metaphorical place at the table. This is understandable:

gay people, as a rule, are so used to minimizing their exposure to homophobia, by living either in the closet or on the margins of society, that for someone—even a fellow gay person—to come along and invoke an image of gay America sitting openly at a table with straight America can seem, to them, like a hostile act. This sense of threat—this devotion to the margin—may help explain the gay-activist rancor toward the movie *Philadelphia*. But most gay men and lesbians were happy to see a movie that showed homosexuality as part of the mainstream, just as most are pleased by the new tendency to depict gay life, in everything from Ikea ads to movies like *Four Weddings and a Funeral*, in a matter-of-fact way, as an integrated part of society.

Am I attacking radicalism? No. I'm saying that the word "radical" must be defined anew by each generation. In the late twentieth century, when radicalism has often been viewed as a fashion choice, it's easy to lose sight of what real radicalism is. It's not a matter of striking a defiant pose and maintaining that pose over a period of years; it's not a matter of signing on to a certain philosophy or program and adhering to it inflexibly for the rest of your life. And it's not always a matter of manning barricades or crouching in trenches. It's a matter of honest inquiry, of waking up every morning and looking at the social circumstances in which you find yourself and having the vision to perceive what needs to be done and the courage to follow up on that vision, wherever it may take you. It's a matter of going to the root of the problem, wherever that root may lie.

And going to the root of this particular problem means going to the root of prejudice. It means probing the ignorance and fear that are responsible for the success of anti-gay crusaders. It means seriously addressing those opponents' arguments against gay rights, in which they combine a defense of morality and "family values" with attacks on homosexuality as anti-God, anti-American and anti-family. Too often, the first generation of the post-Stonewall gay movement has responded to such rhetoric by actually saying and doing things that have only reinforced the homophobes' characterization of homosexuality. The second generation of the movement would do well to respond, not by attacking the American values and ridiculing the religious faith that these people claim as a basis for their prejudice, but by making it clear just how brutal, how un-American, and how anti-religious their arguments and their prejudice are.

And there are a lot of untruths out there to overcome. More and more people understand that homosexuals are no more likely to be child molesters than heterosexuals are, but there remains on the part of many people a lingering discomfort about such notions, and anti-gay crusaders exploit that discomfort with ambiguous, dishonest rhetoric suggesting that homosexuals are (to quote a recent statement published in *The Wall Street Journal* by a group of religious figures calling itself the Ramsey Colloquium) a threat to the "vulnerabilities of the young." That's a lie. But how can homosexuals help heterosexuals understand it's a lie so long as some gay political leaders, in the best Stonewall tradition, feel more comfortable condemning the Log Cabin Republicans than they do condemning the North American Man-Boy Love Association?

Likewise, more and more people understand that homosexuals' lives are no more about sex than their lives are, but there are many who still don't understand that, and the anti-gay crusaders exploit their ignorance by saying (again in the words of the Ramsey Colloquium) that gay people "define" themselves by their "desires alone," that they seek "liberation from constraint," from obligations to the larger society and especially to the young, and from all human dignity. That's a lie. But how can gays help straights understand it's a lie so long as a few marchers on Gay Pride Day feel the best way to represent all gay men and lesbians is to walk down the avenue in their underwear?

Anti-gay propagandists shrewdly exploit the fact that we live in times when there's ample reason for concern about children. American children today grow up in an often uncivil and crime-ridden society, and with a pop culture that is at best value-neutral and at worst aggressive and ugly. Altogether too many of those kids grow up inured to the sight of beggars sleeping on the side-walk, of condoms and hypodermic needles in the gutter, of porno-graphic magazines on display at street-corner kiosks. Anti-gay propagandists routinely link homosexuality to these phenomena, seeing homosexual orientation, and gay people's openness about it, and gay people's desire for equal rights and equal respect, as yet more signs of the decline of morals, of the family, of social cohe-sion and stability and of civilization generally.

One of Stonewall's legacies is that gay leaders have too often accepted this characterization of the conflict and see any attempt to correct it as "sex-negative." The second generation of post-Stonewall gay activism has to make it clear that that's not the way the sides break down at all, and that when it comes to children, the real interests of parents and of gay people (many of whom are themselves parents, of course) are not unalterably opposed, but are, in fact, perfectly congruent. Gay adults care about children, too; and they know from experience something that straight parents can only strive to understand—namely, what it's like to grow up gay.

Homosexuals, of course, are not a threat to the family; among the things that threaten the family are parents' profound igno-rance about homosexuality and their reluctance to face the truth about it. In the second generation of the post-Stonewall gay rights movement, gay adults must view it as an obligation to ensure that parents understand that truth—and understand, too, that accord-ing equal rights to homosexuals and equal recognition to same-sex relationships (and creating an atmosphere in which gay men and lesbians can live openly without fear of losing their jobs or homes or lives) would not threaten the institution of the family but would actually strengthen millions of American families.

It is ironic that, to a large extent, what perpetuates Stonewall-style antagonism between gay and straight are not our differences, really, but traits that we all share as human beings. We all, for instance, fear the unknown. To most straight people, homosexuality is an immense unknown; to gay people, a society that would regard sexual orientation indifferently and grant homosexuals real equality is also an immense unknown. But it is also our humanity that makes most of us long to know and live with the truth, even in the wake of a lifetime of lies. The greatest tribute we can pay to the memory of Stonewall is to work in our own homes and workplaces to dismantle, lie by lie, the wall of lies that has divided the families of America for too long.

The Politics of Homosexuality
ANDREW SULLIVAN

Over the last four years I have been sent letters from strangers
caught in doomed, desperate marriages because of repressed homosexuality and have witnessed several thousand virtually naked,
muscle-bound men dance for hours in the middle of New York
city, in the middle of the day. I have lain down on top of a dying
friend to restrain his hundred-pound body as it violently shook
with the death-throes of AIDS and listened to soldiers equate the
existence of homosexuality in the military with the dissolution of
the meaning of the United States. I have openly discussed my
sexuality on a television talk show and sat on the porch of an apartment building in downtown D.C. with an arm around a male friend
and watched as a dozen cars in a half hour slowed to hurl abuse. I
have seen mass advertising explicitly cater to an openly gay audience and watched my own father break down and weep at the
declaration of his son's sexuality.

These different experiences of homosexuality are not new, of
course. But that they can now be experiences within one life (and

that you are now reading about them) *is* new. The cultural categories and social departments into which we once successfully consigned sexuality—departments that helped us avoid the anger and honesty with which we are now confronted—have begun to collapse. Where once there was only the unmentionable, there are now only the unavoidable: gays, "queers," homosexuals, closet cases, bisexuals, the "out" and the "in," paraded for every heterosexual to see. As the straight world has been confronted with this, it has found itself reaching for a response: embarrassment, tolerance, fear, violence, oversensitivity, recognition. When Sam Nunn conducts hearings, he knows there is no common discourse in which he can now speak, that even the words he uses will betray worlds of conflicting experiences and anxieties. Yet speak he must. In place of the silence that once encased the lives of homosexuals, there is now a loud argument. And there is no easy going back.

This fracturing of discourse is more than a cultural problem; it is a political problem. Without at least some common ground, no effective compromise to the homosexual question will be possible. Matters may be resolved, as they have been in the case of abortion, by a stand-off in the forces of cultural war. But unless we begin to discuss this subject with a degree of restraint and reason, the visceral unpleasantness that exploded earlier this year will dog the question of homosexuality for a long time to come, intensifying the anxieties that politics is supposed to relieve.

There are as many politics of homosexuality as there are words for it, and not all of them contain reason. And it is harder perhaps in this passionate area than in any other to separate a wish from an argument, a desire from a denial. Nevertheless, without such an effort, no true politics of sexuality can emerge. And besides, there are some discernible patterns, some sketches of political theory that have begun to emerge with clarity. I will discuss here only four, but four that encompass a reasonable span of possible arguments. Each has a separate analysis of sexuality and a distinct solution to the problem of gay-straight relations. Perhaps no person belongs in any single category; and they are by no means exclusive of one another. What follows is a brief description of each: why each is riven by internal and external conflict; and why none, finally, works.

I.

The first I'll call, for the sake of argument, the conservative politics of sexuality. Its view of homosexuality is as dark as it is popular as it is unfashionable. It informs much of the opposition to allowing openly gay men and women to serve in the military, and can be heard in living rooms, churches, bars, and computer bulletin boards across America. It is found in most of the families in which homosexuals grow up and critically frames many homosexuals' view of their own identity. Its fundamental assertion is that homosexuality as such does not properly exist. Homosexual behavior is aberrant activity, either on the part of heterosexuals intent on subverting traditional society or by people who are prey to psychological, emotional, or sexual dysfunction.

For adherents to the conservative politics of sexuality, therefore, the homosexual question concerns everyone. It cannot be dismissed merely as an affliction of the individual but is rather one that afflicts society at large.

Since society depends on the rearing of a healthy future generation, the existence of homosexuals is a grave problem. People who would otherwise be living productive and socially beneficial lives are diverted by homosexuality into unhappiness and sterility, and they may seek, in their bleak attempts at solace, to persuade others to join them. Two gerundives cling to this view of homosexuals: practicing and proselytizing. And both are habitually uttered with a mixture of pity and disgust.

The politics that springs out of this view of homosexuality has two essential parts: with the depraved, it must punish; with the sick, it must cure. There are, of course, degrees to which these two activities can be promoted. The recent practice in modern liberal democracies of imprisoning homosexuals or subjecting them to psychological or physiological "cures" is a good deal less repressive than the camps for homosexuals in Castro's Cuba, the spasmodic attempt at annihilation in Nazi Germany or the brutality of modern Islamic states. And the sporadic entrapment of gay men in public restrooms or parks is a good deal less repressive than the systematic hunting down and discharging of homosexuals that we require of our armed forces. But the differences are matters of degree rather than of kind; and the essential characteristic of the conservative politics of homosexuality is that it pursues the logic of repression. Not for conservatives the hypocrisy of those who tolerate homosexuality in private and abhor it in public. They seek rather to grapple with the issue directly and to sustain the carapace of public condemnation and legal sanction that can keep the dark presence of homosexuality at bay.

This is not a distant politics. In twenty-four states sodomy is still illegal, and the constitutionality of these statutes was recently upheld by the Supreme Court. Much of the Republican Party supports this politics with varying degrees of sympathy for the victims of the affliction. The Houston convention was replete with jokes by speaker Patrick Buchanan that implicitly affirmed this view. Banners held aloft by delegates asserted "Family Rights For Ever, Gay Rights Never," implying a direct trade-off between tolerating homosexuals and maintaining the traditional family.

In its crudest and most politically dismissable forms, this politics invokes biblical revelation to make its civic claims. But in its subtler form, it draws strength from the natural law tradition, which, for all its failings, is a resilient pillar of Western thought. Following a Thomist argument, conservatives argue that the natural function of sexuality is clearly procreative; and that all expressions of it outside procreation destroy human beings' potential for full and healthy development. Homosexuality—far from being natural—is clearly a perversion of, or turning away from, the legitimate and healthy growth of the human person.

Perhaps the least helpful element in the current debate is the assertion that this politics is simply bigotry. It isn't. Many bigots may, of course, support it, and by bigots I mean those whose "visceral recoil" from homosexuals (to quote Buchanan) expresses itself in thuggery and name-calling. But there are some who don't support anti-gay violence and who sincerely believe discouragement of homosexuality by law and "curing" homosexuals is in the best interest of everybody.

Nevertheless, this politics suffers from an increasingly acute internal contradiction and an irresistible external development. It is damaged, first, by the growing evidence that homosexuality does in fact exist as an identifiable and involuntary characteristic of some people, and that these people do not as a matter of course suffer from moral or psychological dysfunction; that is, in other words, as close to "natural" as any human condition can be. New data about the possible genetic origins of homosexuality are only one part of this development. By far the most important element is the testimony of countless homosexuals. The number who say their orientation is a choice make up only a tiny minority; and the candor of those who say it isn't is overwhelming. To be sure, it is in the interests of gay people to affirm their lack of choice over the matter; but the consensus among homosexuals, the resilience of lesbian and gay minorities in the face of deep social disapproval and even a plague, suggests that homosexuality, whatever one would like to think, simply is not often chosen. A fundamental claim of natural law is that its truths are self-evident: across continents and centuries, homosexuality is a self-evident fact of life.

How large this population is does not matter. One percent or 10 percent: as long as a small but persistent part of the population is involuntarily gay, then the entire conservative politics of homosexuality rests on an unstable footing. It becomes simply a politics of denial or repression. Faced with a sizable and inextinguishable part of society, it can only pretend that it does not exist or needn't be addressed, or can somehow be dismissed. This politics is less coherent than even the politics that opposed civil rights for blacks thirty years ago, because at least that had some answer to the question of the role of blacks in society, no matter how subordinate. Today's conservatives have no role for homosexuals; they want them somehow to disappear, an option that was once illusory and is now impossible.

Some conservatives and conservative institutions have recognized this. They've even begun to use the term "homosexual," implicitly accepting the existence of a constitutive term "homosexualist," but most cannot do so without a wry grin on their faces. The more serious opponents of equality for homosexuals finesse the problem by restricting their objections to "radical homosexuals," but the distinction doesn't help. They are still forced to confront the problem of *un*radical homosexuals, people whose sexuality is, presumably, constitutive. To make matters worse, the Roman Catholic Church—the firmest religious proponent of the conservative politics of homosexuality—has explicitly conceded the point. It declared in 1975 that homosexuality is indeed involuntary for many. In the recent Universal Catechism, the Church goes even further. Homosexuality is described as a "condition" of a "not negligible" number of people who "do not choose" their sexuality and deserve to be treated with "respect, compassion and sensitivity." More critically, because of homosexuality's involuntary nature, it cannot of itself be morally culpable (although homosexual *acts* still are). The doctrine is thus no longer "hate the sin but love the sinner"; it's "hate the sin but accept the condition," a position unique in Catholic theology, and one that has already begun to creak under the strain of its own tortuousness.

But the loss of intellectual solidity isn't the only problem for the conservative politics of homosexuality. In a liberal polity, it has lost a good deal of its political coherence as well. When many people in a liberal society insist upon their validity as citizens and human beings, repression becomes a harder and harder task. It offends against fundamental notions of decency and civility to treat them as simple criminals or patients. To hunt them down, imprison them for private acts, subject government workers to surveillance and dismissal for reasons related to their deepest sense of personal identity becomes a policy not simply cruel but politically impossible in a civil order. For American society to return to the social norms around the question of homosexuality of a generation ago would require a renewed act of repression that not even many zealots could contemplate. What generations of inherited shame could not do, what AIDS could not accomplish, what the most decisive swing toward conservatism in the 1980s could not muster, must somehow be accomplished in the next few years. It simply cannot be done.

So even Patrick Buchanan is reduced to joke-telling; senators to professions of ignorance; military leaders to rationalizations of sheer discomfort. For those whose politics are a mere extension of religious faith, such impossibilism is a part of the attraction (and spiritually, if not politically defensible). But for conservatives who seek to act as citizens in a secular, civil order, the dilemma is terminal. An unremittingly hostile stance toward homosexuals runs the risk of sectarianism. At some point, not reached yet but fast approaching, their politics could become so estranged from the society in which it operates that it could cease to operate as a politics altogether.

II.

The second politics of homosexuality shares with the first a conviction that homosexuality as an inherent and natural condition does not exist. Homosexuality, in this politics, is a cultural construction, a binary social conceit (along with heterosexuality) forced upon the sexually amorphous (all of us). This politics attempts to resist this oppressive construct, subverting it and subverting the society that allows it to fester. Where the first politics takes as its starting point the Thomist faith in nature, the second springs from the Nietzschean desire to surpass all natural necessities, to attack the construct of "nature" itself. Thus the pursuit of a homosexual existence is but one strategy of many to enlarge the possibility for human liberation.

Call this the radical politics of homosexuality. For the radicals, like the conservatives, homosexuality is definitely a choice: the choice to be a "queer," the choice to subvert oppressive institutions, the choice to be an activist. And it is a politics that, insofar as it finds its way from academic discourse into gay activism (and it does so fitfully), exercises a peculiar fascination for the adherents of the first politics. At times, indeed, both seem to exist in a bond of mutual contempt and admiration. That both prefer to use the word "queer," the one in private, the other in irony, is only one of many resemblances. They both react with disdain to those studies that seem to reflect a genetic source for homosexuality; and they both favor, to some extent or other, the process of outing, because for both it is the flushing out of deviant behavior: for conservatives, of the morally impure, for radicals, of the politically correct. For conservatives, radical "queers" provide a frisson of cultural apocalypse and a steady stream of funding dollars. For radicals, the religious right can be tapped as an unreflective and easy justification for virtually any political impulse whatsoever.

Insofar as this radical politics is synonymous with a subcultural experience, it has stretched the limits of homosexual identity and expanded the cultural space in which some homosexuals can live. In the late 1980s the tactics of groups like ACT UP and Queer Nation did not merely shock and anger, but took the logic and shame-abandonment to a thrilling conclusion. To exist within their sudden energy was to be caught in a liberating rite of passage, which, when it did not transgress into political Puritanism, exploded many of the cozy assumptions of closeted homosexual and liberal heterosexual alike.

This politics is as open-ended as the conservative politics is closed-minded. It seeks an end to all restrictions on homosexuality, but also the subversion of heterosexual norms, as taught in schools or the media. By virtue of its intellectual origins, it affirms a close connection with every other minority group, whose cultural subversion of white, heterosexual, male norms is just as vital. It sees its crusades—now for an AIDS czar, now against the Catholic Church's abortion stance, now for the Rainbow Curriculum, now against the military ban—as a unified whole of protest, glorifying in its indiscriminateness as in its universality.

But like the conservative politics of homosexuality, which also provides a protective ghetto of liberation for its disciples, the radical politics of homosexuality now finds itself in an acute state of crisis. Its problem is twofold: its conception of homosexuality is so amorphous and indistinguishable from other minority concerns that it is doomed to be ultimately unfocused; and its relationship with the views of most homosexuals—let alone heterosexuals—is so tenuous that at moments of truth (like the military ban) it strains to have a viable politics at all.

The trouble with gay radicalism, in short, is the problem with subversive politics as a whole. It tends to subvert itself. ACT UP, for example, an AIDS group that began in the late 1980s as an activist group dedicated to finding a cure and better treatment for people with AIDS, soon found itself awash in a cacophony of internal division. Its belief that sexuality was only one of many oppressive constructions meant that it was constantly tempted to broaden its reach, to solve a whole range of gender and ethnic grievances. Similarly, each organizing committee in each state of this weekend's march on Washington was required to have a 50 percent "minority" composition. Even *Utah*. Although this universalist temptation was not always given in to, it exercised an enervating and dissipating effect on gay radicalism's political punch.

More important, the notion of sexuality as cultural subversion distanced it from the vast majority of gay people who not only accept the natural origin of their sexual orientation, but wish to be integrated into society as it is. For most gay people—the closet cases and barflies, the construction workers and investment bankers, the computer programmers and parents—a "queer" identity is precisely what they want to avoid. In this way, the radical politics of homosexuality, like the conservative politics of homosexuality, is caught in a political trap. The more it purifies its own belief about sexuality, the less able it is to engage the broader world as a whole. The more it acts upon its convictions, the less able it is to engage in politics at all.

For the "queer" fundamentalists, like the religious fundamentalists, this is no problem. Politics for both groups is essentially an exercise in theater and rhetoric, in which dialogue with one's opponent is an admission of defeat. It is no accident that ACT UP was founded by a playwright, since its politics was essentially theatrical: a fantastic display of rhetorical pique and visual brilliance. It became a national media hit, but eventually its lines became familiar and the audience's attention wavered. New shows have taken its place and will continue to do so: but they will always be constrained by their essential nature, which is performance, not persuasion.

The limits of this strategy can be seen in the politics of the military ban. Logically, there is no reason for radicals to support the ending of the ban: it means acceptance of presumably one of the most repressive institutions in American society. And, to be sure, no radical arguments have been made to end the ban. But in the last few months, "queers" have been appearing on television proclaiming that gay people are just like anybody else and defending the right of gay midwestern Republicans to serve their country. In the pinch, "queer" politics was forced to abandon its theoretical essence if it was to advance its purported aims: the advancement of gay equality. The military ban illustrated the dilemma perfectly. As soon as radicalism was required actually to engage America, its politics disintegrated.

Similarly, "queer" radicalism's doctrine of cultural subversion and separatism has the effect of alienating those very gay Americans most in need of support and help: the young and teenagers. Separatism is even less of an option for gays than for any other minority, since each generation is literally umbilically connected to the majority. The young are permanently in the hands of the other. By erecting a politics on a doctrine of separation and difference from the majority, "queer" politics ironically broke off dialogue with the heterosexual families whose cooperation is needed in every generation, if gay children are to be accorded a modicum of dignity and hope.

There's an argument, of course, that radicalism's politics is essentially instrumental; that by stretching the limits of what is acceptable it opens up space for more moderate types to negotiate; that, without ACT UP and Queer Nation, no progress would have been made at all. But this both insults the theoretical integrity of the radical position (they surely do not see themselves as mere adjuncts to liberals) and underestimates the scope of the gay revolution that has been quietly taking place in America. Far more subversive than media-grabbing demonstrations on the evening news has been the slow effect of individual, private Americans becoming more open about their sexuality. The emergence of role models, the development of professional organizations and student groups, the growing influence of openly gay people in the media, and the extraordinary impact of AIDS on families and friends have dwarfed radicalism's impact on the national consciousness. Likewise, the greatest public debate about homosexuality yet—the military debate—took place not because radicals besieged the Pentagon, but because of the ordinary and once-anonymous Americans within the military who simply refused to acquiesce in their own humiliation any longer. Their courage was illustrated not in taking to the streets in rage but in facing their families and colleagues with integrity.

And this presents the deepest problem for radicalism. As the closet slowly collapses, as gay people enter the mainstream, as suburban homosexuals and Republican homosexuals emerge blinking into the daylight, as the gay ghettos of the inner cities are diluted by the gay enclaves of the suburbs, the whole notion of a separate and homogenous "queer" identity will become harder to defend. Far from redefining gay identity, "queer" radicalism may actually have to define itself in opposition to it. This is implicit in the punitive practice of "outing" and in the increasingly anti-gay politics of some "queer" radicals. But if "queer" politics is to survive, it will either have to be proved right about America's inherent hostility to gay people or become more insistent in its separatism. It will have to intensify its hatred of straights or its contempt for gays. Either path is likely to be as culturally creative as it is politically sterile.

III.

Between these two cultural poles, an appealing alternative presents itself. You can hear it in the tone if not the substance of civilized columnists and embarrassed legislators, who are united most strongly by the desire that this awkward subject simply must go away. It is the moderate politics of homosexuality. Unlike the conservatives and radicals, the moderates do believe that a small number of people are inherently homosexual, but they also believe that another group is susceptible to persuasion in that direction and should be dissuaded. These people do not want persecution of homosexuals, but they do not want overt approval either. They are most antsy when it comes to questions of the education of children but feel acute discomfort in supporting the likes of Patrick Buchanan and Pat Robertson.

Thus their politics has all the nuance and all the disingenuousness of classically conservative politics. They are not intolerant, but they oppose the presence of openly gay teachers in school; they have gay friends but hope their child isn't homosexual; they are in favor of ending the military ban but would seek to do so either by reimposing the closet (ending discrimination in return for gay people never mentioning their sexuality) or by finding some other kind of solution, such as simply ending the witch hunts. If they support sodomy laws (*pour décourager les autres*), they prefer to see them unenforced. In either case, they do not regard the matter as very important. They are ambivalent about domestic partnership legislation but are offended by gay marriage. Above all, they prefer that the subject of homosexuality be discussed with delicacy and restraint, and are only likely to complain to their gay friends if they insist upon "bringing the subject up" too often.

This position too has a certain coherence. It insists that politics is a matter of custom as well as principle and that, in the words of Nunn, caution on the matter of sexuality is not so much a matter of prejudice as of prudence. It places a premium on discouraging the sexually ambivalent from resolving their ambiguity freely in the direction of homosexuality, because, society being as it is, such a life is more onerous than a heterosexual one. It sometimes exchanges this argument for the more honest one: that it wishes to promote procreation and the healthy rearing of the next generation and so wishes to create a cultural climate that promotes heterosexuality.

But this politics too has become somewhat unstable, if not as unstable as the first two. And this instability stems from an internal problem and a related external one. Being privately tolerant and publicly disapproving exacts something of a psychological cost on those who maintain it. In theory, it is not the same as hypocrisy; in practice, it comes perilously close. As the question of homosexuality refuses to disappear from public debate, explicit positions have to be taken. What once could be shrouded in discretion now has to be argued in public. For those who privately do not believe that homosexuality is inherently evil or always chosen, it has become increasingly difficult to pretend otherwise in public. Silence is an option—and numberless politicians are now availing themselves of it—but increasingly a decision will have to be made. Are you in favor of or against allowing openly gay women and men to continue serving their country? Do you favor or oppose gay marriage? Do you support the idea of gay civil rights laws? Once these questions are asked, the gentle ambiguity of the moderates must be flushed out; they have to be forced either into the conservative camp or into formulating a new politics that does not depend on a code of discourse that is fast becoming defunct.

They cannot even rely upon their gay friends anymore. What ultimately sustained this politics was the complicity of the gay elites in it: their willingness to stay silent when a gay joke was made in their presence, their deference to the euphemisms—roommate, friend, companion—that denoted their lovers, husbands, and wives, their support of the heterosexual assumptions of polite society. Now that complicity, if not vanished, has come under strain. There are fewer and fewer J. Edgar Hoovers and Roy Cohns, and the thousands of discreet gay executives and journalists, businessmen and politicians who long deferred to their sexual betters in matters of etiquette. AIDS rendered their balancing act finally absurd. Many people—gay and straight—were forced to have the public courage of their private convictions. They had to confront the fact that their delicacy was a way of disguising shame; that their silence was a means of hiding from themselves their intolerance. This is not an easy process; indeed, it can be a terrifying one for both gay and straight people alike. But there comes a point after which omissions become commissions; and that point, if not here yet, is coming. When it arrives, the moderate politics of homosexuality will be essentially over.

IV.

The politics that is the most durable in our current attempt to deal with the homosexual question is the contemporary liberal politics of homosexuality. Like the moderates, the liberals accept that homosexuality exists, that it is involuntary for a proportion of society, that for a few more it is an option, and that it need not be discouraged. Viewing the issue primarily through the prism of the civil rights movement, the liberals seek to extend to homosexuals the same protections they have granted to other minorities. The prime instrument for this is the regulation of private activities by heterosexuals, primarily in employment and housing, to guarantee non-discrimination against homosexuals.

Sometimes this strategy is echoed in the rhetoric of Edward Kennedy, who, in the hearings on the military gay ban, linked the gay rights agenda with the work of such disparate characters as John Kennedy, Cesar Chavez and Martin Luther King, Jr. In other places, it is reflected in the fact that sexual orientation is simply added to the end of a list of minority conditions, in formulaic civil rights legislation. And this strategy makes a certain sense. Homosexuals are clearly subject to private discrimination in the same way as many other minorities; and linking the causes helps defuse some of the trauma that the subject of homosexuality raises. Liberalism properly restricts itself to law—not culture—in addressing social problems; and by describing all homosexuals as a monolithic minority, it is able to avoid the complexities of the gay world as a whole, just as blanket civil rights legislation draws a veil over the varieties of black America by casting the question entirely in terms of non-black attitudes.

But this strategy is based on two assumptions: that sexuality is equivalent to race in terms of discrimination, and that the full equality of homosexuals can be accomplished by designating gay people as victims. Both are extremely dubious. And the consequence of these errors is to mistarget the good that liberals are trying to do.

Consider the first. Two truths (at least) profoundly alter the way the process of discrimination takes place against homosexuals and against racial minorities and distinguish the history of racial discrimination in this country from the history of homophobia. Race is always visible; sexuality can be hidden. Race is in no way behavioral; sexuality, though distinct from sexual activity, is linked to a settled pattern of behavior.

For lesbians and gay men, the option of self-concealment has always existed and still exists, an option that means that, in a profound way, discrimination against them is linked to their own involvement, even acquiescence. Unlike blacks three decades ago, gay men and lesbians suffer no discernible communal economic deprivation and already operate at the highest levels of society: in boardrooms, governments, the media, the military, the law, and industry. They may have advanced so far because they have not disclosed their sexuality, but their sexuality as such has not been an immediate cause for their disadvantage. In many cases, their sexuality is known, but it is disclosed at such a carefully calibrated level that it never actually works against them. At lower levels of society, the same pattern continues. As in the military, gay people are not uniformly discriminated against; *openly* gay people are.

Moreover, unlike blacks or other racial minorities, gay people are not subject to inherited patterns of discrimination. When generation after generation is discriminated against, a cumulative effect of deprivation may take place, where the gradual immiseration of a particular ethnic group may intensify with the years. A child born into a family subject to decades of accumulated poverty is clearly affected by a past history of discrimination in terms of his or her race. But homosexuality occurs randomly anew with every generation. No sociological pattern can be deduced from it. Each generation gets a completely fresh start in terms of the socioeconomic conditions inherited from the family unit.

This is not to say that the psychological toll of homosexuality is less problematic than that of race, but that it is different: in some ways better; in others, worse. Because the stigma is geared toward behavior, the level of shame and collapse of self-esteem may be more intractable. To reach puberty and find oneself falling in love with members of one's own sex is to experience a mixture of self-discovery and self-disgust that never leaves a human consciousness. If the stigma is attached not simply to an obviously random characteristic, such as skin pigmentation, but to the deepest desires of the human heart, then it can eat away at a person's sense of his own dignity with peculiar ferocity. When a young person confronts her sexuality, she is also completely alone. A young heterosexual black or Latino girl invariably has an existing network of people like her to interpret, support, and explain the emotions she feels when confronting racial prejudice for the first time. But a gay child generally has no one. The very people she would most naturally turn to—the family—may be the very people she is most ashamed in front of.

The stigma attached to sexuality is also different than that attached to race because it attacks the very heart of what makes a human being human: her ability to love and be loved. Even the most vicious persecution of racial minorities allowed, in many cases, for the integrity of the marital bond or the emotional core of a human being. When it did not, when Nazism split husbands from wives, children from parents, when apartheid or slavery broke up familial bonds, it was clear that a particularly noxious form of repression was taking place. But the stigma attached to homosexuality *begins* with such a repression. It forbids, at a child's earliest stage of development, the possibility of the highest form of human happiness. It starts with emotional terror and ends with mild social disapproval. It's no accident that, later in life, when many gay people learn to reconnect the bonds of love and sex, they seek to do so in private, even protected from the knowledge of their family.

This unique combination of superficial privilege, acquiescence in repression, and psychological pain is a human mix no politics can easily tackle. But it is the mix liberalism must address if it is to reach its goal of using politics to ease human suffering. The internal inconsistency of this politics is that by relying on the regulation of private activity, it misses its essential target—and may even make matters worse. In theory, a human rights statute sounds like an ideal solution, a way for straights to express their concern and homosexuals to legitimate their identity. But in practice, it misses the point. It might grant workers a greater sense of security were they to come out in the office; and it might, by the publicity it generates, allow for greater tolerance and approval of homosexuality generally. But the real terror of coming out is deeper than economic security, and it is not resolved by it; it is related to emotional and interpersonal dignity. However effective or comprehensive anti-discrimination laws are, they cannot reach far enough to tackle this issue; it is one that can only be addressed person by person, life by life, heart by heart.

For these reasons, such legislation rarely touches the people most in need of it: those who live in communities where disapproval of homosexuality is so intense that the real obstacles to advancement remain impervious to legal remedy. And even in major urban areas, it can be largely irrelevant. (On average some 1 to 2 percent of anti-discrimination cases have to do with sexual orientation; in Wisconsin, which has had such a law in force for more than a decade and is the largest case study, the figure is 1.1 percent.) As with other civil rights legislation, those least in need of it may take fullest advantage: the most litigious and articulate homosexuals, who would likely brave the winds of homophobia in any case.

Anti-discrimination laws scratch the privileged surface, while avoiding the problematic depths. Like too many drugs for AIDS, they treat the symptoms of the homosexual problem without being anything like a cure; they may buy some time, and it is a cruel doctor who, in the face of human need, would refuse them. But they have about as much chance of tackling the deep roots of the gay-straight relationship as AZT has of curing AIDS. They want to substitute for the traumatic and difficult act of coming out the more formal and procedural act of legislation. But law cannot do the work of life. Even culture cannot do the work of life. Only life can do the work of life.

As the experience in Colorado and elsewhere shows, this strategy of using law to change private behavior also gives a fatal opening to the conservative politics of homosexuality. Civil rights laws essentially dictate the behavior of heterosexuals, in curtailing their ability to discriminate. They can, with justification, be portrayed as being an infringement of individual liberties. If the purpose of the liberal politics is to ensure the equality of homosexuals and their integration into society, it has thus achieved something quite peculiar. It has provided fuel for those who want to argue that homosexuals are actually seeking the infringement of heterosexuals' rights and the imposition of their values onto others. Much of this is propaganda, of course, and is fueled by fear and bigotry. But it works because it contains a germ of truth. Before most homosexuals have even come out of the closet, they are demanding concessions from the majority, including a clear curtailment of economic and social liberties, in order to ensure protections few of them will even avail themselves of. It is no wonder there is opposition, or that it seems to be growing. Nine states now have propositions to respond to what they see as the "special rights" onslaught.

In the process, the liberal politics of homosexuality has also reframed the position of gays in relation to straights. It has defined them in a permanent supplicant status, seeing gay freedom as dependent on straight enlightenment, achievable only by changing the behavior of heterosexuals. The valuable political insight of radicalism is that this is a fatal step. It could enshrine forever the notion that gay people are a vulnerable group in need of protection. By legislating homosexuals as victims, it sets up a psychological dynamic of supplication that too often only perpetuates cycles of inadequacy and self-doubt. Like blacks before them, gay people may grasp at what seems to be an escape from the prison of self-hatred, only to find it is another prison of patronized victimology. By seeking salvation in the hands of others, they may actually entrench in law and in their minds the notion that their equality is dependent on the goodwill of their betters. It isn't. This may have made a good deal of sense in the case of American blacks, with a clear and overwhelming history of accumulated discrimination and a social ghetto that seemed impossible to breach. But for gay people—already prosperous, independent, and on the brink of real integration—that lesson should surely now be learned. To place our self-esteem in the benevolent hands of contemporary liberalism is more than a mistake. It is a historic error.

V.

If there were no alternative to today's liberal politics of homosexuality, it should perhaps be embraced by default. But there is an alternative politics that is imaginable, which once too was called liberal. It begins with the view that for a small minority of people, homosexuality is an involuntary condition that can neither be denied nor permanently repressed. It adheres to an understanding that there is a limit to what politics can achieve in such an area, and trains its focus not on the behavior of private heterosexual citizens but on the actions of the public and allegedly neutral state. While it eschews the use of law to legislate culture, it strongly believes that law can affect culture indirectly. Its goal would be full civil equality for those who, through no fault of their own, happen to be homosexual; and would not deny homosexuals, as the other four politics do, their existence, integrity, dignity, or distinctness. It would attempt neither to patronize nor to exclude.

This liberal politics affirms a simple and limited criterion: that all *public* (as opposed to private) discrimination against homosexuals be ended and that every right and responsibility that heterosexuals enjoy by virtue of the state be extended to those who grow up different. And that is all. No cures or re-educations; no wrenching civil litigation; no political imposition of tolerance; merely a political attempt to enshrine formal civil equality, in the hope that eventually the private sphere will reflect this public civility. For these reasons, it is the only politics that actually tackles the core political problem of homosexuality and perhaps the only one that fully respects liberalism's public-private distinction. For these reasons, it has also the least chance of being adopted by gays and straights alike.

But is it impossible? By sheer circumstance, this politics has just been given its biggest boost since the beginning of the debate over the homosexual question. The military ban is by far the most egregious example of proactive government discrimination in this country. By conceding, as the military has done, the excellent service that many gay and lesbian soldiers have given to their country, the military has helped shatter a thousand stereotypes about their nature and competence. By focusing on the mere admission of homosexuality, the ban has purified the debate into a matter of the public enforcement of homophobia. Unlike anti-discrimination law, the campaign against the ban does not ask any private citizens to hire or fire anyone of whom they do not approve; it merely asks public servants to behave the same way with avowed homosexuals as with closeted ones.

Because of its timing, because of the way in which it has intersected with the coming of age of gay politics, the military debate has a chance of transforming the issue for good. Its real political power—and the real source of the resistance to it—comes from its symbolism. The acceptance of gay people at the heart of the state, at the core of the notion of patriotism, is anathema to those who wish to consign homosexuals to the margins of society. It offends conservatives by the simplicity of its demands, and radicals by the traditionalism of the gay people involved; it dismays moderates, who are forced publicly to discuss this issue for the first time; and it disorients liberals, who find it hard to fit the cause simply into the rubric of minority politics. For instead of seeking access, as other minorities have done, gays in the military are simply demanding recognition. They start not from the premise of suppliance, but of success, of proven ability. This is a new kind of minority politics. It is less a matter of complaint than of pride; less about subversion than about the desire to contribute equally.

The military ban also forces our society to deal with the real issues at stake in dealing with homosexuals. The country has been forced to discuss sleeping arrangements, fears of sexual intimidation, the fraught emotional relations between gays, and straights, the violent reaction to homosexuality among many young males, the hypocrisy involved in much condemnation of gays and the possible psychological and emotional syndromes that make homosexuals allegedly unfit for service. Like a family engaged in the first, angry steps toward dealing with a gay member, the country has been forced to debate a subject honestly—even calmly—in a way it never has before. This is a clear and enormous gain. Whatever the result of this process, it cannot be undone.

But the critical measure necessary for full gay equality is something deeper and more emotional perhaps than even the military. It is equal access to marriage. As with the military, this is a question of formal public discrimination. If the military ban deals with the heart of what it is to be a citizen, the marriage ban deals with the core of what it is to be a member of civil society. Marriage is not simply a private contract; it is a social and public recognition of a private commitment. As such it is the highest public recognition of our personal integrity. Denying it to gay people is the most public affront possible to their civil equality.

This issue may be the hardest for many heterosexuals to accept. Even those tolerant of homosexuals may find this institution so wedded to the notion of heterosexual commitment that to extend it would be to undo its very essence. And there may be religious reasons for resisting this that require far greater discussion than I can give them here. But *civilly* and *emotionally*, the case is compelling. The heterosexuality of marriage is civilly intrinsic only if it is understood to be inherently procreative; and that definition has long been abandoned in civil society. In contemporary America, marriage has become a way in which the state recognizes an emotional and economic commitment of two people to each other for life. No law requires children to consummate it. And within that definition, there is no civil way it can logically be denied homosexuals, except as a pure gesture of public disapproval. (I leave aside here the thorny issue of adoption rights, which I support in full. They are not the same as the right to marriage and can be legislated, or not, separately.)

In the same way, emotionally, marriage is characterized by a kind of commitment that is rare even among heterosexuals, Extending it to homosexuals need not dilute the special nature of that commitment, unless it is understood that gay people, by their very nature, are incapable of it. History and experience suggest the opposite. It is not necessary to prove that gay people are more or less able to form long-term relationships than straights for it to be clear that, at least, *some* are. Giving these people a right to affirm their commitment doesn't reduce the incentive for heterosexuals to do the same, and even provides a social incentive for lesbians and gay men to adopt socially beneficial relationships.

But for gay people, it would mean far more than simple civil equality. The vast majority of us—gay and straight—are brought up to understand that the apex of emotional life is found in the marital bond. It may not be something we achieve, or even ultimately desire, but its very existence premises the core of our emotional development. It is the architectonic institution that frames our emotional life. The marriages of others are a moment for celebration and self-affirmation; they are the way in which our families and friends reinforce us as human beings. Our parents consider our emotional lives to be more important than our professional ones, because they care about us at our core, not at our periphery. And it is not hard to see why the marriage of an offspring is often regarded as the high point of any parent's life.

Gay people always know this essential affirmation will be denied them. Thus their relationships are given no anchor, no endpoint, no way of integrating them fully into the network of family and friends that makes someone a full member of civil society. Even when those relationships become essentially the same—or even stronger—than straight relationships, they are never accorded the dignity of equality. Husbands remain "friends"; wives remain "partners." The very language sends a powerful signal of fault, a silent assumption of internal disorder or insufficiency. The euphemisms—and the brave attempt to pretend that gay people don't need marriage—do not successfully conceal the true emotional cost and psychological damage that this signal exacts. No true progress in the potential happiness of gay teenagers or in the stability of gay adults or in the full integration of gay and straight life is possible, or even imaginable, without it.

These two measures—simple, direct, requiring no change in heterosexual behavior and no sacrifice from heterosexuals—represent a politics that tackles the heart of homophobia while leaving homophobes their freedom. It allows homosexuals to define their own future and their own identity and does not place it in the hands of the other. It makes a clear, public statement of equality, while leaving all the inequalities of emotion and passion to the private sphere, where they belong. It does not legislate private tolerance, it declares public equality. It banishes the paradigm of victimology and replaces it with one of integrity. It requires one further step, of course, which is to say the continuing effort for honesty on the part of homosexuals themselves. This is not easily summed up in the crude phrase "coming out"; but it finds expression in the myriad ways in which gay men and lesbians talk, engage, explain, confront, and seek out the other. Politics cannot substitute for this; heterosexuals cannot provide it. And, while it is not in some sense fair that homosexuals have to initiate the dialogue, it is a fact of life. Silence, if it does not equal death, equals the living equivalent.

It is not the least of the ironies of this politics that its objectives are in some sense not political at all. The family is prior to the liberal state; the military is coincident with it. Heterosexuals would not conceive of such rights as things to be won, but as things that predate modern political discussion. But it says something about the unique status of homosexuals in our society that we now have to be political in order to be pre-political. Our battle is not for political victory, but for personal integrity. Just as many of us had to leave our families in order to join them again, so now as citizens, we have to embrace politics, if only ultimately to be free of it. Our lives may have begun in simplicity, but they have not ended there. Our dream, perhaps, is that they might.

A Socialism of the Skin (Liberation, Honey!)
TONY KUSHNER

Is there a relationship between homosexual liberation and socialism? That's an unfashionably utopian question, but I pose it because
it's entirely conceivable that we will one day live miserably in a
thoroughly ravaged world in which lesbians and gay men can marry
and serve openly in the army and that's it. Capitalism, after all,
can absorb a lot. Poverty, war, alienation, environmental destruction, colonialism, unequal development, boom/bust cycles, private
property, individualism, commodity fetishism, the fetishization of
the body, the fetishization of violence, guns, drugs, child abuse,
underfunded and bad education (itself a form of child abuse)—
these things are key to the successful functioning of the free market.
Homophobia is not; the system could certainly accommodate
demands for equal rights for homosexuals without danger to itself.

But are officially sanctioned homosexual marriages and identifiably homosexual soldiers the ultimate aims of homosexual liberation? Clearly not, if by homosexual liberation we mean the
liberation of homosexuals who, like most everyone else, are and will

continue to be oppressed by the depredations of capital until some better way of living together can be arrived at. Are homosexual marriages and soldiery the ultimate, which is to say the only achievable aims of the *gay rights movement*, a politics not of vision but of pragmatics?

Andrew Sullivan, in a provocative, carefully reasoned, moving, troubling article in the *New Republic* a year ago [May 10, 1993], arrived at that conclusion. I used to have a crush on Andrew, neocon or neo-liberal (or whatever the hell they're called these days) though he be. I would never have married him, but he's cute! Then he called me a "West Village Neil Simon," *in print*, and I retired the crush. This by way of background for what follows, to prove that I am, despite my wounded affections, capable of the "restraint and reason" he calls for at the opening of his article, "The Politics of Homosexuality: A New Case for a New Beginning."

Andrew divides said politics into four, you should pardon the expression, camps—conservative, radical, moderate, and liberal— each of which lacks a workable "solution to the problem of gay-straight relations." Conservatives (by which he means reactionaries, I think, but he is very polite) and radicals both profess different brands of an absolutist politics of "impossibilism," which alienates them from "the mainstream." Moderates (by which he means conservatives) practice an ostrich-politics of delicate denial, increasingly superseded by the growing visibility of gay men and lesbians. And liberals (moderates) err mainly in trying to legislate, through antidiscrimination bills, against reactive, private sector bigotry.

Andrew's prescription is that liberals, with whom he presumably identifies most closely, go after "pro-active" governmental bans on homosexuals participating in the military and the institution of marriage. Period. "All *public* (as opposed to private) discrimination against homosexuals [should] be ended and…every right and responsibility heterosexuals enjoy by virtue of the state [should] be extended to those who grow up different. And that is all." Andrew's new "liberal" gay politics "…does not legislate private tolerance, it declares public equality.… Our battle is not for political victory but for personal integrity."

Everyone should read Andrew's article for his sharp critique of the contradictions within right-wing homophobic thought, and for his delicate filleting of what he calls "moderate," know-nothing, blinders-on types like Sam Nunn. Most important, the article is a kind of manifesto for gay conservatism, and as such it deserves scrutiny.

Every manifesto deserves acolytes as well as scrutiny, and "The Politics of Homosexuality" has earned at least one: Bruce Bawer, who appears a year later [June 13, 1994], in last month's *New Republic*, with "The Stonewall Myth: Can the Gay Rights Movement Get Beyond the Politics of Nostalgia?" Bruce, however, is no Andrew. He's cute enough; you can see him looking rueful and contemplative on the cover of his book, *A Place at the Table*, though if you've read the book you'll know Bruce doesn't like it when gay men get dishy and bitchy and talk sissy about boys. He thinks it makes us look bad for the straights. Bruce is serious, more serious even than Andrew, as the big open book in the cover photo proclaims: He's read more than half of it! (Lest anyone think I habitually read the *New Republic*, the playwright David Greenspan gave me Andrew's article, and Andrew Kopkind and several others drew my attention to Bruce's.)

Bruce is not only more serious than Andrew, he's more polite, no mean feat; he's so polite I hate to write that he's also much easier to dismiss, but he is. His article is short and sloppy, and he has this habit of creating paper tigers. Take the eponymous "Stonewall Myth," to which "many gay men and lesbians routinely" subscribe. According to Bruce, these "many" believe gay history started with Stonewall, and regard the riot as "a sacred event that lies beyond the reach of objective discourse." Huh? I don't know anyone who believes that, and I've never encountered such a ridiculous assertion in any work of gay criticism or reportage or even fiction. But Bruce goes on for pages tilting at this windmill and the "politics of nostalgia" that accompanies it. He's also, and I mean this politely, a little slow. It took him five years to figure out that maybe a gay man shouldn't be writing movie reviews for the viciously homophobic *American Spectator*. In his book he is anguished: "Had I been wrong to write for so reactionary a publication? If so, then how did one figure out where to draw the line? Should I refuse to write for the *Nation* because its editors frequently appeared to be apologists for Communism?..." etc.

In the article Bruce decides that our real problem is a fear of acceptance, fear of success, a "deep unarticulated fear of that metaphorical place at the table," and so we march in front of TV cameras in our underwear, confirming for all the world that we really *are* sick. (Clothes, worn and discarded, are always bothering Bruce, spandex and leather gear and business suits and bras, his writing is littered with the stuff.) I'll focus mostly on Andrew's meatier, seminal (sigh!) text. (For a polite but mostly thorough reaming of *A Place at the Table*, read David Bergman in the Spring '94 issue of the *Harvard Gay and Lesbian Review*.)

In "The Politics of Homosexuality," Andrew concedes quite a lot of good will to those farthest to the Right. He draws an odd distinction between the "visceral recoil" of bigots and the more cautious discomfort of those homophobes who "sincerely believe" in "discouraging homosexuality," who couch their sincere beliefs in "Thomist argument," in "the natural law tradition, which, for all its failings is a resilient pillar of Western thought." Bigotry, too, is a resilient pillar of Western thought, or it was the last time I checked. Andrew realizes that bigotry "expresses itself in thuggery and name-calling. But there are some [conservatives] who don't support anti-gay violence..." Like who, for instance? George Will, Bill Buckley, and Cardinal O'Connor have all made token clucking noises about fag-bashing, but the incommensurability of these faint protests with the frightening extent of anti-lesbian and gay violence, which has certainly been encouraged by the very vocal homophobia of "conservatives," might force one to question the sincerity of their admonitions and, further, to question the value of distinguishing "Thomist" homophobes from the "thugs" who in 1993 attacked or killed more than 1,900 lesbians and gay men (at least these are the hate crimes we know about).

Andrew takes a placid view of people on the reactionary Right because he is convinced their days are numbered. But does he really believe that Pat Buchanan is now "reduced to joke-telling"? Such a conclusion is possible only if one ignores the impressive, even terrifying, political energies of the religious Right. Since Andrew decides political discourse can only countenance "reason and restraint," he of course must exclude the Bible-thumpers, who are crazy and *loud*. But the spectrum is more crowded, and on the Right less well-behaved than a gentleman like Andrew cares to admit. His is an endearing reticence, but it is not wise.

Andrew is at his best describing the sorts of traumas homophobia inflicts on its victims (though to nobody's surprise he doesn't care for the word "victim"), yet he's quick to give up on the antidiscrimination legislation of those he calls liberals. "However effective or comprehensive antidiscrimination laws are, they cannot reach far enough." They can't give us confidence, and they only "scratch the privileged surface." "As with other civil rights legislation, those least in need of it may take fullest advantage: the most litigious and articulate homosexuals, who would likely brave the harsh winds of homophobia in any case."

It's unclear whether or not Andrew opposes such legislation which, it seems to me, is worthwhile even if it is only moderately effective. I assume that in limiting the gay rights movement's ambitions to fighting "proactive" discrimination, he is arguing against trying to pass laws that regulate "reactive" discrimination, though I can't find anything in his very specific article that states this opposition specifically or definitively. (In any case, his distinction between *reactive* and *proactive* discrimination falls apart as soon as one considers adoption laws or education or sexual harassment.) Perhaps he's vague because he knows he hasn't much of a case. What worries him especially is that the Right will make effective propaganda out of the argument that "civil rights laws essentially dictate the behavior of heterosexuals, in curtailing their ability to discriminate." And he argues further that this argument "contains a germ of truth."

The argument is unquestionably good propaganda for homophobes, but it's identical to the NRA's argument for giving every nutbag in the country access to a semi-automatic. (Don't curtail their ability to be armed nutbags!) We have to argue such propaganda down, not run away from the legislation that inspires it. As for the "germ of truth," Andrew writes: "Before most homosexuals come out of the closet they are demanding concessions from the majority, a clear curtailment of economic and social liberties, in order to ensure protections few of them will even avail themselves of. It is no wonder there is opposition."

This is a very peculiar view of the processes by which enfranchisement is extended: Civil rights, apparently, are not rights at all, not something inalienable, to which one is entitled by virtue of being human or a citizen, but concessions the majority makes to a minority if and only if the minority can promise it will *use* those rights. Antidiscrimination laws are seen as irrelevant to creating a safer environment in which closeted or otherwise-oppressed people might feel more free to exercise their equality; laws apparently cannot *encourage* freedom, only punish transgressions against it.

The argument that antidiscrimination laws violate "majority" freedoms can be and has been used to eliminate the basis of most of the legislation from the civil rights movement. Affirmative action, housing and employment laws, and voter redistricting can all be said to curtail the freedom of bigots to discriminate, which is in fact what such measures are supposed to do. The connection that such legislation implies between gay rights and other minority rights displeases Andrew, who resists the idea that, as forms of oppressions, homophobia and racism have much in common.

With homosexuality, according to Andrew, "the option of self-concealment has always existed," something that cannot be said about race. (I could introduce him to some flaming creatures who might make him question that assessment, but never mind.) "Gay people are not uniformly discriminated against, *openly* gay people are." Certainly there are important differences of kind and degree and consequence between racism and homophobia, but the idea that invisibility exempts anyone from discrimination is perverse. To need to be invisible, or to feel that you need to be, if there is reason for that fear, is to be discriminated against. The fact that homophobia differs significantly from racism—and loath as I am to enter the discrimination olympics, I would argue that the consequences of racism in America today are worse than those of homophobia—does not mean that people engaged in one struggle can't learn or borrow from another, or that the tools one oppressed people have developed can't be used to try to liberate others.

Andrew is joined by Bruce in his anxiety to preserve the differences among various kinds of oppression, but they both seem less interested in according each group its own "integrity," as Andrew rightly calls it, than in preventing gay rights from being shanghaied by the radical Left. "The standard post-Stonewall practice…indiscriminately link[s] the movement for gay equal rights with any Left-wing cause to which any gay leader might happen to have a personal allegiance" (this is from Bruce's article). "Such linkages have been a disaster for the gay rights movement: Not only do they imply that most gay people sympathize with those so-called progressive movements, but they also serve to reinforce the idea of homosexuality itself as a 'progressive' phenomenon, as something essentially political in nature." Andrew meanwhile warns against the "universalist temptation," which exercises "an enervating and dissipating effect on gay radicalism's political punch."

Gay radicalism's political punch is not something either Andrew or Bruce wishes to see strengthened. Conservative gay politics is in a sense the politics of containment: Connections made with a broadly defined Left are what must be contained. The pair predicts the emergence of increasing numbers of conservative homosexuals (presumably white—in both Andrew's and Bruce's prophecies they come from the suburbs) who are unsympathetic to the idea of linking their fortunes with any other political cause. The future depends not on collectivity and solidarity, but on homosexual individualism—on lesbians and gay men instructing the straight world quietly, "person by person, life by life, heart by heart" (Andrew); to "do the hard, painstaking work of *getting* straight America used to it" (Bruce).

Like all assimilationists, Andrew and Bruce are unwilling to admit that structural or even particularly formidable barriers exist between themselves and their straight oppressors. And for all their elaborate fears that misbehaving queers alienate instead of communicate, there is nowhere in these articles a concern that people of color or the working class or the poor are not being communed with. The audience we are ostensibly losing is identified exclusively as phobic straights, "families" (which one suspects are two-parent, middle class) and gay teenagers.

Bruce and Andrew are very concerned about young gay people. Watching a "lean and handsome" fifteen-year-old leaf through the *New York Native* at the start of his book, Bruce worries that queer radicalism, sexual explicitness, and kink frighten gay kids and the families from whence they come. Probably it is the case that teenagers are freaked by photo ads for The Dungeon. But the *Native* is not produced for teenagers. Images of adult lesbian and gay desire can't be tailored to appeal to fifteen-year-olds and their straight parents. Our culture is the manifest content of our lives, not a carefully constructed recruiting brochure. True, there aren't readily available, widely circulated images of homosexual domesticity or accomplishment or happiness, but I'd be more inclined to blame the homophobic media than gay radicalism for that. Nor does the need for such images mandate the abandonment of public declarations of and *for* the variety of sexual desire, the public denial and repression of which is after all The Problem. Lesbian and gay kids will have less trouble accepting their homosexuality not when the Gay Pride Parade is an orderly procession of suits arranged in monogamous pairs but when people learn to be less horrified by sex and its complexities.

Out of the great stew of class, race, gender, and sexual politics that inspirits the contentious, multiplying, endlessly unfixed lesbian and gay community in America, gay conservatism manages to pick out a majority who are virtually indistinguishable in behavior and aspirations and *Weltanschauung* from the straight world, and a minority of deviants and malcontents who are fucking things up for everyone, thwarting the only realizable goal, which is normality.

Andrew says up front that politics is supposed to relieve anxiety. I'd say that it's supposed to relieve misery and injustice. When all that can be expected from politics, in the way of immediate or even proximate social transformation, are gay weddings and gay platoons, the vast rest of it all, every other agony inflicted by homophobia, will have to be taken care of by some cultural osmotic process of quiet individualized persuasion, which will take many many many years. It's the no-government approach to social change. You can hear it argued now against school desegregation, or any attempt to guarantee equal education; you can hear it argued against welfare or job programs. It's the legacy of trickle-down, according to which society should change slowly, organically, spontaneously, without interference, an approach that requires not so much the "discipline, commitment, responsibility" that Bruce exhorts us to—we already practice those—but a great appalling luxury of time (which maybe the editor of the *New Republic* and the erstwhile movie critic of the *American Spectator* can afford), after the passage of which many many many more miserable lives will have been spent or dispensed with. I am always suspicious of the glacier-paced patience of the Right.

Such a politics of homosexuality is dispiriting. Like conservative thought in general, it offers very little in the way of hope, and very little in the way of vision. We shall soon have gay GIs and same-sex confectionery couples atop wedding cakes. This is important, but it's not enough. I expect both hope and vision from my politics. Andrew and Bruce offer nothing more than that gay culture will dissolve invisibly into straight culture, all important difference elided.

I think both Andrew and Bruce would call this assessment unfair. Andrew's politics may be roomier than Bruce's; Andrew is more worldly and generous (except, apparently, when it comes to the theater). Both men have a vision. They see before them an attainable civic peace, in which gay men and lesbians live free of fear (of homophobia, at least), in which gay kids aren't made to feel worthless, or worse, because they're gay.

But what of all the other things gay men and lesbians have to fear? What of the things gay children have to fear, in common with all children? What of the planetary despoilment that kills us? Or the financial necessity that drives some of us into unsafe, insecure, stupid, demeaning, and ill-paying jobs? Or the unemployment that impoverishes some of us? Or the racism some of us face? Or the rape some of us fear? What about AIDS? Is it enough to say: Not our problem? Of course gay and lesbian politics is a progressive politics: It depends on progress for the accomplishment of any of its goals. Is there any progressive politics that recognizes no connectedness, no border crossings, no solidarity or possibility for mutual aid?

"A map of the world that does not include Utopia is not worth even glancing at, for it leaves out the one country at which Humanity is always landing." This is neither Bruce nor Andrew, but that most glorious and silly gay writer, Oscar Wilde. Because this is the twenty-fifth anniversary of Stonewall, that mythic moment that lies beyond all objective discourse (just kidding, Bruce!), we are all thinking big. That's what anniversaries are for, to invite consideration of the past and contemplation of the future. And so, to lift my sights and spirits after the dour, pinched, anti-politics of gay conservatism, I revisited Oscar, a *lavish* thinker, as he appears in political drag in his magnificent essay, "The Soul of Man Under Socialism."

Oscar, like our two boys, was an individualist, though rather more individual in the way he lived, and much less eager to conform. It would be stretching things to say Oscar was a radical, exactly, though if Bruce and Andrew had been his contemporaries, Lord knows how they would have tut-tutted at his scandalous carryings-on.

Oscar's socialism is an exaltation of the individual, of the individual's immense capacities for beauty and for pleasure. Behind Oscar's socialist politics, wrote John Cowper Powys, is "a grave Mirandola-like desire to reconcile the woods of Arcady with the Mount of Transfiguration." What could be swoonier? Or, with all due deference to Andrew and Bruce's *sober*, *rational* politics of homosexuality, what could be more gay?

Powys also wrote that Oscar's complaint against capitalism and industrialism is "the irritation of an extremely sensitive *skin* [emphasis added]...combined with a pleasure-lover's annoyance at seeing other people so miserably wretched." If there is a relationship between socialism and homosexual liberation, perhaps this is it: an irritation of the skin.

"One's regret," Oscar tells us, "is that society should be constructed on such a basis that man is forced into a groove in which he cannot freely develop what is wonderful and fascinating and delightful in him—in which, in fact, he misses the true plea-sure and joy of living." Socialism, as an alternative to individual-ism politically and capitalism economically, must surely have as its ultimate objective the restitution of the joy of living we may have lost when we first picked up a tool. Towards what other objective is it worthy to strive?

Perhaps the far horizon of lesbian and gay politics is a socialism of the skin. Our task is to confront the political problematics of desire and repression. As much as Bruce and Andrew want to distance themselves from the fact, Stonewall was a sixties thing, part of the utopian project of that time (and the sixties, Joan Nestle writes, is "the favorite target of people who take delight in the failure of dreams"). Honoring the true desire of the skin, and the connection between the skin and heart and mind and soul, is what homosexual liberation is about.

Gay rights may be obtainable, on however broad or limited a basis, but liberation depends on a politics that goes beyond, not an anti-politics. Our unhappiness as scared queer children doesn't only isolate us, it also politicizes us. It inculcates in us a desire for connection that is all the stronger because we have experienced its absence. Our suffering teaches us solidarity; or it should.

Blight and Fruit:
Some Thoughts on Sex, Death, and Censorship
SCOTT TUCKER

1.

All my life I've prided myself on fighting the good fight against censorship, but I've never written publicly about spending two months in a mental ward the summer I turned sixteen, nor about the occasional hustling which helped pay my way until my twentieth year. I've felt free to speak of these experiences in the select company of friends and activists, but I've been reluctant to produce "confessions" from which any bigot might extract meanings which are all too predictable and definite—even though I know very well how profoundly confessional the movements of women and gay people have been, and still remain. Censorship is most fully effective when it succeeds in setting the mechanism of self-censorship in motion; when those who are censored learn to practice self-censorship as a form of self-protection. Censorship implodes identity; confession (witness the "hysteria" of women and gays) explodes it in rage, grief, lust, and laughter.

The personal is political, we used to say, though we often failed to grasp just how variously that might be true. Every social movement is, in reality, plural and not singular—a movement of movements engaged in different strategies of resistance and reconciliation with the existing culture. Some of us have had scruples about making *things* out of our own lives, even if that thing should be a text or book with the power to speak when and where we can't be present in person. Things which can be shaped into weapons against us. We've been reluctant to put messages in bottles which may be translated against our own intentions when they reach some unknown shore, or which may be lost at sea—the very risk which must be taken.

Straight white men, if they are creatures of a certain class and culture, feel more confident of understanding, of a "universal" message they are especially graced to receive and pass on to posterity. Of course they have disputes and polemics among themselves, but this is a fraternity which feels entitled to its fights. "Knowledge is Power"—the words are carved in marble at schools and libraries, and who doubts it? This is why a fierce anti-intellectualism emerges at times among the oppressed, and why "the defense of culture" can also mean the defense of oppression. Now once again the debate about what constitutes the true canon of civilization has broken out in the universities and journals.

It *is* proper to ask, for example, just why or in what way Goethe's poem *Hermann and Dorothea* is more "universal" than Judy Grahn's poem *The Common Woman*. Goethe's poem, beautiful as it is in so many ways, is a classic of class culture and a patriarchal hymn; it was also and therefore written with the dim hope of making a poem such as Grahn's *impossible*—even in the future. The same Goethe ended *Faust* with a paean to "the Eternal Feminine," a notion with a rich and problematic history, including among some feminists, Jungians, and mystics today.

My first truly playful and serious writing was poetry, and maybe all my prose has been a way of returning to poetry. In the course of speaking my mind about culture, I've even been accused of hating art. Much of my published prose so far has really been the more analytical and combative mode of dealing with censorship. In Utopia I'd have spent more time sucking cocks and writing poems. In the real world I spend time writing these sentences.

I return to this section a few days after writing those last words, because in the meantime I've read some striking comments by Cherrie Moraga, a lesbian Chicana writer, which she made in an interview published recently in the gay magazine *Out/Look* (Winter, 1989). "As long as you're writing in resistance," she said, "you're on some level explaining, and having to explain does not produce great art. Though we'd like to think otherwise, it just doesn't... It cost me too much to explain, and it didn't give me what art gives; it didn't give me back, you know?... If I was going to write essays again, I would like to write them the way Adrienne Rich gets to write them. She doesn't explain anything to anybody because, as a poet, she is the voice of authority."

Her words are deeply suggestive, and clarify yet another way in which censorship operates. Goethe, Wordsworth, Tolstoy, and Eliot all wrote expository prose defending their own views and craft, but men of their race and class felt powerfully entitled to the right to write. "High" culture becomes a censorious force when it is used to exhaust those from below in explanations, and when the Pantheon becomes founded upon exclusions. If I were to argue with Moraga's comments, I'd only add that the official canon of great art is problematic, and is *itself* a powerful form of explanation and obfuscation. As for the authority of poets, the number of poets in this century with authoritarian sympathies should give us pause.

2.

In 1933, T. S. Eliot made this statement in a discussion of how a society maintains a "living tradition": "What is still more important is unity of religious background, and reasons of race and religion combine to make any large number of free-thinking Jews undesirable." These words were published in a collection of lectures in 1934 called After Strange Gods. Eliot chose not to reprint the book in his lifetime. Nowadays, many folks (religious and otherwise) feel it is more respectable to proclaim the undesirability of free-thinking queers.

There are some illuminating similarities in the experience of Jews and gays, but here I'll just mention the fact that both groups have been subject to the projections of majorities, and have been accused of exhibiting both selfish tribalism and corrosive cosmopolitanism. Cosmopolitanism was, of course, one of the most common swear-words in the lexicon of anti-Semitism. It is more rarely used against gays, but the word might well describe aspects of gay urban culture which are frequently despised. And patronized, of course—quite literally, as in patronizing the shops, theaters, restaurants, and resorts where gays provide much of the capital, labor, and ambiance. Whenever the left gets lazily general with its class analysis, the animus of the left against the petty bourgeoisie can become a mere sublimation of the right-wing's cruder anti-Semitism and heterosexism. Gentrification, for example, is a real factor in urban life; but the leftists who direct the most passionate fire at gay gentrifiers have hardly been the most passionate defenders of working-class queers or any other kind, whether in Havana or San Francisco.

3.

My lover and I had visited Key West as privileged tourists, but my own particular animus against both the petty and grand bourgeoisie was aroused when I spent three months living there. I worked with a renovation and construction crew consisting of men and women of all sexual orientations. We sculpted and painted the house of a wealthy gay corporate lawyer, also digging through coral to plant his garden. One of my crew mates, an "obvious" gay man, lived in the same slummy apartment block as I did, and was assaulted one night by two straight guys who lived below us. The straight folks at the real estate agency which ran the building threatened to evict us for making trouble— an old story! So we went for help to a gay politician, a gay lawyer, and a gay newspaper editor, all of them notable citizens, and all of them gave us the diplomatic brush-off. What else kept this island paradise afloat if not the solidarity of money? And here, too, there are similarities between divisions among Jews and divisions among gays. Our collective disasters— fascism and AIDS, among others—have not always produced solidarity across lines of class and culture. Gay notables in Key West donated funds to a local AIDS project, but challenging the policies of the island's major realtor was not their line of work.

When I wasn't working I spent my time at the gym and the beach. Given my sexual history, I assumed I was infected with HIV (which was confirmed by a medical test a year later). On weekends I'd dance at the Copa and fuck (rubbered) with friends, sometimes with strangers. I met a porn model I'll call Mike who tried fucking me without a rubber, and when I wrestled him gently away he got pissed and pulled out his works instead. Other than in movies or on TV, I'd never seen anybody shoot up. He watched me watching him and when he offered to hit me with the same needle, I asked him, "Are you trying to shock me?" Afterwards, I kept my distance from him until one of Mike's roommates told me that Mike had been diagnosed with AIDS and had fucked a few guys who neither knew this fact nor had taken any more responsibility for safe sex than Mike. We decided to confront Mike and he denied nothing, responding with physical threats. So we spread the word that Mike could be dangerous. Within two weeks he'd flown to LA, and I don't know whether it was he or the straight thugs living below me who slashed my bicycle tires. I've since heard that a wealthy gay psychiatrist fell in love with him and gave him shelter until Mike died.

That's the kind of story which makes the gay "mainstreamers" jittery, and indeed the more orthodox politicos and religionists tack on their own morals to such stories. I'll say that every person is finally a mystery, but that Mike might have been less destructive to himself and others if the gay movement had been more daring. The "pragmatic" and desexualized politics of polite gay leaders left folks like Mike out in the cold. AIDS has now sexualized queers again with a vengeance; and has also "declassed" some of the more privileged gay people by lumping them with lumpenproles, drug-users, dark-skinned folks, and "resident aliens." Straight progressives who demand some form of national health care have not always been pleased to make common cause with queers; even when they must address the AIDS crisis directly, they often make unsubtle suggestions that this epidemic really matters because people *other* than queers are dying.

Arch-reactionary Jesse Helms intimidated fellow politicians into condemning graphic safe sex brochures by raising the spectre of butt-fucking lepers. In this climate, it's not surprising that some conservatives *and* liberals who once granted gays a place in the arts are now insisting that we had better watch our step even within that reservation.

4.

In May of 1986 I entered the International Mr. Leather contest in Chicago. I only hoped to enjoy a weekend with gay leatherfolk from around the world, but I won the title and my duties included participating in various gay, leather, and AIDS fund-raising events from coast to coast. Riding floats during both the San Francisco and Los Angeles gay pride parades, I had the pleasure of flashing a bare-ass moon at groups of hell-fire Fundamentalists. So I became one of those embarrassments to the Public Relations Department of the gay movement. It was high time, in any case, to demonstrate public solidarity with folks who are often defined as too queer to be gay. For years, I'd opposed censorship inside and outside the gay movement, but diving into the leather scene meant putting theory into practice. Much was new to me, not all of it agreeable. But I want the communities of leatherfolk and drag queens to survive the increasingly upscale conformism of the movement. These communities will not survive intact— AIDS alone has killed so many—but they are, in fact, surviving and evolving. It helps that certain feminists are now producing their own pornography, and have challenged dogmas which reduce all transvestism to misogyny and all sadomasochism to fascism. Still other feminists lead censorship campaigns.

Drugs, alcohol, sex, costumes, pleasure, and pain are all forms of strong natural magic and have been used as such for thousands of years. They should be approached with respect, because all natural magic has dangerous dimensions if abused. Especially in communal settings, the rules of natural magic are likelier to be learned and observed in safety; and it will be a breakthrough for gay culture if communal sexual life can survive and thrive outside of the commercial nexus of bars and baths.

Who says we must choose between a communal life and the equal right to marry and raise kids? Why not both? Once we begin asking such questions, it becomes plain that we can be neither one-dimensional sexual libertarians, nor liberal assimilationists. No sexual revolution can succeed unless it proceeds with a social revolution to secure decent wages, education, housing, health-care, and child-care. Don't hold your breath waiting for the Democratic Party to fight these battles for you. Just remember that Kitty Dukakis brought meals to an AIDS hospice, performing for cameras in San Francisco, while her husband the presidential hopeful resolutely maintained that gays have no right to adopt children. The charity of politicians will always put us quite literally at their mercy. And since the Supreme Court has denied even our right to fuck behind locked doors, this much is crashingly clear: *Our right to privacy will never be secure until the public world is truly free.*

5.

Our right to privacy will never be secure until the public world is truly free. I've said that all my prose is a path back to poetry, but there are people who who will read that sentence and suspect or insist that it has everything to do with politics and nothing to do with poetry. Idiots, you have understood nothing! Poets who have no public world go crazy and sometimes kill themselves, and that, too, is one sign of a censorship so pervasive and invasive that it leads to a final act of self-censorship. "We poets in our youth begin in gladness," Wordsworth wrote, "But thereof come in the end despondency and madness." Well, Wordsworth ended in the contentment of an old fart. It was Hart Crane, the queer Hermetic poet, who died young, jumping into the sea. In my youth I had my share of despondency and madness, but outrageous gladness has won through so far. Artists have sometimes romanticized self-destruction, but why make censorship easy for the censors?

6.

In June of 1969 a police raid on the Stonewall Inn in Greenwich Village became a great deal more than business as usual, though it was news *The New York Times* did not see fit to print. That spark set off a street rebellion, and lesbian and gay militancy arose from coast to coast. "They are different from the rest of us," warned Joseph Epstein in *Harper's Magazine* the following year; and a full decade later, Midge Decter advised heterosexual readers of Commentary, "Know them as a group."

Shortly after Reagan was first elected, Norman Podhoretz examined "the heart of hearts" of "the liberal culture," and came to the conclusion that liberals might be willing to let the right wing do "the dirty work" of attacking gay people and turning back an unfinished sexual revolution, "while of course deploring and disclaiming any responsibility." The evidence that Podhoretz was correct includes the abysmal Dukakis presidential campaign, displaying a liberalism which dared not speak its name and which kept queers at a safe distance.

Aside from liberalism, what about the official left? In a country with no real labor party, leftist politics are often limited to the pages of the left press. This is not always a great loss, since the chief editors are too often the kind of straight men who resent the fact that queers and women have movements of our own; *they* dream of "unity," meaning a movement of working class heroes who have risen above all such secondary and subjective diversions. At *In These Times* and *The Nation*, such editors had to have fires lit under their butts before giving women and gays a poor share of free speech. *In These Times* published the wisdom of editor John Judis: "Society does not have the same responsibility towards homosexuality—whether as sexual behavior or as living arrangement—that it has towards the child-bearing family." That makes one excellent definition of heterosexism. The family is thus a kind of factory, quite in line with right-wing "family values," a sexual economy in which queers can only play the part of saboteurs on the assembly line.

At *The Nation*, the editors saw fit to print the witless bigotry of Robert Sherrill—specifically, his claim that AIDS was the right disease to kill off Roy Cohn, the right-wing gay lawyer. According to Sherrill, "there was something quite fitting in the putrescent ending of this very putrescent fellow." What Sherrill regards as semi-divine justice, I regard as a "progressive" form of moral insanity. Would death from Tay-Sachs disease be specially fitting for right-wing Jews? Or would sickle-cell anemia be specially fitting for right-wing blacks? The editors would never have published racism in that form without comment, but defended Sherrill's literary style when readers protested against blatant bigotry.

Sherrill took special pleasure in "exposing" Cohn's asshole to the world, the pleasure of a He-Man putting down the She-Man, the pleasure of a scandal-monger with a juicy piece to share—in this case, the anal lesion of a dying man. Soon after, *The Nation's* editors also chose to publish without comment a charming dialogue between Sherrill and John Judis in which each accused the other of besmirching the reputation of arch-conservative William Buckley with the dread charge of *effeminacy*. In this case, the brotherhood of heterosexuality crossed political lines; indeed, Sherrill said Buckley would be justified in punching out anyone who questioned his heterosexual manhood. This sort of thing earns leftist He-Men the reputation of cultural dinosaurs.

You have to wonder how much of culture and politics is based on He-Men protecting their rectal virginity. If a cock is the magic sword, then the invulnerable asshole is the magic shield in the full armor of manhood, and this is not inconsistent with the legendary propensity of Marines to bend the rules when "drunk." He-Men know that people who get fucked (women and gays) are fair game to get fucked over. The AIDS crisis has clarified anew some of the more murderous impulses of straight politicians and public figures towards gay people, especially in the willingness to distinguish between "innocent victims" of AIDS and expendable sodomites. Don't take my word for it: in an October 1987 issue of the *New York Post*, Norman Podhoretz assured himself and the world that AIDS is only rough justice for men who "allow themselves (in the striking old Victorian phrase) 'to be used as girls' by other men."

When Joseph Epstein wrote about homosexuality in 1970, he mentioned two men he suspected of "fucking the daylights out of each other," and he admitted, "I cannot get over the brutally simple fact that two men make love to each other." Given the intimately *personal* nature of Epstein's revulsion, he simply overlooked lesbians entirely. Straight men of his kind feel that they must save their own asses with great shows of indignation, and imputations of effeminacy are serious weapons in the arsenal of public abuse. Folks like Judis and Sherrill believe that such weapons must be used *honorably*—that is, only when there is a serious suspicion of a breach of rectal rectitude. Buckley may be effete, but fair is fair, and it's not fair for He-Men to fuck with each other's manhood.

Anal and vaginal sex are each more or less likely means of exposure to specific diseases, but since anal sex is productive of nothing except pleasure and intimacy, it is often regarded as a dispensably dangerous indulgence in the age of AIDS. Patrick Buchanan fulminated on television against "gays who perform suicidal and homicidal gay sex acts." Only a fraction of the bolder right-wingers openly demand the death penalty for sodomites; by comparison, the "moderates" only argue that AIDS is *sufficient* punishment, whose full force must not be mitigated by adequate funding of research and treatment.

In the February 1989 issue of *PWA Coalition Newsline*, Michael Callen has sharply taken the offensive in an article called "In Defense of Anal Sex," challenging both straight and gay people who "may feel only an asshole would defend the asshole in the age of AIDS." Callen quotes Dr. Joseph Sonnabend: "The rectum is a sexual organ, and it deserves the respect a penis gets and a vagina gets. Anal intercourse is a central sexual activity, and it should be supported; it should be celebrated." Yes, and what a shame it still takes the authority of a doctor and scientist to make the point.

The Public Relations Department of the gay movement gave reactionaries a great lead in public discussions of sex. Intent on conjuring up images of hard-working gay doctors and lawyers, they are at a loss when the right conjures up our bedrooms. Guess who practices the stronger magic here? Nor have the "mainstream" messengers of the gay movement been honest about the sexuality of youth. Terrified by accusations of seduction, gay public figures almost never defend the right of gay youngsters to a social and sexual life—a right which heterosexual teenagers increasingly take for granted, whether adults like it or not.

7.

Of the current sexual counterrevolution, Tom Wolfe wrote in *The American Spectator*, "All may be summed up in a single term, requiring no amplification: AIDS." In fact, a great many straight pundits and critics have been busy amplifying and multiplying the morals and meanings of AIDS. Some very telling examples of this trend are evident in the critical reactions to the recent exhibit of Robert Mapplethorpe's photographs. In Vanity Fair, Dominick Dunne suggested that Mapplethorpe's images reflected the kind of sexuality which resulted, "possibly, in the very plague that was killing its recorder." Mapplethorpe was then ill with AIDS, and has since died. In a published letter, Dr. Mathilde Krim tried to remind Dunne that distinctions must be made between a transmissible virus and gay sex as such.

The elision between homosexuality and deadly contagion is now standard political demagoguery. Before AIDS, our enemies spoke of "the plague of homosexuality"; after AIDS, they tend to reduce gay persons to plague-bearing insects and rodents. This is not unique in history, and the inexact parallel is again with Jews. In his book *Toward the Final Solution*, George Mosse wrote, "When the Warsaw Ghetto was stricken by epidemics of typhoid, the slogan 'Jews-Lice-Typhoid' was spread by the Germans among a not unreceptive Polish population." We should resist making crude equations between fascism and present reaction, but certain historical similarities are striking. Gay ghettoes, like Jewish ghettoes and Indian reservations, have been simultaneously quarantine camps and liberated zones—both in times of epidemics and not. Even those who sympathize with our struggles tend to slight this kind of contradictory reality and our own lived experience.

Arthur Danto's review of the Mapplethorpe show in a September 1988 issue of *The Nation* was perhaps the richest and most problematic liberal view of his work. Danto chose to judge Mapplethorpe's images of cocks, orchids, and lovers in leather as an expression of an essential and eternal "homosexual perception." Danto wrote of his photographs, "They are not just of gays at a certain moment in gay history, when it all at once seemed possible for this to become the substance of serious art." I would argue that Mapplethorpe's work is indeed that of a gay visionary, but precisely at a certain moment of history. Even our dreams and utopias are historically specific, and can be nothing else.

"To Generalize is to be an Idiot," wrote William Blake, adding, "To Particularize is the Alone Distinction of Merit." In art, at least, this is spectacularly true. What's interesting about Danto's review of Mapplethorpe is the subtle subtext, the implication that an innate "homosexual perception" is inadmissible to the heaven of universalism, the universalism of heterosexual ethics and aesthetics. The historical contingencies of gay life in the ghetto and elsewhere become products of gay perception, rather than the reverse; and AIDS becomes for Danto the terminus of gay aestheticism.

No one doubts that the urban queer culture of the late 1970's imbued much of Mapplethorpe's work, or that the artist himself made deliberate use of the iconography of death and decadence. His self-portrait as Satanic guerrilla-fighter, with automatic weapon and inverted pentagram, could be taken at face-value only by the kind of cultural arbiters who projected such an image upon queer artists in the first place. Likewise, the high-contrast, close-up facial self-portrait with a death's head walking-stick was both ironic and serious: the artist *was* dying by then, and his own skull was more naked beneath the skin.

Mapplethorpe used dandyism and decadence both as cultural material and as marketing strategy. Whatever mixed feelings we may have about his work, it is striking when an ordinarily sharp art critic such as Danto takes refuge in *clichés*. Thus Danto describes queer cultural resistance in the past tense, a story in which Mapplethorpe serves as an emblematic and elegiac figure: "That was a period in which gays were coming out of the closet in large numbers, defiantly and even proudly, and were actively campaigning not only to change social attitudes toward themselves but to build their own culture."

True enough, yet *the largest civil rights demonstration in twenty years* occurred when over 600,000 people marched on Washington in 1987 for lesbian and gay rights, and when over 600 of us were arrested at the Supreme Court. *The Nation*, like much of the "progressive" press, paid as little notice to these events as did *Time* and *Newsweek*. Meanwhile, gay artists continue to do searching work, and are fighting many crucial battles against censorship. But Danto cannot resist making his own magisterial generalization, and so he plays funeral music for queer politics and culture: "With AIDS a form of life went dead, a way of thought, a form of imagination and hope." How would *he* know? There is a strong element of wishful thinking in this obituary. If queer imagination and resistance will *not* die conveniently, then perhaps it can be put to sleep with such dim-witted diagnoses and sugar-coated sedatives.

One of Mapplethorpe's most androgynous self-portraits reminds Danto of Marcel Duchamp's feminine alias, Rrose Selavy—which is to say: *Eros c'est la vie*. Danto claims to "feel saddened that Rrose Selavy has lost her enduring innocence and changed her name to Rrose Selamort." Danto's sadness is itself considerably less than innocent. The links between sex and death go quite beyond gay aestheticism as such, beyond any resonance of sex with death that Danto may find in Mapplethorpe's images of bondage and sadomasochism, and beyond the AIDS epidemic itself. What may really rattle Danto's sensibility is the equanimity of Mapplethorpe's vision and display: orchids, society portraits, and a bullwhip plugged in the artist's butt.

What sex and sadomasochism have in common is that they play with limitations—skin and senses, toys and tools, cues, caresses, and scenes of all kinds—in order to achieve a temporary transcendence, whether it be particularly intense pleasure, pain, or both.

The final limitation and transcendence is, of course, death. As soon as we mark a boundary between sex and death, we already acknowledge their proximity. Sex has always been a matter of calculated risks and always will be; for good reasons, women have known this better than most men. In the end, the body is deadly for *everyone*; yet there is no essential guilt in disease and decay.

Queers have come to this kind of knowledge through our historical and personal experience, not through some innate "homosexual perception." We are often forced to deal consciously and thoroughly with censorship and self-censorship. To be sure, with resistance comes reaction. Sometimes we are overwhelmed and destroyed, but if we *do* win through to some degree of clarity about the real conditions of our lives and our work, then to that degree we are also better equipped as artists and citizens. Then solidarity is *possible*.

Those who grant queers an ahistorical "homosexual perception" are giving us a very dubious gift, something both sweet and toxic, something shiny which explodes in our hands. What they usually mean is that we may see the particular intensely, but are innately incapable of seeing the Big Picture. For that, you need universality, which is to say, some other sexuality than our own. The universal is idiocy without the particular, just as Blake insisted; and queer particulars are as vital as any others.

8.

Here is an example of universal moralizing which is particularly common among certain "cultured" straight white men, *but by no means limited to them*—in fact, it would have no social power if it were limited to them: "When a society is growing, those things appear and thrive which will make the organism strong, virile, happy, outward-directed—seminal, in short." This is the standard masculine ("virile," "seminal") spirit of confident imperialism. But the author has a social conscience—of a certain kind: "When we look at our large society today we see many problems—overcrowding, the risk of nuclear annihilation, the perversion of the work ethic, the disappearance of tradition, homosexuality, sexually transmitted diseases, divorce, the tenuousness of the economy—and we say, 'What bad luck that they are besetting us at once.'"

For the author, such danger and disorder must be the surface phenomena of a profound order and benevolence. Since the author himself has no traditional faith, he settles for a now fashionable form of organic fatalism: "The problems of the world, AIDS, cancer, nuclear war, pollution, are, finally, no more solvable than the problems of a tree which has borne fruit: the apples are overripe and they are falling—what can be done?... *Nothing* can be done, and nothing needs to be done. Something is being done—the organism is preparing to rest."

The author, I'm sorry to say, is David Mamet, who has shown more intelligence in his plays than in his essays. This essay, "Decay: Some Thoughts for Actors," can be found in his book *Writing in Restaurants*, along with another essay titled "Decadence." In the latter piece, Mamet writes, "We are in the midst of a vogue for the truly decadent in art—for that which is destructive rather than regenerative, self-referential rather than outward-looking, elitist rather than popular." This outward-looking critic then makes a hit-list of his least favorite dramatic themes: "These events, illness, homosexuality, accident, aging, birth defects, equally befall the Good and the Bad individual. They are not the result of conscious choice and so do not bear on the character of the individual. They are not the fit subject of drama, as they do not deal with the human capacity for choice. Rather than uniting the audience in a universal experience, they are invidious." Furthermore, "plays, books, films about homosexuality, feminism" are, according to Mamet, "works about *conditions* rather than about *character*..."

By process of elimination, the people most capable of making choices and having character would have to be able-bodied heterosexuals in perfect health—and if they are women, it would be preferable if they were unconditionally feminine, rather than conditioned by feminism. Mamet nowhere explains why feminism is undramatic, or why gay people, the aged, or the ill are incapable of individuality and choice. Instead, "universal experience" must be defended against the incursions and infiltrations of all such outsiders. Mamet has joined the cultural border police defending Us, the universalists, against Them, with all their decadent particulars, their invidious conditions. Who is it, we might ask, who is really being self-referential and elitist? What is this "popular" culture he defends? In art as in politics, we must always ask: Who does and does not count as a person among The People?

Those who are familiar with the "Gaia Hypothesis" among sectors of the environmental movement will notice the similarity between that notion and Mamet's thinking. "Thus," writes Daniel Keith Conner in the magazine *Earth First!*, "if the Gaia hypothesis is correct, AIDS may be the earth's own response to human-created environmental problems such as the greenhouse effect. If the surface of the earth is in any sense alive, you would expect it to eventually fight back… The AIDS virus may be Gaia's tailor-made answer to human overpopulation." Thinking along these lines, I would have thought sodomy might be Gaia's answer to overpopulation; and in that case, Gaia is a vengeful mother and a warrior with bad aim if she is striking down so many non-reproductive sodomites. But as these men explain her nature, it is obvious that mere logic cannot be her forte—no, hers is the wisdom of Mother Earth, and her favorite mates are these moralists who have taken the role of Our Father in Heaven.

The patriarchal assumptions inherent in many kinds of "organic" thinking (not all) must be exposed. In politics they are dangerously atavistic, even in the guise of liberalism and environmentalism; in cultural work they sometimes appeal to artists, but always result in making art and artists less than both could be. It is artistic work to break through the censorship of "common sense," whether the current modes of thought and feeling are styled "organic" or not. Strong artists require strong intelligence, not just strong feeling. I dare say the imbecilities of Danto, Mamet, and Conner are dangerous to culture in being ahistorical and in making an ethical principle out of irrationalism. They are also specifically dangerous to the well-being of women and queers.

9.

I was the boy standing before the big dictionary in the living room, reading some definition of the word homosexual, transfixed between pain and relief, a butterfly pinned down and classified at last. Today, at the age of thirty-three, I've sat by the bedsides of more dying people than many folks twice my age. Today my parents still find it hard to acknowledge the existence of my lover of fourteen years; and my brother's comment on the whole matter of my sexuality and my politics was, "It's not my issue." Jews, blacks, women, and working people most often grow up with others like themselves; however great their pain and oppression and even self-hatred may be, at least they share it to some degree, so even a child has some sense of solidarity.

And yet I was lucky in so many ways—my dad had been an artist before he was swallowed up and spat out by General Motors, and I learned a lot from my mom's fighting spirit. Our family's entrance into the middle class was tentative, and our exit was abrupt. I did not learn my first lessons in class-consciousness from Marx. Having spent my early youth in Puerto Rico and Argentina, I was also spared from uninterrupted exposure to the more radioactive elements of American culture. Otherwise I, too, might have been another statistic, another of the many suicides among American youth, especially queers.

On scholarship, I was able to attend Loomis Preparatory School, and in my first and only year there I fell in love with another boy, had a serious affair with a married teacher, tried to start a Student

Union, was subjected to an inquisition by a committee of petty tyrants, and half-consciously decided that the easiest route to freedom would be a quiet, non-cooperative breakdown. I was well aware of the movements for civil rights and peace, the movements of women and gays. I was reading Paul Goodman and the French Symbolists. Going crazy (as the saying goes) was not purely volitional, but it was one way out of the hermetically sealed and somewhat surreal precinct of a Connecticut prep school. I was hungry for the *world*.

In the ward of Tower Eleven in Manhattan's Roosevelt Hospital, I felt freer to speak my mind and continue my real education. At that time my motto was, "Burn your bridges behind you," which served that young man quite well. My breakdown was, to be precise, a period of heightened clarity, and therefore of rage and grief. I turned sixteen in that ward, and underlined these words of Albert Schweitzer, which did not and do not strike me as a mere indulgence in *Weltschmerz*, but as the plain truth: "*the world is inexplicably mysterious and full of suffering.*" Like any decent doctor or scientist, we can find particular reasons for particular pains; we can trace cause and effect for good and ill; but suffering as such remains as much an open question as the stupendous fact that anything *exists* rather than nothing at all.

I was befriended in that ward—which was a bleak dormitory in a high-rise hospital, men and women rooming on opposite sides of a long corridor—by a young West Indian woman named Carla. She introduced herself by telling me about her affair with another woman, and made a pass at me at the same time. She'd had a much rougher life than mine, and had come through with so much clarity, fighting spirit, and generosity that she gave me great hope and did me more good than any doctor. We knew each other for only two months, and we lost touch when I left the ward. Maybe she'll find this message somehow? I count her among the lucky events and encounters of my life, and evidence of grace on earth.

10.

Between leaving family, school, and the hospital when I was sixteen, and meeting my lover, Larry Gross, in 1975 when I had just turned twenty, I worked as a potter in Woodstock before moving to Philadelphia, and then worked as a printer with a radical publishing collective, as a janitor and gofer in a gay bar, as a busboy and waiter in restaurants, as a salesclerk in bookstores, and as a sex worker (an "escort") in the circuit of private clubs and cocktail parties. I was usually too beat after work to write, and sometimes had no privacy or quiet to do so where I was living; but I was able to read and take notes. I had no time for any consistent political activism, but was able to attend events and protests organized by others.

Meeting Larry was probably the greatest stroke of luck in my lucky life. Any deprivations and disasters in my life have always been moderated by such luck, and of course by the undue privileges of being white and male in this society. The hazards of being a writer and a queer radical are shared with someone who believes in my work, who comes from a family of Jewish socialists, and who is a *mensch* in his own right out in the world. These facts are worth stressing, because so many others have been silenced, broken, or destroyed. For many people in this country, including queers, the social climate is only tolerable at best, and sometimes murderous at worst. As usual, the wealthiest and most privileged gays can make their closets their castles. More than anyone else, Larry has made my writing and political work possible. After fourteen years together he deserves a love poem; and when I've worked my way through prose to poetry again, he's going to get one.

"Blight never does good to a tree," wrote Blake, "but if the tree still bear fruit, let none say the fruit was in consequence of the blight." I'll say again my life has been lucky, but with sufficient suffering so I don't take my luck for granted. I don't believe all suffering is redemptive; much and maybe most of human suffering is dead-end misery and deformation. I believe there is an irreducibly tragic dimension to life, no matter how near we come to utopia in this life, or to any kind of heaven in any kind of afterlife; but much of the real blight in people's lives is neither natural nor inevitable. And sheer good luck is no substitute for basic solidarity. As I grow older, I become more deeply inconsolable and more sharply unreconciled. Life remains a blessing.

Postscript, October, 1995:

This essay is dedicated to the memory of John Preston, a friend, writer, and editor who gave many queers their first breaks in publication. In 1989, John sent me a copy of a letter soliciting writers to contribute to a new book, *High Risk: An Anthology of Art & Literature*: "The editors of *High Risk* are trying to create a safe forum, within a book, for work that might be deemed unsafe. The repression of cultural expression in these times of the AIDS pandemic under the guise of social responsibility reinforces repression and sexual invisibility... We are asking people to explore such topics as s/m, pornography, public sex, lesbian s/m, hustling, shooting up—those topics which have been part of an aesthetic tradition we hope to keep alive."

John, an avowed pornographer and daredevil himself, urged me to send something new of my own to the two editors of *High Risk*. Soon after I had sent them this essay, the editors called me to say this was just the kind of work they'd been seeking, and even that it would be the final piece in the book. For marketing reasons best known to the editors, this essay finally proved unsuitable—or too risky—for their collection.

This essay is not so very sexy or sensational, yet the form and content still feels very risky to *me*. Certainly this is a work in progress, and in the years since it was first written the shameful retreat of many nominal liberals and "progressives" has been as dramatic as the aggressive advance of the far right. A "cultural war" was *explicitly* declared by Buchanan at the 1992 National Republican Convention, and a battalion of far right politicians swept into Congress in 1994. I chose to edit and polish this essay, but otherwise to keep it intact as a *dated* document. I have more to say—maybe in poetry rather than prose—about the experience of queers in mental wards and in sex work, but at present I would only add the following comments:

In our class and cultural divisions of labor, artists (like scientists and others) often exhibit our very own professional deformations. Sometimes we imagine we can create art works whose form and content will be as indigestible to our enemies as grenades, and as nutritious to our friends as manna from heaven. Thus we advance our own battalions in the cultural war. *Romantic!*

In reality, the more elite galleries and audiences have a capacious stomach for cultural subversion. The more nihilistic artists are even lauded for being *transgressive*, but they are merely surfing the *Zeitgeist*, for nothing beats the nihilism of the "free market," to which they also conform. Meanwhile the mass media rolls on like a juggernaut, itself subject to mass market forces of sensationalism and corporate censorship. Artists can make neither an economic nor a cultural revolution alone. We *can* share in the difficult work of ensuring that such a revolution is genuinely *democratic*.

Finally, as a pinko queer I'm sometimes strongly tempted to get the hell out of the U.S.A. and flee to Amsterdam or Barcelona. In such a mood (which does pass, since we must fight *here*) I came across this passage in one of Kafka's letters to Milena Jesenska (undated, but probably 1922):

"I've spent all afternoon in the streets, wallowing in the Jew-baiting. 'Prasive plemono'—'filthy rabble' I heard someone call the Jews the other day. Isn't it the natural thing to leave the place where one is hated so much? (For this, Zionism or national feeling is not needed.) The heroism which consists of staying on in spite of it all is that of cockroaches which also can't be exterminated from the bathroom.

"Just now I looked out the window: Mounted police, *gendarmerie* ready for a bayonet charge, a screaming crowd dispersing, and up here in the window the loathsome disgrace of living all the time under protection."

Speaking Parts:
Silence, Masculinity, and the Postcolonial Faggot
LAWRENCE CHUA

"What harm is it
to be a woman
when the mind is concentrated
and the insight is clear?

If I asked myself:
'Am I a woman
or a man in this?'
then I would be speaking
Mara's language."
          —Soma Theri, *Therigatha*

Everyone's got a pussy. But we don't all know how to make it purr.
At an early age many of us who will be socialized into men learn that
language, like emotion, is something to keep buried inside our
bodies. Only sissies complain. Men, real men, should be strong. And
keep their mouths shut. Or at least keep big words from forming
there. Silence informs every twitch of our muscles: from enduring
pain on the playground to masturbating in the dark. Silence shapes
our desires. We want the drag queen sharp-tongued and incessant, the banjee boy brooding, brown, and muscle-bound. Just ask
the guy in the sauna at my gym who, after quietly waving his hard-
on at me like a magic wand, suddenly became embarrassed and
ran in wide-eyed terror when I uttered a full sentence. Phallocentric
patriarchy, after all, is about the dick, not the tongue.

In a culture where men lay traditional claims to ownership of
language, the ability to think independently and speak against the
status quo is not a butch thing to do. The violence of domination

doesn't need a soundtrack, doesn't require deep thought about how to perpetuate greed, exploitation, and abuse. Reproduction doesn't require a manual. It comes easy to us not because it's natural but because those values permeate every aspect of our lives. Keeping our minds pure and separate from our bodies is part of the enduring legacy of Cartesian dualism, that separation of Self and Other that brought us here in the first place. The struggle to decolonize our bodies, though, is inseparable from the struggle for our minds, a war of language and speaking. This is not only a struggle over the way we are represented in culture, but a struggle against perfect communication and inflexible translation. It is the struggle to write a narrative that isn't looking to be mastered.

The Uruguayan re-teller of the Western hemisphere's history, Eduardo Galeano, has written, "I sleep on the rim of a woman: I sleep on the rim of a chasm." I am writing from the same abyss, a space that is not a territory to be conquered or owned. I am writing from the intersections of unheard, unseen experience, from the crossroads of Marxism-Leninism, Buddhism and feminism, of theory dialectically engaged with practice. Writing on a machine made by the nimble fingers of Southeast Asian women who will never own one, components made, perhaps by my cousins in Penang, freshly graduated and laboring below minimum wage. Rushing through airport security once, I whipped out my laptop for inspection and the guard, a man as colored and old as me, exclaimed, "Oh shit, homeboy's got a computer!" He didn't need to remind me that I am always writing and breathing against the expectations of who I am: greasy Third World immigrant. Noble savage tainted by Western technology. Awkward faggot with working class lope. Darkie with a laptop.

I was taught early to value writing. While my mother was a public school teacher who brought the written word home with her from work, my father couldn't read or write the language he spoke most often. I discovered that writing was a place where those things I wasn't supposed to, or wasn't able to, say in public, those things that would anger my father, could emerge. In school, writing (a private chore), was something I enjoyed while competitive sports (a public privilege), was something that never held my attention for very long. Writing has been indispensable to the Western myth of difference between oral and written cultures, primitive and civilized minds. It has been indispensable to the justification of colonialism. But seizing the tools of writing has allowed us to intervene in recorded history and myths of origin. To rewind and rework the binary hierarchies of the Garden of Eden: Man and Woman, Nature and Knowledge.

What does masculinity mean in an era of blinding mobility of capital? As multinational corporations remap and redefine our ideas of nation and economy, shifting funds and factories across collapsing borders, we are witnessing both an intensification and erosion of gender. Along with a new global proletariat, the New World Order is producing new sexualities and ethnicities. Whether the workers are men or women, their labor is being feminized. Donna J. Haraway has written that to be feminized "means to be made extremely vulnerable; able to be disassembled, reassembled, exploited as a reserve labor force; seen less as workers than as servers; subjected to time arrangements on and off the paid job that make a mockery of a limited work day; leading an existence that always borders on being obscene, out of place, and reducible to sex…"

It is not a secret that capitalism enforces gender roles that are necessary for the marketplace. The move from food gathering to agriculture to urbanized work and warfare economies has restricted the actions that anoint masculine status. A man is no longer a man because he can put food on his family's table. He is a man because he has a penis and he thinks he knows how to use it. bell hooks writes that in a culture of extreme phallocentrism, "his ability to use that penis in the arena of sexual conquest could bring him as much status as being a wage earner and provider. A sexually defined masculine ideal rooted in physical domination and sexual possession of women could be accessible to all men." Power to the *pinga*. The bigger the better. The refrain that was echoing on the dance floor twenty minutes ago was "Don't need no short-dicked man." But what does small mean in an economy where miniaturization has turned out to be about power: microchips, cruise missiles?

The growing underemployment of poor and working-class black men is often referred to as a "feminization" of black masculinity because in traditional capitalist economies, men worked in factories and women kept house. But the poor and working-class women who nurtured my childhood labored intensively in both public and private spheres. The recent destruction of welfare, the increasing scarcity of full-time payrolled work, the vicious attack on reproductive rights, the tightening of US immigration laws and the ever-present possibility that women's wages will not be matched by a male income, point to enforced poverty growing on a global level. This time, though, it's going to be *with* employment. This scenario is played out in parts of the Third World, like Southeast Asia, that are being forced to make the transition from agricultural to industrialized societies. Land is being bought up or swindled from families who used to work it. The young daughters of these families leave for the assembly lines and red-light districts of major cities like Bangkok, Singapore, Kuala Lumpur and Manila, where they provide the major source of income for their families. One of the first things they learn is that literacy, especially in English, makes them even more attractive to the multinational or the sex tourist. But literacy, contrary to what employers believe, is not simply the ability to read and write. It is the power to intervene. Empower (Education Means Protection of Women Employed in Recreation), an activist group that works with women sex workers in Thailand, recognizes the power of literacy and runs programs in teaching women in bars and brothels to read and write in English and Thai. Noi Chantawipa Apisuk, one of Empower's founders, found that the women she worked with in the sex industry wanted to learn how to read and write Thai and speak English. "We found that those were the basic rights of people to control themselves and to communicate with other people. If people know how to communicate with other people, it means they can take control of themselves and avoid any danger or any exploitation of themselves."

"A man who has a language consequently possesses the world expressed and implied by that language."
—Frantz Fanon *Black Skin, White Masks*

Shortly after the 1994 elections that gave the American right wing unprecedented power over our lives, a male listener called in to WBAI, Pacifica Radio's New York station. The caller identified himself as a liberal. He said he and his wife had been listening to Newt Gingrich on the radio and found themselves seduced by his aggressive masculinity, his virile language and assured promises. This is a nation where macho swagger has always been a sexier premise than intellectual inquiry. But we are living in scary times when thinly veiled fascism becomes an attractive proposition. We want daddy to tell us everything is going to be fine and we don't need to think about our own role in maintaining gender, race, and class inequalities. We want daddy to tell us to just shut up and do as we're told. Sit back and enjoy it, baby.

I am not suggesting a binary relationship between silence and language because silence is a part of any language. People who are reduced to silence may find comfort in it. But when we're able to identify ourselves in crisis and articulate the sources of our pain, silence can be a torture. The contradiction of vernacular language is that it can become so soothing to hear we often use it to reinscribe the same tired definitions, and silence is left to articulate experiences that fall in between the words. I remember the first time I heard the word "faggot." It was something I had heard frequently in the playground of my elementary school, but I didn't really grasp its full meaning. When I asked someone to explain the word for me, I was told it meant a man who loved other men. I recognized myself in the word. I claimed it. The definer tried to dissuade me, but I was insistent.

I cling tightly to definitions like that, even knowing that they don't have much to do with where I come from or where I'm going. Knowing the communities based on those definitions do not always share my interests. During the twenty-fifth anniversary of the Stonewall Rebellion, an uprising initiated by black and white drag queens and lesbians during the struggles against racism, imperialism, and patriarchy of the 1960s, the theme of unity was invoked repeatedly. As the month-long festivities wore on, it became clear that this precarious unity was based on the erasure of difference. Multiple voices were routed into one monotonous chorus. "Big Guns!" promised the posters, inviting lesbians and gay men to dance on a U.S. warship. The tiring model of masculinity invoked by Stonewall 25 resembled nothing more than the kind of ticker tape celebrations of muscle and carnage televised during the Gulf War. I am not suggesting that the eroticism of uniforms, muscles, and "big guns" can't be pleasurable, but that pleasure always belies broader, economic, contradictions. Would we celebrate those things in the same way if economic power didn't inform them as symbols? Or if there wasn't a giant "health and beauty" industry selling product so that we might one day resemble or own them? Dancing on battleships during pride week wasn't a subversive celebration of masculinity, but a celebration of militarism by gay men. This desire was spoken in language not so much erotic as obscenely patriotic, casting the massacre of Iraqi civilians as something heroic, something to fall in love with. Perhaps because gay men have traditionally been excluded from the territories of masculinity, we overcompensate for it in tragic ways, replicating abusive models of power relationships in our own lives. Or perhaps, as the heady commercialism of Stonewall 25 suggested, the ultimate any faggot can aspire to is to be part of white supremacy, multinational capitalism, and phallocentric patriarchy.

New Year's Eve. Miami Beach. 1995. Goodbye cruel world. At four-thirty A.M. I am locking my bicycle to a parking meter outside a gay bar. The street is flooded with pedestrian traffic. Revelers. Party boys. A white man and woman pass by, laughing. The woman points to the Tina Turner look-alike drag queen on the car next to me and says, audibly enough: "Look at the nigger." My mouth falls open, forms an imperfect circle before it snaps, but the words coming from my throat land on a cushion of drunken silence. None of the mostly light-skinned Latino and white nancy boys waiting around the entrance of the bar register this comment with anything more than an uneasy silence. When I bring this incident up in a small cluster of Latino and white men the next afternoon, no one says anything either. Just little pained looks of regret before we all turn our faces to the sun and close our eyes. When language is used to efface humanity, the response is often coded in silence. But one question will always dig deeper than the sand on my back. Why did this woman feel comfortable expressing such violent hatred, garlanded in mirth, in this crowd? When white supremacy raises its head visibly, we click our tongues, shake our heads, and express regret that it has happened. But anyone who has been to a gay bar knows that racism is not just an unfortunate incident, a bizarre deviation from the enlightened norm. It is a constant practice.

Foucault said there was no such thing as a homosexual, only homosexual acts. Perhaps, then, there is no gay community. Perhaps, after the smoke and pink balloons settle, there is only a gay marketplace. All the Pride Beer and pink triangle T-shirts and gold pendants of Stonewall 25 underscored the economic stake of projecting creamy unity. What does it mean to be a colored faggot in a culture that is continuously telling you you're not worthy of love: that no matter how many hours you devote to the gym, how hard you bleach your skin and pinch your nose that you'll never be as beautiful as the posterboy for the White Party. Never be cute with three k's. Not that you'd want to be anyway, but to reject those tired models of masculinity and beauty also means that you will not have access to the same wealth of resources as someone who's buffed and blond. This is not an issue of whydon'tyoulovemewhiteman but of white privilege being built on the backs of black people. Anyone with even the most basic under-standing of history can see how black bodies are constituted in the commercial marketplace: from the cane fields to the playing fields. By teaching us that we shouldn't value our dark-skinned selves, it leaves others free to exploit us and then deny us the fruits of our labor. The Lesbian Avengers did a gender/race breakdown of gay and straight coverage of Stonewall 25 events. Men were represented at a ratio of 12 to every one woman. White men were represented at a ratio of 50 to every one black man (and I am using the term here politically but also because I am tired of calling myself a person of color). Black lesbians were ignored. Part of the problem of building community around identity lies in what it excludes. Like those without perceived spending power.

Ruptures along every possible fissure have made the concept of a gay community elusive. Stonewall 25 was instructive in that it responded to difference by calling for a new essential unity. That unity served the interests that totalizing sameness usually serves. In the wake of that travesty, we can only work toward a deeper understanding of coalition: one that underscores affinity rather than identity. The Venerable Thây Thich Nhat Hanh has writ-ten about "communities of resistance," affiliations that transgress the socially imposed categories of gender, race, and class. The struggle against patriarchy, white supremacy, and multinationalist capitalism, after all, needs to be carried out by sisters and brothers, by comrades. Not by clones.

In 1917, addressing the First All-Russian Congress of Trade Unions, Bolshevik Alexandra Kollontai said: "The class-conscious worker must understand that the value of male labor is dependent on the value of female labor and that, by threatening to replace male labor with cheaper female workers, the capitalist can put pressure on men's wages. Only a lack of understanding could lead one to see this question purely as a 'woman's issue.'" The rising influence of "unity" based on marketplace ideas of identity can represent a step further away from challenging the status quo. I'm not arguing that class affinities override other forms of solidarity, but that these things are interdependent on one another. What would it be like to imagine a feminist movement comprised of people as diverse as everyone who is oppressed by patriarchy? Or a lesbian and gay rights movement where most of the people don't even buy into the binary structures of gay and straight? Or an anti-racist movement where people of European descent can divest of their whiteness and play an active role in dismantling white supremacy?

> "Silence can be a plan
> rigorously executed
> the blueprint to a life
> It is a presence
> it has a history a form
> Do not confuse it
> with any kind of absence."
> —Adrienne Rich

Contemplative silence in capitalism has always been a dangerous thing. Idle hands are the devil's plaything. But traditional Southeast Asian cultures have always made the space to vibe and meditate. The myth of the lazy native. The refusal to work in colonial capitalist production was also a form of resistance to European conquest. Silence can be a fierce opposition to the lurid practice of needing to know and own the mind of the native subject. Silence is a useful answer to stupid questions: questions that begin with "As a black man, how do you feel about…?" Silence is the place where speech is made.

Acharn Sulak Sivaraksa, the Thai social activist, has written that "Buddhist practice points toward the development of full and balanced human beings, free from the socially-learned 'masculine' and 'feminine' patterns of thought, speech, and behavior, in touch with both aspects of themselves." To transform the relations of power based on that split is to create liberated space across the socialized categories of race, gender, and class. An unconquerable place for people to develop their abilities.

Silence can be the moment we take to clear our minds, focus on breathing and mindful dialogue. To control our own breathing is to control our own bodies and minds. Radio silence. Dead air. The gathering of dust and light. One of the five precepts of *panca sila*, the ethical guide of Buddhism, is to abstain from false speech. To live with ethics in this world is to know that it's right to rebel. Don't mistake my silence for cuteness, complicity, or ignorance. In the space when all you hear from me is my breathing, deep and steady, I am thinking of new ways to overthrow you.

Miami Beach, 1994–95

SEX

Gay men are famous for talking about sex. We talk about it in bars, over dinner, cruising the streets; we talk about it with lovers, tricks, friends, and strangers. We write about sex in poems, and novels. In many ways sex-talk is the thread that holds gay male culture together—it is a presumed commonality, a shared social and psychic experience that we all understand. But all too often our talk of sex, for all of its exuberance, is limited by our inability to be completely honest; we are encouraged to be explicit without necessarily being truthful. This is not surprising in a culture which, though it actively promotes sex to sell consumer products, disregards most attempts to think or discuss sexuality in an honest manner. While heterosexuals face many of these same restrictions on sexual honesty they, at least, receive constant affirmation that their sexuality is productive and good. Gay men and lesbians live in a world that continually denigrates homosexuality as being nothing more than an unnatural and unhealthy sexual activity.

It is not only the dominant culture and the mainstream press that discourage—or overtly ban—frank discussions of gay sexual issues. There are many in the gay community and the gay press who would as well. Sometimes these reactions, on the part of gay people, are precipitated by the ever-present fear that any admission of sexual nonconformity will hurt gay people's chances of being "accepted" by mainstream society. (This position overlooks the reality that *all* gay sexuality is regarded, by many, as an objectionable form of "sexual nonconformity.") Often the gay media shy away from controversial sexual topics because they are afraid of losing advertising or subscription revenue. As a result, honest writing about gay male sexuality—writing that poses hard questions and that conveys, truthfully, the intricacies of sexual feeling and experience—is rare.

The sexuality of young people has always been a difficult topic for our culture to discuss; even more so when that young person is gay. Vestal McIntyre's "Naming the Addiction" tells of the author's experience growing up as a gay youth in a conservative religious family in rural Idaho. From its opening lines—"The first time I saw my own cum I didn't know what it was. I thought I was going to die"—we can feel the heat and the fear that newly discovered gay sexuality can generate. In recent years it has become more and more fashionable to celebrate how some gay men and lesbians have found ways to reconcile their sexuality with their traditional religious beliefs. In "Naming the Addiction" Vestal McIntyre reminds us how frightening and destructive "tradition"—be it religion, the community, the family—can be to gay sexuality.

The main reason the sexuality of gay youth is a charged topic is that gay men have been, and continue to be, vilified for having sex with, and corrupting, minors. It is no surprise then that intergenerational sex—particularly between men and boys—is an explosive topic. The North American Man-Boy Love Association (NAMBLA) has been a center of controversy since its founding in 1978.

Condemned by Jesse Helms on the floor of the Senate, by the gay Republican Log Cabin Club, and forbidden to march in gay pride parades in New York and Los Angeles, NAMBLA has also received enormous support from such people as Harry Hay, the founder of the Mattachine Society and considered by many to be the father of gay liberation, by poet Allen Ginsberg, and by writer and social critic Camille Paglia. The intensity of the attacks upon and support received by NAMBLA illustrates not only to how difficult it is for us to think and speak about children and sexuality but raises other issues as well: Who gets to define who is part of the gay community? Has the pressure of conservative attacks on gay rights lessened the gay movement's support of a variety of forms of sexual expression over the years? What is the historical relationship of male pedophilia to gay male culture? What does the gay movement do when its members honestly and vehemently disagree about where to "draw the line" about certain types of sexual behavior?

Jesse Green's "The Men From the Boys" is a personal, investigative piece about the role NAMBLA now occupies in the popular imagination as well as in the gay movement. Interviewing NAMBLA members, their critics and supporters, Green paints a complex portrait of a gay organization under fire. And perhaps more importantly he presents us with a picture of how—in this specific instance—sex, fear, politics, power, and media prejudice are played out in the gay movement today.

Bill Andriette's "Dumbed Down and Played Out: The Gay Movement and the Liquidation of Boy-Love," is less a rejoinder to Green's article than an analysis—from the inside—of where NAMBLA fits into the context of contemporary gay politics. Andriette, a longtime NAMBLA member (he is interviewed by Green in "The Men From the Boys") and spokesperson, places the organization in a historical context and seriously questions how the mainstream gay movement deals with political dissension, sexual freedom, the rights of children, and the deeply ingrained prejudices against non-traditional forms of sexual expression.

Sex between boys and men is at the heart of John Preston's "What You Learn After Thirty Years of S/M." As a one time hustler, an s/m top, and pornographer, Preston made a career out of being a sexual outsider. Here, in one of the last pieces he wrote before his death in 1994, he describes an early sexual relationship with an older man and how it influenced his entire life. "What You Learn After Thirty Years of S/M," is an elegiac remembrance and a personal and political investigation of what it means to be a man in our culture. Preston's essay might be subtitled "Everything I Ever Needed to Know I Learned in Bed" and is something of a cross between Flaubert's *A Sentimental Education* and the Marquis de Sade's *Philosophy in the Bedroom*. Alternately sexy, smart, and meditative, it is some of the best writing John Preston ever produced.

"Making Sex Public" is the text of a speech that Michael Lassell delivered at Flesh and the Word: A Celebration of the Work and Life of John Preston, a conference held at Brown University in the fall of 1995. Lassell speaks less about John Preston's life and work than about the increasingly contentious role that sexuality plays in our lives and culture. Lassell is concerned here—as Preston always was in his writing—with the ways in which sexuality, a force he considers the wellspring of imagination, politics, and love, is continually denigrated and dismissed in our culture. Lassell charts how the Greek god Eros—a potent and dangerously radical figure; only a distant relation to our watered-down and sentimentalized Cupid—is now used to sell commercial goods and shopworn, repressive ideas about sex. "Making Sex Public" celebrates the life and work of John Preston, but it also places John Preston, and other sexual liberationists, in a new, broader, cultural context.

While much of John Preston's writings detailed the habits, practices, and politics of the S/M community, the tacit understanding was that such activity is always consensual: erotic theater in which leather and chains, menacing poses and threats, were props to increase sexual pleasure.

Craig Hickman's "Deliverance" deals with the harsher realities of violence and eroticism. Written (and presented) as performance piece, it is, at heart, an essay on that dangerous intersection where sex and violence, hate and eroticism, inexplicably cross. Assuming the persona of Jeffrey Dahmer, Hickman attempts to understand the private man behind the public monster and imagines Dahmer's complex, destructive—and, possibly— loving relationship to his victims. Because he has written it as a performance piece and not a traditional essay Hickman takes risks that most other writers would never dare. Poetic, frightening, and problematic—Hickman's Dahmer suggests that his victims came to him, and death, to find love and comfort—it pushes us to think and deal with ideas most of us would rather ignore or avoid.

Naming the Addiction
VESTAL MCINTYRE

The first time I saw my own cum, I had no idea what it was. I thought I was dying. I had been playing with myself, in the bathtub before school, which was my habit in the sixth grade, and all of a sudden my heart was beating in my ears and bits of white were flying out of me and I couldn't help but make splashing noises because my skinny, too-hairy-for-my-age body was writhing out of control, in a fit of what could only be thought of as possession, or death, or some sin that had no name. Afterwards, as I lay there panting, conscious of those bits of white sinking through the water to my skin, I wondered if my mom, who was making breakfast in the adjoining kitchen, had heard all. I stood up, pulled the plug, and quickly began to dry off. And I realized this white stuff was sticky and the more I tried to dry it off the stickier it got, and I suddenly understood sex. I understood how babies were made. (Sex was, of course, never mentioned in my house. Neither was *Three's Company* watched or the Lord's name used in vain.) So in those moments, dizzy with having just experienced some sort of insanity and with thinking rapidly, fearfully, I understood what it was that men and women did. There was some relief in this mystery being solved (before I had thought that maybe a man and woman sleeping in the same bed over a period of time caused the woman to become pregnant, or maybe some exchange of urine was involved) but there was also the terrible suspicion that I was the only person in the world who had done it with himself. As I pulled on my clothes and combed my hair, I muttered an apology to God.

"Hurry up, Vessy!" Breakfast was ready.

I went into the kitchen, kissed Mom good morning and sat down to an egg sandwich, instant oatmeal, and hot chocolate, while Dad, in his brown paisley bathrobe and drooping eyelids, began reading to me from a daily devotional. I was still spinning, and the new sin I had just invented was weighing heavily, and cowering there over my breakfast, I vowed to myself and to God that I would never ever do that again.

I rode to school with my brother Evan, who was in eighth grade, and at that time Idaho law allowed fourteen-year-olds to drive during daylight. The ride to school took us between wide, flat fields of mint or wheat, past the sugar beet factory billowing smoke, a series of trailer parks and subdivisions, into town. Nampa is small, with streets named after other states or presidents. The buildings downtown are made of old brick; their cornerstones say "1910," "1895," and many have brightly colored aluminum facades. Southern Idaho being flat and dry, the sun shines on Nampa constantly, palely, with an almost artificial kind of light. The lawns are big and treeless. There are few buildings with more than two stories. There are no dark alleys.

The boulevard, lined with used-car lots and farm supply stores, led to our school—Nampa Christian, a Protestant, non-denominational school; a small, ultra-conservative school in a small, ultra-conservative town. (When I visit Nampa now, from Boston, I can't resist the temptation to drive by Nampa Christian at least once. As I pass I don't turn my head, but glance only sideways at those three yellow brick buildings that seem so much smaller now. It's silly, I know, but the fear of being seen, perhaps even recognized, haunts me still.)

It was here, at school, in a stall in the boys' bathroom that I first broke my vow, less than two weeks after having made it. After battling the urge all through reading period, I surrendered, walked quickly to the bathroom (which was empty) and soon I was swooning, gasping, holding myself up against the wall with my free hand.

And as I wiped the evidence off the floor and toilet seat with a piece of toilet paper, I told God that this was really the last time. It was out of me. Never again. I flushed and returned to class.

On the bookshelf of my sixth-grade classroom there was a row of Christian comic books. Some were illustrations of Bible stories, some were the true-to-life adventures of missionaries, and some, the most popular, had "for ages thirteen and above" printed on the cover. In one of these comics two tall, muscular men with those comic-book cheekbones and shadows beneath their pectorals were roving witnesses of the gospel. They came upon a town where devil worship was rampant. "What…WHAT is that old man EATING!?! Oh my…it's HUMAN FINGERS!!!" There were detailed drawings of a young boy, possessed by Satan, writhing in a cloud of dust. Another comic book, about Catholics, had on the cover the silhouette of a bishop, his body dark except for glowing red eyes. On one of its pages was a single frame—a Protestant heretic bound to a stake in the center of some pavilion and, frozen ten feet before him, a bull mid-charge. The Protestant's head was bowed, accepting his martyrdom peacefully, reverently. And there was a comic on "the gays"; it began with the hulking, hairy men of Sodom gathered with torches at Lot's door, demanding the angels, and went on to men in grotesque make-up, and the lambda—a secret symbol used by members of the homosexual underworld.

These frightened and delighted me. I read every one and re-read my favorites. They were Christian publications—guilt-free satisfaction for my taste for gore and the deliciously perverse. They told me "this is where your sin can take you" but also, "yes, you may sin but at least you're not screaming, clawing, possessed, or watching your skin melt as a result of an L.S.D. flashback, or a man in women's clothing, or Catholic."

Friday afternoons at Nampa Christian, during the hour usually spent on math, the fifth graders would come into our classroom for singing and discussion. We were extra careful to behave because once there was too much whispering or if a note was caught being passed, the fifth graders would be sent back across the hall and the math would begin. So we sang loudly, attentively "Kumbaya," "Zacheus Was a Wee Little Man," or a song whose name I forget:

> I'm no kin to the monkey
> And the monkey's no kin to me
> I don't know much about his ancestors,
> But mine didn't swing from a tree.

And the discussion that followed often had the feeling of ghost stories told around a camp fire:

"My cousin got a Ouija board for her birthday, and she knew it was evil and so she threw it into the fire. She could hear the demons screaming as they burned."

"I read that astronomers found something way off in the galaxy, heading toward earth. They say it might be Jesus, returning."

"My big brother played his Led Zeppelin record backwards and it told him to worship the devil. So he broke it in two and threw it away."

"My mom told me, in the future, everyone will have to have a bar code tattooed on their arms and they'll have to scan it when you go to the store for you to be able to buy anything. That'll be the Antichrist; every number will end in 666."

And one Friday our teacher, Mrs. Stanley, who was tall and thin and had glasses with lenses that became dark when she went outside, but were never completely clear, told us about her recent visit to her son in San Francisco. "He asked me if I wanted to see the part of town where all the gays live, and I thought it would be interesting, so I said yes." Mrs. Stanley had a large key chain that fit around her wrist and she would finger the keys, twisting her wrist, jingling, as she spoke. "Well, driving there he told me to roll up the window and lock the door, and when we got there, there were all these men in women's clothing. My son told me that they all have to wear women's clothing. All except for one called the "Queen Bee," who's in charge. He wears men's clothes."

At night, after prayers and before sleep, these stories haunted me. I believed them all. They made the world colorful and magical and terrifying. And yet I was still good, safe, God was still on my side. Up until that morning in the bathtub I had led a fairly sin-free life. I had cursed only three times in my life. I had never fist-fought with anyone outside my family (and with six older brothers and sisters, one must defend oneself). And I had always immediately turned away from those scenes of exposed bodies, sometimes shamelessly touching each other, which were always flashing before my mind's eye. I ignored the fact that these figures were nearly always male (sometimes Rick Springfield, or one of the Hardy Boys, or one of the members of my brother's basketball team). Naturally, there was no link between these flashes and the men pounding on Lot's door. Nothing in my mind had anything to do with dress-wearing San Franciscans. Certain sins are much less grave before they are named.

But it was during that sixth-grade year that things became more complicated. I lingered on sinful thoughts longer than I should. And that one sin—the one I had invented on that morning in the bathtub—was becoming a problem. I had started a cycle of promising God to abstain, resisting the urge for perhaps a week, then giving in. I told God I was sorry, but I really couldn't help it; I'd limit myself to once a week, and that I'd only think of girls while I did it. And only four days into the week I'd find myself in the bathroom of Dad's office, hunched in guilty pleasure, holding a tissue in my free hand so as not to make a mess, pretending that for this moment I was shaded from God's view. "I'm afraid I'm going to have to do it more often...Once every other day, but only thinking of girls...Three times thinking of girls for every once thinking of boys." I began to wonder how all this would affect my health. I wondered if I would run out of this white stuff. I considered keeping a record of how often I did it. And my negotiations with God continued. "Whenever I want, trying not to think of anything at all...Okay, never again...Thinking about boys, but only once a week...I'm sorry, God." But these agonized negotiations with Him who was silent, whose position was unchangeable, could not succeed. I was addicted to my sin and to boys and was left to do nothing but apologize. "I'm sorry, God."

(Within a year or two I would quit talking to God about it altogether. Christians are instilled with the need to confess, but for us Protestants, of course, there is no confessional. The idea is to confess to God, who's seen all already, or to let sin upon sin pile up on your soul until, later in life, you confess them to your friends as titillating anecdotes, or to someone on the other end of a phone sex line, or to a lover as the required information, or to a reader. For me, they piled so high that my soul finally collapsed and my sins lost their names again, and all of a sudden the spotlight that was God burned out, and my sweat dried, and I began to learn to see in the dark.)

For my brother Roy the world is still lit by God. Ten years older than I, a Southern Baptist minister, he and his wife recently left for Bangladesh to spend the rest of their lives as missionaries. (I, too, had once planned to be a missionary. It was in sixth grade, during those negotiations with God, that I abandoned that plan.)

Roy and I have the same eyes, the same nose, our mannerisms are similar, and we're often mistaken for each other on the phone. When he started losing his hair, I became nervous. In the evening after his wedding two years ago, five of us seven kids—my two lesbian sisters, my gay brother, the straight one who doesn't care, and I—escaped the stiff atmosphere of a Baptist wedding reception to a bar by the water, just south of San Diego. The baby of the family, finally old enough to order a drink, I made the first toast: "To the *hope* that Roy is straight, because in this family he doesn't have much of a chance."

Roy and I never talk about religion. Needless to say, I wonder about him a lot. What did he do with his sins? Is he happy? How does someone as whiny and negative as one of us preach the gospel? And it makes me wonder where I'd be now if my soul hadn't collapsed.

The sin that I invented was finally given a name, at a roller-skating party in the seventh grade. My best friend at the time was Suzanne who lived in Boise and dressed cool and listened to Iggy Pop. Suzanne was an excellent source of information—it was she who explained menstruation to me and, in her description of "a 'daisy chain'—something men in prison do"— gave me my first mental image of anal sex. (Soon after this I dreamt of having anal sex with a man in that same bathtub where my addiction started. I woke up angry. I was surprised at the things that were coming out of my mind. I hated them, hated loving them.)

"It's called masturbation," said Suzanne in her lisp which would disappear a year later when her braces were removed. She was bent, lacing her roller-skates. "It's like having sex with yourself. Only gays do it." Again, that dim sense of relief in a mystery being solved, and in knowing masturbation was actually someone else's invention. But also the numbing horror of having, myself, been named. "Gay." The monsters that Nampa Christian had warned me about, in high heels and too much lipstick, crowded into my mind.

Over the next few years, I would be named again and again. When I dropped out of the football team, in eighth grade, my teammates named me "gay." It was whispered in the Nampa Christian halls. It was also in eighth grade when my friend Tom spent the night and, for the first time, I played those intoxicating games, and felt for the first time that amazing, hard-yet-soft feeling of someone else in my hand. Lying in the dark afterward, he on the bed and I in a sleeping bag on the floor, he started talking about unimportant things in a quick, cold voice. I didn't want to talk; I was thinking of too many things at once. For the first time, there was the hint of a realization that it wasn't just me putting one over on God, that He had cheated me too, forcing me to explore by myself in locked bathrooms what everyone else got to explore with others, behind the gym or in a dark corner at the roller rink. Then, out of nowhere, Tom asked in a bitter voice, "So when are you gonna tell your parents you're gay?" My thoughts froze. I had, once again, been named and Tom lay there, silent, comfortable in the bed, not naming himself. And suddenly it wasn't dark enough.

The Men From the Boys
JESSE GREEN

Funny Clowns Together

The chairs we sit in—many of them—have been stenciled with an inscrutable logo. We are attending an ACT UP meeting…a Pacific Islander lesbian conference…a 12-step program for recovering codependent transsexuals. We are fighting, crying, dishing; and all the while the letters GMSMA tag our backs. On any given night, very few of us at the Center—New York's Lesbian and Gay Community Services Center—are actually members of Gay Male S/M Activists; a good number of us would probably even find that world vaguely sinister and disreputable. But no one fusses. GMSMA has bought the chairs—and a place in the community. For a dona-tion of $1,200 a year they even get to call themselves Founders, and indeed they were among the first to meet in the semi-decrepit building on West Thirteenth Street. Still, it's surprising that a group whose interests are so outré (last April [1994] at the Center you could attend their evening of "fantasy and fetish" on the sixth, or "urethral play" on the twentieth) is accepted so calmly. Perhaps that's because they know—it's part of their scene to know—where to draw the lines: If the Center forbids live frontal nudity, GMSMA stays clothed. They've learned the advantage of playing by the rules.

Not that the gay and lesbian community, as a whole, seems to have many rules. There are odder things than GMSMA at the Center, and in our papers and in our parades. Who can say which is more disturbing: "Water of Life" urine therapy workshops, or Saturday afternoon meetings of "Funny Clowns Together"? Some activists find it appalling that the Gay Officers Action League ("successors to the cops who beat us at Stonewall") are welcome; some conservative types would be just as happy if Dykes on Bikes disappeared from the movement, if the Radical Faeries flounced off into obscurity. But no serious action has been undertaken to expel or disclaim such groups. As far as the Center goes, only one organization has ever been denied access. Neither Center President Steve Powsner nor any other current employee will discuss it on the record ("It's a lose-lose situation," whispered one), but former board member Steve Ault is blunt: "There was a feeling that to have *them* meet at the Center would be very dangerous for our ability to raise money." And so, despite the board's stated desire to accommodate "all groups that consider themselves part of the gay community," NAMBLA—the North American Man-Boy Love Association— was left to fend for itself.

Strange Bedfellows

Success has many parents; failure is an orphan. Though "boy lovers" played a significant role in the formative years of gay liberation, NAMBLA, the largest (and virtually the only) pedophile group in the United States, has been condemned, with biblical vehemence, by most mainstream gay and lesbian organizations— even by some its members helped to found. This has not been a clean excision; after all, the gay movement in its inception valued expressive freedom over political power and thus embraced any like-minded comers. The rioters at Stonewall weren't interested in looking respectable in order to gain a place at the table. They didn't want a place at the table. They wanted universal sexual freedom, and all desires were equal before the god of liberation. But that god has become a lot more finicky since 1969. Pedophiles, once standard-bearers, have become an embarrassment, anathema, a blot. How this has happened, in the last few years especially, makes for some kind of fairy tale, complete with battles, betrayals and fire-breathing dragons.

The tale begins in July 1993, when, after years of failure, the International Lesbian and Gay Association (ILGA), a Belgium-based umbrella group representing more than 300 organizations worldwide, finally got the UN Economic and Social Council (ECOSOC) to grant it third-tier consultative status. Much rejoicing was in the land: A gay voice (however feeble) would be heard (actually, only written statements are permitted) at the UN. But Jesse Helms got wind of the fact that one of ILGA's signatories (and earliest members) was the evil NAMBLA; he fulminated, and his bill threatening to cut UN funding unless it expelled all pedophile groups passed the U.S. Senate, 99-0.

The war shifted ground. ILGA, jealous of its hard-won status, returned NAMBLA's 1993 dues and strongly suggested it quit the federation, but NAMBLA stood its ground. After all, NAMBLA claimed, its positions and ILGA's on intergenerational sex were all but identical. Much comparing of documents and an unpleasant airing of gay linen ensued. ILGA's early statements on the matter *were* a bit vague: A 1990 resolution declared that "major power imbalances" between adults and youth "create the potential for child abuse"—leaving open the possibility that some pedophile relationships would not fulfill that "potential." But NAMBLA immediately condemned this position as "another tired example of adults deciding what's best for kids." Whatever common ground originally existed, by November 1993 it had completely eroded: ILGA released a statement saying unequivocally that it "objects to the political aims of NAMBLA" and announced it would attempt to expel NAMBLA at its annual meeting, in New York in June 1994. Expulsion requires an 80 percent majority however, and so it seemed likely that NAMBLA would remain in ILGA, ILGA would be expelled from ECOSOC, ECOSOC would retain its U.S. funding—and Jesse Helms would have tasted blood.

In the wake of all this, HRCF, NGLTF, P-FLAG and GLAAD, among other acronymic gay rights organizations, have all more or less endorsed the sentiment expressed by Stonewall 25 co-chair Pat Norman: "Those who advocate or engage in the sexual abuse of young people are not welcome in the family of gay men and lesbians who lead upstanding and honorable lives." The statement does not specify how young is young, or what kind of sex is sexual abuse. But making clear policy was not the intent. The intent was condemnation—necessary, as Franklin Whitworth, administrative director of Colorado's human rights organization Ground Zero, has put it, to "take away that tool" the radical Right has been using against the community for years: the hammer of child molestation.

Whitworth is right to worry. As early as the 1930s, newspapers used the infrequent "sex murders" of boys as an opportunity to lecture the public on the dangers of homosexuality. Anita Bryant did much the same in her 1970s crusade, and today Colorado for Family Values, in its guide to anti-gay initiatives, flatly states that "73 percent of homosexuals incorporate children into their sexual practices." Even the most mainstream gay groups get tarred with that brush: A 1992 article in *The Jewish Advocate* capped its argument against homosexual marriages by salaciously, if inaccurately, revealing the existence of "support groups called *lambda* for men with sexual appetites for children." Such confusion requires a clear political response. But the intent of those gay groups condemning NAMBLA is not just political. It also involves the desire to protect children and a seemingly personal need to position homosexuality safely in the mainstream of American values and far away from dangerous fringes. Rich Tafel, national director of Log Cabin Republicans, the conservative gay lobbying group, has called for organized opposition to NAMBLA as a way of demonstrating that, contrary to right-wing smears, gay Americans have high moral standards and will enforce them. "One of the signs of a politically mature movement is its ability to clearly articulate what it is and what it isn't," Tafel wrote. "NAMBLA marching under our banner of gay equality is a travesty. We need to say it and we need to stop it."

To make his point, Tafel retails some right-wing smears of his own—alleging that NAMBLA produces how-to guides for seducing boys with alcohol and pornography, and promotes travel packages to countries where underage sex partners may be procured without danger of disease or entrapment. (These topics are occasionally discussed in NAMBLA publications, but are hardly promoted.) Other half-truths or outright falsehoods making the rounds are that NAMBLA advocates forcible rape, that it produces a color catalog of boys who can be bought by credit card and delivered by Lear jet, that its motto is "Sex before eight, or it's too late." Such canards make NAMBLA easier to target, but the tactic suggests the fear that a more rational examination would not produce the desired result.

And therein lies the story. Despite the veneer of unanimous condemnation by the community, there are, beneath the surface, gaping and unexamined divides. For every Pat Norman there's an Allen Ginsberg, who expressed solidarity with NAMBLA by saying: "I love boys, too. Everybody does who has a little humanity." For every woman who says she was forced into sexual encounters with adults, and feels she has suffered as a result, there's a man who sought such sex, enjoyed it and reflects fondly on the memory.

(And vice versa.) The issue raises all sorts of contentious questions about privacy, power, and the meaning of consent. Is pedophilia inborn? Chosen? Sick? If it was good for Greece, is it good for us? If we merely fantasize about boys or girls are we the same as pedophiles? Are we thus hypocrites? Must the gay community throw in its lot with any group that says it is gay, with any group that will pay for the chairs? Who are we of all people to condemn a sexual minority? And who are we of all people *not* to condemn sexual predation? What in fact is NAMBLA?

What in fact are we?

It's a shame that these questions, long ignored or debated sub rosa, have come to the fore only in response to forces external (and hostile) to the community. Jesse Helms was probably inspired in his ILGA crusade by a right-wing anti-gay journal disingenuously named *Lambda Report*. And it was WNBC's John Miller, a muckraking TV journalist usually assigned to mob cases, who filed the sensational hidden-camera reports in March 1993 that led to the removal, pending investigation, of Peter Melzer, a New York City high school teacher whose only crime appears to have been membership in NAMBLA. Had the gay and lesbian community dealt earlier and more directly with the moral dilemmas concerning this subject, it might not be faced with such public-relations dilemmas now. As it is, the organizations that say they represent us have been left scrambling for cover, often ending up in bed with our worst enemies as a result. But then the question of who gets to be in bed with whom is what the whole business is finally about.

A Charming Hat

When the TV cameras suddenly appeared, their lights blaring, everyone cowered—not just the pedophiles. We had come to the New York Underground Film Festival on this damp March night to see a documentary about NAMBLA, not to stand as emblems of perversity on *American Journal*. But with pedophilia so much in the public eye recently—Michael Jackson, Woody Allen—perhaps we should have known that the monster-hunt was on. In any case, the packed theater erupted in shouting; a bunch of middle-aged men near the front covered their faces. "Go! Go! Get out!" people screamed. "We could get in trouble for this!" The uproar lasted for three minutes, until a man, laughing at the scene, announced, "We're just at the movies, people." This man turned out to be filmmaker John Waters; I hope he was taking mental notes on the hysteria for use in some future delirious romp.

I had been embarrassed to ask the box office clerk for a ticket to *Chicken Hawk: Men Who Love Boys*. I had even been embarrassed by the way I learned about it in the first place. "Hey, there's something about pedophiles you might want to check out," my father, who knew I was researching the subject, said on my answering machine. "*Men and Boys in Kitty Hawk?* Something like that." In fact, I had been embarrassed to tell people that I was writing about NAMBLA at all. The subject rattled me. The *name* rattled me. Still, I was unprepared for the vehemence of other people's reactions. "They should be shot," said more than one friend I'd considered open-minded and liberal. Others turned their faces away, as if overcome by nausea. And then, one by one, each admitted his or her own experiences with intergenerational sex—good, bad, and indifferent. How had something so apparently common gone so far underground?

Of course, most of these people had never met a member of NAMBLA. They were not talking about the professional (if unfulfilled) pedophiles who would join a club, but rather of the teacher they'd fallen in love with, the uncle who'd fiddled with them, the pickup who (surprise!) was only sixteen. The revulsion turned into something much more complex the minute they considered individual situations. "It fucked me up but I was fucked-up anyway," said a woman. "It ruined me but it saved me," said a man. The mixed feelings of the community seemed to be represented precisely in the mixed feelings of its constituents—as long as the focus was personal. When the focus returned to NAMBLA, certainty resurfaced. Just as some people who support the group willfully ignore its documented positions, some who decry the group willfully ignore their own experience.

Chicken Hawk would not have helped them resolve their confusion. In the documentary, made by a film student named Adi Sideman, a series of men, almost all of whom showed obvious signs of emotional immaturity, talked about their love of boys in terms that made me cringe. One man in particular seemed painfully naive in his conviction that something so good as boy-love—as he and other NAMBLA members call it—would be embraced if only people opened their hearts. Amazingly, this former missionary allowed the camera to follow him as he chatted up a 14-year-old named Jason, whom he found playing games at a pay phone in West Virginia. "Let's see how you did that!" he cooed. "Hey, not bad!" "That'll be our secret, then." Afterward, in tones of evangelical ecstasy, he described the encounter as if it had been with the young Jesus himself—or as if *he* were the young Jesus himself. "This is what life is about, this is what real life is about!" he exclaimed, driving away with a huge smile on his face. "And I would say he was in bloom, and that's it: The flower is responding to warmth. That is, I as a human being am bathing him in a certain kind of celestial warmth, and he feels that and he responds to that and he thinks, 'Oh, how nice, how wonderful that there's someone who is appreciating what I am and who I am!'"

Though the movie included heartbreaking scenes of the loneliness suffered by those pedophiles who choose celibacy rather than risk indulging an outlawed sexuality, it was this man, Leland Stevenson, completely misconstruing the passing attention of pubescent boys as erotic interest, who lingered in my mind as the lights came up. Then, suddenly, there he was in person, participating in what was meant to be a discussion with one Tom

McDonough, who represented an anti-NAMBLA group called Straight Kids USA. McDonough and his street-tough cohorts had appeared in the film, picketing the apartment of a NAMBLA member and leaving this message on his answering machine: "You fucking babyfucking motherfucker. Your mother was a whore; you know who your father was? A fucking pimp, you low-life son-of-a-fucking, cuntlicking....You low-life prick, you kike, you....Wait till the fucking parade: Gonna put a bullet in your fucking head, you cocksucking babyfucker. Die of AIDS, babyfucker, die of fucking AIDS, you fucking low-life son-of-a-fucking, cuntlicking whore!"

Members of the audience quickly ferreted out McDonough's larger, anti-gay agenda—Straight Kids USA seemed to be a reformulation of a group that called itself, rather too tellingly, the National Traditionalist Coalition. But the crowd was no friendlier to Stevenson, who, as the discussion disintegrated into a brawl, kept returning to his image of pubescent boys as exquisite flowers about to "bloom." When I introduced myself to him afterward, he seemed to try to make *me* bloom, too. "My, what a charming hat that is," he said. "That is one very lovely hat. I think it's *very* becoming." Perhaps it was too dark for him to notice the gray hair creeping out from under that hat, but then I didn't feel as if I were actually present in his experience of our conversation anyway. Present or necessary. As he had in West Virginia, Stevenson seemed to be playing both roles in a purely interior seduction (since no one was really there to reciprocate): lover and beloved, predator and prey. Amazingly, he was himself the boy he desired, embodying both the *M* and *B* of NAMBLA in one victorious act of imagination.

Smiles Imply Consent

It is commonly held, and fervently reiterated, that 90 percent of pedophiles are straight men. Unfortunately, there is little reliable information to support this claim. A 1984 study titled "The Gender Gap Among Perpetrators of Child Sexual Abuse" did show that men who identify themselves as heterosexual are responsible for 95 percent of the sexual abuse of *girls*; but since girls are the reported victims in only two out of three cases, that leaves some 37 percent of pedophiles unaccounted for. Are they gay? Not necessarily. Many psychiatrists who study the subject believe that pedophiles, whatever they call themselves, are neither gay nor straight, but their own category entirely: people in whom age replaces gender as the dominant factor in desire. Such theories are meaningless, though, once you move beyond the textbooks. NAMBLA is a hodgepodge of individuals whose orientations, ideations, and affiliations lie all over the map. Though many are gay, some—refugees from extinguished straight pedophile groups—are not. Perhaps more oddly, not all are men, nor even pedophiles; a handful of women have been active, as well as the occasional teenager and a few wayward libertarians and Trotskyites. Talking about NAMBLA as a pedophile group (or as a gay group) is thus, in a way, misleading: It represents only a minority of pedophiles, a minority of gay pedophiles and an infinitesimal minority of gays.

Just look at the parades. The NAMBLA contingent, when permitted to march, is instantly recognizable amid the fabulousness by its homely pathos: four or five men comporting themselves with the outward probity and glazed looks of Rotarians. NAMBLA does, in fact, operate legally, whatever the malfeasance of individual members, and, as even *Lambda Report* admits, "has survived several investigations, including one by the FBI." Were there even a hint of organizational misconduct, NAMBLA would have been shut down ages ago. Not that there's much to shut down. At this point the organization, which has no office beyond its members' homes but is listed in the Manhattan phone book, is little more than a publishing collective, producing its *Bulletin* eight times a year, along with a few other manifestos and broadsides. Thanks to more stringent laws and more aggressive stings, twelve local chapters have been winnowed to none; the national group subsists on an annual income of about $60,000—mostly derived from gifts, publications, and the twenty-five dollar dues of one thousand members. (Another eighty-five, in prison, are comped.)

In the early days, around 1980, members believed that NAMBLA would quickly outstrip its original incarnation as an ad hoc anti-witch-hunt cadre and take its place at the leading edge of liberation politics. If this never happened, it was not for want of a radical vision. "Sex is a good, healthy, and for most people, a necessary part of life, and should not be denied to children any more than they are denied nourishment," a NAMBLA position paper trumpets—radical enough, but radically disingenuous. Sex is not always a good and healthy part of life; it *can* and *should* be. How do we ensure, even for ourselves, that harm will not come to us as a result of our desires? We often can't. A child has even less of a chance. Surely some young people are more prepared than others to test their sexuality in an adult world. But *which* young people? Describing having anal sex with a boy in his early teens, Leland Stevenson nominates any child who's willing: "He positioned himself in such a way that nature would take its course and he would experience within himself a part of the body of his friend. And so, laying [sic] as he did on his side and producing the natural consequence of this event—I may say that this was sufficiently stimulating that no lubricant was desired, er, required—that is, nature or life simply produced its own for this occasion—he experienced what he wanted to experience, and I certainly on that occasion experienced something that was very precious and fulfilling to me as well." Such repellent circumlocutions do not make one eager to entrust the decision to a person whose lust is engaged—whether that's the man or the boy. And parents, especially parents of homosexuals, might choose never to let their offspring have sex. State governments, too, have made a mess of their attempts to codify the age at which a person may make his own mistakes, but even if they could agree to agree, is the answer 9, 11, 14, 16, 18, 21?

NAMBLA's answer is none of the above, which reflects its general anarchic leanings. Indeed, the organization is not notably coherent. When you're this far beyond the fringe, and under attack from all sides, it's hard to be picky, but the result is that a group of people who do not necessarily even share the same goals share the same name—and the same onus. The biggest split is between those whose taste runs primarily toward adolescent boys and those whose taste runs younger. Nevertheless, as a demonstration of solidarity and "ideological purity," NAMBLA has steadfastly refused to draw distinctions between the case of a twenty-year-old who falls in love with a seventeen-year-old while at college, say, and a sixty-year-old who has sex routinely with compliant-seeming boys of eight. (It's the former example they publicize, though.) Since children develop uniquely, NAMBLA says, no rational age-of-consent line exists and the principled approach is thus not to draw one. A photograph in a recent *Bulletin* of a happy-looking boy lying naked on his stomach bears a caption that defines their position: "Smiles imply consent."

The picture, if it appeared in a gallery or in your family album, might not be disturbing; here, abstracted amid bad poetry and treacly softcore porn, it seems like grist for the masturbation mill. Still, it's all kept mild; the typical article describes relationships that are mentoring, cuddly, and "nonpenetrative." This is a rare instance of delicacy on NAMBLA's part; elsewhere, "ideological purity" has pushed the group into some uncomfortable (and laughable) corners. Among the grab bag of positions adopted over the years and appended to its constitution are statements opposing the military draft, corporal punishment, intervention in El Salvador, circumcision and clitoridectomy, compulsory schooling, age-based curfews, and laws prohibiting child prostitution, employment, and pornography—though children should be compensated for their work. In addition, NAMBLA explicitly endorses the right of children of any age to serve on juries, vote, hold office, choose from a variety of living arrangements (including residences operated by children), design their own education, divorce their parents and receive explicit sexual information and contraceptives—"in appropriate smaller sizes," of course.

Today, a jury of eight-year-olds awarded a divorce on the grounds of circumcision to the honorable Senator Macaulay Culkin.... The mind reels. NAMBLA's agenda, meant to strengthen and elaborate its fundamental argument for allowing sex with children, instead exposes that argument as the product of massive rationalization, just as all the talk of cuddling and empowering children evaporates in the heat of Leland Stevenson's descriptions of fucking them. Thus the glazed looks. It takes a lot of hard work to deny the very words coming out of your mouth, and the unmistakable deeds of your hands.

New Math

Sexual relations with people below the age of consent are prohibited in the U.S. by forcible sodomy and statutory rape laws, which are written by state legislatures and thus vary widely. An adult man can have (unforced) intercourse with a thirteen-year-old girl (though not with a boy) in Virginia; in California, the girl must be eighteen. Two fifteen-year-old boys may legally have sex in Connecticut, but not across the border in Massachusetts.

This is inconsistent, but not uniquely so; remember that in Georgia, and fifteen other states, *any* oral or anal sex is illegal, regardless of age or gender. (In five additional states, that prohibition applies only to homosexuals.) In several states, the crime is deemed more or less severe according to the age differential between the partners: In New York, unforced sex between someone who's twenty and someone who's sixteen is a misdemeanor (which carries a maximum jail sentence of one year); make the older person twenty-one, and it suddenly becomes third-degree rape (which carries a maximum of four).

The rest of the world is no less confusing. The age of consent is eighteen in Germany, fifteen in France, twelve in Spain. In England, Parliament recently lowered the age at which a male can have sex with another male from twenty-one to eighteen; it's sixteen, however, for heterosexuals, and lesbians don't count. NAMBLA's Canadian chapter shut down when that country dropped its age of consent to fourteen, so if you were sixteen on the day the law changed, you could have been having sex two years ago. Unless it was anal sex—then you'd be illegal until eighteen, so college freshmen could be prosecuted, while seniors could not. In the Netherlands, the ages between twelve and sixteen are a semi-legal gray area: If the child doesn't object and the parents don't either, the police can't initiate a prosecution.

In the United States, prosecutors sometimes take such niceties into account, but the punishments can often be formidable (especially in comparison to more overtly violent crimes) and are levied inconsistently. According to Evan Wolfson, who prosecuted sex crimes for the Brooklyn District Attorney before becoming the senior staff attorney at Lambda Legal Defense and Education Fund, age-of-consent laws are used, "if not more frequently" against homosexuals than heterosexuals, "at least more harshly."

Klismaphilia, Anyone?

We are all doomed to become experts in our own sexuality and ignoramuses of everyone else's. Those who make it their professional business to study what other people do with their bodies are prone to compensate for the stigma attached to that endeavor with long words and categorization schemata that seem to defy our actual experience of love and perversion. In its standard diagnostic reference, the American Psychiatric Association dryly defines pedophilia (from the Greek for "boy-love") as a recurrent, intense sexual desire—acted upon or causing distress—for prepubescent children. Adults who are drawn to older children, thirteen or so and up, are called ephebophiles (from the Greek for "youth-love") and are more likely to identify themselves as gay or straight, since the objects of their desire have adult sexual characteristics. In terms of psychiatry, they exist in a gray area. Not so the "true" pedophiles. Though their orientation, like all orientations, is considered immutable, they are classed in a scary group called paraphilias, which until 1973 included homosexuality and still includes sado-masochism, bestiality, necrophilia, voyeurism, and many others too odd to mention. (Klismaphilia anyone? Look it up.)

For scientists, classifying and judging are not the same thing. John Money, sometimes called Mr. Paraphilia for his ground-breaking work on these unusual desires, records cases of man-boy love in which he finds no harm, and even finds value. He attributes a lot of the damage that results from pedophilia to society's over-reaction when the liaison is revealed—the boy is traumatized by his rude introduction to the criminal justice system. The main harm of pedophilia, he posits tautologically, is that it may produce new pedophiles. For these insights, Money has won hero status among boy-lovers; he's constantly quoted in NAMBLA materials. ("If I were to see the case of a boy aged ten or eleven who's intensely attracted toward a man in his twenties or thirties, if the relation-ship is totally mutual…then I would not call it pathological in any way.") But Money is being taken out of context. His scenario of beneficial pedophile relationships does not mean that such rela-tionships are the norm. It only means they are possible.

In fact, Money's expertise derives largely from clinical work with pedophiles who wish to *control* their appetite for boys. Professionals who work with the boys themselves often have a less tolerant perspective. Joyce Hunter, president of the National Lesbian and Gay Health Foundation and a longtime youth coun-selor, says, "A young person, if he has a stable living situation, money in his pockets, and friends he feels safe with, is not gener-ally interested in older men. It's the kids on the streets, abused or unloved, I worry about. The pedophiles say they're helping the kids deal with their problems, but in fact they're *contributing* to the problem. They're *perpetuating* what the parents have done. The reaction of these kids is to get very depressed, angry and scared. In the long term they often are unable to be intimate as adults with their partners. That's why, if we get a call saying a kid is coming to New York and getting off at Port Authority, we get someone there within a half-hour. Because if he's on the street for more than that, he'll get picked up by one of these guys. I've never seen it where it's a good thing. The kind of idealized mentor they talk about, well, he's not living in New York City."

Where *is* he living? In ancient Athens, in tribal New Guinea, in fifteenth-century Japan. As Gary Remafedi, assistant professor of pediatrics at the University of Minnesota, points out, love is culturally defined, as is childhood. "Many societies have prohibitions against sex with prepubescent children," he says. "In others there's a great deal more variance. Whether it's considered a disorder or not depends on who's doing the judging. Sex between a young man and an older woman is highly valued in our society; sex between a young woman and an older man is sometimes considered a feather in the older man's cap. Whereas sex between men and boys is automatically considered wrong and is illegal."

Remafedi, who has studied the sexual patterns of gay male adolescents and found that, on average, their partners were seven years older than they, has seen the emotional damage caused by pedophilia. "In societies where there's an extended period of adolescence, such as ours, there's usually a wide power difference between the adolescent and the adult, and it's very difficult for the two to meet on equal terms; in a sexual relationship between them, most often one or both are damaged. In non-industrialized countries, where there isn't this prolonged adolescence, it has not been uncommon for young people to marry and have children, particularly young girls with older males. But we live here. And in my view, when an adult is *only* able to form relationships with youngsters, it speaks to some underlying emotional problem."

Condemned ourselves, we find it hard to condemn anyone whose minority status reminds us of our own, especially in the same terms traditionally reserved for us. But it is possible to examine the situation without malice. "You can make the point that people are different, they don't choose their orientation, and shouldn't be hated," says Fred Berlin, founder of the sex disorder clinic at Johns Hopkins, "while also spelling out that you have to look at consequences. Objectively we find that in some pedophile relationships the kids aren't hurt: That's good news. But that should not be turned into an endorsement. One has to distinguish between whether it's harmful and whether it's wrong. I could give a kid drugs, and he might luck out and not have anything bad happen; but morally I'm playing Russian roulette, and I don't think he should be exposed to that risk. On the other hand, we shouldn't make it self-fulfilling. I went to court recently: A twelve-year-old had been involved with an adult, and the prosecutor was saying he would never be the same, his childhood had been stolen from him, he'd never have a normal life. And I was thinking: *This* is child abuse. The message to the kid should have been: 'You've done nothing wrong. The man may have loved you, he just did it wrong.' I mean, if God forbid I was given a choice of my child being hit by a truck or touched on his penis by an adult, I'd choose the penis!"

Berlin has treated some 400 pedophiles at his clinic, using synthetic hormones and psychotherapy to control what he calls "a craving disorder." For obvious reasons, NAMBLA is not happy with this kind of work, nor with research that attempts to locate the origin of pedophilia in childhood sexual trauma. Money's theory of the "vandalized lovemap" posits unnatural interference in juvenile sex play as the set-up; the pedophile's erotic development is arrested at the point of interference and never advances beyond it. For NAMBLA members, the set-up is irrelevant because the result, as they see it, is not a disease. To them, trying to pinpoint the etiology of pedophilia is as insulting as similar attempts to explain homosexuality. With some justification, they decry the modern medicalization of desire, in which every erection or lubrication becomes a symptom instead of a pleasure. Gay people especially should be wary about relying on psychiatric theory and statistics for legitimacy; the same theories once labeled us sick, based on statistics similarly derived from studies, like Kinsey's, of convicted sex offenders. Hormone treatments are still used to "cure" homosexuals. But however flawed, the study of sex has done, on balance, more good for homosexuals than liberal blandishments and pious toleration. It's thanks to such work as Kinsey's that homosexuality itself was finally declassified as a disorder, thus indirectly but profoundly altering not only the way we are looked at but the way we look at ourselves. Unfortunately for pedophiles, science has not proved as beneficial to them as it has proved to homosexuals. Nevertheless, as E. M. Forster wrote at a time, not long ago, when the two groups were thought to be virtually synonymous: "Science is better than sympathy, if only it is science."

My Own Private Athens

Bob Rhodes tells me I will recognize him because he is "grotesquely overweight," and so, for forty minutes, whenever an even moderately chubby person enters the restaurant where we've agreed to meet, I wonder if maybe he's a pedophile with a bad self-image. I know that NAMBLA believes we're all pedophiles, covertly at least: "Scratch your average gay man, find a boy-lover," is a phrase I've heard more than once. It's true that one gay male ideal, embodied by Marky Mark, among others, is a hairless though muscular sun-kissed dope. And the female supermodel of the moment, Kate Moss, is a woman whose physique and demeanor are that of a ten-year-old. Pedophiles merely act out the attraction we all feel for youthful beauty—that's what NAMBLA members say. Well, exactly.

And murderers merely act out the anger we all feel for our benighted world.

Not to equate love and death. But the arguments fail in the same way. In fact, most of the arguments I've heard in favor of pedophilia fail elementary tests of logic. The Athenians did it. (They also forbade adult homosexuality.) If a child is allowed to say no, he must be allowed to say yes. (Why? Do we let children drive because they want to?) It's innately human. (So is violence.) Many of the arguments against don't hold up much better. Children are powerless to make reasonable decisions in the face of love. (Who isn't?) Pedophilia's a perversion: Psychiatrists say so. (That's what they said about homosexuality.) It's innately inhuman. (The Athenians did it.) And back again.

I have plenty of time to consider these conundrums because Rhodes never shows up. When we finally do meet, a few days later, in the Christopher Street office of Heritage of Pride, where Rhodes is a longtime member of the committee that plans the annual New York City march, he proves to be a conundrum himself. He is, as advertised, quite overweight, and faintly resembles W.C. Fields— a notorious child-hater. He has light brown hair, pale eyes behind pale glasses and, at forty-eight, the friendly but defensive expression of a retarded child. Though his teeth are rotten and badly spaced, like ancient gravestones, he isn't really unappealing; his intelligence, which he makes quite evident, leavens him considerably. To underline this attribute and substantiate his ideology, he has brought sheaves of documents, which he tosses sloppily to me and picks at from time to time. Still, he seems prepared for the worst—and helps promote it. Soon after we begin talking, for instance, he suddenly plops himself onto the floor, where he sits for the rest of the interview, rocking back and forth as he talks and occasionally lifting his sweatshirt to scratch at his formidable belly.

I try not to stare, but I wonder if these are unconscious provocations—like Stevenson's gaudy metaphors, like NAMBLA's name itself. I'm reminded of the riveting photograph that accompanied a *New York* magazine article about Peter Melzer, the teacher under investigation for his NAMBLA membership. In it, Melzer is captured, in his shabby Bronx apartment, wearing sandals over threadbare socks through which poke his pink little toes. How artless can a person be? It's as if we are being dared to comment, dared to judge. But philosophies are not discredited by the ungainliness of their proponents. Sometimes people who live in scorn are odd and provocative not because of inherent turpitude but because of their being scorned in the first place. Actions that seem like provocations may just be tics, the strange compensations a person evolves when his every drive must be diverted, when the only solace in the world is a ghetto in his own private Athens.

In any case, despite the rocking, Rhodes turns out to be thoughtful and frank. "The typical NAMBLA member is someone overeducated, underemployed, and not terribly sexually active," he says, though he himself works for the federal government as a disability specialist and has had what he calls a wide range of experiences with "senior-high-school-aged boys." One was a sociopath who stole three of his VCRs; another, whom he met twelve years ago and still has an occasional sexual relationship with, is now the vice president of a brokerage firm. "What he sees in me I have no idea," Rhodes says, raising his sweater and scratching himself. "I generally need to be hit over the head to understand that someone is flirting with me, because of my self-image problems. One kid on the street, he was about sixteen or seventeen. If he didn't want to have sex, at some point he would have sent out negative signals. I've had some people change their mind. Do I let them go?" He stares for a moment. "No, I blend them in the Cuisinart—that's a joke."

A joke and a challenge. Though Rhodes has a fanatic's encyclopedic knowledge of his subject, he complains that the rest of the world takes sex too seriously. He waves off every example I produce of damage done to children by pedophiles: "Providing that the sexuality is at a level both parties can accept, there's no reason it cannot be mutually pleasurable." The question of consent irritates him, too. "There is no question of consent," he sneers, "beyond *Does he say yes?*" Like all NAMBLA members, he cites the victimology craze as the source of such groundless concerns. "Right now we are undergoing a stage where we believe that everybody should be accompanied throughout life by a therapist. We're going from protecting children to protecting adults. What this ignores is that people are autonomous and should be allowed to make their own decisions, some of which will have painful consequences. If you're highly dependent on one person and that person ends up leaving you, then that's going to happen and you had best get through it."

Granted, America has become hysterical on the subject, and violent pedophilia, though highly publicized, is extremely rare. But this attitude just seems hard-hearted. Are there really no victims? Isn't a man, in choosing to have sex with a nine-year-old—even one who "smiles his consent"—choosing to put his pleasure above the child's unknowable long-term response? Isn't that a pathology?

"Any sex that doesn't interest you," Rhodes says, "you find ridiculous or disgusting. Beyond that, it's not more inherently pathological than any other orientation. What we're interested in is pleasure, gotten into voluntarily, and that can be gotten out of if they don't want it. Yes, there can be individual tragedies, but sex between adults and boys is not generally a tragedy in the making." The way he describes it, pedophilia sounds like macrame: a harmless odd hobby. (Or, if there is harm, it is usually to the man, who is the one more likely to be abandoned, according to Rhodes.) No wonder he sees himself as an "upstanding and standard" member of society. "I read the *Economist*, I'm a government employee. Only in a few peculiarities do I stand out, and only when counterposed against the public norm." He sighs and rocks.

"Until then you don't realize that you're a figure of personal horror, which I find quite shocking and surprising still."

The Men From the Boys

Vaughn Challingsworth was trying to listen. As chair of the Youth Constituency of the U.S. Steering Committee for Stonewall 25, he had invited two NAMBLA members to explain, in March 1994, why their organization should be permitted to participate in the rally at the UN that June. Stonewall 25 had voted to ban groups that "advocated sexual exploitation of children," but NAMBLA argued that it advocated empowerment, not exploitation; love, not abuse.

Whatever they were advocating, Challingsworth wasn't buying. Earlier that weekend, he says, the same NAMBLA members had "infiltrated" a social event meant only for Stonewall 25 youth and their invited friends. As a result, the meeting was tense. "A lot of my caucus were very scared of them. You should have seen the eight of us all squoze on top of each other." Additional debate before the full steering committee produced two separate votes that left everyone confused. Stonewall 25 says NAMBLA is not invited. NAMBLA says it is, and will come. A group called Spirit of Stonewall suddenly materialized to act as a beard for NAMBLA at the march. Contemplating this, Challingsworth holds his heart and shakes his head. "As an individual, I believe every person has a right to be heard, even if I disagree with them, even if they stand for principles I don't find pleasant. But I swear to God it'll be a setback for young people. I am going to try to see if I can have NAMBLA arrested. I will take them through hell."

Challingsworth (like the other members of his caucus) isn't even underage. He's twenty and, at first glance, self-possessed. When I meet him at the Neutral Zone—the Christopher Street drop-in center for gay and lesbian youth where he says he works as a counselor—he's decked out in a stylish green blazer over a white T-shirt, flowing black pants and dressy shoes: halfway between a night at Limelight and a day at Merrill Lynch.

"Most young gays can't stand older gay people," he says. "For the simple reason we think they only want to come near us for sex. 'He loves me, he loves me,'—yeah, whenever he wants to roll over and have sex with you. Otherwise he has no time. Right now I'm searching for a young person who was in this relation with an older adult. I'm afraid he's killed himself. A large number of my kids here, and at other youth centers, have had sex with adults. Most of the experiences are one-night events; very few go into the realm of relationships. The real damage is to the kids' perception of the gay community. If this is how it's set up, then I don't see a future for us in it." Challingsworth pauses darkly.

"You can't empower me by fucking me," he continues, "but by showing me the things I need to know. NAMBLA is thinking what we need is sex, when what we need are job workshops. Sex is going to come knocking at your door in its own time. You'll find some-one. But kids thrown out of their homes are looking for ways to find stability. And what do they run into? A bunch of older gay men who are just out there to get kids into their car and into their pants. When NAMBLA says the kids come on to them, that's an easy way for the older community to justify what they want. Yes, there are some who have survival sex because that's how they get food in their stomach. And some, because of the rejection from their fami-lies, are looking for someone to love them, care for them, and guide them.

"I know what *that's* about! When my mother said, 'Vaughn, you're gay and I'm not paying to send a gay boy to college,' I searched desperately for someone to care about me." He suddenly goes quiet. "I myself trusted an older man in the gay community. I used to go to church with him. Then one night I turn around and the trust got my arm pinned behind my back and my legs spread open and in the hospital with the police and a whole rape investigation going on.

I contracted AIDS from him." He stares across the table at me, with blame in his eyes.

Challingsworth's blustering confidence—all his talk of "my kids" and "my caucus" and taking unilateral, earthshaking action— has mutated into a kind of hysteria that makes me question some of his stories. Indeed, officials of the Neutral Zone later tell me that Challingsworth has never been employed there. But the feelings behind his fabrications are real enough: anger at the damage done by people who are supposed to be mentors and role models and supports. Of all the divisions within the community, the age division may be the most problematic because it must be solved anew with each generation. That's why Challingsworth laughs off NAMBLA's argument that the rejection of pedophiles will lead to the rejection of drag queens, people of color, and other subgroups. "Honey, I'm black and was named Miss Pittsburgh, and nobody's trying to cut me off for *that*." The danger he sees instead is the danger of cutting off youth. But it's a two-way street. Even as we speak, a guard at the door watches for people who seem over-age and shoos them off as if they were beggars.

Women and Children Last

There are no organizations for lesbian pedophiles. This is not to say that adult lesbians do not have sex with girls; some do. There are no reliable figures on the subject but, anecdotally, such relationships, especially with younger children, appear to be very rare. This may reflect a fundamental difference between males and females: Men are said by sociobiologists to have a "wilder"—that is, more unfocused—sexuality. Or it may reflect a double standard, whereby acts considered pedophilia when committed by men are understood as something else when committed by women. In any case, a group called NAWGLA does not exist.

Quite the opposite: Lesbians are generally much more vocal and adamant than men in expressing their disapproval of NAMBLA. An exception to the rule is Pat Califia, longtime *Advocate* sex columnist, who wants it made clear she's speaking for herself and not her publication. "Women's traditional role vis-à-vis sexuality is to act as the guardians of young people and as a bulwark against toxic male sexuality," she says. "As long as this debate gets cast in terms of predatory men and helpless victims—seeing any form of male sex as a thinly veiled form of rape—it would be very difficult for women to take any different position than to condemn pedophilia." Since Califia finds this analysis dubious and homophobic, however, she rejects it outright; in fact she is a NAMBLA supporter. But she seems misinformed—in exactly the way NAMBLA wants her to be. She talks about the wimpy gay community cooperating with a state-sponsored campaign of hate against "sexual minority youth and their adult friends and lovers," but she keeps referring to eighteen-year-olds.

"But many reasonable people genuinely feel that a twelve-year-old is rightly protected from having that kind of relationship," I say.

"That's not what NAMBLA's about," she snaps. "That's a distortion. They're not talking about twelve-year-olds."

"Yes they are. That's what they say to me. Twelve and, theoretically, much younger."

Califia backs down, at least for a moment. "I have to be really clear here. Most of what I'm focusing on are postpubescent, older teenagers; I have a hard time envisioning a consensual relationship between a child and an adult. But this is the choice: Either we can cling to the ideal that we are offering a radical critique of mandatory heterosexuality and the nuclear family—and that what we're about is creating alternative institutions for human interaction—or we can say that our movement is about joining the mainstream and duplicating those institutions, only with same-sex relations included."

NAMBLA members, echoing Califia's jargony belligerence, also call for the abolition of the "proto-fascist" nuclear family; they consider bourgeois values, especially homosexual bourgeois values, inherently poisonous. Betraying a surprising streak of misogyny, they portray women who speak out against pedophilia as harpies, envious of male sexual freedom and eager to put an end to it. The possibility of a principled opposition is never admitted; only pedophiles take an intellectually defensible stance. In *The Boston Sex Scandal*, a history of the emergence of the pedophile movement, the author, who signs himself only "Mitzel," goes so far as to compare crusading boy-lovers to Tom Paine. "The so-called molestation of the young," he writes, "is the start of politics."

Boy For Sale

The three-story Brooklyn brownstone is run-down but livable. A handwritten sign on the buzzer tells you its name is Madrigal House. Since it opened in August 1993 as a residence for throw-away lesbian and gay youth, twenty-three kids, mostly boys, have called the place home. Right now, because it's mid-afternoon, most of them are at work or at school. This is already a major achievement. In his office, founder and director Steve Ashkinazy—who has worked with gay youth for more than twenty of his forty-four years—is telling me that almost every boy referred here has been exploited by some kind of arrangement with a pedophile.

Most of the kids I've been able to talk to about their experiences with pedophiles have already been processed by social service agencies; their stories, however true, sound a little preprogrammed. NAMBLA literature (as well as some psychiatric case histories) provides positive testimony, but I want to know more objectively what the typical story is. What I've discovered, though, is that few gay males of a certain age, say forty and older, are objective. Like the street boys Ashkinazy has just described, they all came out with older men, and see themselves as victims, survivors, or beneficiaries of the experience. I figure that Ashkinazy—who, with his graying beard, crocheted yarmulke, and open plaid shirt, looks like he should star in a show called *Street Rabbi*—will have a less personally inflected perspective. But he sure doesn't talk like a rabbi.

" 'No kid has ever been hurt by a blow job'—that's what Damien used to say." Damien Martin co-founded the Hetrick-Martin Institute, a New York City agency whose services for gay and lesbian youth include counseling, socializing, and the Harvey Milk School. Ashkinazy interprets his statement to mean that sex between a teenager and an older man is not always, by itself, a disastrous thing. "A relationship, however," Ashkinazy continues, "becomes problematic. And when someone is pretending to be a mentor, but is also involved with his protégé sexually, the young person always—*always*—suffers. Think about the damage *parents* do; now imagine taking that and mixing it up with sex, and it's damn confusing. They say they have the best interests of the kids at heart, but what I invariably have seen is that it's against *their* better interest to make these kids independent. What they really want is to keep them under their thumb. Deep down, they know that if the kid achieves independence he'll leave them. I know this as a result of dealing with a lot of kids who are involved with NAMBLA people, and from the NAMBLA people themselves, who don't even realize what they're telling me. I always ask them this: 'If Joey decides to stop sleeping with you, or if you find out he's having sex with someone else, will you let him continue to live with you?' I don't remember anyone ever saying yes. Even if they're well-meaning people, I think NAMBLA is a dangerous organization. I think it's justified to cast them out."

Is that my objective answer? Just to be sure, I ask Ashkinazy if, as a boy growing up in Brooklyn, he himself had encounters with adults. At first he doesn't respond. He sips a cup of tea; the wind through an open window blows some papers about his disheveled office. The radio plays "Saving All My Love for You."

"When I was fourteen, I read in *The New York Times* before going to school one morning that they were going to clean up Times Square because there were drug addicts and homosexuals and prostitutes there. It was the first time I'd seen the word 'homosexual' in print and I blushed: I was terrified that my whole family would be able to see that I was looking at that word. I went to school but I didn't hear a thing; it was a pointless day spent worried that by the time I got to Times Square all the homosexuals would be cleaned up. I took the bus to the subway, which I'd never been on before. Every three stops I looked at the map. It wasn't until we hit Thirty-fourth Street that I realized I had no idea what I would do when I got off. But not to worry, because between Thirty-fourth and Forty-second, a man approached me. He said hello. I was so nervous I couldn't get my voice to work.

"He was twenty-eight. I was clearly a kid. First he took me to a movie theater on Forty-second Street; we sat in the back row. Then we went to his place on Seventy-second and had sex—oral sex and a lot of fondling. I wasn't attracted to him, he was really kind of disgusting, but it didn't occur to me to turn down any offer. We made a date to go out a few days later, and afterwards I went to Forty-second Street again. This time I found someone I thought was really attractive, and we had much better sex, but as a person I found him really despicable."

Ashkinazy pauses and sips more tea. "In the next two years I probably had sex with well over a thousand people, most of them much older than myself. When I was sixteen, I couldn't go to a bar, and there weren't drop-in centers like there are now where I could meet gay people my own age, so I'd cruise the Statler Hilton, in jacket and tie, hang out in the lobby. What started to happen is I met people and went with them several times. It would usually be someone in town for several days, looking for someone to take to the theater and go to nice restaurants. It was very exciting and glamorous. I got to see *Oliver!*"

I am shocked to hear him describe these events so blithely, nostalgically, his eyes almost twinkling. "And that's all?" I ask. "Only good things?"

Ashkinazy smiles a moment longer, then suddenly falters. "It was the swings between feeling exalted, on a pedestal, and feeling like a piece of shit that were unbearable. One minute you were being treated royally, the next like a piece of flesh. I certainly got handed around from person to person a lot. People turned me into a hustler, sent me out for money. Most of my memories are of the good things, learning about ballet and opera, but…" He trails off. "I couldn't share the experience with my peers. The depression from having to lie! Fortunately, I managed to keep my grades up and function at a level so that no one knew what was going on. I never accepted drugs, though they were thrown at me. Very few kids would have gotten through it: people always trying to tell me to run away from home. But I had a perfect sitcom family. And at sixteen I went into therapy—I didn't mention the three suicide attempts, did I?" He's suddenly stricken and starts to cry—that is, his eyes water over, but no sound breaks through.

"The therapy saved me. I guess I'd have to say, if I'm a survivor that's why. And my father, who wanted to know why I had to see a psychiatrist, was footing a very expensive bill, even though he was kept totally in the dark. It's very clear to me all of a sudden that the shrink saved me." The tears come harder, but still no sound. "Until I hit thirty I didn't know what a real relationship was. I still deal with the issues and the damage that was caused at that time."

He never does wipe his eyes; the tears are left to evaporate, which, eventually, they do.

Them and Us

Of any public event involving our people, my family used to ask: Is it good for the Jews? My parents seemed to think that anything done by a member of the extended clan, or by someone perceived to be a member, reflected directly on our own moral standing, and betrayed or advertised us to the world. Ruth Bader Ginsburg: Good for the Jews. Joel Rifkin: Well, he was adopted.

At least we were clear on who our clan was. The gay and lesbian community has no such clarity. Andy Humm, policy and communications director at Hetrick-Martin and a co-anchor of Gay Cable News, says: "Some of the papers cover any incident of a man found having sex with a boy as if it's a gay thing. I don't think it's a gay subject, and I don't cover it." But Bill Dobbs, who accurately describes himself as a tiresome gay activist, takes it for granted that pedophiles are us. "NAMBLA is treated like the Commie Party in the 1950s: *Are you now or have you ever been?*" (Dobbs himself is not a member.) "Take the Melzer case. The only people who were willing to go to bat for him were [*Village Voice* columnist] Nat Hentoff—a straight, white, Jewish man; Howell Raines on the *Times* editorial page; and [New York Civil Liberties Union executive director] Norman Siegel—a straight, white, Jewish man. Siegel said to me: 'I really earned my pay today,' and I said: 'You've got more fucking guts than those creeps at Lambda.' The gay legal establishment will throw members of its own community to the wolves when it's expedient to do so," Dobbs concludes.

It's obvious that Melzer's dismissal from the classroom, with no evidence or even the accusation of wrongdoing, is a gross violation of his civil rights. And it's true that few gay community organizations have spoken up about it. But it's not just expedience, as Dobbs would have it. Organizations like Lambda do not have the freedom to spout off at every provocation—that's why we need tiresome activists—but feel they must jealously conserve their resources for the battles they are best armed to fight.

"It is a minefield," says Lambda executive director Kevin Cathcart. "Believe me, I'll get nothing but grief for talking to you about this. Unless I say absolutely that people in NAMBLA don't even have a right to exist, I'll get letters saying, 'I will not renew my membership.'" Cathcart nevertheless tells me that Lambda has had internal discussions about the issues raised by the Melzer case, and decided not to go near them. "Our reason for being is to expand the rights of lesbian and gay people and people with HIV," he explains. "As a community organization we also have an obligation not to take cases that are going to *harm* lesbian and gay civil rights over the long run. Our clients have to be the best of the best. The soldier with the bronze star, at the top of his class. And NAMBLA"—he raises his eyebrows—"does not fit that category."

Throughout our conversation, Cathcart has been playing with a Slinky, letting it fall from one palm to another and then back again. It seems an apt metaphor for the on-the-one-hand, on-the-other-hand dilemma the gay community faces in NAMBLA. If we disown them, are we disowning a part of ourselves? It's not as if Jesse Helms will be appeased by our casting NAMBLA out; even "good gays" are unacceptable to him. Mightn't we suffer for drawing such lines?

Yes we might, says Frances Kunreuther, executive director of Hetrick-Martin, but that doesn't mean we can avoid our responsibilities. "Let's be clear. NAMBLA is about adults and children having sex. Adults have power, age is power, and to deny that is to deny reality. To say that young people are making informed decisions—in the context of an anti-gay society, where children and teenagers have no power or the financial resources and other rewards that come with that—is false. You don't say to a six-year-old: I'm going to empower you by telling you you can cross in the middle of the street or not. Our role should be helping young people to come to fruition as healthy, productive adults. In the gay and lesbian community, we sometimes don't know how to take on that role, and the parents of lesbian and gay youth don't either. So there's a vacuum, and sometimes sexual relationships end up filling that vacuum. But a sexual relationship obstructs the healthy development of a child; you wouldn't give a six-year-old a job. There are reasons for child-labor laws, for minimum driving ages. There are stages of cognitive development, documented for years and years and years, that make different activities appropriate at different ages. Adults who have sex with children are exploiting them; it's just that simple. Here at Hetrick-Martin, we're absolutely clear on this, and that position has never wavered."

Damien Martin, those innocent blow jobs notwithstanding, knew this firsthand. In an interview shortly before his death in 1991, he told me that his own adolescent experiences with pedophiles were profoundly damaging. He told me too how dismayed he was when the gay men he approached to help fund his new agency ran off in droves, as if someone had threatened to pin them with a scarlet *P*. One man who did support him insisted on delivering his $50,000 cash contribution in his cowboy boots, lest anyone think he was a pedophile. Of this reaction, Martin wrote: "We are frightened because, as a charge, it has been used against us so effectively. We also fear those in the straight world who condemn NAMBLA so vociferously; we know they can, and probably will, turn on us in the same way." Nevertheless, he banned NAMBLA members, or any pedophiles, from the new organization, despite their efforts to join. Now, with hundreds of young clients passing through its doors each day, Hetrick-Martin has an extremely strict non-fraternization policy that requires staff to obtain permission to take a kid out for coffee.

Drawing the Line

In anyone's book, twenty-five passes as old enough. Old enough to say yes, old enough to say no, old enough to live with the consequences of either. I don't just mean a twenty-five-year-old person. If you count from Stonewall, we are twenty-five this year. Are we old enough to make choices? "One of the signs of a politically mature movement is its ability to clearly articulate what it is and what it isn't," Rich Tafel said, and just because he's a Republican doesn't mean he's wrong. NAMBLA has us trained to fear guilt by association. We act as if we are tainted by the mere existence of pedophiles—is it good for the gays? And we reject ideas as tainted too if they resemble ideas held by our enemies. But finding ourselves in agreement with conservatives on one issue does not mean we agree with them on others, any more than sitting in the chairs of the S/M activists requires us to pierce our nipples. Political positions are not owned by blocs; as individuals we choose our views, some of which may come from Trotskyites and some from troglodytes and some from our own souls.

It does mean choosing, though. NAMBLA claims that difficult and arbitrary lines are better left undrawn, but this is an error of logic. Drawing a line nowhere is as arbitrary as drawing a line somewhere. If nothing is excluded, what can inclusion mean? Jewish federations need not include a group like Jews for Jesus just because they call themselves Jews. In fact they must be *excluded*, because their goals are too divergent. In a paper titled "The Death of Gay Liberation?" NAMBLA co-founder (and longtime gay activist) David Thorstad gets it exactly wrong. "Your case against discrimination is weakened," he writes, "if you yourself discriminate." Well, no. You must discriminate (it means "to distinguish")— fairly, rationally—to have a case at all.

NAMBLA knows this. In adopting selected standards of antiquity (like boy-love) and not others (like woman-hate: ever see *Medea?*) they are picking and choosing among historical precedents. They are discriminating. So should we, but we have failed, at least in public. No one wants to stake a position, no one wants to make a move; it's a lose-lose situation and let's not talk about it. But refusing to talk means refusing to acquire the knowledge that allows us to make mature choices. Seen that way, the NAMBLA controversy is not a lose-lose situation at all, but an opportunity to further define ourselves, to decide what we are and what we are not. Perhaps we're afraid to recognize that NAMBLA, which may disturb or disgust us, has some interesting questions to raise, even if our answers are irreconcilably different. Not just about age-of-consent laws. In a larger sense, NAMBLA provokes us to ask: What are the limits of liberation? Have we reached them? Have we passed them?

"The gay movement has gone down a certain path that's proven to be very successful in certain respects," says Bill Andriette. "We've claimed that sexual desire is something that takes place solely in someone's skull, and that society has to give people space to explore these feelings and be happy. It's worked, but I think it's wrongheaded. Homoeroticism is a part of human *culture*, part of the human glue. We all have a stake in homosexuality—and hetero-sexuality—being expressed in the proper way. This is where the sex liberationist rhetoric that got us started meets its limit. Sex for sex's sake, dissociated from relationships, may have reached its endpoint. I sometimes wonder how helpful gay liberation and sex liberation has been altogether."

You might think Andriette was one of those Log Cabin Republicans, or a guppie neo-con. Handsome, slim, his short brown hair flecked with gray, he peers through silver-rimmed glasses at *The New York Times* while sipping chamomile tea at a coffee bar in Boston. But Andriette, Cornell philosophy grad and features editor of Boston's *Guide* magazine, is in fact a member of NAMBLA. At twenty-eight, he is part of its second generation. Talking to him, I do not get the feeling of someone deformed by his desires, perhaps because his desires are broad. Though he fantasizes about boys as young as eight, it would be suicide, he says, to act on such fantasies and so he makes do with men his own age. Telling me this, he looks me straight in the eye, doesn't euphemize, and generally acts like someone's bookish boyfriend. I'm reminded that part of the problem with NAMBLA is, unfor-tunately, aesthetic. If pedophiles looked more like Bill Andriette than Bob Rhodes in our imaginations, we would be more tempted to tolerate them.

Andriette is keenly aware of this. He is not only the editor of NAMBLA's *Bulletin* but of a publication called *Gayme*. Designed to sneak around the stigma of NAMBLA (though it's published by Zymurgy, which is NAMBLA's corporate name), *Gayme* tweaks the age of its models up a few years, uses color and glossy stock, avoids the words *boy-love* and *pedophilia*—and walks off the news-stands. Andriette sees this as proof that gay men are attracted to boys, regardless of arguments about age of consent. "If people are troubled by the idea of an adult having sex with a child," he says, "it's only because they don't have any image except a very ugly one of what that can be like. What's missing is any understanding of what *value* there is in this love. NAMBLA has been terrible at this, at articulating a vision of the *value* of pedophilia."

To counteract the ugly image, Andriette proposes a model of boy-love that is public, safe, and voluntary: a "room" with windows through which society may watch, padding to soften any falls that occur, and doors so that participants may enter, or exit, at will. In some ways it resembles the astonishing, little-known, pedophile culture that flourished, with the tacit approval of the community, in some working-class neighborhoods of Baltimore in the 1950s and 1960s. In some ways it resembles the moon. As he paints the scene, Andriette looks as if he might get a cramp in his head from imagining so hard. He's had plenty of time to think about the subject: He's been a member of NAMBLA since he was fifteen. (His interest in boys younger than himself was already established.) Perhaps growing up so far on the fringe is what has given him such an intensely wishful and yet gloomy outlook. "The experience of NAMBLA's rejection by the gay community has been a very terrible one," he says. "To embrace and feel embraced by the gay world and later to have people you feel you share a history with and a common quality of oppression with—to see them reject you with this sort of intense hatred…" He trails off. "Well, civil wars are the most intense." He looks straight at me. "It's final proof of the co-optation of the gay movement into what its proponents will say is a more liberalized and humanized culture, but one that still depends for its legitimacy on an inquisition against its demons."

Andriette does not accuse me, but I feel accused. And manipulated. I'm reminded of what psychiatrist Fred Berlin told me: "If

I had an orientation where society said I could never be intimate with the kind of person to whom I was attracted, it would be awful. But if pedophiles want us to be sympathetic to the facts of their desires, they have to be sympathetic to society's justifiable concerns." So far, neither side has shown much willingness to do anything but provoke or look the other way. Perhaps we need to remember that sympathy is not endorsement. Refusing to demonize members of NAMBLA does not mean embracing them. There are middle grounds, choices, and finally there are lines; after fair examination—discrimination, in fact—we may draw them. NAMBLA will not like it; NAMBLA never wants to take no for an answer. But we need not let ourselves be coerced, nor let a smile imply consent. The gay community, such as it is, is now old enough to be allowed to choose for itself whom it will get in bed with and whom it will decline.

Update—September 1995

Shortly before this article appeared in the September 1994 issue of *Out*, NAMBLA was in fact expelled from ILGA. ILGA thus retained its consultative status at ECOSOC, and ECOSOC retained its U.S. funding. NAMBLA did march in New York City's Stonewall 25 parade, bearded by the ad hoc Spirit of Stonewall group, and was met with the usual assortment of boos and laughs. Though public pedophile hysteria has appeared to die down since then, the mail received by *Out* in response to "The Men from the Boys" was anything but temperate. Those correspondents who felt I had not adequately demonized NAMBLA accused me of being a pedophile myself or, alternatively, of hating children; those who felt I had demonized NAMBLA too much accused me of being an anti-sex fascist. I found this response ironic. Since my intention had been to show that there are ways of making distinctions without demonization, the hysterical accusations only proved the necessity—and the futility?—of making these points in the first place.

Dumbed Down and Played Out:
The Gay Movement and the Liquidation of Boy-Love

BILL ANDRIETTE

Three days in the life of the editor of the North American Man-Boy Love Association *Bulletin*:

On Tuesday, I get a collect call at work from Richard (I've changed some identifying facts). He was well known in his local gay community and on the arts scene, and used to do volunteer work with gay youth. Once the charges hit the papers, many of his friends wouldn't call him. I wrote him back in February, in the first days of his sentence, but I had not heard from him. He's serving eleven-to-fifteen for sex with two teenage boys, and clings to the hope that in five years he might get parole, but sex offenders today almost never do.

On the first night in prison, he tells me, the guards stripped him naked and put him in a cold, padded cell with just a thin blanket. They announced his crime to the men on the tier, and for hours the prisoners pounded the walls, screaming that they would kill him. Richard says he pulled the blanket over his head and managed to fall asleep.

Wednesday morning, 12:30 A.M. I am wakened by a call from a man in Chicago. A friend of his in Michigan got thirty years for consensual sex with a thirteen-year-old boy. The man plea-bargained to spare the boy a trial, but the judge reneged on the sentencing agreement. The caller is trying to help his friend appeal. Do I know of any helpful legal precedents? Their relationship came to light, he tells me, after the youth got caught in sex play with another boy, and was taken to a therapist, who pressed him for details of his sexual experiences, and then reported them to the police.

Friday afternoon, I go to my post office box, and get the latest letter from my friend Abraham, a psychiatrist and rabbi. He has been on the inside for about three years, and at the earliest, he might get out around 2005. Probably because of writing I helped him publish, Abraham was moved recently to one of the worst prisons in New York. "Things have blown up pretty badly here," he writes. "There is one other observant Jew here, who is also in for a sex offense, although not involving children. To make a long story short, he and I were walking in the yard last Friday when someone 'bumped' into him and slit his neck open with a razor. Fortunately the carotid artery was not damaged, but it was close. He now has sixty-eight stitches, and is in 'involuntary protective custody.' A confidential informant told the officers that yours truly is next on the list to be cut." In the meantime, my friend Abraham writes, he is locked twenty-four hours a day in his five-by-nine foot cell.

Also in my box is a letter from Edward, who is serving ten years in a Kentucky prison. He spends his time studying and writing hauntingly sad short stories and earnest essays about what is wrong with how psychologists and social workers treat boy-lovers and their boys. His latest essay comes with a cover drawn by Kevin, thirteen years old, the boy for whom Edward is in prison. They still keep in touch. "I was thinking about you when I drew this picture for you," Kevin writes. "I just want to say before I go, I love you."

The Founding Moment

In December 1978, when thirty-four men and a handful of teenage boys caucused at Boston's Community Church to form the North American Man-Boy Love Association (NAMBLA), they had reason to feel optimistic. Among the group were veterans of the anti-war, civil rights, and gay liberation movements. If there was one thing they'd learned, it was that social change was possible through organizing and activism. As the voices of black people, gays, and the anti-war protesters had begun to be heard, couldn't the same be possible for men and boys who shared erotics and affection?

Hope was in the air that day, because the gay community in Boston had successfully fought off a witch-hunting district attorney, who was exploiting a man-boy sex case for his reelection bid. In Revere, a gritty northern suburb, there were men who were giving blow jobs to some local teenagers, with beer, pot, and pocket money thrown into the bargain. The scene had been going on for as long as anyone could remember.

After seeding the media with intimations that this was the scandal of the century, DA Garrett Byrne established an anonymous tip line to clean it up. Boston was the home of *Gay Community News*, then the movement's *de facto* national paper, and its activists were skilled and sharp. They saw the danger the unfolding panic and the hotline could pose to gay men. Over a kitchen table in Dorchester, a handful of activists organized a defense committee to combat the witch hunt. The Boston/Boise Committee (named after a famous Boise, Idaho, scandal in the 50s), didn't take a public position on sex between adults and youths, but it was clear where its sympathies lay. Over the course of a year of demos and press releases, and a gala fundraiser starring Gore Vidal, the committee succeeded in putting the DA on the defensive, quashing the hotline, and, come election day, helping defeat Byrne. The scandal of the century fizzled out in two dozen plea bargains, mostly probationary sentences and fines.

In the meanwhile, the publicity the committee attracted brought to it a critical mass of men who identified with their feelings of affection and desire for boys. As one of its final acts, the Boston/Boise Committee (BBC) sponsored a one-day conference on "Man-Boy Love and the Age of Consent." An Episcopal bishop from Connecticut, a well-known Boston University psychiatrist, and social workers from the state prison for sex offenders were among the 150 participants. At the end of the day, some conference-goers caucused, and NAMBLA was born. Its work done, the BBC gave its remaining bank balance to found Gay and Lesbian Advocates and Defenders (GLAD), New England's gay legal group.

There was a brief opening that NAMBLA enjoyed. A few gay social workers in Boston worked with NAMBLA members to help place homeless teenage boys. The social workers at the state prison kept in touch with NAMBLA to provide housing and support for boy-lovers finishing up their sentences. When Boston's lesbians and gays contemplated setting up a community center in the late 70s, NAMBLA was in on the discussions.

But the optimism of NAMBLA's founders proved off the mark. There was to be no cultural opening for pederasty. Indeed, in the new regime of sexual repression then taking shape, boy-love, and adult-youth sexuality generally, would become pivotal evils. GLAD, founded to help defendants and youths in cases like Revere, today won't touch with a ten-foot pole gay men in legal trouble with boys. GLAD even sanitizes its official history to cover up the fact it shares a parent with NAMBLA.

What Happened?

In 1976 and 1977, as the Christian right was beginning to feel its oats again and America's first "born-again" president took office, there was a small surge of media attention given to kiddie porn and teen prostitution. But soon after Reagan took office, the wave became tidal, saturating the media with stories and images about a profound sexual danger to children and adolescents.

The discussion about sex abuse that emerged from the feminist consciousness-raising movement in the 70s came from women who had incest experiences. The aim of their initiatives was getting men who had sex with their young daughters to stop what they were doing and acknowledge what they had done, but to keep police and prisons out of the picture. But with the Reagan revolution, the right wing seized on sexual dangers to the young as a political icon. The rhetoric became sharply punitive, and the attention now refocused on a threat to children coming from outside the family.

By the mid-80s, many TV watchers had been brainwashed into believing that there existed a vast "child porn" industry involving, on some accounts, billions of dollars and hundreds of thousands of youngsters, that bands of pedophiles snatched tens of thousands of children off the streets annually, that bizarre conspiracies of men and women had infiltrated day-care centers and were involving toddlers in Satanic sex rites with horses, elephants, and decomposed corpses. Millions of milk cartons carried photos of missing children, more than 99 percent of them runaways or taken by the losing parent in a custody dispute. But milk cartons just gave the name and the "DOA," or "date of abduction," ghoulishly imitating hospital shorthand for "dead on arrival."

These claims were mostly fabrications and distortions, as even the media began to realize. But they left a sediment of draconian new laws and networks of cops and social workers dedicated to rooting out "abuse" that "victims" and "offenders" didn't realize was going on.

Laws requiring corroboration in court of illegal sex were abolished, and new ones were written allowing hearsay, making prosecutions of consensual but taboo sex easier. Therapists, teachers, and other professionals were legally mandated to report evidence of illegal sex involving minors. Statutes of limitations for prosecuting such relationships were abolished, and rules of evidence weakened.

Across the board, sentences for consensual sex offenses were increased, and life terms for sex play with teenagers or children are now commonplace. Under California's "one strike" provision, that punishment can be mandatory. Starting with Washington, many states have passed laws allowing for permanent civil incarceration of sex offenders, including those guilty of completely consensual relations with minors, after any criminal sentence has been served. With the number of persons jailed for sex with minors already swelling and set now to skyrocket, the *New Yorker* suggested in March 1994, that the state reinstitute castration, underscoring that this is a demonization of male sexuality.

The Supreme Court declared in 1982 that porn depicting minors was a wholesale exception to the First Amendment, and Congress has taken advantage of the loophole to expand continually the definition of child pornography. Under guidelines issued by Clinton's Justice Department in 1995, "child porn" can include an image of a person younger than eighteen, fully clothed, and engaged in no sexual activity whatsoever— in other words, any photo of a boy a NAMBLA member has in his house. Penalties for possession range up to ten years in prison.

The 1994 federal crime bill criminalizes sex with persons under sixteen (and under eighteen if a gift is given) outside of the U.S. or across a state line, even if the relationship is perfectly legal under local laws. The mere intention to travel to have legal sex with a minor, as revealed by a letter or conversation, is punishable by up to ten years in prison. The crime bill also requires that states establish public registries of sex offenders, so that persons found guilty of consensual sex with minors are marked for life, and can be thrown back in jail if they fail to update their address, or if the cops misplace their annual re-registration. In states where already in effect, public registration laws have led to death threats, beatings, and firebombed homes.

The Metamorphosis

The sexual coercion of children was a crime often underplayed before the 70s. But the attempted solutions to the problem that came out of the child sex panic are soaked with hate, retribution, and dishonesty, like a rag with gasoline.

Our culture's fixation on the sexual dangers to children and youth can be compared to the fixation on black rape in the post-Reconstruction South. Interracial relationships then, like inter-generational relationships today, were forbidden and scandalous. White Southerners' response—beatings, lynchings, castrations, rhetoric about sullied purity, a generalized climate of terror for black men and boys— had little to do with the genuine problem of rape and coercion in the South. Most Southern rape, after all, was probably intra-racial, and when inter-racial, its victims were predominantly black women at the hands of white men, not white women raped by blacks.

The purpose of the South's war on the black rapist— a war that loaded with suspicion all contact between black and white, much as every interaction between man and boy is loaded today— was to preserve the color line. It was a matter of keeping secure the crown jewels of white privilege, at a time when the social order founded on it was under threat.

What has been the latter-day "reconstruction" that has provoked and shaped the child and adolescent sex panic? An answer lies in the anxieties and dislocations caused by the liberalizing economic and social transformation that American society (and the West generally) undertook in the 60s and 70s. The racial equality, feminist, and gay movements are emblems and were engines of this change, revolutionizing sexual mores, race relations, and freedom of expression. But the fuel powering this transformation was the intensifying and globalizing economy, which integrated American society (and increasingly all of the West) into a single market wired by networks of commerce and media. This dulled regional economic and cultural differences, and generally limited the role of small and medium-scale social structures—communities, neighborhoods, families—to define, constrain, and establish the meaning of individuals' lives.

This transformation was a triumph of liberalism, not the liberalism that Democrat and Republican alike today vow to bury, but the basic, historical liberalism of free markets and individual autonomy that is the West's political ether. These ideals were asserted originally back in the Enlightenment in defiance of feudalism, with its given, fixed roles, and limits on individual action. It wasn't philosophy, but the emerging market's dynamism that did feudalism in, by means of the opportunities the market opened to individuals outside the old constraints of manor, guild, and church. The social transformation of the 60s and 70s was similarly about a dissolution of historically-grounded social and economic structures, which the developing market deprived of economic function and dissolved.

Consider the pre-Stonewall male homosexual life in New York City that historian George Chauncey has chronicled from 1890 to 1940. Chauncey uncovers a rich tapestry of homoerotic scenes, varying with and incorporated into the city's patchwork of ethnicity, religion, trade, race, and class. There was no general gay consciousness, but in neighborhoods there existed many vibrant homoerotic subcultures. What made them possible, and blocked a general gay movement, were the solid ties within neighborhoods that had a clear economic and cultural function. As the market developed, these neighborhoods gave up most of their economic structure. Mom-and-pop stores gave way to chains, the local factory shut down, the children grew up and moved to New Jersey. These communities lost the boundaries that had defined them, lost the differentials of information flow, commerce, friendship, religion, and ethnicity—boundaries high enough to evolve distinctive cultural forms and hold people within them.

Take also the South's peculiar institution of race segregation. Across America, small agricultural towns flourished because of the need for a large population to work the land. In the South, the predominance of small-scale agriculture and slavery's legacy made segregation useful to local land-holding elites to keep poor whites divided from blacks. But as the U.S. market developed and grew more unitary after World War II, small-scale agriculture declined and with it the South's local elites. The Southern economy became more like other regions', weakening the pillars of Jim Crow and paving the way for the civil rights movement's eventual success.

These examples illustrate the distinctive, and potentially illiberal, cultural forms that can be spawned within an organic community—a group of people living in a given place who deal with each other over time within a stable context of production. The social arrangements that develop here are not governed by abstract rights. They grow, rather, out of the necessity for people in a community to accommodate each other. The processes of "getting along" are familiar. Office workers, for example, often post family pictures on the walls above their desks. They don't have the formal right to do it—the walls are not theirs—but custom dictates they can, and woe to the boss if she asserts otherwise.

People who have direct control over a space have a lot of say over how it's used. We tend to leave people alone who aren't bothering anyone. We overlook bendings of rules that don't threaten basic structures and where everyone involved seems content. If something has gone on before, there's a tendency to let it happen again. Such are the guidelines governing the precise allocation of powers and control over spaces in organic communities. The rules are pragmatic, context-bound, sensitive to precedent, and, to be sure, reflective of larger social forces and relations of power—class, race, sex, and sexuality.

Out of this informal process of communal negotiation, often not even transacted via language, come arrangements that accommodate considerable deviation from stated norms—witness New York's rich pre-Stonewall homoerotic scenes, which had no "right" to exist, enjoyed no legal protection, but survived and often flourished anyway. These arrangements, not decided by reference to abstract rights, can also violate liberal standards—witness segregation. Even in societies with a highly developed market, much of the social realm is left to these informal processes. But organic communities, in contrast to mass market societies, are characterized by the breadth of social space given over to them.

As the market developed—the post-World War II period seems decisive—organic community declined, and with it, the capacity to sustain informal, locally-based arrangements. The factors contributing to community's undermining are many, but they reflect the elaboration and intensification of the market: suburbanization, the automobile, television, the demand for labor mobility, declining need for manual labor, the weakening of unions and other institutions of working-class solidarity, the expanding private sphere of middle-class consumption, the growing power of social workers, and the fracturing of the nuclear family, itself a shard of the old extended family. Where these changes did not directly enhance the autonomy of individuals vis-a-vis the community, they simply weakened the latter.

The decay of community is registered in our use of the word. In phrases like "gay community" or "IV drug-using community," the term is a vaguely positive or euphemistic way of referring to a group of people with something in common. These are communities of special interest, defined usually by a pattern of consumption, rather than organic communities, with shared locale, a density of material connections, and human-scale rules of engagement. The developed market allows broad scope for these virtual communities, because commerce becomes ever more specialized and the capacity grows to narrowly target information. But these communities of special interest can individuate less than organic communities. They don't have the space, continuity, or boundaries to develop very distinctive social forms. They exist essentially as a segment of the larger market. The models aside, the same liquor ads appear in a glossy gay magazine as one for Hispanic businesswomen. Indeed, it is only after the market has safely dulled the knife's edge of cultural difference that a rhetoric celebrating "diversity" can take hold.

The market created the opportunities of which the postwar social movements deftly made use. It did so by softening up communities, reducing their ability to channel individuals into particular roles and forms. The market also increased opportunities for individuals to connect with each other and gain access to resources—such as money and media—outside the old collective structures. The frustrations these social movements voiced, while not new, were felt all the more keenly just because of the diminished capacity of community to contain and repress them.

The social movements of the 60s, felt throughout the Western world, were not revolutionary, but based squarely on Enlightenment principles. These movements' contribution to liberal theory was a variation on nineteenth-century liberalism's concern with national self-determination: it was a focus, instead, on the ways liberal ideals are blocked for distinct kinds of people, as defined particularly by their race and sex. The changes these movements wrought were profound, but overdetermined by the sun of liberal ideology, which has kept the West in its gravitational orbit since the Enlightenment. From the American and French revolutions, it took many generations for the solar currents to heat the air enough to get the market's winds blowing. But once they blew, they dissipated the clouds of local custom and local elites that had blocked from so many places liberalism's light. It has taken even longer for the warming rays to begin clearing the fog of overt racism, sexism, and anti-gay feeling. But the same light— radiating from

TV sets, beamed by courts and social campaigners— now increasingly shines everywhere, exposing the hidden, homogenizing what it illuminates, and realizing conditions that approach total visibility.

Backlash in Code

The 60s social movements triumphed in short time, transforming the political and cultural landscape all around the West. Blatant racism, common in public less than a generation ago, is totally politically anathema. If not yet rare, it is no longer routine for police to beat confessions out of suspects. Contraceptives, abortion, and sexually explicit images and writing are widely available. For adults, the written word falls now essentially beyond state control. Homosexuality is effectively decriminalized and widely visible. None of these were settled questions a generation ago, but they are now.

Yet for all the apparent ease the speed of these changes might imply, they were profoundly disruptive. They challenged many people's sense of order and normality, even as they opened up opportunities. They struck deeply into the home, bedroom, and workplace, and established new codes of conduct and expression that many find alien. In jobs and relationships, men face new expectations of treating women as equals. A new racial code of conduct took hold, backed by state authority and elite opinion. The gay movement's prominence put men kissing men on prime-time TV and won avowed sodomites and sadomasochists invitations to the White House. Like it or not, everyone is forced to acknowledge a sexual identity. Technology and the market's segmentation increased the media's bandwidth, turning broadcasters and publishers into competitive commodity producers. Where previously the media tended to directly serve elites, now with life-or-death rivalry, they serve the mass market first. TV shows and rock bands compete to up the ante of the shocking, eating away at the sense of public decorum that social contention already helped rupture. The global warming of market competition has kept incomes stagnant in the

U.S. since the early 70s, sharply increased inequality of wealth, and pushed women *en masse* into the paid workforce. Demand for manual labor is drying up, excluding a swathe of the population from any economic function. These are the inflammatory catalysts at work on the body politic's seething underbelly.

Yet liberalism's ideological triumph makes it impossible to address these anxieties directly. It is remarkable, given the right wing's ascendance since 1980, how little is on the table. A rollback to 1950s-style censorship is not in the offing. Jesse Helms doesn't talk about throwing homosexuals in jail. The right wing homes in on the symbolic margins, such as public funding for gay-themed arts, but is stymied in pursuit of a broader agenda. Meanwhile, politicians of all stripes hail the free market as a social and economic cure-all. Thus the primary backlash to the 60s reforms takes a coded form: the just-under-the skin racism of the Willie Horton ad, the war on crime and drugs, the attack against persons on welfare, anti-immigrant campaigning, and the child sex panic.

Like these other flavors of backlash, the child sex panic is a symptom of the underlying social inflammation. One of the hallmarks of the market's development is its expansion into areas of social life formerly outside of economic exchange. We all need goods that intrinsically can't be bought and sold— affection, love, friendship, family, neighborliness— but children need them most of all. Indeed, children are oblivious to exchange relationships: hire a nanny for a child and he'll fall in love with her anyway. Children feel especially keenly the market's erosion of family and neighborhood.

The market has crowded out these non-market goods with its own products. A portion of the six hours a day Americans spend watching TV used to be spent hanging with friends, family, and neighbors. Bringing incessant murder and mayhem from around the country into every living room, and dramatizing more of the same, is TV's tattle-tale strategy to forge intimacy with viewers. The media's obsession with deviance, a boon to social movements that embody or claim to combat it, adds to the manufactured spectacle of social breakdown that is grist for the mills of law and order. Since children need an island of stability to gain their footing, all of this tends, reasonably enough, to focus fears on dangers to children. The anxieties women felt as they went to work and left their children in strangers' care outside the home were key, for example, in fueling the daycare center sex hysteria of the 80s and 90s.

But it is liberal ideology most of all that has scripted the child sex panic, and made it a theater for the expression and pseudo-resolution of our social contradictions. Liberal theory builds the edifice of individual freedom from the brick of the solitary, rational adult, able to maximize his or her self-interest. Aside from stipulating them by default as not rational, liberal theory doesn't know what to do about children. Enlightenment ideology is consistent with a wide and disturbing range of positions about the young. On the right wing is the idea that children are the property of their parents or the state until they reach an arbitrary age of reason. The left position regards children as essentially rational, and deserving virtually full autonomy. The conflict between these stances gets expressed throughout American society, but basic liberal ideology doesn't offer an answer.

Conservative perspectives, by contrast, don't suffer this gap. Whether one's fundamental obligation is serving tribe, the gods, or the fatherland, what is good for children is pretty much good for adults. Liberal theory's generational chasm gets exacerbated by the modern economy, which has no productive use for the young and creates few spheres where children or adolescents engage with adults outside the family. This turns children into ciphers, voids filled willy-nilly by adults' projected fears and dreams.

With the demise of community, which is intrinsically conservative, the rules governing social life have fallen explicitly in line with liberal standards. Those who argue for, say, legalizing drugs, will out-boast each other about the draconian penalties they want exacted for those who sell pot to minors. This grandstanding substitutes for recognition of the moral problems, the dangers of misuse, that attend the freedoms they seek. Drugs, porn, or sado-masochism offer extreme experiences; their dangers flow from the same source as their great potential value. The left implies that whatever the moral risks of these activities, they are washed away by the fact that it is rational adults who are choosing them.

The left, therefore, has an ideological stake in polarizing the contrast between adults and children, because it is key to unlocking the freedoms they want. The right wing has a stake in the distinction, too, because it is the one limit to freedom built in to liberal ideology. For them, it offers a starting point from which to win broader controls, as the current debate over Internet censorship illustrates.

The child sex panic is a sort of HIV of liberalism, in that it infects the ideological immune system that normally insures freedom and keeps bigotry in check. This immune breakdown is worsened by the mass market's dissolution of community, whose interdependencies normally serve as a separate limit on hate.

At a White House press conference in January 1996, President Clinton announced a new initiative to display pictures of missing children (most of them nabbed by feuding parents) at post offices nationwide. The president then offered the podium to a child protection activist, who homed in on the evils of pedophilia. The only cure for pedophiles, the man declared to the national media with Clinton standing by approvingly, was "the Dahmer treatment;" that is to say, killing them. In an era fixated on rituals of sensitivity to minorities, the call for killing pedophiles, sanctioned by the office of the president, was remarkable. It was as remarkable as the fact that among our usually vigilant guardians of political correctness and civic decency, nobody noticed.

Whither the Gay Movement?

The mainstream lesbian and gay position is that homosexuality and "pedophilia," as it is usually called, are totally different and unrelated: historically, psychologically, and morally. The claim aspires to be obvious, a matter of logic and definitions. And can we please now change the subject? But like apartheid's insistence on the essential difference between black and white, what is cast as a simple truth requires a burdensome repressive machinery to keep afloat, a rewriting of history, a habitual wariness and dishonesty. By first isolating and then trying to cast off pedophilia, the lesbian and gay movement is marked increasingly by its relationship to it.

Pedophilia and homosexuality are inextricably bound, which is exactly why many feel impelled to segregate them. The term "pedophile" entered the pop lexicon suddenly in the 1980s, on the coattails of the concept/ "sexual orientation." It was not because people suddenly started coming out as pedophiles that the idea came into currency; of the hundreds of boy-lovers I've known, only a handful embrace the term. Rather, it was right-wing social campaigners who put pedophilia on the map. The right took to the tabloids with this obscure term from psychiatry's diagnostic manuals as a counter-example to the gay movement's positive assertion of sexual orientation. Whereas *child molester*, like *sodomite*, implies a person who commits a certain act, *pedophile* denotes an unchanging, unchosen, unfixable condition of which the sex act is only a sign. And that is exactly what the gay movement said that homosexuality was.

Gay activists had advanced their cause by arguing homosexuality to be a sexual orientation, and sexual orientation to be a morally neutral category—everybody has one!—deserving legal protection. That claim rested on the similarity of sexual orientation to race, both being, on this view, a fixed, unchosen quality of an individual.

Ah, but the right wing countered, waving the Medusa's head of pedophilia, "Here is a sexual orientation that is pure evil." It was as if, just at the time white America finally began confronting its racism, anthropologists on expedition in the Himalayas had found a hitherto isolated and distinctly inferior race of human—let's dub them the Yirks—who were incontrovertibly, inveterately, and congenitally stupid, lazy, and amoral. America in 1958 would have received news of the Yirks with great interest, and proponents of racial segregation, then besieged, would have enjoyed a fresh boost. Black people would forge on, to be sure, contending that they, at least, were a race the moral equal of whites. But undercut would be the strong claim that racial discrimination was always fundamentally wrong.

The emergence of the pedophile into the menagerie of sexual minorities transformed politics on the Animal Farm. In one respect, *pedophile* was a more successful category than *homosexual*, of which it was a back-formation. While homosexuality remains an ambivalent concept in the wider culture, provoking disgust even among people whose politics prescribe tolerance, pedophilia currently enjoys a status of glittering, untarnished repugnance. As such it has become a sort of gold standard of sexual value—negative value, to be sure—in relation to which other sexual groupings, with more uncertain position, can denominate the coin of their virtue.

The consequences sometimes are amusing. For a magazine article on bestiality, I've been talking recently to people who have sex with animals. A number of zoophiles gave me sophisticated arguments about how consent does not require rationality or language, how animals can readily convey whether or not they enjoy fondling or fellatio, and how a person with basic empathy can have sex cross-species without crossing any troubling moral boundaries. These are arguments directly relevant to the debate about children's capacity to consent to sex play. But then these bestialists, who have regaled me with tales of their encounters with cows or cats, go on to say how they draw a strict line in the barnyard against erotic play with calves and kittens, which they regard as totally unethical.

For homosexuals, asserting virtue by abhorring pedophilia gets complicated by the intertwining of man-boy and androphile homo-eroticism. Most gay men, like most straight ones, feel desire, overt or covert, for persons younger than eighteen. This intermixing is a problem, but an opportunity as well: it provides a stage for a theater of purging and sanitizing, by which homosexuals can prove their fitness for liberal society. Thus the expulsion of NAMBLA in 1994 from the International Lesbian and Gay Association, after ten years of membership. In porn magazines there are the fine-print declarations that references in stories to *boy*, *youth*, *youngster*, etc. absolutely do not signify a person under the age of eighteen. A number of gay and lesbian academics recently discovered that pederasty in ancient Greece, ever since a model for expression of male homosexuality, has in fact nothing whatever to do with it. Ancient pederasty, they say, was simply a naked will to power, an assertion of the Greek citizen's right to penetrate the bodies of his inferiors. Aside from adding that Greek love was high in choles-terol, it would be hard to paint a more unflattering portrait, even if it means ignoring all those Greek love poems to boys that express a familiar desire and affection, and which gay readers today still enjoy.

The most common strategies for segregating boy-love and homosexuality do not call attention to themselves, but are famil-iar to gay people because they are the same ones used over the centuries to cover up and deny all same-sex desire. *Out* magazine sponsors a CD of music by "gay" composers, such as Tchaikovsky, Schubert, and Britten, but ignores the centrality of boy-love to their eroticism and creativity. Authors of triumphalist gay histories revel in the personages whom they can place in the homosexual pantheon. They don't add that Michaelangelo or Walt Whitman would face years in prison and demonizing as "pedophiles" in today's America. Physique magazines from the 50s and 60s casu-ally mixed images of men and boys. Through the 70s, the *Advocate* classifieds were a shopper's paradise for boy pornography. But the adolescent is totally absent today in American gay erotica. Even the word "boy" is verboten in *Advocate* advertising, though that doesn't stop FBI agents from using the magazine's classifieds for running kiddie porn stings. Pulp sex novels with lusty schoolboys, commonplace in the 60s and 70s, also have disappeared— all in an effort to pretend that the politically troublesome desires that spawned them have also vanished.

The Ideological Collapse

For a test case to investigate the effects of this dishonesty on the queer body politic, we could do worse than consider OutWrite, the annual gay and lesbian writers conference. The event draws around 1900 people, and is sort of an annual parliament for those who articulate and transmit gay and lesbian culture and history to ourselves and the wider world.

OutWrite is a project of the parent of *Gay Community News*, which in the 70s and 80s helped shape the U.S. lesbian and gay movement, first as a newspaper and crucible of political thought and contention, and then by sending out from its ranks many of the first generation of national gay and lesbian leaders. *GCN* anticipated the pattern of gay and lesbian solidarity that today is the most visible face of homosexual politics and culture. It worked to situate the gay movement within a broadly progressive agenda that pays attention to issues of race, sex, class, as well as sexual orientation. That contribution, too, is today part of the broader movement's basic furniture.

As befits that history, it is the aim of OutWrite's organizers, and the expectation of participants, for there to be careful attention to political symbolism. A good deal of the of the work of the conference's organizing committee is balancing panels by race, ethnicity, and sex. Sensitivity to nuance is such that the major issue at the conference a few years ago—the occasion for outraged speeches, an emergency "town meeting," and mortified apologies—was the racial composition of a subcommittee that had chosen the finalist for an award for a book by a lesbian or gay writer of color, along with the process by which the name of the award had been selected. It is just this attention to detail that makes OutWrite a useful case for examining the implications for gay ideology and politics of the child sex panic.

OutWrite wears its willingness to discuss man-boy love as a badge of its commitment to openness and diversity. For two years, at a time of growing gay hostility to NAMBLA, I was on the OutWrite organizing committee, which testifies to this commitment. The committee was clear in wanting to insure that the discussion of boy-love be civil and polite and, indeed, declared as much one year in the conference program book.

In trying to push the question of man-boy love on the organizing committee, I took advantage of this opening. As I saw friends disappear off to jail and censorship's maw grow ever wider, I felt word had to get out. I went to sleep at night thinking that for our writing and publishing, I and my fellow activists risked years in prison. The gay movement's progressive wing needed to recognize that we faced repression spiraling out of control, threatening all.

As if to illustrate my point, while I was on the committee, Canada passed a sweeping child pornography bill, targeting words as well as images. The 1993 legislation criminalizes texts that "advocate" sex with persons younger than fourteen. The NAMBLA *Bulletin* was the law's explicit target, but prosecutors declared they intended to go after fiction as well. The penalty for writing illegal texts ranges up to ten years in prison; for possessing them, five. Across Canada, gay people were scrutinizing their bookshelves, and burning novels, like Kevin Esser's *Streetboy Dreams* and Hakim Bey's *Crowstone*.

I regard my intervention in OutWrite as a failure, and the gay left's stated willingness to discuss this issue as a dishonest front.

The willingness to discuss man-boy love might seem like OutWrite's openness to dealing with other controversial issues that provided focuses for the conference: AIDS, class, ethnicity, gender, race. But in each of those cases, discussion took place against a backdrop of moral concern: for diversity, fighting racism, comprehending the monumental loss from the epidemic. These commitments did not force discussion into a mold; indeed, presenting a range of opinions and experiences was the means of expressing and deepening them. But there was no question of debating these fundamental commitments. There were to be no panels at OutWrite asking "AIDS: Clearing out the rot of sexual compulsives?" or "Black lesbian writers: Why so hung up on race?"

In the case of man-boy love, OutWrite's pledge to open discussion was a substitute for any moral commitment. OutWrite welcomed writers and representatives from publications who had argued for the purging of boy-lovers from the community, for the appropriateness of long prison terms for people who break age-of-consent laws, and even for boy-lovers being killed. Presumably, these opinions were to be expressed at the conference politely, so as not to obstruct the free flow of ideas. But the purpose of "open discussion" in this context was not to express an underlying moral commitment, so much as to show its absence. The issue had the status of a troubling aesthetic dispute, on which opinions were strong and contention sharp, which needed to be handled with care, but on which nothing significant rested.

On the organizing committee, I tried to shift the terms of debate. We needed to state clearly, I felt, that the rhetoric of violence and hate against boy-lovers was morally wrong, as were long prison sentences for noncoerced sex, and the widespread censorship of man-boy love in lesbian and gay bookstores and media. Only once these positions were established could open discussion be useful. But my fellow committee members regarded this as special pleading.

What happened at OutWrite reflects generally the way man-boy love gets discussed among lesbian and gay progressives. There is a willingness to debate "Can children consent to sex?" a question that, within the framework it is posed, can't be resolved. The failure to reach closure is taken not as sign of the limits of liberal theory and our need to ask the question in new ways, but of the problem's permanent intractability. This eliminates the need to do anything, or to monitor the relation between our beliefs and what is happening in the world. There has been almost no change in the nature of the discussion of this issue in the gay community since the late 70s, when the problem in its current form first was posed. This is despite the fact that today life sentences are routine for consensual sex, many of the legal safeguards that once existed for defendants now are gone, sex offenders must list their names on public registries for life, and writing an essay in support of man-boy love can get you ten years in a Canadian prison. If after *Kristallnacht* a German journal of letters devoted an issue to "the Jewish problem," and took pains to be fair and express the best case for all sides in the debate, we would have no trouble seeing its moral inadequacy. But that is how man-boy love is treated in the gay movement today.

For me, the perniciousness of the situation came home while hearing the welcoming speech at the 1995 OutWrite conference, given by veteran activist Urvashi Vaid, former director of the National Gay and Lesbian Task Force. On one level, she was a logical choice—she had just won a $200,000 advance for a book on gay politics. Her speech, loudly cheered, dealt eloquently about the need for lesbians and gays to embrace a broad vision of justice. But under the policies that Vaid has supported, many of the most important homosexual writers of the past century would today face years in prison in the U.S. Vaid has campaigned for the elimination of boy-lovers from the gay movement. She may say that she is trying to protect girls from abuse and unwanted sexual attention, but that doesn't explain why the laws she has supported or been silent about would condemn writers like André Gide, Walt Whitman, and William Burroughs. Along with Congressman Barney Frank, Vaid has said that she thinks that "homosexual pedophiles," her phrase, deserve "civil rights." But Frank voted to extend federal child pornography laws to cover images of fully clothed minors, around the same time Vaid was urging the International Lesbian and Gay Association to boot NAMBLA.

The Gay Movement and the Market

The fundamental problem is not cowardice and opportunism among gay and lesbian leaders. The problem's roots, rather, go to the expression of homosexuality that has prevailed in the West. That is a homosexuality essentially a product of Enlightenment ideology and the market economy that it spawns. In its developed state, that economy dissolves all other social and cultural forms— including all other forms of homoeroticism. The gay movement should be understood as a product of the market both in terms of its structure, and the dynamics by which it has played itself out.

The first basic element of modern homosexuality is its equation of sex acts and identity. This is the position that persons who have same-sex sex are, in a deep sense, a distinct kind of person. Ideologists for homosexuality adopted this claim, and it succeeded in the marketplace, because it mimicked the answer to a central crisis of twentieth century liberal capitalism: the race question. As the developing market dissolved the local structures that had perpetuated racism and sexism, liberal ideology faced the discrepancy between its fundamental legitimizing ideals of equality and its racist and sexist reality. The solution involved elevating to an ideological tenet the realization that liberal ideals were failing because of persistent inequality for specific classes of people. In order for homosexuals to benefit from the forms of recognition and redress that thus became available, they needed to have a status as distinct and deeply rooted as race and sex were understood to be. They didn't have to create such a status, but merely assume and de-pathologize one that psychiatry had already fleshed out. This provided the ideological structure of contemporary homosexuality.

The second basic element of modern homosexuality is its material existence as a community of special interest existing in the broader market. The market provided the matrix for the growth of gay identity. When we talk about "gay community," we refer mostly to institutions located within the chain of commerce: bars, bathhouses, porno cinemas, publications, and bookstores. The chance for homosexuality to develop a commercial locus reflected the growing capacity of the market to sustain narrowly tailored segments that served, not just particular neighborhoods, but entire cities or regions. The gay community's informal organizational network emerged from these same capacities. They expanded the ability of individuals to link up with others of common interest, and to publicize homosexuality so as not to stamp out its locales, but aid its spread.

By taking up residence in the market and the political sphere, homosexuals committed themselves to an explicit public presence. This required developing and pursuing an ideology, something people in pre-Stonewall scenes did not have to do. Once you open a bakery on the public square, you can't then refuse to put a brand name on your bread, or fail to respond when the newspapers allege rat hairs in your rye. Elaborating and promoting a gay ideology was necessary for, and served the interest of, gay businesses owners and aspiring activists, whose careers depended on the success of homosexual identity.

Pursuing a gay politics has consequences. For one, it forces a dialogue with those who represent prevailing norms. The challenger in such a dialogue, for there to be any point in it, has to maintain that, despite surface disagreement, there is a commonality underneath that all can work toward. That baseline, for homosexuals confronting a bigoted society, was underlying liberal ideology. But dialogue engenders a subtle shifting of the challenger's position so that it comes closer, where it can, to prevailing norms. The point of political dialogue, after all, is to gain something. That shift is not risked when discussion is avoided in the first place.

Another effect of this turn by homosexuals toward discourse and ideology was the gay movement's claim to jurisdiction over all same-sex eroticism. The assertion that act equals identity not only grounded gay political legitimacy, but offered an olive branch to hostile heterosexuals. The claim of gay identity made homosexuality easier to take, because the depth and boundaries of that identity insulated non-gay people from becoming personally implicated in homosexual acts, even if gay sex were to cease to be taboo. If acts equal identity, and I don't have the identity, then I don't desire the acts.

But this ideological strategy burdened gay identity to account for *all* homosexual acts, at the risk of losing legitimacy. From this comes the movement's hostility to those who have homoerotic relations without joining the gay fold. Thus, it is said, married men who suck dick at highway rest stops haven't dealt with the truth of their lives, football players embracing on the field aren't kidding anyone, and every queer has the civic duty to come out of the closet, or, perhaps, face an outing.

By immersing itself both in the market and in ideology, homosexual politics has served essentially the interests of the middle class, which dominates the gay movement. Gay identity strongly correlates with middle-class status, in the U.S. and internationally. It was middle-class persons who benefited commercially and politically by the movement's expansion. From the middle class have come most of those making careers as activists or administrators. But most important, middle-class homosexuals needed a public ideology of homosexuality to have sex. The respective sexual cultures of the working class and rich are based less on guilt and more on shame, a fear of being found out. The ideological structure of the gay movement, its demand for a fixed identity and aboveboard commercial venues, its need to convince doctors and parents of homosexual normality, reflect peculiarly middle-class preoccupations with status.

The gay movement's structural and ideological path succeeded because it was selected by the market in a society increasingly market-dominated. But these choices, like all market choices, are not thereby the best outcomes or neutral ones. This is evident at OutWrite, which, like any trade show, aims to grease the market. In this instance, it is the market that wrings fat advances, literary fame, and crossover success from selling homosexual identity via books. Those goods involve exploitation of a natural and collective resource: the past and present of homoeroticism. This exploitation, as epitomized by Urvashi Vaid's speech, is actually a savaging of homoeroticism. It involves undermining its actual history, normalizing a campaign of liquidation against its most vulnerable practitioners, and putting a palatable and progressive gloss on the whole affair to anaesthetize discussion.

These are normal market processes. They are comparable to the conditions that make the destruction of Brazilian rainforests by cattle ranchers economically rational for those engaged in it. The preconditions for disaster are set in place by the market itself. They include the erosion of community and loss of its ability to impose traditional agricultural techniques, which tend to be sustainable just by having survived the test of time. These preconditions include the fact that market societies value materialism above all other goods, and the fact that the market, once in place, gives individuals who serve it extraordinary rewards. With wealth and success come the means to buy legitimacy. Who remembers East Timor?

The market intensifies the present by destroying the communal continuity that culturally inscribes the past and future in the now. At the same time, it rewards decontexted individuals for serving its immediate demand, and elevates the value of its prizes above all others. The emptying out of history, the reduction of all time and space to a totalizing present, can be seen in the stubble of the rainforests, as well as the complicity our gay and lesbian leaders with a campaign to extinguish eroticism between men and boys.

The Market's Limits

At a dinner party recently, a forty-five-year-old gay man told me about the sex he had growing up in Florida with all the teammates on his high school football squad. Sex like that happens much less these days, because the gay movement has draped the albatross of identity around the neck of same-sex erotic play.

The homoerotic play of boys is part adolescent hijinks, part male bonding, part erotic rehearsal, and at once affection, aggression, and their containment. These games are a constant across cultures and eras, and they have nothing to do with identity. Their continuity with similar play among young male animals is obvious. This is the natural field of man-boy erotic interaction. It is not always genital or involving sexual penetration, and for myself and most men I know who like boys, it does not need to. But if the mock-fighting, grappling, and roughhousing on the bed does not lead occasionally to clothes coming off and naked romping, it's usually from conscious direction or years of drilling in body hate.

Sexuality's forms are historically constructed. But on the scale of accident and necessity, whose furthest point of determination is *that I eat*, and whose contingent extreme is *what I ate today*, man-boy eroticism falls toward the essential. Even in a culture now less gendered, this homoeroticism can be eliminated only at society's peril. Until recently, man-boy scenes flourished silently, often within or contiguous with forms of pre-Stonewall homoeroticism. The decline of man-boy solidarity and affection, corresponding with the child and adolescent sex panic, is registered, I think, in the sharply increased rate of boys' suicide (which nearly doubled for males ten to fourteen from 1980 to 1992).

The incompatibility between boy-love and market-based homosexuality is not simply the imposition of identity. It is also the politicization of sexuality. The gay movement is based on a gamble that playing the market would pay, and indeed for some it has. But making sex so ideologically contentious and buying symbolic rights with the inflated coin of liberal values has led to some big-time winners, a mass of losers who've lost their shirts, and resentment all around.

But more than anything else, boy-love is hurt by what is more a precondition than an effect of the gay movement: the dissolution of community. To ask in the abstract about consent in sex between men and boys is an endless merry-go-round of indeterminacy, one the gay movement likes to ride if it has to address the question at all. Liberal theory, which gives us the powerful concept of consent, doesn't know how to apply it to the young. It's a permanent muddle. Boy-love needs to be considered in the context of community, which provides structures of visibility, on-going connections, mutual obligations and dependencies, a context in which reputations can register and transgressions exact consequences. This is where man-boy relationships most naturally and beneficially occur. While market-based homosexuality requires the demise of organic community, boy-love flounders without it.

What Next?

A question that markets raise, but cannot answer, is "What happens to losers?" Markets reward winners and punish defeat. If otherwise unchecked, the market's natural tendency is to create a few very rich people, and masses of poor. In the cultural marketplace of the capitalist West, modern homosexuality has prevailed, and man-boy love has lost. In August 1995, when a federal judge struck down a law in Washington allowing for permanent civil incarceration of persons who have consensual sex with minors, the right wing screamed about liberal courts that coddle criminals. The question soon will fall to the Supreme Court. In America's current ideological and political climate, there seems no limit to the blood that can be exacted for those who have sex with minors, not mandatory life sentences, perhaps not the death penalty. The left and the gay movement, a repository of relevant history and experience, have so far put up no resistance. Gays have simply exploited the hysteria as an opportunity to purge the boy-lovers, present and past, from their ranks.

Another question the market raises, but cannot answer, is whether it can sustain itself. The market, like people, depends on goods that cannot be bought or sold, such as the ecology and culture. The market economy, whose wealth and pitch of individual autonomy underlies modern homosexuality, is not sustainable on a global scale, or perhaps even for the rich West. But the cultural effects of capitalism are felt far beyond those who enjoy middle-class pleasures. What are the prospects for preserving erotic forms existing outside the market? What will the market sever first? Its ecological root? Or will it break its root to culture by its erosion of accumulated knowledge and custom? Can there be a smooth transition to a new, sustainable structure? And when we have to reconfigure, will the traditions we need to unearth be lost?

These are vital questions for the lesbian and gay movement, because it has cast its lot on a wager: that the liberal market represents the end of history. That the market perfectly expresses our nature and protects our rights, a realm of pure positivity. That the full penetration of a regime of total visibility is freedom, not slavery. That we can throw ourselves into the market's sun as if it were a light that will not consume us.

Now that we know our true identities, we know we are not sex offenders. With our sexual ideology at last rational and grounded, we can make every crime capital, punish real sex offenders forever into the future for transgressions that occurred any distance in the past. Our system of sexual control exists outside of politics or morality, in a realm of pure administration. Sitting at its end and on the top, history reveals no form of eroticism that we cannot finally comprehend.

Every age, to be sure, asserts its hubris and casts wide the web of its preoccupations. But we are unmoored by our loss of what has been throughout history the primary realm of human freedom: the informal unspoken spaces within organic community. Destroyed by the market, they leave us with language, ideology, and identity. With the market's total spatial inflation, the present moment's absolute intensification, no age has been so unconscious of history's weight, so marooned by the structures of recollection. As we stand, our hubris is our doom. That is why the lesbian and gay movement is morally and intellectually bankrupt, and that is why we must reclaim our history to imagine ourselves anew.

What You Learn After Thirty Years of S/M
JOHN PRESTON

Pedro was my first boyfriend. Well, I was the boy; he was my first lover. He was at least fifteen years older than I was. I met him in a gay bar in Providence, Rhode Island. I haven't a clue how I got in; I was only seventeen. I had learned my way hustling around some mean streets in Boston and I had found men to have sex with by hitchhiking the back roads around my rural hometown in Massachusetts. I already had a range of homosexual experience and, since lots of information passed between people who lived in a hidden culture, I had already begun my initiation into gay life. Somehow that all got me to Providence, about forty miles away from my parents' house.

The bar was pretty tawdry—this was long before gay ghettos and gay style. It was, in fact, the cocktail lounge for a Chinese restaurant, up on the second floor of the building. Pedro was the only man there I wanted, and he knew it from the very first time he looked at me and saw the hunger on my face. He broke into a smile that I can still see—bright white teeth against his olive Portuguese skin. He didn't even really come on to me, he just gestured with his head, telling me to come over to him.

I did, and as soon as I did, his hand cupped my ass. He didn't talk to me at first, he simply continued a conversation he was having with another friend.

There was never a question about who was going to fuck whom. I was the one who was going to get planked. That night was magical for me for many reasons, but one stands out. I had been torturing myself reading psychiatric and sociological texts trying to find out about my sexuality. The recurrent term was: unnatural. I had somehow always found the need for lubricant to be a proof that sex between men was, in fact, artificial. Pedro, though, in those far pre-AIDS days, had something to show me. He leaked so much precum from his uncut cock that he didn't need any of that stuff. He just jerked off a bit and there was a thick layer of ooze all over his dick.

"Time for me to climb on, Pup," he said, giving me a private nickname. He slipped into me more easily than any K-Y-ed man ever had.

He fucked me wonderfully. I kept thinking: It is natural! It is natural! I was transformed.

Pedro was important in lots of other ways. Sex had been hidden for me. It was something that you did with men who didn't want you to know their names, those men who'd hire a teenager in Park Square or else who would drop a hand on a hitchhiker's thigh. Pedro talked dirty. He talked dirty a lot. And he didn't separate himself from the rest of my life.

I was an overly bright, even precocious, high school student with a shock of blond hair. I went about my life in my hometown quietly, aware I shouldn't draw attention to my other life. Sex was something I never did at home. Pedro changed that. He didn't fuck me at my parents' house, but he called for dates after the first time we were together and, when he came to pick me up, he'd come in to visit. He drank with my father and the two of them talked sports. I was amazed. I thought for a while that he was playing with my parents—that he was daring them to talk about the fact that he, a man well into his thirties, was about to leave the house with their teenaged boy. Maybe. I think it's more likely that he didn't think in those terms. He, like my parents, was a working-class guy, friendly; what my mother calls people of any age whom she likes, "a good kid." My parents liked him. They really did. Maybe, in some working-class tradition—I've seen this played out with other people—they decided that, if their son was going to be gay (and, by then, they knew I was) he should at least have a "good kid" to show him the ropes, forget the age.

Pedro changed my ideas of what a male homosexual acted like, of how a male homosexual lived. Pedro was a Portuguese truck driver and, by God, that's just what he looked like. He was as tall as me. He was well-built, but not in the way we think of today in the midst of our gym culture—he had muscles, but they were under a layer of firm fat. He didn't have a pot belly, but he had a stomach with substance to it, dense, with no visible abs. His arms were the place where it really showed up. They were big beefy arms with thick wrists and heavy biceps. I loved those arms.

After a few dates, I became a regular at Pedro's house. And, once I became a regular, the sex started to escalate. "Take off your clothes, Pup," Pedro said one weekend afternoon when he'd fetched me down to Rhode Island. "I want you naked."

Undressing in front of another man who was going to enjoy the sight in the full light of afternoon was so compelling, I nearly shot from the idea of it, and from the way he said it to me. I stripped down. My cock was stiff and hard, spearing out in front of me. Pedro opened his pants.

"Come suck it, Pup. On your hands and knees."

I can still taste that dick and I can still feel the way it filled my mouth.

Pedro liked to take me to parties. I would stand there, a painfully shy boy, and he would tell me to turn around and show off my ass. "That's my piece!" he'd tell his (frighteningly open) homosexual friends at their barbecues.

He slapped me a couple times. At first on the butt, just before he fucked me. Once across my face. That one came out of nowhere; there was no fight, no conflict, he just wanted to slap me, and he did. He liked to make me react.

I never, ever even dared *think* about seeing anyone else when I was dating Pedro. Oh, no.

That wasn't going to fly. He never really said anything about it. He didn't have to. I would stand in the Providence bar, or at his friends' parties, and he'd put his arm around me and there was no question that he was doing far more than being affectionate; he was establishing ownership. It was the way he stood, the way those stocky biceps fell on my shoulder, the way he looked at other men who might look at me that told me he was calling on some primal male thing...

That's not true. I did once flirt with an unsuspecting man who had eyed me. He was innocent. It was my doing when the man came over and touched me. I got what I wanted: Pedro beat him up, on the spot, no questions asked, no quarter given. Pedro's friends had to drag him off the poor unsuspecting man and pull Pedro out of the bar.

"Get naked, Pup," was the first thing he said when we got inside his house. "Get naked fast." Pedro had to fuck me to reclaim me; it was just what I wanted him to do.

I eventually went to college. It broke Pedro's heart when he learned that I wasn't going to stay near him, but was going to the Midwest to school. He stalked me for a while, following my mother and me when we went to the supermarket, parking his car on our block and just staring at our house.

You can deconstruct this all you want. I'll help you: Pedro was close to being a child molester; though, given my precocity and my aggressiveness in making myself available, it's really stretching the point to say that. He was violent. He was manipulative. And then there was the stalking…so dangerous.

Go through it all and challenge it step by step—why the role playing? Was it class-based behavior? Was he claiming his privilege as an older white male by asserting the role of "the aggressor" in the sex we had?

It doesn't make any difference what analysis you come up with. Here's my truth: There is no question in my mind that he was the first man who loved me. If I have a regret from my youth, it was that I left him so easily. This is what is important: Pedro was my first great passion. He taught me that fulfilled desire can be its own reward.

The next years of my life were filled with more expected forms of homosexuality. I went to bars in Chicago, near the college I attended. I was part of the pre-Stonewall gay world that was laying the foundations for gay activism—simply by going to parties, joining groups at bars where we talked about our lives, that kind of thing. We were making the essential series of connections that would eventually become what we call a community.

The sex was pretty uninteresting stuff. Every once in a while I used to drive north to Kenosha, Wisconsin, to go to the bars there. The men were blue-collar working men from the huge American Motors plant who would come to The Roadhouse when they got off second shift.

They were more comfortable for me than the more sophisticated homosexuals of Chicago. They had the smell of Pedro about them. But I never found anyone quite like him.

I went on to be a gay activist in the seventies. Sex got even more bland. The boards of the organizations I worked for in Minneapolis, for instance, had only one rule about my personal life: I must not be seen in the baths. It would not do for a public figure of gay liberation in Minnesota to be seen sucking cock in public.

Some of my friends were beginning to be intrigued with other things. I remember once standing in a bar and watching my friend Kris's face when the first leather man we'd ever seen walked in dressed in full regalia. Kris had seen a new god and he wanted to do homage. He did. The next day he showed me the bruises on his ass. He was very proud of them. We were in our mid-twenties by then.

I was intrigued and I began to know—or suspect—what I wanted. I took a vacation to San Francisco to find it. His name was Brent. I found him in a leather bar on Folsom. They were having a charity slave auction that night. I was stunned by the idea of it—stunned into a hard-on because it turned me on so much. Brent saw what was happening and began to play with me. "We'd probably get a lot of money as a pair—me the top, you the bottom." It was the first thing he said to me. I was so swept up in the idea of actually going on the stage and having someone choose me that I nearly went for it. Brent decided to go for me instead. He was the first man whose piss I drank. He had me kneel in a cubbyhole in the back of the bar and he took out his dick and he just let go. I hated it; I loved it.

Sex was pretty hot with Brent that night. He came complete with every leather accessory you could imagine. I learned a lot, both in the bar where he went about a ritualized claiming of me (placing a collar around my neck), and then at his apartment where he beat me harder than I imagined I could stand.

Wouldn't you know it? Brent turned out to be a drag queen. He was part of the Cockettes, a political gender-bending theater troupe that was beloved in the Bay Area. He taught me a lot during that vacation. I learned that his role playing was playing a role. (He did it well, whether he was on stage in a dress, or in a bar in leather.) Brent believed in authenticity, it's just that his authentic self changed with the stage on which he stood.

Brent was a good guide during my explorations. I wasn't all that surprised—nor was he—when I ended up on top by the end of the week. Once I'd learned the ropes, I knew how to tie them. It felt...comfortable to be the top. I've stayed there pretty much since then. Oh, there was one tryst a few years later when I bottomed for playwright Doric Wilson, with whom I went home from the old Eagle in New York, but basically, I figured out where I stood during that week with Brent.

My trip to San Francisco was an invaluable learning experience. It could not have happened—given my professional life and given the limitations of visible gay life there—in Minneapolis. This was true for me, as well as for other gay men. But I don't think that many gay men really want to live their lives in the major ghettos. After a young man I know from New Hampshire recently visited San Francisco for the first time, he came back and announced that he couldn't take the men on Castro Street seriously. He kept on thinking they were paid actors, just stage props for some adult theme park. His observation struck a cord. People in San Francisco seem to think they are the ultimate beacon, the light at the end of every other gay men's tunnel. They're not. It's easy to dismiss the place by saying that, but I also think the ghettos—New York, San Francisco, West Hollywood, Key West, Provincetown, you know the list—are important as places to visit, sometimes for a long time. I like to think of them not as end posts, but as finishing schools. We should send our young men off to those places so they can learn to wear their harnesses correctly and to have the proper slave attitude, etiquette, and dress. These are such important lessons in life.

That's what the ghettos were for me—a place to learn, a place to take some risks with myself, my lovers, and life on the edge. I immersed myself in them for about ten years—I was a very intense student. My school buses were Harley Davidsons and BMWs. Class lectures were held in dungeons. Leather was my major; I graduated with honors. I was hired to be the editor of the *Advocate* in 1974; I arrived in West Hollywood wearing leather chaps; it wasn't really expected; but I wore them well. Later I moved to San Francisco and became a hustler—a leather top for hire. I did a little of that when I moved to New York. I was into it.

I learned that tops learn from bottoms. The basic S/M is easy stuff—you slap some butt, you talk dirty. You say the things the men read in the porno magazines and that's all they want — the same show as Brent's, just leave out the depth. But when you go further, ah, then you learn.

A lot of the lessons, I began to realize, I should have learned from Pedro, and maybe I did. It was obvious that the man was on to something. "Take off your clothes, Pup," he used to say. Get naked. Strip it off. But it wasn't just the clothes, it was all the accumulated baggage as well—all the hidden features of our lives that we wanted to expose in a context we trusted. It was about being a man, and learning what that meant. It was about letting go of some of those false things we had been taught about masculinity.

I learned some devastating techniques during this time. I remember the first time I had a man suspended from chains hanging from the ceiling and I whispered in his ear, "You wouldn't want to disappoint me, would you?" He absolutely did not. "I want to give you ten strokes with this paddle. It would disappoint me terribly if you told me to stop. I will, if you ask. But it will disappoint me…terribly." I not only got to give him ten, I got to give him thirty by the time it was done and he was so happy about it all. He was so proud. He came back the next week for more. And he paid me for it. Life can be pretty wonderful.

There are other lessons. All men are competitive. If you really want to be able to go at it, get two bottoms together—lovers, fuck buddies, strangers, any two bottoms who're interested in a three way. Move back and forth between them. "Jack just took twenty. Are you going to take less?" Never. The playground's open and there's no teacher monitoring recess.

Here's a strange truth you can use to achieve your pleasure: Many men want to be made to cry just so you'll comfort them afterwards. S/M is a world of boys and fathers, pain and relief.

When I became a writer and began to chronicle what I had learned and seen in the S/M world, I had in mind a simple truth: The drama of S/M is all in the bottom's mind. American men have such layers of defense that it becomes spectacular when you help them rip them away. For an American man to submit openly to another man is one of the most dramatic rituals he'll experience. Open the door to that experience and a good bottom will walk through.

Why be a top then, if all the fun's on the other end? It's partially an aesthetic experience. I adore men's bodies. I love them when they're naked and exposed to my gaze and my touch. I love to see them throw their muscles into stark relief when they're responding to pain. I like claiming them. I like to see my bruises on their skin, knowing that I put them there and they let me.

There's the intimacy. It gets messed up in S/M because it happens in different ways than in the rest of society. S/M intimacy is harsh and fast, it produces a rush of emotion that most people want to turn into something more. Few people know how to read the roadmap to show them the way through the new terrain. You've stripped a man naked; you've hurt him; you've consoled him; he has gone through more for you than anyone else ever has; you want to get married. Unfortunately most people are not like Brent: They're authentic, in terms of the stage they're on at the moment, but they know they're going to move onto another stage.

Maybe that is why so many men are trying to turn S/M into a lifestyle. I stopped wearing leather for about ten years because of the lifestyle stuff. For me, S/M had all been about living on the edge, being on the very cusp, being an outlaw: roles were something to be tried on, mocked, challenged. Suddenly, in the late 1970s, men were taking S/M and leather and turning it into an organizing tool, demonstrating for "leather rights," and in the meantime imposing exclusionary dress codes and holding workshops on how to do it right. What a mess.

Now, there's a group in New York that has a Slave School and a Master School. Don't drool, these are the most anti-sexual things you could imagine. After "students" go through a prescribed number of lessons, the two classes get together for a final examination and the newly graduated tops pour melted wax on the newly certified bottoms. I think it's all ridiculous, this over-codification of our lives.

I don't mind the fact that leather men come together in groups. I was one of the founders of the Harbor Masters here in Portland, Maine. I think most men who happen to be gay—even when they're into leather—also want to be in a club. The tribal instinct in men is strong. So we formed a tribe. When we first started we were the only gay organization in Maine that had two nickels—we charged everyone two dollars at every meeting and it built up. We funded a gay/lesbian youth group, we co-sponsored a gay/lesbian cultural festival. Here's the truth: We were more like the Rotarians or the Masons than anything else. There was some sex going on, but, like most leather groups, the Harbor Masters were more of a fraternal benevolent organization than anything else. Nothing wrong with that. But it's hardly an outlaw posse.

I decided the best way to get back to the fringe was to go straight, in a gay kind of way. I figured a good bottom would recognize a good top no matter what he wore. So, when I went to New York, I'd show up at the Spike wearing chinos and loafers and oxford cloth, a parka on a cold night. My hunch was correct, getting bottoms was more in the eyes then the leather jacket; but it was harder, and didn't happen nearly enough. I've given in and gotten some leather again, but someone's going to pay the price. I'm pissed off about it.

People often ask me how a slave might train himself. I think he should shave his body and keep it shaved. None of this easy gym-bunny stuff where you shave your chest and say you're just showing off your development. All of it. The ritual alone is worthwhile in this under-ritualized world we live in. Preparing your body for a master—real or imagined—is a task of its own value. It's good for a slave to wander around with his nuts in silky skin without protective covering, smelling his sweat without his armpit hair to soak up his perspiration. All of it. Do it regularly and be more aware of being stripped. (When a top does reach down into your pants for the first time and finds a shaved cock and balls, he'll know he has something; you'll know it was worth it.)

I often think the fact that I am the oldest of five children—and that my brothers are fourteen and seventeen years younger than I am—has a lot to do with my being a top/Daddy/even a sadist. I'm used to being in control. I got taught how to do it. It fits. I like it. I know how a boy should act and what makes him happy.

That's a great thing to have in your experience when you hit my age—forty-seven and, I hope still counting, at least for a while. Back in the seventies the guy who then owned *Drummer* came across that daddy thing. He turned it into a major fetish; he created the "daddy" and the "boy" as desirable media objects. The models in the skin magazines became much older all of a sudden.

Today, as I realize what he's done for me, I realize it was a godsend. Age—such a controlling factor in our everyday, consumer lives—is much less a factor in S/M than it once was. The Daddy image showed a respect for age that the rest of our culture does not.

But it's not just media hype, for beneath the Daddy image lay a truth: Daddy has some lessons he can show a good boy who wants to learn. He knows how to put a bottom through a rite of passage, a bit of endurance that lets him test his manhood, something the boy is in danger of never discovering in this white bread world. Daddy knows where the edge is, he's been there. He can take you there, if you trust him.

That is what I like about being a Daddy. And what I don't get enough of. Not nearly enough. A lot of that is because I live in

Maine. It's not that there isn't S/M in a rural state; there is. I interviewed Edmund White back in the seventies, just when he had come back from the research trips that eventually comprised his groundbreaking travelogue, *States of Desire*. I asked him what had really surprised him. He told me that he had been amazed at how much S/M there was out in the hinterlands. He had thought it was a subcultural thing, that there had to be the symbols and costumes of the ghetto world to carry it out. But he discovered he had been wrong. There were all these farm boys in middle America who were doing it with incredible ingenuity. S/M just might be something that American men do, he decided. My limits are set in Maine just because the population's so low. There have been many men to whom I've taught many lessons here. Some of them were as accomplished as the men in the sex clubs of the ghettos. They were good boys. There's one walking through the streets of Portland with his body shaved as I write this. I still look for more.

All my journeys have been worthwhile. As Isak Dinesen has said: "One must, in this lower world, love many things finally to know what one loves the most ..." I've learned what I like: A firm body with enough resilience to take some strokes over its butt and shoulders; a submissive man who understands the knowledge he can find in his acceptance of himself as a bottom; clean jockey shorts stretched over smooth, hairless skin. Those are the ingredients I want. I want to at least see the potential for them when I look at someone and try to decide whether or not I want to take him on a ride on the leather trail. I want him to know what it takes to be a man, and what it does not take. I want him to know what it is like to cry and be consoled, to give and not just take. I want him to know himself, his authenticity, his pain, and his pleasure.

Making Sex Public:
Remarks Relevant and Irreverent
MICHAEL LASSELL

When a friend and colleague asked me the topic I was addressing for this John Preston celebration weekend, I responded (half in jest, half having forgotten the exact rubric): "Having Sex in Public, I think." She was suitably shocked: "I'm sure that's not it," she replied (half in jest, half hoping I had forgotten the exact rubric, I'm sure). And, indeed, "Having Sex in Public" is not exactly right. "Making Sex Public," is something far tamer than the assertion that one ought to go rutting around in the street—although, we might well ask ourselves, at some future conference, just what would be so hideous about having sex in public, given the truly disgusting things that can be seen every day. So Bruce Bawer, Andrew Sullivan, and their odious apologist ilk can just relax... for the time being.

"Making Sex Public" seems so unassailable a goal, I wonder why it is even necessary to give it any energy in 1995, which is more than a few calendar years since the invention of sex, even of public sex, much less the artistic representation of sex—which, the historians among us can document, were once not forbidden at all. It took the three great evils of the Middle East—Judaism, Christianity, and Islam—to institute an official dichotomy between body and spirit, between society and the basic biological realities of human existence, between the individual and God (except via a priestly class getting fat on the agony of its flock).

So… "Making Sex Public." This little phrase contains two major assumptions: one, that sex is not now already public (about which many would disagree); two, that it would be a good thing to make it public if it is not already.

Is not sex already public? Is this not, in fact, the big gripe of the censorious martinets of the political right?—Christian, Jew, and Muslim alike—that there is too much sex available to the public, and that sex will corrupt the morals of children and hence undermine Western civilization (making their own assumption, of course, that Western civilization is, for some unspecified reason, worthy of preservation). The answer, of course, is yes… and no.

Never has there been on earth, I suspect, a society—a culture, if you prefer—as obsessed with sex and as ignorant. One might even legitimately cite obsession in conjunction with ignorance as one of the cardinal traditional American values. Does it not relate equally, for example, to sexuality, race, and class? Is it not exactly the quality brought to the Westward Expansion, the Industrial Revolution, and foreign policy from the Spanish-American War to the debacle the propagandists in Washington call "Desert Storm"?

Of course, it is precisely the point of obsession to remain ignorant of reality, to immerse oneself in obsession rather than take the intellectual, emotional, and even spiritual recess from obsession necessary for meaningful dialogue, the step-back from our own position we must take for analysis—perhaps even for the resolution of differences, or the possible means to live serenely in the presence of unresolved differences. After all, confrontation and resolution are only two constructs among many. But I digress, as usual. (Think of it as the adjectival lifestyle.)

So is sex already public? Yes, it is, quantitatively speaking. Qualitatively speaking, no, it is not—at least from the point of view that diversity (a word I now use with trepidation in its non-ironic sense) is a good thing. I believe in diversity. I believe in multiculturalism. If the words have come to stand for imperfect solutions to real social problems, that is not my doing. Given everything else the world has to contend with, of course, the imprecise application or devaluation of words is probably not even in the top ten— although when the Republican Party starts demonizing words like "liberal," we enter the kingdom of manipulation, some miles removed from misguided misuse or intentional misrepresentation.

So sex is everywhere: films, television, videos—even on the Internet—and I am not even talking about pornography, per se (not even by the right wing's far too promiscuous definition of erotica). However, it is grotesquely significant that what is being decried by the phrase-makers in their mad scramble for attention is *not* the use of sex to hawk wares in the marketplace of product (the right being pro-business in the extreme): "Yes," we say as a culture, "sex sells; please feel free to attach a wallop of unexamined sexuality to every product from diet cola and toilet cleaners to the latest Janet Jackson tune."

No, the objection is not to the commercialization of a highly prescribed and limited kind of sexuality—(different in degree, but not in essence from the hypocritical rigidity Hawthorne wrote about in *The Scarlet Letter*). No, the objection is to the introduction of sex, sexuality, sexual orientation, sexual practice, sexual representation, gender deviance (and other such "minority" issues) to the marketplace of *ideas*. (Even though, when you add up all the "minority" concerns you might find yourself with a "majority" of people who are not monogamous heterosexual couples engaged exclusively in missionary-position procreative sexuality.)

I am generalizing, of course, partly for effect, partly because these are things I believe to be true. Among the most interesting turn of events lately has been the public outcry over the Calvin Klein ad campaign that featured extremely young (or apparently young) half-clad kids in poutingly provocative come-hither poses. I despised the ads myself—not because I found the pictures disgusting (I found the pictures genuinely and legitimately erotic—teenagers *are* sexual creatures, the self-hypnotic blindness of their parents notwithstanding), but because old Calvin is using teenage sexuality to sell jeans. I couldn't care less if Calvin Klein is a pederast, whether or not he comes clean about it, so to speak. I just hate him for exploiting the innocent sexuality of his models for personal gain; for pushing the envelope not of public sexuality, but of profit.

But I digress.

It is because those in power derive their power from the control of bodies not their own that the Helms posse wants to shut down the NEA. Because politics cannot control art any more than it can control hunger or thirst—the clearest evidence you can muster for the very logical proposition that government is less necessary than creativity. And the more unnecessary the people in control feel, the more necessary they feel it is to exert control. (George Wolfe, the gay African-American director of the Public Theater in New York takes this as a good sign, as the pathetic flailings of a ruling class that knows its days are dwindling down.)

Censorship, one of the favorite toys of fascism, is what happens when you put heterosexual men in charge, of course. As a group, they seem synonymous with patriarchy and patronage, hierarchy and hegemony. Also, they don't clean up after themselves in locker rooms. (If women had even an inkling, in their worst nightmares, of the things men say about their wives, lovers, and girlfriends in male-only environments, there would *be* no heterosexuality.)

It is the conceit of the power mafia that some sex is good sex and some sex is bad sex, as opposed to, for example, a construct that holds that some sex works for some people and some sex works for others. Faced with diversity and multiculturalism, the powers that be write laws that undermine affirmative action and define as obscene everything different from their own sexual practices, which—to read the news—seem frequently to involve the nonconsensual participation of female employees, including minors.

It is at this juncture crucial to note that the issue of public obscenity is as old as recorded Western history. The word itself—obscene—refers to the stage house of the Greek amphitheaters that flourished in the fifth century B.C. The *skene* was the building itself, in front of which the actions of gods and heroes unfolded. OB-*skene*—literally, off-stage, behind the scene house—was where things took place that were too dangerous, difficult, or potentially harmful for the audience to witness. In Athens, seat of Hellenic culture in its apogee, what was considered obscene was not sex, but violence. When Oedipus puts out his eyes to punish himself for his crimes, he goes behind the stage house, because self-mutilation in Greek society was considered obscene. Times have changed. "They gave me a medal for killing a man," says the gravestone of Leonard Matlovich, "and a court martial for loving one."

We must also realize as we come to the end of this millennium that sex has always been a central component of art. Oedipus is the story of a man who kills his father and sleeps with his mother—who fathers children with his mother. Most of the other extant Greek tragedies involve some sort of transgressive sexuality—as do all the comedies of Aristophanes, which are not only overtly and comically sexual but political as well, taking contemporary politicians and political situations to task in frequently scabrous language.

Less known, except to those of us who thought it might be a good thing to spend the Seventies in drama school instead of in Vietnam, is that these most noble Greek tragedies were performed in trilogies that were followed by satyr plays. These broadly sexual farces were burlesques of the tragic plays that had directly preceded them, and included choruses of highly sexualized beings called satyrs—half men, half goats—who wore little except extremely large leather phalluses. The Greeks, who were repressive enough in their own way, did not seem to think it wise to repress sexuality.

So we do not need to ask ourselves the question whether or not sex and/or politics is and/or are appropriate to art: sex and politics are not only inextricable one from the other—as the women's movement taught us: *Sex is political* (and this is not a passing observation relevant only to the Seventies; it is one of the most profound statements ever made)—but sex and politics are equally inextricable from art. It is worth noting, further, that these raucous satyr plays—like the more familiar dramatic forms of comedy and tragedy—were performed as part of an annual *religious* festival, a community-wide homage to the god Dionysus. So sex and politics are, in a traditional Western sense, inextricable also from religion. No wonder "Thou shalt not" Christianity was greeted with such hostility by the Romans.

The twin problems we then face are how to introduce the full palette of sexuality to contemporary art—and thus into the public dialogue—and how to rescue from the politicians the right to make art about whatever we want to make it about: sex, politics, and religion, in any combination we chose.

Not to get too esoteric, let's put it this way: How do we stop people who do not know anything about sex from censoring those of us who do?

Another question—and it's their question, of course, not ours—is, why do we insist on *writing* so much about sex?

There are several obvious responses here: We write about sex because it is exactly our sexuality that seems so to bother those who base their careers on being bothered by other people. The more they want us to shut up and go away, the more we need to keep blabbing. Making artifacts that record the self-important nonsense of the powerful is one of the historic roles of artist/liberators. We give it up to our own peril.

We write about sex because we have a mischievous streak that makes us want to thumb our noses at authority (much the way Henry Fielding did in *Tom Jones*, for example, in the first half of the Eighteenth century), and I am, as usual, only partly joking. As Julia Cameron writes in her very persuasive *The Artist's Way: A Spiritual Path to Higher Creativity*, the artist part of creative individuals is a child, the inner child, if you will, to borrow yet more jargon from the contemporary scene. This artist-self behaves as a child—which is precisely why it is invaluable: It has not bent to the socialization that kills creativity in favor of the status quo, in favor of those things that make the most people feel the most comfortable. A reminder to comfort Christians: The Bible records Jesus as saying he does not come to bring comfort, but to shake up the comfortable. That Jesus was something of a scalawag.

Defying authority is not only an adolescent or immature gesture. That's what they kept saying in the Sixties, those who were in control of the money and the rules they could buy with it: That the peace movement, the youth movement, the women's movement, the black movement, the sexual revolution, the gay/lesbian movement, were adolescent. What they meant was, they had the money, and it pissed them off that we managed to acquire power without it—in our numbers (just like in a democracy).

Additionally, we write about sex because it is a normal thing to write about. We write about our kind of sex because it is the normal thing for us to write about. We write about sex because our perspective on sexuality as outsiders is precisely the piquant ingredient we have most legitimately to offer the conformist socio-cultural stew. Conformity is another favorite toy of fascism.

But there is a fundamentally more important reason for writers to write about sex, for writers of minority sexuality to write about minority sexuality, and the reasons are so fundamental they go back, again, to Greece, to a prehistoric period that predates the writings of Fifth-century B.C. Periclean Greece, to the very origins of the god Eros. Now Eros, of course, is the root of the word erotic. Like many words, it has come to have a specific cultural meaning that entirely eclipses the breadth and depths of its roots in the culture from which ours derives.

In fact, there were two different gods called Eros in Greek mythology, one familiar to us, having descended through the renaissance as a chubby little kid on St. Valentine's Day cards. This pudgy putito is a total emasculation of the original Greek god, who belongs to the creation myth, before the Olympians, before the Titans who sired the Olympians. Let me read a passage from the *Dictionary of Mythology*:

"*Eros*. The god of love. In early Greek mythology he is the child of Chaos, antedating the Olympian gods. In later legends he is son of Aphrodite—by various fathers: Zeus, Ares, or Hermes— and he is represented by a winged boy. The older view sees him as a great creative, cohesive force in men's lives—the builder of cities, the establisher of friendships, etc. The later view saw him more exclusively as the god of sensual desire and, as such, cruel and imperious. The Romans saw him almost entirely in this role, a winged child with a bow from which he shot the arrows of desire. Their name for him was Cupid and their concept has almost entirely replaced the older one in the modern mind."

It is because the Renaissance received its classical information from the Roman interpretation of earlier Greek culture that we have lost this far more complex and authentic notion of Eros as the force in nature of all creation, associated naturally in the pre-democratic agrarian Greek imagination with sexuality, but transcending sexuality. Eros therefore came to stand for the life force in nature, that which opposes Thanatos, or the force of death.

As many of us have learned far too early, in this age of AIDS, life consists of coming to terms with the shifting balance of these forces of life and death. It becomes increasingly necessary to preserve this original notion of Eros as the force that embodies all creativity, including sexuality, because this is the very notion that is now under increased attack. It is a mistake to separate body and spirit, and we have suffered from that schism because the Roman Catholic Church held a jealous hold on scholarship for the millennium between the fall of Rome and the Renaissance. We got used to half-lives because the clergy demanded mega-lives for itself.

If one suppresses sexuality, one suppresses creativity. If one suppresses creativity, society dies. If society excludes those of us who have by virtue of our outsider status a more complete understanding of sexuality, then society will inherit more network sitcoms and fewer works of literature.

It's as simple as that, whether one invokes antique precedent or the common sense of personal experience: I am not creative when attacked: I am angry. I am not moved to build bridges or write poems or even to make love. I am moved to hurl a live grenade in the direction of Congress, or in the direction of the Pope— who is currently infecting my home town of New York City with his homophobic genocidal murdering Christianity—or in the direction of Colin Powell.

Has anyone read anywhere in the mainstream press that Colin Powell would make a bad president because he refused to let gay and lesbian military personnel acknowledge their sexuality while in the service? Ignorance, bigotry, and hatred are not qualities one admires in a leader—even though they are traditional American values—because ignorance, bigotry, and hatred do not negotiate; they retaliate (which is why Colin Powell is a general, and generals do not like exceptions; they like conformity and obedience and consequently make excellent dictators, as Latin America learned, sadly, many years ago).

Among the many reasons to make sex public, or at least to put it on public record, is to rescue future generations from the ignorance of those that went before them. I know I am not alone when I say that when I grew up there was no information in my local library on homosexuality—or on sexuality at all—that was not entirely disapproving. If I had wanted disapproval, I would not have needed books; I had my parents for that—Republicans and Christians as well as heterosexuals, and therefore members of all three major enemy camps.

One of our great responsibilities here, of course, is to make sex public *accurately*—which is to say, in its wide variety, and in its real-life role, which includes sexuality inside committed relationships. I understand the tendency to revel in pure sexual expression—both in life and on the page—to bring into the light the full weight of our imagination and experience with unmitigated sexuality... in other words, erotic writing, or pornography, if you will—our John Preston used the terms interchangeably (or at least took the public position that the two were interchangeable). It is *normal* for us to want to get it into the canon that pure sexuality exists and that it is or can be a good thing.

God knows I have had enough experience with and written frequently enough about it to state categorically that there is nothing demeaning, unusual, or less-than-wonderful about the anonymous sexual encounter between two men who never exchange sun signs—or who never actually see each other. God knows, and entirely approves (it is the lunatics who cash in on misinterpreting him who get their cassocks in knots about it).

One of the most liberating moments of my own sexual education—back in the, yes, glorious Seventies—came at a West Hollywood bathhouse called the 8709. The 8709 had a dimly lit maze in it, and its denizens frequently doused even the dim lights, to create a labyrinth of pitch darkness. Freed from prejudices about visual attraction, I came to understand that chemistry does in fact exist. In that totally dark corridor it was possible to come into contact with hundreds of naked men in a single night, and eventually to happen upon a single arm, or leg, nipple, earlobe, or cock (there, I said a pornographic word) that created an absolutely uncensored and uncensorable chemical or electronic or, for all I know, spiritual erotic charge. Had I not "transgressed," I would still be ignorant about my own body.

But sex can become addictive. As an oppressed minority—as the only single minority whose oppression is still a matter of law— our community has come to include a disproportionate number of alcoholics and drug addicts, addiction being a function of, among other things, low self-esteem. We endanger ourselves with other self-destructive behaviors, too—including sexual compulsion, obsession, and addiction. The pursuit of sex has led many to unnecessary deaths. When we talk about making sex public, the temptation is to assume, as I usually do, that we are making *our* sexuality public for *their* consumption, as if among gay men and lesbians sexuality is already known, that we cannot each inside the community profit from information about sexuality other than our own, about leather sex, for example, if we do not walk in that part of the forest, or transvestism, or any other kind of sexual expression— including sex inside relationships both traditional and nontraditional. As my friend Paul Monette said in an interview I did with him once, "Being in love is not the only way to be happy," and I'm sure I'm paraphrasing here, "but it's the only way for *me* to be happy."

The gay male community, and an increasing segment of the lesbian community, has lost itself, or is losing itself, in the pursuit of sexuality per se, and not putting sexuality in the context of lives larger than sex alone. And this obsession with sex, with youth, with body parts, is a direct result of buying the heterosexual lie, that we dykes and fags *are* our sexuality and nothing more.

Which brings me at long-winded last to John Preston. It is my experience of John that his genius was to acknowledge the importance of sexuality, the legitimacy of all forms of minority sexuality— *Franny, the Queen of Provincetown* and *Mr. Benson*—and to integrate sexuality into a life that included not only queer politics, AIDS fund-raising, and a public identity as a novelist, editor, and columnist, but as a community figure who loved his family, his friends, and the people he knew even casually in Portland, Maine.

John Preston may have been a fierce leather top; I have no experience of him in that regard. He may have been a vital organizer; I don't know a thing about his political activities. I know John as an intellectual, as a witty and keen observer of the literary world we shared, as a brilliant editor and a tireless steward of literary excellence. He was, for me, not a model writer, but a model man of letters, who extended the realm and reality of letters, and who gave me permission, by his example, to continue to explore sexuality, spirituality, and politics in my own work. Because of John, among others, I have come to regard my own experience as totally legitimate material for my work—whether it's poetry or prose, fiction or nonfiction. And that's a great gift.

I first met John because of some poems I had written about a notorious burlesque house *cum* brothel in New York, poems that seemed completely natural to me to write (having been given permission to be a gay poet by an early association with Constantine Cavafy), but which seemed shocking to others, even to others who embraced them and who became friends. John was the person who best understood my work, who gave me a place in *Hometowns* to write about not having had a hometown, and a place in *Flesh and the Word* for a little porn story I tossed off in an afternoon because it had, to him, just the literary qualities he was looking for—thus liberating my "nonpornographic" work even further—and who gave me a place to write in *Friends and Lovers* anonymously, because that's what I needed to do.

John Preston was a great enabler… and I mean that in the best possible sense of the word. When I was fiercely depressed in the summer and autumn of 1993, and I turned to my friends for emotional and even financial support, John knew what I needed more than money. He knew I needed a book, and with a flourish of his phone, pen, or fax—I don't know which—he made *The Hard Way* happen. And for that I am, of course, grateful beyond words. In this way, John Preston's friendships were erotic, in that classical Greek sense I spoke of earlier: They were creative, supportive, positive, and life-affirming. They sometimes embodied Eros in our later sense, too, the sense of sexual attraction, whether or not sexual expression—genital contact (which *they* call sex, and which we know is only a small part of Eros)—was part of the alliance. John was the *compleat* friend.

The problem with most pornography, of course is not that the content is *wrong*, but that it is badly written. The truth is never wrong. It can be painful and damaging. It can inflict sorrow and suffering. That does not make it nonhuman. "I do not write to shock," said the great Tennessee Williams, one of our tortured forebears, "I write the truth, and the truth shocks."

But all writing, whether it is about sex or anything else, ought to aspire to great expression, because it is the expression that makes the experience live. Writing—pornographic, indecent, noble, or pedestrian—that takes as its model other writing will likely fail. John Preston, no great stylist by his own admission, made the impact he has made because he put himself into his own books and the rest of us into the books he edited. It is authenticity in this world of mendacity that speaks louder than Senate resolutions, and we must continue to be authentic even after we become legitimate, which is inevitable.

Deliverance
CRAIG HICKMAN

For Jeffrey Dahmer

I grew up in Milwaukee and went to elementary school with one of Jeffrey Dahmer's victims. The day I saw Dahmer's face on the cover of Newsweek, I realized that I'd had an encounter with him back in my precocious adolescent days. As a Black gay youth, I could have easily become one of Dahmer's victims.

Shortly after the story broke, I wrote a piece to examine the slaughter of Curtis, my elementary schoolmate. A year and a half ago, I sat down to try and make some sense out of all the madness. I did not know what form it would take.

What follows is the result of that transforming experience. It is a meditation of sorts—an imagined or channeled essay Dahmer might have written himself to explain his actions. I have presented this text as a performance piece on several occasions, and it has been placed on the page in this way to represent how it is delivered.

I don't know why, but I'm feeling so sad
I long to try something I've never had
Never had no kissin', oh what I been missin'
Loverman, oh where can you be?

That's what their eyes sang to me
when they stared into mine.
All those young, colored faggots
wore their loneliness as
a reeking, putrid odor,
and I breathed it in,
let it tingle in my nostrils,
let it ignite the fires in my blood.

I was chosen to offer them
the thing they never had.

Now,
Newsweek,
Time, *Inside Edition*,
and every newspaper across
this forsaken land features my face,
and they tell the tale that
I'm the Devil himself.
But the Devil would never
have been as
kind
as I was.

I called my attorney a fool
for playing that plea of insanity,
knowing any number of jurors in
their right minds
could ever believe me
insane.

I knew exactly what I was doing.
No one—no one—thought Abraham
insane
for preparing to carve up his son
and offer him a burnt,
a burnt! sacrifice,
claiming
the voice of God
ordered him so.

Well,
I had my voice,
and it was much more
powerful than God's.

All my Isaacs
came to me
willing,
needing,
begging to be delivered.

LITERATURE

Writing as cultural and sexual outsiders, gay men are forced to reevaluate the literary world that surrounds them, to challenge the status quo by providing both a critique and an alternative.

Tony Kushner is famous both as a playwright and activist. Here, in "on pretentiousness," he combines his literary background and role as a social critic to explicate the philosophical implications of style, sexuality, and making lasagna. Kushner's essay—delivered as a keynote address at OutWrite '95, the national gay and lesbian literary conference—is a dense and textured look at how the personal and political, literature and life, writing, and eroticism are inseparable from one another. Through the lens of his gay identity and sensibility Kushner transforms "traditional" literary concerns and ideas into a phantasmagorical tapestry of insight, politics, cooking tips, and cultural revisionism that challenges and provokes.

Kushner's investigation into style and politics is continued by Reed Woodhouse in "Five Houses of Gay Fiction," an attempt to understand and categorize contemporary gay male fiction. By combining standard literary criticism with a newer sense of political analysis, Woodhouse manages to re-view gay male writing to find out what makes it tick, or more precisely, what makes various authors and books tick in different ways. Woodhouse's taxonomy may rankle and perplex—all literary criticism is, after all, a more formal attempt to convince the reader of why she or he should like a favorite book—but it indisputably demands that we take gay male fiction writing seriously as expressions of political thinking and activity.

The hidden agendas of writing is also the topic of Christopher J. Hogan's "What We Write About When We Write About Porn." Hogan, a reviewer of video pornography, deftly delineates the practice and the problems of watching and writing about sex. "What We Write About When We Write About Porn" looks at what goes unstated when we write about sexuality in a culture that would prefer us to ignore the broader considerations of how sexuality touches all parts of our lives. Pornography is a constant in the lives of many gay men, and Hogan's essay is an attempt to locate those points where pornography has become so ingrained in our lives that we ignore the myriad messages it conveys.

An important impulse of gay sensibility is that it allows us to see what really lurks beneath the accepted innocuousness of everyday culture. Mitzel's "How to Write a Short Story" is a succinctly written, beautifully constructed piece of subversive humor in the tradition of Thorne Smith and Dorothy Parker. Ostensibly a primer for writing the "short story," Mitzel's piece, with its light-hearted tone and innocent chat, soon becomes a nightmare version of traditional American values and the politics of sexual repression. "How to Write a Short Story" is a fierce and prime example of gay wit: Mitzel—like all great gay satirists—takes a time-honored genre that has always been used to promulgate traditional values, and grabbing it by the throat shakes it until it reveals its true agenda.

on pretentiousness
TONY KUSHNER

Everything I say to you tonight, indeed everything discussed at the conference this weekend, is overshadowed, if not actually overwhelmed, by the fact that down the seaboard, in D.C., the scariest Congress this country has ever elected is energetically, industriously, enthusiastically dismantling the federal government. The America we live in today, still racked, starved, burned, brutalized, and unrecovered from the pillaging it endured in the eighties, this present ravaged America will seem in ten years' retrospect a paradise; that's an easy prophecy; the future that's being legislated into existence in these last few weeks is as we all know no future at all. All the important accomplishments of struggle, all the benchmarks of agonizing progress, are going up in great puffs of unregulated uninvestigated nicotine-laden tobacco smoke. In ten years' time public education through high school will be nothing more than overcrowded indoctrination in rightist political cant, supervised by Bill Bennett and his ilk, with no bad-tasting non-nutritional but at least free lunch. Affordable public higher education will be virtually nonexistent. This will help make people even more docile when faced with downsizing, which surely must produce prodigious rates of unemployment; and there will be no organized labor and no social net. Multinationals will have near-absolute sway over the workplaces and breathing spaces and landscapes and mindscapes and airwaves and informational pathways; corrupt and unaccountable state legislatures will be big business's eager foot-servants; minorities will have no legal protectional guarantees and will be ruthlessly dominated and policed by a pseudo-majority whose real power derives, not from brute numerical superiority, but from an unchallengeable stranglehold on realpolitik financed by multinationals. Progressive taxation will be a memory; the rich will be very rich. Searching police will need no warrants, recent immigrants will have no rights, the rights of the rest of us will go next, civil liberties will be lost, abortion rights will be lost, civil rights legislation will be lost, health care is lost already. Laws that protect children from abuse will be lost. Laws that reinstate death penalties and limit the number of appeals a death-row inmate gets; laws limiting the possibility of suing miscreant corporations, or the government—these will be passed in every state. Guns will be available. Prisons will mushroom. Sodomy laws will mushroom. Public discourse will have degenerated to such abysmal depths George Bush will seem to have been eloquent; there will of course be no federal funding for the arts or humanities. Colleges will offer courses in hokey-scientific theories of race-based genetic superiority, and on the history of the failure of feminism, and though abortion will be illegal, eugenics will be a coming thing. Research on AIDS, research on breast cancer will have stalled; pharmaceutical corporations and managed care corporations and insurance giants will control the medical front, concurrently racking up astronomical profit—the FDA, deeply flawed as it is and has ever been, will be a thing of the past and, dare I say it, missed.

Some wizened Republican horror will occupy the White House, and whatever his name is he will be Nixon, he will be Reagan, he will, perhaps in name as well as in spirit, be Newt. You went to bed in 1994, and wake up: It's morning, 1953! Except in 1953 things were better.

And it is no exaggeration to say that as a direct result of the laws and amendments these criminally reckless, criminally stupid, mendacious neo-barbarians are enacting, millions of people will die.

So from underneath this lightless, lengthening, deepening, icy-cold shadow, it's hard to talk about writing. I have even in the best of times only the shakiest faith in art, in the political power of the written word, and in times of political extremity writing seems to me a luxury. It is only because I am in utter helpless thrall to luxury that I continue writing, and reading. We have written a lot, and read a lot, and a lot has been changing, and some of it for the better, and then suddenly you discover that the decisive battle was happening behind you, and though you may have won the skirmish before you, the enemy is swarming up from the rear. And you are fucked. And not pleasantly. Suddenly someone who is the antithesis of what a writer ought to be, someone whose every word is a lie, someone who can't spell "potato" even, has carried the field. So what, my despair asks me at such times, is the use of writing?

The other thing that makes it hard to talk about writing tonight, besides having spent too much time listening, on C-SPAN, to the Götterdämmerungian Shit-Hits-The-Fan Overture also known as the proceedings of the 104th Congress—the other thing that makes it hard to talk about writing is that this is a roomful of writers I'm talking to; some of you, terrifyingly enough, are very good writers; a few are even great; and I yearn for the moral and aesthetic superiority with which I could protectively enfold myself were I addressing, say, the Heritage Foundation. You *look* fabulous, I admire you I adore you you are my sisters and brothers but you are *writers* and you scare the shit out of me.

The danger I face tonight is that I am back in psychoanalysis and I am in a confessional mood. Forgive me my sins: My problem is fraudulence. As a person who calls himself an artist in the face of the world's determined aggressive downward spiral, I feel a fraud, for this is an era of emergency, of crisis, and art is a self-indulgence; and then when I am among other people who are artists I abandon my ambivalence about *being* an artist and become aware only of how insufficient an artist I am.

For instance: The past two years I've participated in readings in New York City to raise money for the people of Sarajevo. These have, on each occasion, left me depressed—it would be histrionic and rhetorical to say suicidally depressed, but I *am* histrionic and rhetorical and so I say I have felt suicidally depressed. For the reasons mentioned above: In the face of the Bosnian horror, words, art, admirable sentiment, ideas, memory, history, hope—everything fails, or seems to fail. The gap between the words we write and read and the need for action so much greater than any individual has the power to perform—that gap grows too large and I despair. Despair is a sin, I really believe that, but I am as I say a miserable sinner, and there are days after some nights I can't get out of bed. And what made each of those Sarajevo evenings even worse was that my despair and I were surrounded by *writers*, my scrivenophobia excited to its utmost. On both occasions, in fact, I had to sit next to or immediately behind Joseph Brodsky, Big Daddy, the man who told Brezhnev poets always have the last laugh, and he was right. I smiled shyly at Brodsky. He didn't smile back. It took me months to recover.

Last year I dreaded this speech and this conference so much I didn't even show, that's how much I dreaded it. Instead of coming I sent a note of apology, which I believe was read aloud:

October 8, 1993

Dear Michael, Mark, and the OutWrite Conference:

Perestroika, Part Two of *Angels in America*, is a play about the difficulties of change, and true to its subject the play and its productions,
both here and in London, keep changing in the most difficult ways
imaginable. Because of delays in the schedule, the OutWrite
Conference falls, not on the second weekend of previews, which was
the case when we spoke several months ago, but in the middle of
the most arduous and tension-filled technical rehearsals since the
Trinity Test at Los Alamos in 1945. Unlike J. Robert Oppenheimer
and Company, we are hoping not to produce a bomb.

I am as disappointed and sick at heart about being a no-show as
I was honored to be invited to speak. I feel like the World's Biggest
Rat Fink, and I think you should collectively reprove me by hiss-
ing as one for fifteen seconds, and then forgive me by praying for
me—forgiveness is the secret to maintaining one's youthful looks,
and I need the prayers.

And when you're next in New York you should all come to
dinner. I'll bake a lasagna.

I'm really really sorry; I send you my deepest apologies, regrets,
gratitude for your forbearance, and much much love.

Yours,
Tony Kushner

Even a year later, even now, the fear, the sense of fraudulence, the
doubt that I have anything of value to teach anyone, is so great that
coherence, as such, is startled out of hiding like game birds from
the underbrush, in panicky bursts, and I find I must talk about
writing to you writers only obliquely.

So let's talk about lasagna.

Why, my analyst might ask me, did I choose lasagna for last year's palliatory offering? One obvious answer is that it's my favorite among the dishes my mother prepared. I loved it so much that I learned how to do it. I can cook various things now but for a while lasagna was the only thing I could cook and this is how it's made:

Stewed tomatoes, wide flat lasagna noodles, thyme, basil, bay leaves, oregano, black and white pepper, salt, yellow onions, scallions, garlic, green and red peppers, AT LEAST four kinds of cheese: one bland and milky (I prefer cottage cheese to ricotta because the curds have more heft), one white and stinky, one yellow and stinky and one yellow and mellow—AND Parmesan—and beef, fennel pork sausages, olive oil, mushrooms, olives, and a deep Pyrex dish. And parsley for the garni.

Lasagna is about opulence. Lasagna should be garlicky garrulous, excessively, even suspiciously generous, promiscuous, flirtatious, insistent, persistent overwhelming exhaustive and exhausting. Perfection in a lasagna I think ought to be measured by the extent to which it effects a balance between fluidity and solidity, between architecture and melting. It is something between a pie and a mélange; there are membranes but they are permeable, the layers must maintain their integrity and yet exist in an exciting dialectic tension to the molten oozy cheesy oily juices which they separate, the goo must almost but not completely successfully threaten the always-discernible-yet-imperiled imposed order.

Baking lasagna has long been my own personal paradigm for writing a play. A good play I think should always feel as though it's only barely been rescued from the brink of chaos, as though all the yummy nutritious ingredients you've thrown into it have almost-but-not-quite succeeded in overwhelming the design. A play should have barely been rescued from the mess it might just as easily have been; just as each slice of lasagna should stand tall, while at the same time betray its entropic desire towards collapse, just as the lasagna should seem to *want* to dissolve into meat and cheese stew, so you can marvel all the more at the culinary engineering magic that holds such entropy at bay, that keeps the unstackable firmly, but not too firmly, stacked. A good play, like a good lasagna, should be overstuffed: It has a pomposity, and an overreach: Its ambitions extend in the direction of not-missing-a-trick, it has a bursting omnipotence up its sleeve, or rather, under its noodles: It is pretentious food.

Pretentiousness, overstatement, rhetoric and histrionics, grandiosity and portentousness are, as much as they are also the tropes of fascists and demagogues everywhere, American tropes, gestures of habitual florid overstep common among those practitioners of American culture to whom I have always been most instantly attracted. It is an aspect of American history and the culture we have developed that I am keen to possess, to transform for my own purposes: the writing of Declarations, Constitutions, Epics, Manifestos. Consider Chapter 18 of de Tocqueville's *Democracy in America*, which is entitled "Why American Writers and Speakers Are Often Bombastic," and which is remarkable for its insight, less so for its French antidemocratic snottiness:

> I have often noticed that the Americans, whose language when talking business is clear and dry, without the slightest ornament, and of such extreme simplicity as often to be vulgar, easily turn bombastic when they attempt a poetic style. They are then pompous, without stopping from beginning to end of a speech, and one would have supposed, seeing them thus prodigal of metaphors, that they could never say anything simply.
>
> The reason is easily pointed out.
>
> Each citizen of a democracy generally spends his time considering the interests of a very insignificant person, namely, himself. If he ever does raise his eyes higher, he sees nothing but the huge apparition of society or the even larger form of the human race. He has nothing between very limited and clear ideas and very general and vague conceptions; the space between is empty....
>
> Writers, for their part, almost always pander to this propensity,

which they share; they inflate their imaginations and swell them out beyond bounds, so that they achieve gigantism, missing real grandeur....Writer and public join in corrupting each other.... Finding no stuff for the ideal in what is real and true, poets, abandoning truth and reality, create monsters.

I have no fear that the poetry of democratic peoples will be found timid or that it will stick too close to the earth. I am much more afraid that it will spend its whole time getting lost in the clouds and may finish up by describing an entirely fictitious country. I am alarmed at the thought of too many immense, incoherent images, overdrawn descriptions, bizarre effects, and a whole fantastic breed of brainchildren who will make one long for the real world.

So when I began work on *Angels in America*, I felt that the outrageousness of the project I was attempting—offering itself like a fatted calf to critics who loved to feast on pretentiousness and grandiosity—I felt that this selfsame pretentiousness and grandiosity was my birthright as an American, and rather than pointing to some serious deficiencies and flaws in my character—although such deficiencies and flaws undoubtedly exist and are complicit in all of this—my artistic obstreperousness indicated to me, on good days, that I was heir, no matter how puny an heir I might be, to a literary tradition that had produced some of my favorite books.

Chief among which was, and still is, *Moby Dick*—we know de Tocqueville never met Melville but he might have been describing him in advance. I have always loved the daring, the absurdity, the frequently hair-raising success, and occasional hair-raising failure, the passion and the onrushing grandiloquent devouring recklessness of Melville's writing. It gives me license to try anything.

Melville's first taste of critical disregard came with his book *Mardi*, which is, in my opinion, one of his greatest, clearly a warm-up for *Moby Dick*, which also failed critically. In *Mardi* a fictional Polynesian archipelago, called Mardi, is a stand-in for the entire world. The book begins as a slightly fantasticized version of Melville's early, successful South Sea adventures; but winds of metaphor, the heritage of English literature and contemporary national and international politics soon fill his sails and blow the author, by about a fourth of the way into the book, out of the realm of realism and into a new kind of entirely literary, philosophical, symbol-laden, book-of-a-book—a planet on the table.

The novel is deliriously endless; in Chapter 180 we encounter a character who is the Mardian Homer or Virgil or Dante, and his sufferings to produce his masterpiece, an epic called *Koztanza*, are described. But clearly Melville is writing about himself, in a perfectly splendid lament over the high-wire perils, the anxieties suffered by a writer—even a great writer—tilling the vasty fields of pretentiousness:

> Sometimes, when by himself, he thought hugely of [his book]…but when abroad, among men, he almost despised it; but when he bethought him of those parts, written with full eyes, half blinded; temples throbbing; and pain at the heart—He would say to himself, "Sure, it can not be in vain!" Yet again, when he bethought him of the hurry and bustle of Mardi, dejection stole over him. "Who will heed it," thought he; "what care these fops and brawlers for me? But am I not myself an egregious coxcomb?
>
> Who will read me? Say one thousand pages—twenty-five lines each—every line ten words—every word ten letters. That's two million five hundred thousand a's, and i's, and o's to read! How many are superfluous? Am I not mad to saddle Mardi with such a task? Of all men, am I the wisest, to stand upon a pedestal, and teach the mob? Ah, my own *Koztanza!* Child of many prayers!—in whose earnest eyes, so fathomless, I see my own; and recall all past delights and silent agonies—thou may'st prove, as the child of some fond dotard: beauteous to me; hideous to Mardi! And methinks, that while so much slaving merits that thou should'st not die; it has not been intense, prolonged enough, for the high meed of immortality.

Pretentiousness is risky; a vast, amorphous, self-generative anxiety comes with the equally vast and amorphous territory one has chosen to cover. One is highly susceptible to ridicule and possessed of such a number of flanks that it is impossible to protect them all. Since the size of one's ambitions is laid bare for the world to see, being thin-skinned is a predictable consequence and symptom of pretentiousness: One's skin is, after all, so painfully stretched over such a very large area. Implicit in grandiosity and pretentiousness is an unslakable desire to embrace everyone. The impulse to make work that contains the world surely stems from an infantile impulse to swallow it whole, and to be universally adored for having done so. These desires are even more doomed than the desires you develop as an adult, and to carry the appetite of an infant into middle age is to risk a certain indignity, to say the least (the way, for instance, that this speech attempts simultaneously a self-defense and a self-critique, and is I fear tangling itself up in knots). We pretentious writers of the Left share this unfortunate flaw, of being excessively thin-skinned and rapaciously greedy, with other control freaks, people we'd probably rather avoid any association with— Rush Limbaugh, Bob Dole, Adolf Hitler....

Pretentiousness is, I sometimes think, a form of hysteria that manifests itself as listing, cataloging; manifests itself in a panicked strained effort towards the encyclopedic, lest the important ideas, which the pretentious writer doesn't feel she or he truly or deeply comprehends, escape while writerly attentions dazedly malinger over some bit of inconsequence.

But the joys of pretentiousness are more alluring than its humiliations are forbidding. It is, as de Tocqueville says, a profoundly democratic gesture, or failing, though not entirely as he understood it. Pretentiousness is in one sense a Promethean, protean liberation of the imagination, and anyone is capable of it, provided we pretenders can inure ourselves sufficiently to the shame that is heaped upon us when we are caught in the act of pretending. Pretentiousness consists in attempting an act of bold creation regardless of whether or not one has sufficient talent, emulating the daring of which only genius is truly capable—daring to see how close to the moon we are capable, all our insufficiencies and limitations notwithstanding, of soaring. Embracing pretentiousness as a trope, as a stratagem and a tool, becoming ironically aware rather than ashamed of grandiosity, enables us to make literary and perhaps political hay out of the distance between what we would like to have done, and what we have actually accomplished. The success and the failure both are part of the story, the success celebrating our gloriousness, the failure nobly demarcating our tragedy, but in both glory and tragedy, we pretenders are fabulous.

Pretentiousness is Camp, it is Drag, perhaps this is why it's most resplendently at home in the theater. Pretentiousness, *if it's done well*, performs a salutary parody of carving out, in the face of the theorilessness and bewilderment of our age, meta-narratives, legends, grand designs, even in spite of the suspiciousness with which we have learned, rightly, to regard meta-narrative: By pretending that such grandeur is still possible, we acknowledge how absolutely necessary, and indispensable, an overview, a theory, a big idea still is. Such Pretense will have to do, until the real thing comes along.

People fundamentally lacking a sense of humor when confronted with pretentiousness miss the irony and the fun and are left with flared nostrils indignantly aquiver at the *tastelessness* and the *presumption*. Invariably, such people are themselves guilty of pretension, and are drearily unaware of it.

To make political art is always to risk pretentiousness, because you can only ever fail to formulate answers to the questions you pose, if those questions are big enough—and really, if they aren't, why bother posing? To make overtly political art you must, I think, always declare more than you can prove and say more than you can know: You must speculate, and so risk the pretension all participatory political discourse is heir to. C. L. R. James values this most in Melville: the fact that Melville arrives at a place of self-confessed

unknowing, that his art goes beyond his powers to explain, addressing issues of such depth that "to explain would be to dive deeper than
Ishmael can go."

I suppose I am speaking here specifically of a tradition of public
art that consciously engages itself with civic debate, a tradition of
writing that, presumptuously, aspires to position itself among other
grand American texts, each of which is not without its overreach.
The Declaration of Independence is pretentious. So is the
Constitution.

There is, of course, art that is not pretentious, just as there are of
course good foods that are not overstuffed. There is, for instance,
the matzoh: thin where the lasagna is fat, flat where the lasagna is
thick, cold and dry and desert food where the lasagna is wet and
steamy and Mediterranean, somber where the lasagna is meretri-
cious; poverty versus richness. The matzoh is not pretentious; it is
hard, brittle, transportable, it has been carried through the worst
times imaginable, it is imaginably present, preparable, consum-
able in even the most dire of circumstances, and it evokes those
circumstances even in the best of times. The matzoh is so
formidable that no sooner does it make its appearance at the
Passover Seder table than we slather it with a ragout of nuts, apples,
honey, cinnamon, and Shapiro's Kosher Wine ("*So thick you can
cut it with a knife!*")—because the matzoh reminds us: political
success, stability, security, the luxury of time and ingredients needed
to bake a lasagna, a play, a rounded identity: These things can and
most likely will be stripped away, and you will be faced with hard
choices. Cleave as bondsmen and women to the dangerous false
beauty, the unrighteous magnificence of Mitzrayim; or go into
the desert, liberated slaves, starved-tough and nourished on the
harsh simple bread of haste and affliction.

The matzoh is a spiritual discipline, and it rebukes me each
time I contemplate it that I am, or believe myself to be, incapable

of such discipline; my instantaneous reflex when confronted with such ascetic, anhedonic, bony reality is to grope blindly for the condiments, for the butter and salt, settling for whatever spice and lubrication comes first to hand. So as a playwright I find myself a determinedly optimistic baker of sloppy and runny and voluptuous concoctions, worried all the while that the exigencies of our times require a sparer, more sinewy approach. Leo Bersani and Ulysse Dutoit, in their wonderful book *Arts of Impoverishment*, describe the writing of Samuel Beckett, that matzoh of a playwright, this way: "In the ill-humored privacy of his art, in its defiant unrelatedness, Beckett reinvents our somewhat incomprehensible passage from the masochistic jouissance of self-enclosure to the fictional confusion of the 'I' and 'non-I.' At its very highest, art perhaps knows nothing but such confused beginnings, and in pushing us back to them it beneficently mocks the accumulated wisdom of culture."

For all that I have publicly decried the dangers of assimilationism, for all that the assimilationism of the lesbian and gay Right infuriates me, I have long been guiltily aware of the extent to which my work and even my politics betray an assimilationist penchant for "the accumulated wisdom of culture," evident perhaps no place as clearly as in my ardent embrace of pretentiousness as my birthright as an American citizen, third generation, ambivalently and only partially enfranchised—because queer—eternally implacably diasporan inhabitant in what my immigrant ancestors called Di Goldene Medine: land where even Jews get to bake lasagna—pork fennel sausage a weighty cultural and theological decision of course, and beef replaced by roasted eggplant if you're keeping milckedik and fleyshedik separate. Which, once they dismantle the FDA, kosher vegetarian might be the only way to go.

Recognizing the accumulated wisdom of culture as a repressive ideological apparatus is easy to do—read one of Bill Bennett's books, if you really hate yourself—but a radical rejection of aforesaid culture is more difficult. Imbedded in this culture is a history tending, though not deterministically, not without struggle, towards some plausible, workable, realizable version of radical, pluralist democracy. In American history and culture there is a liberal individualism which a radical anti-individualist progressivism relentlessly critiques and reshapes; a nonviolent, pragmatic revolutionary politics predicated on a collectivity of individuals reinventing themselves into something new; a social and economic justice emerging, fitfully; and for all our arrant and arid Puritanism, a sensuality and a socialism of the skin. In American millenarianism I see the anticipation of the break that will finally come when, even in this hard-hearted, bloody, and mistrustful land, necessity finally submits, to borrow from Akhmatova, and steps pensively aside.

I see the contradictory motions of this politics in Melville; it's why he turns me on. Let me read you two passages from his novel *White-Jacket*. These follow close upon one another in the book: "Depravity in the oppressed is no apology for the oppressor; but rather an additional stigma to him, as being, in a larger degree, the effect, and not the cause and justification of oppression."

This is formidable wisdom, arrived at in 1853; no one in Washington today seems capable of it. But only a few pages later Melville delivers himself of this vatic, imperial pronouncement: "We Americans are the peculiar, chosen people—the Israel of our time—God has given us, for a future inheritance, the broad domains of the political pagans....The rest of the nations must soon be in our rear....With ourselves, almost for the first time in the history of the earth, national selfishness is unbounded philanthropy; for we cannot do a good to America but we give alms to the world."

Here is something more congenial to the drafters of the Contract With America. Melville at moments such as these reminds us that pretentiousness, again, is an expression of a certain luxuriousness, and hence perhaps of privilege, and it is also an expression of aggressive power, of dominance—in this case, of a hegemonic

Manifest-Destiny-huffing-and-puffing that drowns out the truths and the histories of noncitizens, of which the writer is otherwise remarkably sensible. Both truth, and also the lies State Power tells itself are present in Melville; like Whitman, he contains multitudes. This naked, exposed working-through, this public-arena-wrangling, is the cultural inheritance (more multiracial, multigendered, multipreferenced an inheritance than the Right has ever understood) I cannot bring myself to abandon. Do I, in this reticence, betray myself as, God forbid, a liberal?

Many years ago in the famous AIDS issue of *October*, Leo Bersani, one of the authors of *Arts of Impoverishment*, published a provocatively titled, and provocative essay, "Is the Rectum a Grave?" Now Professor Bersani has published a new book called *Homos*. Let me read you a paragraph found on page 69:

> To move to an entirely different register, Tony Kushner's *Angels in America* has analogous ambitions. For Kushner, to be gay in the 1980s was to be a metaphor not only for Reagan's America but for the entire history of America, a country in which there are "no gods...no ghosts and spirits...no angels...no spiritual past, no racial past, there's only the political." The enormous success of this muddled and pretentious play is a sign, if we need still another one, of how ready and anxious America is to see and hear about gays— provided we reassure America how familiar, how morally sincere, and, particularly in the case of Kushner's work, how innocuously full of significance we can be.

Allow me to pause, before explaining why I am quoting this passage, to state that ten years have passed since that issue of *October* and I still don't know if the rectum is a grave, but I now think I have an answer to the question: Is Leo Bersani an asshole?

Yes, obviously, though not a stupid asshole. A college sophomore should know better than to try to build a case that being gay is, in my plays, a "metaphor" for anything, and hopefully that sophomore would be warned against the literary malpractice of quoting a character in a fiction as though he reliably speaks in the author's voice, especially while ignoring a context as laden with irony, and as significant to the reception of what the character is saying, as is the context in *Angels in America: Millennium Approaches* in which those quoted words are uttered. This nasty attack is uncharacteristic of the tenor of the rest of *Homos*—it's hurtful, of course, it's intended to be, but it's not the "muddled and pretentious" bit that bothers me especially. Muddled and pretentious are I think among the plays' *charms*, and as I said, people with no sense of humor don't like plays like mine; like de Tocqueville, Professor Bersani simply doesn't get it (he is, I might point out, a professor of French). I was more disturbed, and intrigued, by Professor Bersani's consternation over the fact that I offered the straight world representations of gay men who are "morally sincere." I plead guilty.

The reason I've decided to go through this, in addition to being, as I warned you, preternaturally, even *prenatally* thin-skinned, is that *Homos* offers itself as a critique of bourgeois lesbian and gay politics from a profoundly radical, subversive perspective. And as I have already pleaded guilty to assimilationist tendencies in my work, it would be disingenuous, now, to try to cast my plays as radical-as-they-ought-to-be. What's disturbing about *Homos*, and it seems to me disturbingly representative of at least a considerable portion of gay male radical thought, at least as it is expressed in literature, drama, and queer theory, is that the antidote to the gay liberalism of which I am, perhaps, a deeply ambivalent example, is not, apparently, to be found in either socialism, or in more actively seeking and building common cause with other communities of the oppressed, or in the idea of community *period*.

In his penultimate chapter, "The Gay Outlaw," the professor begins with the question "Should the homosexual be a good citizen?" We already know, from the parts of the book we've already gotten through (and it is, I regret to say, a rather marvelous, exciting, infuriating, and important book which raises a number of extremely important questions and formulates the problematics of identity politics elegantly) that Professor Bersani is going to answer this question, "Should the homosexual be a good citizen?" in the negative. He moves immediately from this question to the following statement: "…gay men and lesbians have been strenuously trying to persuade straight society that they can be good parents, good soldiers, good priests." Professor Bersani then confides that he "find[s] none of these options particularly stimulating…" The equation of good parenting with good soldiering is telling, as is the use of the word "stimulating." Moral sincerity is clearly not on his agenda. It is only a few pages later that we find Professor Bersani deep in an encomium to Jean Genêt, specifically stimulated by Genêt's "revolutionary strength": "Both [Genêt's] abhorrent glorification of Nazism [in *Funeral Rites*] and his in some ways equally abhorrent failure to take that glorification seriously express his fundamental project of declining to participate in any sociality at all…. *Funeral Rites* seeks to detach evil from its oppositional relation to good…. It would replace the rich social discursiveness of good-and-evil with what might be called the empty value of solitude."

In his preface, Professor Bersani has promised us a replacement for the "micropolitics of participatory democracy and social justice," which are to him "political ambitions as stirring as those reflected on the bumper stickers to 'think globally' and 'act locally.' " Instead of the *unstimulating* pursuit of democracy and social justice, Professor Bersani offers us this: "the most politically disruptive aspect of the homoness I will be exploring in gay desire is a redefinition of sociality so radical that it may appear to require a provisional withdrawal from relationality itself."

If you are confused, as I was, as to how a "provisional withdrawal from relationality," or as he later calls it, an "anti-communal mode of connectedness" can lead to effective oppositional politics, well, it doesn't. He continues, "This is not a political program. [The characters in *Funeral Rites*] are positioned for a reinventing of the social without any indication about how such a reinvention might proceed historically or what face it might have." This rejection is important, apparently, for "without such a rejection [of relationality], social revolt is doomed to repeat the oppressive conditions that provoked the revolt." Collective or communally based political engagement, in other words, is not simply insufficiently titillating, it is ultimately doomed, as Foucaultian complexities tuck opposition and resistance back within the inescapable context of those social practices against which resistance was conceived and initiated.

Homos, like the postmodernist texts it is heavily indebted to, is infinitely richer and more valuable than I perhaps understand and certainly more than I have time to explore. But there is something to be gleaned from the fact that the book begins as a critique of a political movement, begins by making queer theory's as-yet-to-be-redeemed promise of articulating notions of "the political productivity of the sexual," and concludes as a politically defeated, or at least politically *muddled*, celebration of books. If we were permitted to categorize Professor Bersani's politics as politics, we might venture ego-anarchism; as a psychological category (recognizing, of course, that such categories merely serve policing functions), sociopathy or autism comes to mind. Finally, though, this is a vision which, it seems to me, imprisons political struggle inside the pages of literature, from whence it does not emerge.

Beginning with a very important question for politically active homosexuals, namely "What is our *unique* contribution to progress to be?"; seeking to interrogate the life of desire as it flows through the Polity, and the subversive potential desire it was once presumed to possess; recoiling from a politics of politeness that is willing to pathologize any and all desire that refuses to ape heterosexual norms, in exchange for lethal, powerless existence as recipients of *tolerance*—Professor Bersani arrives at a position in which, I would imagine, one would only avoid despair if one didn't care very much about the world to begin with.

Against the library-stillness of Professor Bersani's revolutionary defeatism ("This is Genêt's ingenious solution to the problem of revolutionary beginnings condemned to repeat old orders: he dies..."); against this ascertainably Left but not particularly invigorating implosional nonresponse to the present crisis, we can balance the spectacle, from the assimilationist camp, of one prominent gay citizen recently visiting a large Catholic midwestern campus, ostensibly for the purpose of critiquing the Church's homophobia, and in the process complimenting Joseph Cardinal Ratzinger for his "usual intellectual acerbity and indeed intellectual honesty," while the *New York Times* reporter covering the speech enthuses over the speaker's politeness, in the process equating ACT UP's anger with Operation Rescue's. Or another prominent gay citizen, one I admire a lot and who really should know better, offering the readers of the *New York Times*' Op-Ed page his opinion that ACT UP and GMHC share "some of the blame" for the fact that far too many of us have stopped practicing safe sex. ACT UP bashing, in fact, seems near-epidemic these days. Let's hope we aren't witnessing in such instances the beginnings of an old bad propensity for progressive people, when confronted with triumphant political evil, to take careful aim and shoot themselves in the feet.

We posit against these any politics, any theory, that galvanizes action, that produces common cause, that is not self-defeating; perhaps, even, half-facetiously, half-seriously, a politics of literary pretentiousness, in which a book, or a play, muddled though it may be, is willing to sacrifice form and coherence in a determined effort to escape the library and become literature no longer—to become, instead, life. That this effort is also doomed, because writing will always remain writing, doesn't mean that the ultimate struggle is doomed or that writing has no contribution to make to a practical politics, to a ready response to the current unbelievable onslaught. The yearning displayed in pretentiousness may have its political uses, for one of the greatest dangers in times of reactionary backlash is that the borders of utopia appear to have been closed. When even bodily necessities are denied us we can too easily surrender the necessity of aspirations, dreams, hope—the future. Isn't any art that seeks to inspire or provoke or excite yearning likely to be, in some fashion, pretentious? And for a *sexual* politics, as our politics must necessarily be, is pretentiousness and its concomitant stirrings of no interest to the excesses of desire?

A politics that seeks to dismantle normalizing categories of gender; that seeks to retrieve a history from a violently enforced forgetting; a politics that seeks enfranchisement not only for new kinds of citizens, but for Sexuality itself, that seeks to introduce fucking and sucking, licking and smelling, kink, sleaze, clits and dicks and tits and assholes and the games people play with them, into the previously chaste Temple of Democracy; and even more daring still, a politics that seeks a synthesis between desire and transformation, that seeks some union between the deepest recesses and cavities of the human heart and body and soul, and the sacrifices and responsibilities building communities and movement, building progress and power entails: This politics needs its writers, and its writers had better be capable of extravagance, had better not be tame.

Oh well, who knows, really? Talk about pretentiousness!

I have to end, I have to end, last year you couldn't get me here and now you can't get me to shut up. The offer for lasagna still stands. Last year, a few weeks after OutWrite, I was stopped on lower Broadway by two adorable men who demanded that I take them home and feed them lasagna. I, sexually flusterable as always in the face of a challenge or opportunity, let them slip away, but the encounter has left pasta charged with scintillations of the erotic. You should all come over, I will cook for you all. Except now I'm vegetarian. *Oh I am so glad this is over!* If I've made a fool of myself, I have at least made of myself the kind of fool I want to be: That is the virtue and power of pretentiousness.

I'll wrap up with Blake, that most unpityingly pretentious or rather *grandiose* of poets—because it can't really be called pretentious if it was dictated to you by angels: "I pretend not to Holiness; yet I pretend to love....Therefore dear reader, *forgive* what you do not approve, & *love* me for the energetic exertion of my talent."

I promise you I will love you all for the energetic exertion of yours.

See you in Washington. See you on the Internet. See you on the streets.

Thank you.

What We Write About
When We Write About Porn
CHRISTOPHER J. HOGAN

I write reviews of gay porn videos. The guidelines from my editor
are simple. I am to write reviews of approximately a dozen videos
each month. Each review begins with a "slug" that starts with the
title; credits the studio, director, and any other significant members
of the production team; lists the cast; and gives the running time
and information for ordering the video. The body of the review that
comes after the slug is to be no longer than two hundred and fifty
words. That's it. After that, what I write and how I write it is pretty
much up to me.

This is the kind of freedom most writers crave. I, on the other
hand, would like more of a formula to follow. I read other gay
porn reviews and re-read my own in search of what the structure
and content of writing within this genre should be. I learned that
porn reviewers—like all critics—actually write about much more
than the tapes we review. The pieces may vary in length from one
hundred and fifty words to several pages, but all draw upon the same
eclectic list of subjects.

This is what we write about when we write about porn:

Sex

Well, duh.

One would think it would be impossible to write about pornography without describing sex. Oddly enough, I often finish a review, re-read it, and discover that I have mentioned no specific sexual acts. I have read books and essays that engage in the discourse on the politics and meaning of pornography where the writers get away without explicitly describing what is depicted in it. My job is not necessarily to elaborate on the theory of pornography; it is definitely to evaluate the actualization. When I have written a sexless review, I go back and insert at least one reference to the sex in the video. We reviewers must say what happens. It is the one thing our readers expect of us. They want videos that will turn them on and look to us to find them.

Reviews of pornography become pornography themselves. It may be the only medium in which the review becomes part of the genre of the product reviewed. A restaurant review never becomes a restaurant, and no play review has ever—to my knowledge—been adapted for the stage. The longer porn reviews (which generally appear in glossy magazines with sexually explicit stills from the videos) give detailed play-by-play accounts of the sex scenes. If one were to lift selected paragraphs out of these reviews, it would be nearly impossible to distinguish them from sections of "erotic fiction." We reviewers then are tied to the producers, writers, and directors of adult videos by the common thread of being pornographers.

The relationship between the artist and reviewer is inevitably symbiotic. The reviewer depends upon the artist to create work to be reviewed, and the artist depends on the reviewer to generate a market for the work. Mainstream film reviews are regularly quoted in movie advertisements. Advertisements for blue movies and other sex industry services (such as phone-sex lines) are a major source of income for most gay magazines, especially those that run reviews of pornography. This symbiosis is heightened by both the work and the review needed to turn the consumer on.

How then can a reviewer honestly describe a film in which the sex is mediocre and still keep the review erotic? Answer: By fudging it. For example, the fact that penises are often only semi-erect or even flaccid during sex is simply skipped over. Performers a reviewer finds attractive will be described in great detail while other, less appealing, actors are mentioned in passing. This isn't to say that all porn reviews are a tissue of lies used to market the product. Most critics will be honest about videos that don't meet their standards. Some writers are downright vicious. The fact is that most porn videos contain quite a bit of mechanical sex in which the actors seem to have only a passing interest. If the video is halfway decent, the general practice is to accentuate the positive.

The Limitations of Language

Pornography is not sex. It may depict sex graphically. It may arouse sexual feelings. It may even aid in masturbatory, couple, or group sex. In the end, however, it remains inanimate and thus not a sexual act.

Pornographic videos simulate sex by being only one step away. They display, in this case, men having sex. The cum shot is critical as it proves that these men on some levels were not acting, but were filmed having a genuine sexual experience. It is so central to the industry that it is referred to as "the money shot." Reviews of porn videos are, then, two steps removed. They attempt to simulate the videos which simulate sex by depicting with words the real sex these men had. Just as the cum shot is emphasized in videos, it is dwelt upon in reviews. Inordinate amounts of column space are spent on who shoots, when they shoot, how much they shoot, and how far they shoot. Using written language, reviewers must try relate the physical intensity of experiences they have only seen in two dimensions.

Words are fragile vessels in which to transport sexual experience. Not only do they rarely convey the fullness of the physical feelings, but there quite simply aren't enough of them to last for several pages of writing intensely about sex. Clinical terms are generally avoided in pornography because they are so clinical. Who's going to rush out and rent a video that features lots of "oral-anal contact" or "erotolalia"? Once those are eliminated, there are very few common terms left. For example, to say that two men have anal sex, one could write that they "fuck," "screw," or, as the hopelessly romantic might say, "make love." One must get dangerously creative after that, and that's not easy. Few people can use terms like "baton of joy" or "poop chute" and sound reasonably intelligent. I certainly cannot.

Aristotle's "Poetics"

Just as the makers of porn movies seem to feel compelled to give their works dramatic form, we reviewers cannot help but commenting on their efforts. By and large, the consumer doesn't give a fuck about anything except the fucking. Still, the self-esteem of everyone in the industry is wrapped up in maintaining the illusion that these skin flicks have plots, characters, themes, and everything else dramatic narrative entails.

Aristotle wrote "On the Art of Poetry," also called the "Poetics," sometime in the fourth century B.C.E. Ever since, the text has essentially defined the terms of dramatic criticism. Anyone wishing to analyze drama must either use Aristotle's work or consciously reject it. Those who reject it tend to be those brainy "lit. crit." types who write impenetrable articles for arcane academic journals. Porn reviewers, on the other hand, stick with what's been around for over two thousand years. It would be a waste of time to deconstruct "character" before discussing Hunter Scott's performance in *The Big Score*.

It is either absurdly ironic or supremely appropriate that Aristotle's treatise is now applied to what surrounds the screwing in videos such as *Hip Hop Hunks* or *Born to Please*. Read almost any porn review, and you'll find that at least one of Aristotle's six elements of tragedy (spectacle, character, plot, diction, song, and thought) is mentioned. Aristotle's exact terms aren't always used. A reviewer may, for example, refer to the "special effects" rather than the "spectacle" or "dialogue" instead of "diction." Nonetheless, the reviewer is taking an Aristotelian approach. When porn film makers take the bold step of showing a bunch of sex without pretense of dramatic form, the reviewers invariably comment on the fact that there are no characters and no plot. We are left with "song." My Ivy League education in dramatic theory really pays off when I'm critiquing the soundtrack of Bijou Studios' *Stop in the Name of Sex*.

Aristotle's concepts of "terror and pity" as essential elements of tragedy are also critical to pornography. "Terror" as Aristotle uses it might more accurately be called "recognition" today. It is the intangible quality of a story, play, or film that allows the audience to see some part of themselves in the characters and, therefore, to identify with them. In tragedy, this evokes "terror" or fear because if we are like the characters, we too could meet their tragic fate. In pornography, it should cause arousal by leading the audience to believe that we are enough like the characters, that we could meet their sexual fate. "Pity" is an even deeper projection of the audience into the story. Because we recognize ourselves in the characters, we may empathize or at least sympathize with them. We experience their condition on some level. Again, this is painful in tragedy and erotic in pornography. When a reviewer says something is "hot" or a "turn on," the video must have created a sort of sexual "terror and pity" to allow that visceral connection.

Film Making

The difference between a good porno movie and a bad one is rarely the actors, the script, or the setting. It usually comes down to the technical proficiency of the people behind the cameras. The reader may think a reviewer pretentious to discuss camera work, lighting, or sound quality. Watch a few badly filmed, poorly lit videos in which the performers are inaudible but the ambient sound comes through loud and clear, and you'll realize just how critical the craft of film making is to the porn producer.

Editing is by far the most important of the production values. A sex scene in a porn film should be structured to correspond with whacking off. The action should set a nice pace for the viewer's own rhythm. Ideally, the performers come at about the same time as the viewer. If they shoot too soon, the viewer must go through the whole thing again with another scene. If they last too long, the viewer might feel he suffers from premature ejaculation. Good editing also engages us in the sexual fantasy by clearly showing who is doing what to whom. Too often videos are cut so that we see several minutes of footage in which it is impossible to discern what is going on. This lack of basic craft can be devastating to a film. It precludes the viewer recognition and projection (see "terror and "pity" above) necessary for successful pornography.

Porn Stars & Movie Stars

Siskel and Ebert gush about the latest performances of stars like Meryl Streep and Denzel Washington. Porn reviewers content ourselves by extolling the qualities of Ryan Idol and Cody Foster. Porn stars inhabit a smaller galaxy than their big screen counterparts, but they are stars just the same. Their fans are fewer in number but at least as intensely dedicated, nor are reviewers immune from becoming enthralled by a particular artist. Porn reviewers more readily admit their prejudices than mainstream critics do. It is expected that we will figuratively drool over some actors in our reviews implying that we may have done so literally as we watched them perform. Our consumers want to know the drool level of a video.

Reviewers bring the parallel worlds of "real" movie stars and porn stars closer together. Movie stars set our culture's standards for acting, image, and beauty; therefore, they are often used to describe the performances and looks of the men in adult films. A ruggedly handsome actor might be compared to a young Paul Newman in *Cat on a Hot Tin Roof*, and an actor who comes off as fiercely aggressive may inspire mention of Elizabeth Taylor in that film. The porn studios encourage these comparisons with the *noms de lube* they give their boys. The recent proliferation of porn actors with the last name "Baldwin" is no mistake.

Hollywood films, to some extent, construct the mainstream culture's definitions of "masculinity." Gay pornography, like the rest of gay culture, expresses deep ambivalence about the definitions Hollywood puts forward. On one hand, it embraces them. Porn uses Hollywood's images and language to signify characters as essentially masculine. The easiest use to see is adaptation of mainstream movie titles to create porn video titles like *Hidden Instincts*, *An Officer and His Gentleman*, and *Big Guns*. Sometimes, things are a little more subtly done, and we simply see a Hollywood motif in an adult film. Jungle warriors, for example, have been staples of gay porn since the first appearance of *Rambo*. Gay porn does not, however, take Hollywood definitions of masculinity at face value. Heterosexuality is integral to masculinity in mainstream culture. Queer pornography must subvert this conception to present homosexual fantasies. *Stryker Force* follows two groups of Ramboesque men who take time out of their perilous adventures to screw each other. By changing just this one element of masculinity, porn completely redefines it to include its audience.

Gay Men & Sexuality

Gay porn creates a world of men. Women are so rare in this world that they might as well be extinct. Those of us who review "mainstream" gay porn (videos that depict only man-to-man sex) must ask ourselves how the film makers define and represent "gay men." What are the messages they send about masculinity and sexuality?

There has been a major shift in gay porn over the past fifteen or twenty years. Simply put, there is now more of a presumption that the characters are openly gay. Videos are set in the context of the gay subculture, and the characters navigate through that rather than the surrounding straight world. Plot lines including "straight" men engaging in gay sex are rarer and rarer. Now, we even see videos that follow the agony and the ecstasy of gay couples. We now see stories in which a gay man may trick outside his primary relationship, hire a hustler to act a third for his lover and him, or be a sex industry worker himself and still be committed to one partner. Some videos have even forced us to examine if monogamy can be sexy. In addition, more performers publicly define themselves as gay. In both interviews and videos in which the actors "play" themselves, we are seeing greater numbers of men not only embracing but also celebrating their homosexuality.

In a genre that once glorified mainly the butch, the fag has emerged as a powerful icon. For reviewers, this means we are not so rigidly confined in describing men. Words like "beautiful," "cute," and "lovely" are no longer applied only to chicken in videos. Leather boys can be "adorable" and waify, young boys can be "handsome." Similarly, we are able to explore the erotic potential of a wider variety of gay sexuality as the film makers do. When discussing videos like *Lovers, Tricks, and One Night Stands*, we can examine whether it's certain physical acts gay men perform or relationships between men that turn us on.

A growing genre of queer porn includes not only women with

bisexual men but also transgendered people. These videos further challenge our notions of gender and sexuality. They are still generally considered either separate from or marginal to gay video, but this seems to be shifting. The 1995 *Adam Gay Video Directory* includes Lana Luster (a.k.a. Vince Harrington) and Kelly Michaels (who plays the title role in *Mr. Madonna*) in its performers index. Reviewers who are often charged with the task of categorizing videos (as "all-male," "bi," "fetish," etc.) face a challenge with the so-called "new wave" of gay pornography. Is sex between a man and a pre-operative male-to-female transsexual gay, bisexual, or what? Can homosexual men view anyone with a penis as a potential sex partner? These are the questions those of us who write about porn will have to answer more and more.

Power & Roles

How gay porn defines and represents sexual roles has also shifted. Traditionally, there has been a division between the butch top who is insertive in anal intercourse and the either young or effeminate bottom who is receptive. Recently, these roles have become more fluid. We now see a number of beefy "manly" men like Rip Stone or Tom Katt getting fucked and enjoying it on video. We also have a proliferation of both young and "queeny" tops who are very aggressive.

Much of this change can be attributed to the increase in homogeneous couplings that are represented. When two muscle boys get together, at least one of them has to be a bottom. More importantly, the receptive partner is no longer portrayed as weak or passive. He can now be strong. Likewise, the current spate of European videos, most notably those by director George Duroy that feature only nubile young men, requires that some of them be tops. Boys, therefore, stop being the sexual possessions of older men who initiate them by fucking them. They are more in control of their own sexuality whether they choose to be tops or bottoms. Less frequently, but more frequently than in the past, we see couples in which there seems to be a traditional top/bottom dynamic that gets switched, completely blurring the connection between persona and sexual role.

Again, this all allows porn reviewers to discuss a greater range of sexual possibilities. We can allow tough daddies to fantasize about getting fucked by some Czech boy, and flaming pansies to get off on dreams of screwing rough trade. The shift of roles in pornography has also allowed us to exalt the erotic power of the bottom. Joey Stefano was one of the biggest stars in gay porn until his death. He reached a higher level of recognition and adoration than any other bottom has; however, with the rising recognition of bottoms in both pornography and what is written about pornography, there are sure to be many more bottom divas.

Camp

Where fags and bottoms have risen in prominence, can camp be far behind? Camp, broadly defined, is a humorously ironic commentary on culture. Since we are in the United States, Land of Dichotomies, we can say that there are two kinds of camp. First, there is that which was not intended to be campy but is read as such by at least certain audiences. *Whatever Happened to Baby Jane?* and Karen Black's early works fall into this category. The second category of camp includes those things that are intended to be campy by their producers. Examples of this would be drag queens and Bette Midler's early work. Many people believe that gay porn has always been camp. Recently, however, some video makers moved from the first kind of camp to the second.

Gay porn reviewers can also be roughly divided into two categories, determined by how they handle the camp value of their subjects. There are many reviewers who still take adult videos as seriously as the producers once took them. They tend to focus on what sexual acts are performed, the cum shots, and how hot it all is. A growing number of reviewers appreciate the lighter side of pornography. Sometimes, they write in a traditionally dishy style. Other times, they are highly ironic. These writers have always been around, but in the past they were marginalized. Now, however, they are gaining strength in the industry because they are working with other people in the porn media rather than against them. With screenwriters and directors like Chi Chi LaRue (who sometimes appears in drag playing "non-sexual" roles in porn videos) making meta-porn films that poke fun at the industry, there is more freedom to treat the videos as fun little *divertissements* rather than hard-core turn-ons. Both the film makers and the reviewers with this new camp sensibility still take sex and sexuality seriously. They have simply reframed the context using a lighter outlook.

This is a chicken/egg situation. Which came first? Intentionally campy porn or a more ironic and camp approach to viewing porn? It's nearly impossible to say. The porn video industry is highly responsive to the market. The films are made and distributed so quickly that they can easily cater to their audience. As soon as it became evident that a large enough number of people enjoyed skin flicks that had fun with themselves, more and more of those videos were made. In turn, porn helps establish what gay male culture defines as erotic. If humor and a somewhat playful approach to sex are put into porn, humor and playfulness will, for some people at least, become sexy, and if people find it sexy, it will show up more often in pornography.

Fashion Trends

Because gay porn is so market sensitive and because it is made by and for fags, it is easily blown by the winds of fashion. Hollywood movies also continually define, then react to trends, but because porn videos are made much more quickly than big-budget films, they do so much more quickly. Consumers and reviewers of porn are both the beneficiaries and the victims of this. When something new is done in a video, the very novelty of it can be a turn-on. The positive feedback producers get for this novelty almost instantly creates a glut on the market. For example, when Calvin Klein underwear first appeared in videos, reviewers raved and the fag public couldn't get enough. Now you can't swing a cat in a dirty video store without hitting a box with a picture of a boy or boys in fashion briefs. Reviewers are bemoaning the lack of creativity in the industry for putting all the actors in tighty-whiteys. We have no one to blame but ourselves.

Since videos are being set more firmly in the context of the gay subculture, the impact of fashion trends is being felt more strongly than ever. The broader gay media currently tend to cast the gay community as one that shares a "lifestyle" defined by material possessions. The largest glossy magazines targeted at gay men all include fashion sections. In this market, porn producers must use gay clothing, hair, and decorating trends to indicate that characters are gay. Thus, pornography promotes gay commercialism while it remains controlled by market forces.

Politics

Politics are in style right now, or so it seems. To respond to the times, gay porn directors have been putting more political themes into their work. The military has, of course, always been a staple of pornography. Now, instead of contenting themselves with showing guys fucking in the barracks, screenwriters and directors feel they must address the injustice of the ban on homosexuals serving in the armed forces. It is, however, difficult for the characters to discuss the nuances of this complex issue in the videos because they have dicks in their mouths half the time; therefore, the analysis of this national policy goes something like, "Gay boys are regular guys who can be good soldiers that just happen to like taking it up the butt, and it's not fair we can't be in the army."

We must ask ourselves about the use of porn as a forum for

political issues. Do we really want people active in a movement for social justice whose philosophy was formed by watching *Secret Sex II: The Sex Radicals* and reading *Manshots*? Given the state of the gay movement, maybe we do. While the analysis pornography offers may be simplistic, it is, in some ways, more radical than that any other mass-produced gay medium puts forward. During the national debacle that was the debate over whether homosexuals should be allowed to serve in the military, gay "leaders" refused to discuss the sex lives of queers in arms. Some even said that gay men and lesbians could and should remain celibate during tours of duty. Pornography, on the other hand, contended that someone could screw an entire brigade and still serve admirably. Rather than denying sex, porn put it at the center of the issue.

When writing about a political porn video, a reviewer has two options. The first is to avoid sounding as shallow as the video and not mention the political overtones. The second is to try to seriously analyze the issues raised. The former is the easier option, but one runs the risk of sounding ill-informed and apathetic taking it. The latter is much more difficult. There is the very real danger of sounding just plain silly discussing the military-industrial complex and *Honorable Discharge*, especially in a two-and-fifty-word review. It's really much safer to comment on the double meaning of the title. The reviewer can effectively circumvent this dilemma by taking the same approach as the videos. By simply putting forth pro-sex positions, as simple as they may be, the reviewer adds to political debates in a way that is both appropriate and credible.

AIDS & Safe Sex

While politics may (or may not) be just a passing trend in porn, AIDS has become a permanent fixture. It is a silent but powerful presence. After the FBI warning, gay videos scroll a message reinforcing the importance of safe sex. Producer/director Sam Abdul has taken this one step further by starting each of his films with a porn star talking as himself and urging viewers to practice safer sex. That's as far as the explicit mention of AIDS goes. Still, it permeates every video.

In the mid 1980s, men were sometimes thrown off porn sets for refusing to have anal sex without a condom. Ten years later, condoms are *de rigueur* in gay porn. (Unfortunately, straight porn has still not caught up to the times with safer sex.) Usually these condoms appear as if by magic. In one shot we see a naked penis about to breach an anus. After the plunge, there is a rubber on the dick. The intention is to keep the fantasy progressing undisrupted; however, this sudden change is quite jarring and really draws attention to the condom. Since pornography presents sexual fantasies, we can suspend our disbelief about any number of unrealistic elements. The magical appearance of condoms has become one of those things for many viewers. Scenes in which we see the condom being put on are popping up here and there. Usually, it's done rapidly and is purely functional.

On rare occasion, the donning of a rubber is vaguely eroticized, but the condom as turn-on may be a future trend in gay porn. In the video *Do Me Dirty*, there is a scene in which a top pulls out of the bottom, rips off his condom, drops it on the bottom's back, and proceeds to shoot his load on his partner. The used condom remained in the shot—right on the guy getting sprayed with cum— until nearly the end of the scene. The image was so unique in porn that it was startling. For a moment this porn film dropped out of the realm of pure fantasy and looked like actual sex in the age of AIDS. Interestingly, this image was clearly unintended. The actor was about to come, and getting that shot is essential. Where the condom ended up was a fluke; however, the editor later chose to keep that image in the video. If this kind of image creates more recognition and projection for the viewers without detracting from the fantasy, we may begin to see used condoms more often.

Beyond safer sex, we see the subtle effects of AIDS throughout pornography. It can hardly be a coincidence that the depictions of gay sexuality, definitions of roles, camp value, and political overtones of the medium all changed from the mid-eighties to today. Certainly, this is partially attributable to the natural evolution of any form of expression. The timing also meshes with the boom in the home video market. Films were simply made much differently when they were intended to be shown in movie theaters. It could be argued, however, that evolution and change of venue simply meant that porn had to change and that AIDS shaped how it changed.

In a time when getting butt-fucked was being equated to death, is it any surprise that gay men needed to celebrate this act? I believe the connection was largely unconscious, and perhaps that made it even more compelling; therefore, we witnessed the ascendancy of the bottom. The AIDS crisis, meaning not the disease itself but the government and health industry's reactions to it, demonized fags and made gay rights a more highly visible national issue than it has ever been for a sustained period of time. With nowhere else to go, gay men turned to porn not only for their jollies but also for validation of their lifestyles. Videos responded by exalting both gay sex and the men who have it. Finally, AIDS has devastated the collective psyche of the gay community. Pornography may well be the most escapist of all mediums, and fags have needed to escape to someplace fun. A little camp humor in a video will not make AIDS disappear, but it may ease the pain of it for a little while.

These same changes can be seen in the media that surrounds the pornographic film industry. Since critics along with AIDS activists led and won the battle to have condoms used in videos, AIDS is rarely explicitly discussed in their writing. It has become simply the context in which everything is written.

Each Other

In some ways, porn videos are the fairy tales of gay culture. The characters in both are simultaneously larger than life and two dimensional. Often they are not characters at all but archetypes, the evil stepmother, the horny hitchhiker, the charming prince, the leather top, etc. Both fairy tales and pornography are set in worlds like our own, but clearer and more magical. Finally, they both satisfy us by providing the expected yet desired endings, everyone is happy ever after and everyone gets laid. While many people think of fairy tales as simplistic, moralizing stories for children, they are incredibly complex. A body of scholarship has grown out of the works of Max Lüthi and Bruno Bettelheim that examines the deeper meaning of folk and fairy tales. These stories probe the human psyche and shed light on our basic nature. They also contain sharp criticism of social and economic institutions. Many carry subversive messages and flourished without censorship because they were oral tales told by women. They were also protected by the pretense of being removed from reality and by the fact that all of their deeper meaning was imbedded into them in such a way that no one was fully aware of it.

Pornography has become the safest forum in which gay men can examine their culture. Like fairy tales, it is largely ignored by the larger power structure. The great pornography debates in feminist, liberal, and conservative circles have focused almost entirely on straight porn, including the gay media only as a side-bar. Within the gay community, men who avoid overt political or cultural discussions are engaged in these issues through porn. Screenwriters and directors will create images of gay archetypes, sex, lifestyles, and interactions. Consumers respond either positively by buying or renting certain videos or negatively by avoiding them. In trying to determine what gay men want to see, pornographers are commenting on what they think gay men are. The images, however, are limited to what the consumers will readily accept.

Market forces therefore both inform and restrict any cultural commentary in pornography.

The dynamics of the porn market have, then, become an intricate underground discussion of what gay men think of each other. The reviewer mediates this discussion. Part advocate for the consumer and part promoter for the producer, we analyze the messages sent both ways. Sometimes we see deep cynicism, and other times great affection. In the end, the entire exchange is about developing a vision of a sexual utopia for gay men—our happily ever after. There will never be an end to this. No singular fag nirvana will emerge as a communal desire, nor should one. It is the process that matters. Through it, we learn about each other's fantasies and fears.

Ourselves

All critics reveal certain biases and predilections in their work. Doing so is the very essence of reviewing any medium. Writing reviews of pornography inevitably exposes something about the writer's sexuality. I shun the first-singular in my reviews, preferring to operate under the delusion that if I don't say "I," "me," or "my," I will not reveal myself. I neither believe in nor want to perpetuate the myth of the dispassionate critic. I simply worry about showing too much of myself to readers who are largely strangers to me. In reality, I know that even if I weren't evaluating pornography but simply describing it, I would be opening myself up to the reader. What I noticed and chose to relate would be as subjective as how I felt about it.

The job of the reviewer is an exercise in egomania. One must assume that one's taste is representative of all consumers. The ego and, since we're talking about pornography, the id of the writer can hardly be hidden. While "Is this a turn-on?" and "Does this turn me on?" are vastly different questions, to the reviewer they become essentially the same. No matter what other sexual tastes we have, all porn reviewers are exhibitionists to some degree. A positive review undeniably implies that watching the video gave the reviewer an erection. Porn reviewers' erections or supposed erections are, therefore, publicly displayed. If nothing else, at least we have that in common with the porn stars.

Five Houses of Gay Fiction

REED WOODHOUSE

The composer Virgil Thomson once said that when he was working on a new piece he kept at it until (as he put it) the piece "composed itself the same way" three days in a row. Several years ago, my friend Michael Schwartz and I began teaching a course at the Cambridge Center for Adult Education called "Gay Male Fiction"—literature (as we put it) "by, for, and about gay men." Our course has confirmed Thomson's experience, for it has now composed itself in basically the same way three times. Each time, we have come back to the same core of texts, around which we then situate certain others. This core I am calling "ghetto literature"; its periphery I am dividing into various categories: closet, proto-ghetto, assimilative, and "queer."

When we first conceived this course, we were faced in the most practical sense with the question of a "canon." Which books *had* to go on the syllabus? Which would be fun to teach if we had time? Which were irrelevant or bad? Further questions occurred to us:

What is the essence of a "gay" fiction? Are the gayest books necessarily the best books? Or does the book's "gay-density," so to speak, have nothing at all to do with its literary value? What follows is my own attempt to justify the "canon" we have repeatedly composed, and in so doing to make a rough-and-ready taxonomy of modern gay male fiction.

It is not, I hope, a restrictive, let alone a prescriptive, taxonomy, though I am aware of having left out a great deal. I am, for instance, deliberately confining myself to American gay male fiction of the post-World War II period. I have done this mainly because I think it is almost impossible to speak of openly gay fiction—books "by, for, and about gay men"—before this period. There are exceptions, of course: Parker Tyler's *The Young and Evil*, for instance. But most books claimed for gay literature from earlier periods (e.g., Van Vechten's *The Blind Bow-Boy*) are so severely coded as to require sophisticated literary cryptography: they are not the focus of this essay. For the same reason, I do not attempt to bring out the homosexual meanings of Melville, James, or Proust: a task which literary historians like David Bergman, Eve Sedgwick, and Robert Martin have undertaken. The tradition I am invoking is far more recent and far less grand. Whether its works will be seen by future readers as "great" remains to be seen. They are, nonetheless, *our* books in a way that *Billy Budd* and *À la recherche du temps perdu* are not; and as such they attempt a synthesis of homosexuality into literature that earlier writers, no matter how great, simply could not have imagined.

I believe that there is a distinguishable body of first-rate work "by, for, and about gay men," a literature I am calling "ghetto" or "proto-ghetto" fiction. I further believe that this fiction ought to be considered the trunk, not a mere branch, of our particular literary tree. By "ghetto" fiction, I do not mean only the books whose authors lived in the gay ghettos of San Francisco, Los Angeles, or New York; nor those whose characters did. In a sense, it would be more accurate to say they are books whose *readers* did indeed live there, but that even that residence need not have been a literal one. The more important reason this is "ghetto" fiction is that it occupies a place in literature analogous to the place occupied in the city by the gay ghetto; a place where homosexuality is both taken for granted (and thus invisible) and at the same time easily identifiable (and thus highly visible): a sort of parallel city, in fact. "Ghetto literature," then, is in one sense literature "by, for, and about gay men." In another, wider sense, it is literature that resembles the ghetto by extolling the virtues of separateness and pride, by insisting on a gay identity, and by existing for itself alone, not for the straight world.

These are not books, in other words, whose characters "just happen to be gay"; any more than the ghetto can be defined as a place whose residents "just happen to be gay." Its characters (whether truly or mistakenly, comically or disastrously) see their sexuality as a key to their lives. These books, like the gay ghetto itself, represent a gay world at its furthest point of self-definition, and are an expression of homosexuality at its most concentrated: that is, as nearly as possible without normative reference to the straight world. The proto-ghetto books differ from ghetto books mainly by lacking a gay community, and sometimes even the *name* "gay" for who and what the characters are. They nevertheless belong with ghetto literature, rather than with either closeted or assimilative fiction, sharing with ghetto fiction an astonishing, sometimes arrogant disregard for the surrounding straight world. Some of the works I would put in the ghetto or proto-ghetto category are: Tennessee Williams' early and amazingly unabashed short stories ("Hard Candy," "Desire and the Black Masseur," "Two on a Party" and others); Christopher Isherwood's masterpiece, *A Single Man*; James Purdy's novels of rapturous violence, *Eustace Chisolm and the Works* and *Narrow Rooms*; Andrew Holleran's *Dancer from the Dance*; Ethan Mordden's three volumes of short stories on gay life in Manhattan in the late 70s and 80s; and, most recent and one of the best, the English author Neil Bartlett's beautiful *Ready to Catch Him Should He Fall.*

Ghetto literature was preceded by, and in some ways formed against, something we might call "closet" literature: fiction, that is, which saw homosexuality as something defining indeed, but horrifyingly so. One wants to say that this is literature so remote from an ordinary modern gay man's experience that it is now irrelevant. But such a judgment would not be quite true, for in a sense the closet can never die. So long as homosexuality continues to be defined (as, in an obvious sense, it must) as a *sexual* identity, books about it will be quintessentially sexual and thus quintessentially threatening. That is the source of closet literature's truth and power. ("Queer" theorists and artists insert their skewer precisely here: the closet *can* die, in their view, if sexual identity—being "gay" or "straight"—is no longer considered defining or constitutive. Hence their eager embrace of bisexuality as theory and practice; and their extension of "queerness" to forms of identity that are non-sexual.) James Baldwin's *Giovanni's Room*, the closet novel *par excellence*, is a reminder of where we have come from, and where most of us, at some point in our gay lives, have been: alone, scared, fearful, disgraced. It is also true, in some horrible way, to an *ongoing* sexual need and sexual shame that are never entirely erased. Gloomy and unfair as much of it is, closet fiction is at least not Pollyannaish. It has the great virtue of taking sex seriously. It does not whimsify it, nor denature it of moral meaning.

Both ghetto and closet literature have been replaced, in recent years, by different kinds of gay fiction, most of it very polished, much of it popular, and some of it well-reviewed in the mainstream press. The two main branches of this new literature I call "assimilative" or "homosexual," and "transgressive" or "queer."

Assimilative gay literature embraces many of the best-known gay writers in America, including the late Robert Ferro, David Leavitt,

Stephen McCauley, Christopher Bram, Michael Cunningham, and others. This literature breaks away from the ghetto tradition by placing its gay characters either outside the literal gay ghetto or in a hostile relation to it. But the characters are also outside of the symbolic literary ghetto: Nothing but their inclusion of a gay character would make us think these were gay books. Assimilative stories are deliberately integrative and frequently concern a gay character's coming to terms with his family, living with straight friends (often women), or finding a lover and settling down in a monogamous relationship. An astounding number of them are about raising children.

Assimilative literature is fiction about gay men for straight readers. It shows gay life within the implicit or explicit context of mainstream life, and tacitly appeals to mainstream values—especially those of the family, or of monogamous love—to bless its gay characters.

It is not the same thing as closet literature, for it claims the right of gay people to exist—provided they resemble straight ones. These books, while well-written, are rarely brilliant or witty. (Stylistic brilliance of the Wildean sort is perhaps too identifiably "gay.") Their strength lies in an appeal to a common humanity: "We're all looking for love" or, "We're all trying to figure out our parents." These novels *are* about people who "just happen to be gay." Some homosexual titles: Gore Vidal's brave early novel, *The City and the Pillar*; David Leavitt's *Equal Affections* and *The Lost Language of Cranes*; Stephen McCauley's *Object of My Affection*; and Michael Cunningham's beautiful *Home at the End of the World*. Perhaps the most popular of all gay books (among both gay and straight readers) would fall into this category: Armistead Maupin's *Tales of the City* series.

The transgressive, or "queer" writers are quite different, at least on the surface, from the assimilators. And they too number some respected, if less-known gay writers, many if not all from the West Coast: Dennis Cooper, Robert Gluck, Kevin Killian, Paul Russell, the late Sam Dallessandro. Their stories are frequently ones of horror, dissociation, or emotional numbness. They are often shocking in their presentation of extreme psychological states and extreme sexual acts, such as mutilation and murder. They are like the assimilators in disdaining the ghetto, though for a different reason: what they loathe is its bourgeois complacency, indeed its rather vulgar success. And indeed, they seem to be assimilative themselves—only to a different larger group.

The queer writer is queer first, homosexual second. "Queer" in this context does not primarily mean "homosexual," but "estranged," "marginal." He is in reaction against not only the straight world, but the gay one as well, especially the middle-class ghetto. He is a professional distruster of authority. Queer writing is peculiarly contradictory about sex. On the one hand, because it sees homosexuality as "transgressive," it can present gay characters as heroes of the sexual margin. On the other, "transgression" takes so many forms—including cross-dressing, bisexuality, radical or reactionary politics, or mere anomie—that it's hard to keep the homosexuality as such separated from the general transgressiveness that is praised. If the characters are gay, their gayness is not as central as their boredom.

The queer writer *par excellence* these days is Dennis Cooper, whose novels *Closer* and *Frisk* exemplify the frightening coolness and unemotionality of radical narrative. In *Frisk*, for example, one of the characters asks another to shit in the toilet and not flush. He adds: "I'm not being abject … It's not, 'Ooh, shit, piss, how wicked,' or anything. It's, like I said, information." Queer writing is often pornographic or parodic of pornography; and brilliantly captures the dissociation of sexual obsession. Its other great insight is that, just as "love" can be put in ironic quotation marks, so can something seemingly real and objective like "sex." Nearly all the sex scenes in Cooper are fascinating—the right, obsessed word—

because they are mechanical. In no case do they call forth irrelevant words like "beautiful" or "ugly," "good" or "bad." "Queer" titles might include Killian's *Shy*, Gluck's *Elements of a Coffee Service* and *Jack the Modernist*, Paul Russell's *The Salt Point*, Sam Dallesandro's collection of stories, *The Zombie Pit*.

Neither the assimilationists nor the queers are attempting quite what the earlier gay authors attempted: namely, to create a literature of gay awareness, heroism, and separateness. Neither ones seem to proceed from a sense of *joy* (even privilege) in being gay. None of them finds the "world well lost" for it. The assimilative books, while completely un-abject and "pro-gay," continue a narrative of *acceptance* by the straight world that was present in earlier, more lachrymose works like the saccharine *The Lord Won't Mind*. The transgressive titles repudiate the straight world (construed as something much larger than the mere mass of heterosexuals), but in that repudiation continue its power, and assign homosexuality a position only on the margins of society—powerless, undignified, desperate. In both assimilative and transgressive texts, homosexuality loses all particularity of social reference; the gay characters don't act or talk "gay." Whether insiders or outsiders, they are virtually indistinguishable from straight ones.

Is this a step forward? Many would say yes; I would disagree. It seems to me that there is a tremendous, and unacknowledged, pressure on gay writers to tone down the sexuality of their characters and their story, to make them more "universal." I am an Aristotelian in this matter, and believe that universality, if it is to be found, must come in the form of particulars. I do not think that a literature, or a life, that blurs the outlines of our gay identity represents us fully to ourselves or to the straight world. While assimilative or queer texts may be excellent books, therefore, they are only partially "gay" books. However interesting or beautiful they may be in other respects, they are not the books I would recommend to someone, gay or straight, who wanted to know what a *gay* life was like.

The ghetto writers, by contrast, do insist on a gay particularity and are thus as necessary (I would argue) as the actual ghettos many of us inhabit. Both fictional and urban ghettos "stand for" an identifiably gay life, and thus are living refutations of the belief that gay people don't really exist, or are not really different. Both institutions, ghetto and ghetto literature, make a radical and complex claim: that gay life is different from straight life in some important ways; and that that difference won't go away. Ghetto writers have posed, if not solved, the peculiar difficulties and triumphs of gay life by insisting on three things. The first and most important is that sexuality must be central; to make it peripheral or adventitious risks erasing the characters' homosexuality altogether. Second, and related to the first, is the insistence on the characters' slight, but important, separateness from the straight world. Third, they insist on joy, even arrogance, in that separateness, rather than shame or guilt. The sexual and social particularities of their characters may be social disabilities, but are personal advantages.

What I am calling "ghetto literature" is then gay, not incidentally but essentially. It is not enough that it simply take place *in* the ghetto; it must, as it were, be written *for* the ghetto. It is not intended primarily for a non-gay audience: like life in the actual ghetto, it will take homosexuality for granted, and will not explain it. It is not enough for there to be one or two gay characters swimming in a welter of straight ones, even if the gay characters are "good" and the straight ones "bad." The purpose of ghetto literature is not to award points for sensitivity.

The gay protagonist will see himself in only incidental relationship to the straight world: George in Isherwood's *A Single Man*, for instance, teaches with straight people at his state university. But they are not the important people in his life. Even his best friend Charlotte, who *thinks* she is more important to George than she is, is kept at a distance. These books describe a homosexuality which sees itself as separate, confident, un-self-pitying.

By the same token, they see heterosexuality and the life of the straight family as interesting, perhaps, but essentially irrelevant.

The separateness the gay character feels, in other words, liberates him more than it enchains him. It is the condition of his particularity, and he would not give it up, even if he could.

It has been noticeably easy for critics to praise a fugitive and cloistered vice: that is, to give their blessing to a homosexual fiction which represents few gay characters, few gay tropes (irony or camp), and few gay sexual acts. David Leavitt's *Equal Affections*, for example, seems to have won acclaim for its representation, not of the gay son, but the dying mother. (A reviewer for the San Francisco *Chronicle*, carried away by exaltation, compares him to Tolstoy.) Stephen McCauley's *Object of My Affection* tells the *Times Book Review* "what it is like to be young in these crazy times." ("Young," not "gay.") And at the opposite pole, the cold horror of Dennis Cooper has proven almost equally tolerable, at least to the avant-garde. ("A minor classic," says the Washington *Post* of *Closer*.) In much recent writing, the homosexual love is purged of lust (as in Leavitt), or nihilistically reduced to it (as in Cooper). In the older books, by contrast, specifically gay desire is important, romantic, and—most dangerous of all—attractive.

To give an idea of the different branches of gay male fiction from the last fifty years, I have taken descriptions of five homes from different branches of gay literature: the closeted, the proto-ghetto, the assimilative, the transgressive, and the full ghetto fictions. Each shows the gay protagonist in a particular relationship with himself, with the outside non-gay world, and with the outside gay world. The kind of place it is, the way it's described, the sort of person who's living there (and the sort who is not) are all indications of the author's vision of homosexuality. They will help us focus on some larger generalizations I'll make about these branches of gay fiction and what I see to be their main trunk.

The Closet

The closet is not quite invisible: that is its glory and its terror. It is not quite *enough* of a hiding place. It is consequently a place of shame, and the closet novel focuses on that shame as its main topic and emotional effect. If it damns homosexuality, at least it does not trivialize it. The story of the closet is also surprisingly long-lived: we see late and unworthy versions of it in *The Boys in the Band* and the strangely gloomy life of John Rechy's "sexual outlaw," so promisingly bold in claims of liberation, so unecstatically guilty in fact. (Ecstatic guilt, as in James Purdy on the other hand, is quite alien to Rechy's depressed sex-hunt.) The closet narrative will always hold some interest for us, as will its more upbeat relative, the coming-out story, because we can all remember a time when we dreaded to see, acknowledge, or express our homosexuality. Further, the strength of the closet novel, which is intensity of feeling, will always be more popular than mere happiness, or the complex perspectives of irony.

The great novel of the closet is, of course, James Baldwin's *Giovanni's Room*, published in 1956. We say "coming out of the closet," but *Giovanni's Room* is about entering it. We should perhaps remember that in the bad old days, a closet was at least in part a good place: the place where you were private. Even so, Giovanni's room is plainly a symbol not so much of privacy as of imprisonment. It is described as a pool of standing water: "Life in that room seemed to be occurring underwater." Everything there is blurred and softened and distorted: light doesn't quite penetrate it, action is impossible in it. Its waters are the amniotic fluids of a perverse, unnatural womb, one that kills rather than brings to life. It is a place not of ordering but disordering: things spill onto the floor—violin music, wine, empty bottles. The horror David feels at the sight of this room is the horror at a sinister life-in-death, at something that cannot or will not die. The past is artificially preserved here, symbolized in stacks of old newspapers. What was lively and intoxicating once—a bottle of wine, its contents spilled on the floor—is now deadening, though paradoxically not dead itself. Its "sweet and heavy" aroma hangs over the room. An old potato—that gift of the New World to the Old, like David himself—is so neglected that even its sprouted eyes have rotted.

The thing that is most symbolically rotten is sex. The half-torn wallpaper, for instance, depicts a "lady in a hoopskirt and a man in knee breeches perpetually walking together, hemmed in by roses." Only in a closet could we be asked to think of a rose garden as a prison. Even the light fixture is repellent: it "hung like a diseased and undefinable sex." The disease we might have expected; the characteristic Baldwinian twist is that the narrator cannot tell what *kind* of diseased sex organ it is, male or female. Deformity, unnaturalness, indecisiveness, and sexual confusion thus hang over the bed on which David and Giovanni make love.

Inside, then, is intense shame. But outside is danger. The courtyard "malevolently pressed" against the windows, "encroaching day by day, as though it had confused itself with a jungle." Passing shadows make Giovanni "stiffen like a hunting dog ... until whatever seemed to threaten our safety had moved away." You can't see or be seen through the translucent, whited-out windows, but you can nevertheless hear the voices of singing children, a mocking code for the "natural," and thus a continual reproach to Giovanni, who bitterly wants to be straight. These voices are like a parodic inversion of that voice St. Augustine heard at the moment of his final conversion: the voice of a child ("whether of a boy or a girl, I don't know") chanting in sing-song fashion: "Tolle lege, tolle lege": "Pick it up, read it." Augustine at that point opens the Bible to *Romans*, where he reads: "Let us walk honestly, as in the day; not in rioting and drunkenness, not in chambering and wantonness..." But there is no honesty for Giovanni; he is condemned to "chamber" in his room, to live outside of the day. The children's voices damn, and do not save him.

The world of normality, of family, heterosexuality, nature, is thus shown to be the homosexual's enemy. But the space Giovanni has built to protect himself, a kind of male womb, is no protection. Not only is it precarious, it is itself diseased. Nature itself is not wholesome; for outside his window even the man-made courtyard (another anti-womb) threatens to "encroach." Inside there is a rose garden gone to seed. The jungle of Nature is not banishable; it has invaded his room like a virus. All he can do to ward it off is maintain himself in a perpetual timelessness. He is a sinister Sleeping Beauty around whom a monstrous forest has grown up, and who hopes in vain to be rescued by the inadequate Prince Charming, David.

The Fortress

To turn from *Giovanni's Room* to Christopher Isherwood's great proto-ghetto novel, *A Single Man*, is to travel more than the eight years that separate its publication from that of *Giovanni's Room*: it is like coming out again into the light. It tells the story of a middle-aged Englishman, George, now living in Los Angeles, where he teaches at a third-rate state university. A year earlier, his lover Jim has died in a car accident. George is now alone, the "single man" of the title. The novel, based loosely on Joyce's *Ulysses*, follows George around through the day, from his waking up to his falling asleep—or perhaps dying.

As a "proto-ghetto" novel, *A Single Man*'s main difference from the full-blown variety is its protagonist's isolation from other gay men. The only ones that might count are the hustlers George spots "scowling" on the street corner, with whose youth and sexual energy he claims a distant kinship. For all his isolation, however, George is quite free of self-pity or self-doubt—at least about his homosexuality. He is in many ways part of the outside world. His archetypally straight neighbors, the Strunks, know he's gay, for instance. "Mr. Strunk, George supposes, tries to nail him down with a word. *Queer*, he doubtless growls. But, since this is after all the year 1962, even he may be expected to add, I don't give a damn what he does just as long as he stays away from me." Mrs. Strunk "is trained in the new tolerance, the technique of annihilation by blandness...(Shame on those possessive mothers, those sex-segregated British schools!)" They leave him alone, and treat him with respectful hostility.

George's house is a symbol of his kind of homosexuality. It is, first of all, *separate*: "They loved it because you could only get to it by the bridge across the creek." It is cut off, too, by trees; but not the "jungle" that "encroached" on Giovanni: *this* house is safely "in a forest clearing." To live there would be like "being on our own island." (Indeed islands, like Fire Island or Manhattan, are typical and frequent presences in ghetto and proto-ghetto literature. They are signs of gay autonomy and identity.) The forest is not menacing here, but rather protective. Devouring Nature is comically represented by the ivy, "half-alive, half-dead," which overgrows only the old inadequate garage they don't care about and which will be consequently "useful for keeping some of the animals in." Furthermore, by placing Jim's animals there, Isherwood effectively reclaims nature for this unnatural couple. He rightly sees that the only unnatural thing in their house and garage is their cars, so he has George and Jim keep them on the sagging bridge.

This house is one you can see out of, but not into. It is literally elevated above the other houses in the neighborhood, permitting George to gaze contemptuously down on the Strunks' house below (as he sits on the toilet reading Ruskin). He can see the Strunk-world more completely than they can see his: the gay viewer forms the truer opinion. (Giovanni, by contrast, could neither see nor be seen.) The very smallness of the house has a different meaning in this novel from that in *Giovanni's Room*. Giovanni's room was "not large enough for two." George's is "cozy," "tightly planned...." He often feels protected by its smallness; there is hardly room enough here to feel lonely." Finally, even George's love for Jim is characterized by a sort of separateness. There is a marvellous description of them lying at opposite ends of their couch reading, "the two of them absorbed in their books yet so completely aware of each other's presence." They are mutually aware, but not indistinguishable. Love, then, like his house, is built upon a self-respect that preserves boundaries.

The Bridge

One of the most popular gay novels of recent years was Stephen McCauley's *The Object of My Affection* (1987). It is what I would call an assimilative or "homosexual" book. It literally and symbolically places the gay protagonist almost entirely in the straight world, in this case making him the roommate of a heterosexual woman with whom he dreams of raising the child she is carrying when the novel begins (not his child, of course). Indeed the fact that the hero is gay disappears from sight over large stretches of the novel, especially the first half. As most of its reviewers noticed, *The Object of My Affection* is determinedly pacific and bridge-building, its message seeming to be: "All of us, straight and gay, are lonely and looking for love."

The story concerns another George, George Mullen, a 27-year-old Bostonian who moves to New York to do graduate work in history at Columbia. Quickly realizing he has no passion for the subject (or indeed for anything else), he drops out; but not before he's begun an antiseptic affair with Robert Joley, a professor of Victorian history. Joley is an unpalatable sort of fellow, emotionally closed and unable to sleep *with* George, or *without* the whirr of a white-noise machine. If they have sex, it's not mentioned. They quickly break up. Glad to be rid of him, George remembers a woman he'd met at a party who said she had a room for rent in Brooklyn. He crosses the bridge from Manhattan to Brooklyn Heights, and leaves the gay world behind.

What do we notice about this move? The first thing is the narrator's social viewpoint. He is glad to be moving out of Manhattan (unfairly symbolized by Joley's apartment, which was as prissily clean as Nina's is warmly disordered). He is making a trip across a bridge *out* of gay space and into the straight world: an exact reversal of what Isherwood's George had done. At first George Mullen is wary of Nina's street because it's "far more ostentatious than I'd expected." Luckily for him, it gets grittier: "the brownstones were less elaborately decorated here, narrower and flatter and without the polished look of restoration." We note in passing that words like "elaborately," "polished," and "restoration"— queenly terms—have negative meanings in the Mullen glossary, and "narrow" and "flat" positive ones. He likes the fact that the only "ornamentation" is the "trash barrels chained to the fence in front." George's relationship with outward beauty is always problematic, as though he were warding off a suspiciously gay aestheticism.

We notice, too, some morally telltale children—always a sign in this book of virtue and naturalness. Significantly, there are no children around the "ostentatious," "ornamented" brownstones near the park. Children appear, as if on cue, only in the poorer neighborhood, as an earnest of its greater fidelity to "life." Would it be rude to ask who lives in those "ostentatious" Brooklyn Heights brownstones? Could it be gay men, the selfish beasts? If so, it would not be the first, and will not be the last, slur George makes against his fellow homosexuals.

The inside of Nina's house is cozily lived-in; and the reflection that "more than one generation of children has run amok in this place" reassures George, as it is intended to reassure the reader. As George priggishly says, "It was unlike any apartment I'd been inside in Manhattan." We might notice, too, the honorable place assigned to dirt and grease. Like a sort of inversion of Giovanni's room, Nina's apartment is desirable precisely *because* "the air was heavy and intoxicating." It is perhaps no accident that the building is owned, and presided over, by a warm-hearted stage Italian, Mrs. Sarni, the smell of whose motherly cooking has been absorbed by its greasy walls. Her presence "naturalizes" George's perversity in more ways than this, for she herself has a gay son who lives in the Village that George has spurned. She is, in other words, a sort of fag-hag. If Baldwin's poor Giovanni had only had *her* for a mother, none of his suffering need have happened!

Nina's bedroom itself George pronounces to be "feminine," which apparently means "messy." But Nina's messiness, unlike Giovanni's, is found eccentrically charming. And not only messy, but isolated: McCauley even bestows on her the same blocked-out windows Baldwin's David was so horrified by! The cards crowding the mirror tell us that she doesn't actually use it and is thus innocent of "narcissism" (that gay neurosis). The detritus of her bedroom is the sign of whimsicality, not (like Giovanni's) of despair: "feather necklaces, yellowed lace, wind chimes, and a little girl's straw bonnet with a sky-blue ribbon." They are props that testify to Nina's childlike soul. Not Giovanni's violin music (too arty?), but clothes spill from her bureau. In place of the undead potato are "three vases of dead flowers" and "four coffee cups with spoons sticking out…"

George tells Nina, after surveying this scene of squalor, "You know what, Nina? I could easily live here." He could, and does; for this place is George himself writ large. Notice that by fitting himself into this "feminine" space, he effectively neuters himself. And indeed his sex drive vanishes as soon as he moves in. (Not that there was much to vanish: the first event in the book is George's decision *not* to go on an arranged blind date.) Indeed there is very little sex or sexual identity in the book. His best friend Timothy, for example, lives not in Brooklyn but off Sheridan Square, and could be a representative gay urbanite. But he is unfortunately neither butch enough to be a clone, nor witty enough to be a queen. He's merely (like Joley) a self-absorbed neatnik. But George's attitude toward other homosexuals is really worse than indifference. On a trip to Vermont, for instance, he does find the "object of his affection," a solemn former hippie named Paul; but until then George doesn't mind trashing every other gay person in Vermont: "I recognized our host standing at the far end of the bar... I crossed the narrow room, choking briefly on the smoke, and shook his sweaty hand. The top of his head was covered with a greasy, pitch-black toupee that drained the color from his face and gave his complexion a jaundiced shine. 'I want you to meet Tommy,' he said in a drunken slur. 'He owns this dump with me.'" Grease, so honorable in Nina's apartment, is apparently disgusting when associated with a gay man.

It is no accident, finally, that Nina is pregnant, that Paul has adopted a child, and that George works as a teacher for a snotty East Side elementary school. Children are invoked as a kind of sanction for his sexuality, removing its perverse sting. They make his homosexuality acceptable. When he finally settles down with Paul, he is not so much embracing homosexuality as allying himself with a superior version of Nina: sexier, but just as much a shield from the gay world he fears and despises. In an odd way, George's supposedly extinct Catholicism re-surfaces in his assumption that sex for the sake of children is permissible, but not for pleasure. While George doesn't literally procreate, his story is about becoming a father: an act whose moral beauty apparently redeems the perversity of his homosexuality. While it would be untrue to call *The Object of My Affection* a "closet" novel exactly, it is astonishing how much its fundamental premise resembles that of, say, *Giovanni's Room*. That premise is, of course, that homosexuality needs to be redeemed. The main difference between Baldwin's and McCauley's books is simply the possibility or impossibility of such a "redemption." And one may feel that George Mullen's happy ending is bought at the too-heavy price of squeamishness about the actual gay world, and other gay men.

No Place

As an example of "queer" storytelling, I'm going to take a beautiful, if little-known story by a writer who died at the horribly early age of thirty-one of AIDS, Sam Dallessandro. Its appropriateness will be obvious from its title, "Giovanni's Apartment." The story, to the extent that there is one, is about an unnamed narrator who is followed home one night by Giovanni, a handsome man whom he'd seen in a movie. Giovanni takes him to his apartment, where the narrator stays for the next eighty days, leaving only to walk in zombie-like straight lines through the unidentified city. For the first thirty-two of these days, he never leaves, content to stay among Giovanni's erotic but semantically blank possessions. On the thirty-third day he goes outside and "zombies" into a dime store, where he strikes up a conversation with the clerk, a dwarf named Mary. He immediately invites her to dinner. From that point on, Mary, Giovanni, and he become friends and spend all their time together. The narrator has dropped all his previous friends, as well as his job. At the end of the story, there is a suggestion that he'll go back to work, not because he's bored—he's literally incapable of boredom—but in order to buy Giovanni a VCR: "Then we can all watch 'The Flintstones' and 'Our Miss Brooks' reruns at night. Except Tuesdays, cheap beer night, Gio's pool night." And there the story ends.

Giovanni's apartment has "black walls," and is illuminated only by the erotic red light of a lava lamp on the floor. It is "a warm and luscious hell." Its only furniture besides the lamp is a "fat mattress on the floor," the scene of Giovanni's nightly "killings and revivings." There is no day or night in this place; time is suspended. But who needs day? "If I tired of sunbathing on the floor, I could go to the window and look out. Flowers, trees, dirt, garbage, a child's swingset but no child, two women having coffee on an iron table. I couldn't be bored." It is, like Giovanni's room, a womb, a place of rebirth into "emptiness." As the narrator says, "I felt clean for the first time since I was born."

As the title suggests, we are invited to consider this place in the light of Baldwin's classic room. There are obvious similarities, including the allusion to being underwater, the womb-like timelessness. But how different is his reaction to that timelessness! Far from being horrified by it, as David is, he is enchanted by it; it frees him (to be happy? or is the word irrelevant?); it purifies him. The very tone of the passage is unemotional and unemphatic.

And if he's clean, he's plainly different too from McCauley's George Mullen. Giovanni's apartment has none of the warm eccentric squalor of Nina's house in Brooklyn or the upright orderliness of Paul's house in Vermont. Though he might recognize himself in the narrator's passivity, George would not be happy here. For one thing there's too much sex, and it seems too violent and too ecstatic: "killing and reviving" would hardly have appealed to Mullen. For this gay man, unlike Mullen, is both physically and emotionally *penetrable*. Indeed, he is *nothing but penetrability*: he has no boundaries of any kind. He is totally invadable by the world. Unlike Mullen, he has no dishevelled charm with which to joke away passion. The room itself offers no distraction from the "fat mattress" on the floor. While George Mullen can lose himself in the sheer random proliferation of things in Nina's apartment, the minimalism of Giovanni's apartment keeps the narrator focused on sex. This place is sparely furnished, and becomes more so as the story continues: Giovanni gradually and without explanation gets rid of most of the existing furniture, though leaving the mattress and the lava lamp. The lava lamp, which would have been only a social marker in McCauley—something he and Nina could feel superior to, something that would further clutter and conceal their lives—is completely functional here. It is not meant to be whimsical. Indeed there is no wit in this story at all, as there is no judgment. Judgment of all kinds is suspended, as being part of the dirt the narrator sloughs off. The dirt in Nina's apartment, we may now realize, was ironically what prevented George from seeing how dirty he thought his own sexuality.

This is a "queer" place for several reasons. One is, simply, that it is not a ghetto place: there are no other gay men in the story; the only other person who joins them is the presumably heterosexual Mary. At the same time, it is not a closet, for no one feels shame, guilt, or indeed any other strong emotion. Nor finally is it an "assimilated" world. The presence of Mary, for example, far from heterosexualizing, and thus naturalizing, the narrator's relationship with Giovanni, makes it seem even weirder than it already is. These characters all share an isolation from the world which is the antithesis of the integrative assimilating vision.

Another way Giovanni's apartment is queer is its utter and essential lack of boundaries, names, and definitions. We never know where it takes place, what the narrator's job used to be, or even what his name is. Such details, essential to the bourgeois realist tradition, are irrelevant here. What would it mean for such a narrator to call himself "gay" and someone else "straight?" His dissociation from the world goes far beyond that of mere sexual identity. Finally, the point of the story really is not the narrator's homosexuality, but his aloneness and Zen-like indifference. Sex is crucial to it, but not gay sex. Do we even know for sure that the narrator is male?

The Ghetto

By their drugs ye shall know them. If "Giovanni's Apartment" is like being "drowned in heavy waves of barbiturate-like nothingness," Andrew Holleran's *Dancer from the Dance* seems written on speed, its co-protagonist Sutherland's drug of choice. It is brilliant, funny, melancholy, and exact. It is not content to be dissolved in a postmodern "emptiness," like Giovanni and his lover. Neither is it a closeted fiction, for the character lives an openly, obviously gay life.

Finally, it completes, and complicates, the proto-ghetto journey by moving its main character, Malone, into the heart of gay New York. And this is the symbol of a far more profound narrative move: the experiment of imagining a gay character who is, for once, almost totally *free*, unconstrained by small-town mores, cowardice, social disability, or a novelist's need either to "doom" or "redeem" him. Malone, in other words, can theoretically choose happiness. That he doesn't, or that the happiness he thinks he has chosen turns out to be delusive, is the source of the book's ineradicable melancholy and its wit.

The world Malone comes to inhabit is both straight and gay, both public and private: that of post-Stonewall New York. (Indeed, in the Bantam paperback edition he arrives on Sheridan Square promptly in 1969, three months after the Stonewall Riots.) His journey there is a coming-out story and, like all coming-out stories, also a homecoming—to a place he has never been before. It is mostly a catalogue of *wrong* places, of anti-homes. They include the seemingly paradisal tropical island where Malone spent his dutiful childhood; the Vermont prep school, where he "studied diligently and postponed happiness to some future time"; the suburban home of the "widow of an ambassador who had been a friend of his grandmother's when they were girls," where he lives on a "vast floor of empty rooms in whose hallway outside his own the odor of cold cream, the sound of a television program being watched downstairs, hovered." New York City, which will become his true home, "he saw…with the eyes of most of his classmates: an asphalt slag heap baking under a brown shroud of pollution."

The half-comic, half-poignant moment when Malone finds his home in the new gay ghetto comes when he is visiting New York, working late on a "promissory note for the Republic of Zaire." When a messenger comes into his office, he looks up: "How could he know that his desire, his loneliness, were written on his face as clear as characters on a printed page?" The messenger, less inhibited than Malone, bends over to kiss him, and Holleran writes, with half-amused exaggeration: "It was the kiss of life." The messenger leaves him "with an expression on his face such as the

Blessed Virgin wears in paintings of the Annunciation." It is because of this kiss that Malone finally decides he must become gay, that he must throw in his lot with the gay men he had previously seen, desired, and feared. With a touching, ridiculous hope he moves to Sheridan Square, the heart of the nascent gay ghetto, where on a late-summer evening he "watched the Puerto Rican boys unloading soda pop for the Gem Spa on his new corner.... And so the last Sunday evening of August 1969 found him sitting on his stoop like a monk who comes finally to the shrine of Santiago de Compostela—devoted not to Christ, in whom he no longer believed, but love."

The half-comic, half-rueful religious vocabulary is telling. For what is it to make a pilgrimage to a shrine? It is to make yourself public, to declare yourself. It is to remind yourself of your true home, and of your long exile in a false one. (It is no accident that Malone, on the night of his "engagement" and death, is brooding over St. Augustine in Point O'Woods.) "The false years of dutiful behavior" can now "fall away." The great cry of triumph that is present even in Holleran's most muted, wistful phrases is an almost religious one, then: the realization that those early, respectable years *were* simply "false."

Coming out since Stonewall brings you to your own stoop, your own new corner—that is, a place which is simultaneously public and private. One consequence of his move to the ghetto is that Malone becomes real for the first time to himself. Before, he had been what he calls a "ghost"; now he has a body, and can therefore be *seen*. Seen, furthermore, *as gay*. If we could imagine the men who are unloading soda pop turning their heads in his direction, they would see not just "Malone," but a gay man, emblem of an unmistakable homosexuality. In fact, the whole city of New York, in page after brilliant page of Holleran's novel, becomes a gay neighborhood—as indeed it is, to the eye of erotic faith.

Here, then, are examples of five important kinds of gay male literature. Let me conclude with a few generalizations about each, and a brief defense of the centrality of ghetto literature.

I would be disingenuous if I didn't admit that I find most of the non-ghetto works limited in their ability to tell the truth about gay life. The closet novel finds doom too easily, and indeed unnecessarily: the terrible self-laceration of David in *Giovanni's Room* was already in 1956 (after the stories of Tennessee Williams, after Vidal's *City and the Pillar*) a mere stage-prop. Closet texts are like baroque arias: exciting in a way, but monotonous in their single-mindedness. There is absolutely no other voice in Baldwin's novel but the tragic one, and its story is uncontaminated by contradiction or by life.

The queer alternative is as un-ironic as the closet novel, if for completely different reasons and with far different effects. The lack of irony here stems from the narrator's, author's, or character's radical un-self-consciousness. There is in fact no self to be conscious *of* in "Giovanni's Apartment" or in Dennis Cooper's *Frisk*—except by the most minimal, detached definition of "self." The characters can watch their thoughts as intently as a Zen Master; but they scrupulously, phobically avoid the dimension of the self one might call "deep": the moral, the æsthetic, suffering dimension. There is certainly nothing so old-fashioned as a Faustian double-soul dwelling, alas, in a single, tormented breast. Interesting, indeed brilliant as this inner minimalism can be, its effects seem to me strictly limited. In this style one can "speak" only a few passions: numbness, boredom, suppressed hysteria. Far from being primitive or elemental, queer fiction is an example of what George Santayana called in 1922 "Penitent Art," an art which "childish as it may seem at times, is a refinement, perhaps an over-refinement ... not so much crude or incompetent, as ascetic or morbid."

This leaves the "homosexual" or assimilative novel: Leavitt's or McCauley's, for example. Assimilative writers are the Human

Rights Fund of gay literature: decent, politically and socially middle-of-the-road, interested in the "naturalization" of homosexuality and the satisfaction of rational desires. Their work is neither ascetic nor morbid, but bouncingly healthy, liberal, generous, common-sensical. Its characters are generally as well-observed as they are well-behaved. Many "homosexual" writers seem determined to prove gay life just as dull as straight: a useful corrective to gay arrogance and inflation, I suppose, but pallid fictionally and untrue historically. For many of us, after all, living in a gay world has been anything but dull: promiscuity made it thrilling in the 70s, deadly in the 80s; political battles have made it restless, heroic, or absurd; friendships make it precious. Assimilative fiction tends to mock or otherwise "punish" the passionate. In *The Object of My Affection*, for example, Nina's boyfriend Howard, who actually loves his job, is made to seem ridiculous for it. Similarly, in Leavitt's short story, "AYOR," the narrator's friend Craig gets into predictable trouble by cruising in dangerous areas: his sexual adventurousness is primly called "tragic" by the writer/narrator. Sometimes these authors, in their automatic preference for the prudent emotional compromise, seem prematurely middle-aged. They are able to tell a certain valuable truth, but throw away something yet more valuable in the process: namely, that separateness, that sense of an identity which both liberates us for political and personal action, and from complacency. From doubtlessly good motives they take the gay label from us, finding it divisive rather than liberating. Like Rilke in his famous response to Freud, however, I found myself wondering if getting rid of one's devils (anti-gay stereotypes, for instance) means also getting rid of our angels (our sense of election and joy.)

It is a choice we ought to be hesitant to make. However rightly we desire acceptance and rights, we need to insist on preserving in literature, and also in life, the "slight angle to the world" that Forster saw in the (proto-ghetto) poet Cavafy. Indeed I would claim that a certain apartness is essential to a full homosexuality, as well as to the literature that celebrates it. The actual gay ghettoes of American cities remain not merely places where a gay man can be among others like himself, and thus find a workable happiness, they are also places that *straight* citizens can identify *as being gay*. They thus serve a double purpose, both private and public. The private life being lived in the ghettoes, and made possible by them, is also a public symbol of homosexual existence. The great impediment to our success in the past has been our invisibility, or our reluctant visibility. The ghetto makes the presence of gay people in the big cities a simple and undeniable fact of urban life.

Ghetto literature is performing an analogous feat. It is not only a place for gay readers to find images of themselves that are neither simplistic nor demeaning. It is also an identifiable literary site. In the most concrete sense, it means sections in mainstream bookstores called "Gay and Lesbian." In a deeper sense, it means there is now fiction that refuses to make homosexuality invisible—not simply by presenting sexual talk, sexual acts; but by insisting that its characters are gay, first and foremost. They are not generically "queer," they are not "just people," and they are certainly not "closet cases." Ghetto and proto-ghetto fiction is the only place in literature where this is true, with the sole, and limiting exception of pornography.

Is ghetto literature then necessarily better than non-ghetto literature? Yes and No. There are undoubted successes in all the genres I have listed, and there are many failures or partial-successes among the ghetto texts. The claim I would make is that *when* the ghetto texts succeed, they are more complex, more audacious, and more lifelike than the non-ghetto texts when *they* succeed. For if, like Holleran's Malone, many of us have come to the ghetto as to a shrine, we come with a complex and contradictory burden: that of a past we do not wish to jettison and a present which that past would not understand. Ghetto fiction does not simply lament this burden, nor simply celebrate it. It tries to hold it in a creative tension. Ghetto literature is, so far, the fullest expression of that tension. Thus, though ghetto texts are often deeply contradictory, indeed precisely because they are, they do more complete justice to gay life *qua* gay, than assimilative, closet, or queer fictions.

Dancer from the Dance is, to my mind, the best of all modern gay novels, not because it is formally the most perfect, but because it is simply larger in its scope: large enough to risk contradictions. Its "failures" have to be measured against its far greater ambition. Its most radical attempt is to bring together Malone's past and present, his straightness and his gayness, without disparaging or eliding either; to give him, as it were, more experience than he can possibly contain. That both he and the book fall apart is therefore hardly surprising. To me it means only that Holleran has tried to do something impossible, and therefore interesting. While other perfectly good books have presented a more coherent view of homosexuality, they have usually, to my mind, simplified it out of recognition. They have either seen homosexuality as a terrible doom, thus leaving out irony and happiness altogether (like *Giovanni's Room*); or they have so blurred it that its "happy endings" seem virtually heterosexual (like *The Object of My Affection*); or they have made it a mere special case of marginality (like *Frisk* or "Giovanni's Apartment.") In none of these other categories does gay life seem desirable in and of itself, but either a damnation, a *pis-aller*, or a sardonically desired disintegration. Even Isherwood's great novel *A Single Man*, while technically far more accomplished than *Dancer from the Dance*, attempts less than Holleran's. George is finally content to be "single," to take what he can get, "eating his poached eggs humbly and dully, a prisoner for life." Malone, ridiculously, pathetically, and heroically demands more.

The Victorian novelist George Macdonald once wrote: "Home is the only place where you can go out and in. There are places you can go into, and places you can go out of, but the one place, if you do but find it, where you may go out and in both, is home." Neither wholly public nor wholly private, neither entirely solid nor evanescent, the ghetto is the closest we have yet come to a "home." It has both an inside and an outside, and we enter and leave it freely. And what I have called "ghetto fiction" is like the actual ghetto because it is neither hermetically sealed, nor overly porous, but flexibly distinct. When it works, ghetto fiction thus seems to me the largest and most livable of the existing "houses" of gay fiction.

How to Write a Short Story
MITZEL

The Short Story

The short story is a genre of writing that has a long and prosperous history in our literature. Practitioners of the short story have included men and women, boys and girls, students and professionals. Many short stories have been published to acclaim in magazines and other periodicals, as well as in commercial and academic anthologies. The short story has brought fame and a healthy reputation to many who have dedicated their talents to it. In one sense, we can say that it was Mr. Edgar Allan Poe who most recently invented the modern short story as we know it today, even if many of his stories have a dark and almost a revengeful or morbid slant to them, and, of course, Mr. Poe, a notoriously unadjusted personality type with no history of acceptable role models, died, drunken, in a gutter in Baltimore when he was only forty years old and was promptly forgotten. This is how the short story began in its current incarnation.

Still interested?

Choosing a Subject

When setting out to write your short story, please remember to select a subject with which you are comfortable. It is very difficult to write about things with which you are unfamiliar, despite the huge outpouring of the Science Fiction literature, so-called, in the past fifty years, most of which is harmless enough, though much of it did lead, finally, to the pot-smoking craze of the 60s and ruined the minds of generations of children, and many of these Science Fiction writers, so-called, became ex-patriates, and cries to Congress to investigate them have gone unheeded, leading to further voter anxiety and deep citizen resentment over the drift in our culture. Perhaps you would like to select from among topics such as "First Prom Night," "Work Experiences," or, even, "The Neighbor's Big Dog." These may not seem to you to be new or fresh topics, but it is the genius of the short story that each writer can bring an individual voice and a unique perspective to tried, trusty, and true universal themes. Always remember that you, as a writer, have a responsibility to the reader who will want to read your short story for the satisfaction and sense of reward that you hope your short story will provide.

Point of View

Each short story must have a Point of View. This is very important. Let us say, for example, that you have chosen to write a short story about "First Prom Night." This is an excellent topic. But, before you begin to write your short story, you must select from whose Point of View you will narrate your story. Will you tell it from The Girl's Point of View? Or will you tell it from The Boy's Point of View? Let's say you want to be The Girl, we'll call her "Betty-Lou." You will want to imagine all her girlish excitement as she gets ready for Prom Night, her intimate chats with her sister and all her girlfriends, those long tension-filled minutes as she daintily pulls on her silky, lacy underthings, her sweet joy in fastening the tight bodice of her swirly pastel Prom Gown, the giddy agony of her three-inch heels, and all that loving time spent applying makeup. Tonight is going to be her night! And, just before the doorbell rings, announcing her beau, we'll call him Todd, your Girl just might stop and wonder: Will He Kiss Me Good-Night?

If you choose to be The Boy, other thoughts might enter your short story: can he get Dad's big new car to drive to The Prom? Will he be able to sneak a few drinks from his flask that he is carrying concealed inside a coat pocket in his tuxedo? Will he be able to steal out in the middle of the dance with some of his school chums and smoke a cigarette without being reprimanded by one of the dance's official chaperones? And, while driving Betty-Lou home from the Prom, after that misfortune where she broke off one of her heels after doing that mad Watusi number, will Todd think: how far can I make it with this babe? First base? Second base? All the way? To engage your reader, you will want to fully develop areas of human interest that will relate to your reader's real life experiences. Issues of moral depravity, such as those developed in many of the short stories by Mr. Tennessee Williams, should be considered reprehensible and be avoided, as they do not connect with a normal reader's world view or with his expectation of what the arts community should be offering to the reading public at large, instead of this outpouring of filth, degradation, and all manner of exploitation for its own sake.

Plot and Other Devices

It is important to have something happen in your short story. This is called A Plot. In The Prom idea, you could develop a plot wherein Todd gets too drunk to continue to dance with Betty-Lou, and Chance comes to her rescue and takes her home after her heel breaks off. In the Neighbor's Big Dog, you could develop a plot wherein Rover, who usually seemed so friendly, has secretly mauled and murdered baby Mary-Ann and buried her body in the back yard and, when discovered, Rover is dragged off to be destroyed. In Work Experiences, you might develop a plot wherein a co-worker is caught stealing to feed his drug habit, or perhaps infiltration of a high-clearance government work area by agents of a secret cabal of highly-trained but "normal-looking" thugs bent on world-wide terrorism and enslavement of freedom-loving peoples everywhere on the planet. Or you might have Betty-Lou secretly training Rover to maul and murder baby Mary-Ann who Todd told her was her cheerleader rival's secret OW child from one of the "normal-looking" thugs, the one who was also having a secret homosexual dalliance with Todd, who, it could turn out, has a weakness for beefcake-type pornography and has fallen down a deep moral abyss. One thing modern short story writers agree on: Avoid The Trick Ending. The Trick Ending is when you, as the writer, set up your short story so your reader, in the full and completely understandable expectation that you are observing your responsibility as a writer in society, will be reading along, only to discover Things Are Not What They Seem, and, of course, the inevitable disappointment sets in and, for many, resentment. The Trick Ending is a cheap tactic and undermines the integrity of the short story form. For example, in the Prom story idea, the reader would not enjoy finding out on the last page that after Todd, completely drunk, had taken Betty-Lou home, nearly killed them both in a disastrous car crash, and then, while dragging Betty-Lou's unconscious body from the tangled wreck to a nearby tree and ripped at her tight bodice and pretty, lacy underthings and attempted acts that made Oscar Wilde notorious, it was all just a masturbatory fantasy that Todd, alone in his room, had been rolling around in his mind as he reclined naked on his bed, the sheet kicked back as he stroked his firm, hard, male member. The Trick Ending was made familiar by the late O. Henry (not his real name) who, prospective short story writers should know, was a ne'er-do-well, a bankrupt, a cynic, an alcoholic, and because of his early death under mysterious circumstances, was almost certainly suffering the terminal effects of one or more sexually transmitted diseases, which medical science at that time could not correctly identify, though years in psychoanalysis, begun at an early age, might have made an enormous difference.

Rewriting

As a new writer, it is understandable that you will be impatient with the loving and precise skill of editing and rewriting your short story. But experienced short story writers all universally recommend at least three rewrites of each story. As a beginner, you may need more than this number. The important thing is to reach a level where you feel confident with what you have written within the tight constraints of this difficult but very rewarding form. For example, in Todd's attempted rape of Betty-Lou after the car wreck, you will want to make certain that all the facts you introduced in the beginning of the story have continuity throughout your work. If Betty-Lou lovingly put on a pair of bright pink nylon panties and a sky-blue uplift bra while dressing for the Prom, it is important to make certain that Todd is not ripping off a pair of plain old white cotton panties and tearing at a scarlet bra that pops open in the front. Readers get a kick out of catching writers who make mistakes such as these. And if Rover is described as a big happy Alsatian bitch on your first page, she cannot be a Labrador at her public execution, what with those thousands of animal-rights activists picketing outside after it is revealed that all along Rover had been trained by one of the "normal-looking" thugs. And if baby Mary-Ann is really an OW child, it would be unfair to the reader to announce only after the dismembered carcass is dug up that she was born a Mongoloid! If you want the baby Mary-Ann to be a Mongoloid, it is your responsibility to readers to tell them up-front, and work it into the plot, as perhaps divine punishment on the cheerleader for practicing her dissolute sex life. Remember:

no tricks; no surprises. Just life as it is. Perhaps it would be wise to inform your readers that Todd, lost in his masturbatory fantasies, might have a copy of a book of short stories by Tennessee Williams, E. A. Poe, or O. Henry on his bedside table. This might establish the depravity of his character. As would the jar of Vaseline and the small, encrusted towel he keeps hidden under his bed. And it might be important to you, in establishing Todd's behavior, that he has lately become obsessed with oral-genital sex. You might introduce, in a flashback, the scene where one day Todd is watching Rover lick her private parts and then deciding he can make poor Rover lick his! Betty-Lou's thoughts on oral-genitalism would only be appropriate in this flashback if you were telling it from Betty-Lou's Point of View, but, remembering your commitment to continuity, you must also recall that Betty-Lou is probably out cold when Todd attempts the act. But this might explain why Chance so quickly came to Betty-Lou's rescue after that embarrassing broken heel incident. Could it be that Chance, who is very tall and good-looking, had heard that Betty-Lou gives the best head at Dorksville High? And if, in one of your numerous rewrites, you want to give Betty-Lou a reason for choosing fellatio as a way to satisfy the boys and keep herself "popular" in a very competitive high school environment, you might write an interior monologue for Betty-Lou in which she weighs the pros and cons of performing this particular sex act, thinking that a few quick blowjobs might involve less loss of social status as compared to "putting out," as did her cheerleader rival, who got knocked up and had the OW baby, without, you might add as an interesting detail, missing even one day of cheerleader practice!

Selling Your Short Story

Congratulations! You have now completed your first short story. It should be a very satisfying experience! And you now have joined the ranks of short story writers! All writers want to share their creations with a potential readership. This means: Selling Your Short Story. It is here where so many young writers face inevitable disappointment. But do not become discouraged! Many fine short story writers have known rejection not just at the beginning of their careers, but often all throughout life. Many went on to glamorous heights of acclaim. There are many fine and reputable small literary journals which are eager to entertain manuscripts from young and aspiring writers. Your local friendly librarian will be pleased to assist you in locating lists of literary magazines which welcome submissions by unknown writers. Each writer must, however, face the very real prospect that success will not come overnight, as there are also many other writers out there with their own short stories to submit. The literary agents, the editors, and the publishers, in many ways play gate-keeper to which new talents will be acknowledged and which will be made to wait. Times do change, and with patience, most writers find the right outlets for their work. But the rejection notes will come; mature writers never take these personally. You may receive a sweet rejection note from a literary journal, usually on finely embossed stationery, often handwritten, expressing interest in your work, but stating that your short story is just not "right" for their current editorial needs. Each publication must keep its focus and has a dedicated readership accustomed to a certain style or "school" of writing. If, however, your rejection note comes back signed by "Betty-Lou," you will quite naturally wonder about issues regarding fairness and paranoia as the writer's lot. Imagine poor Betty-Lou! After the shock and humiliation of Prom Night, what with Chance trying to force her to go down on him, fleeing in her broken heel to drunken Todd's arms, then the near-fatal car crash, where, you might add, they ran over Rover, who had been "freed" by the animal-rights loving mob at the site of Rover's imminent immolation, and then the attempted rape, and Betty-Lou got herself into a community college, with an emphasis on "communication skills," and then just lucked out and landed a job as a reader and receptionist for a small and very toney literary publication run by an old letch who liked leggy girls with great looks and perky attitudes, and there, on her desk, comes your short story, "First Prom Night." Betty-Lou, being young, won't yet think of legal action or leg breakers, but what a shock for her to have to read her very own story of degradation thrown back in her face as "literature." Her "communication skills" have taught Betty-Lou grace and forbearance, and she has rejected your short story. Frustrated at the idea that the "Betty-Lous" of the world have now taken over the entrances into some of the smarter magazines, you might want to seek out a Literary Agent. Be sure to select one who specializes in the kind of work you do best, and not someone who shills those Science Fiction stories or media exploitation biographies of sports figures up on murder charges. Agents work on a "commission"— often ten percent—so The Agent you select will be eager to place your short story. Friends might recommend, say, "The Lanahan Agency," well known to be friendly to up-and-coming authors. Your initial query letter has been warmly received, and you have been invited to meet with the agency's head. Do not be surprised if, at this meeting, you find out that "Mr. Lanahan" is actually Todd, who, it turned out, had a secret trust fund all along and didn't care where his depravity led him, which, of course, was to the biggest and most wicked city of them all, where he was doing quite well for himself. Todd will charm you and tell you how much he likes "First Prom Night." He may make suggestions for an additional rewrite, recommending to you that you make Betty-Lou sluttier, going on a bit more with the blow jobs, emphasizing the size and shapes of the various genitalia, etc. Todd may tell you he can line up publication in a high-paying skin magazine, which can pay up to $15,000 upon acceptance. A young writer will be eager to jump at this opportunity, but a smart short story writer should also take into consideration the preferred path you will want to choose for your short story's presentation. Would "First Prom Night" be appropriate "literary cover" for a magazine that is essentially nothing but bosoms and gash? Retreating to a bar-and-grille after your meeting with Todd, you might consider your options. Chance, who now owns this smart bistro, though deep in debt to The Mob on account of his cocaine habit, his gambling addiction and his taste for cheap floozies who hang out in his place, can offer "street advice." As a short story writer, you must be prepared for your new role in life and that other people will take an interest in your career, even if many of them are profligate and degenerate. At home that night, while deciding whether to let "Mr. Lanahan" place your short story in the skin rag, you might see on the television that Rover has become a martyr to human viciousness to animals and the dog's supporters have got the government to issue a stamp in her honor, in which case you might want to remove the scene where Todd gets Rover to lick his cock. Is it really all that important? And The Evening News might also report that Betty-Lou's cheerleader rival has just been elected governor of a small state, on a winning campaign against Single Moms and illegitimacy. At this point, some short story writers have often committed suicide, and won't Betty-Lou and the dog's owner just love reading your obituary? There are gas, pills, and jumping from high places. Sometimes a successful suicide can be a useful career move, but such a decision is best postponed until any short story writer is more intimately familiar with The Marketplace.

In Conclusion

Assuming the life of a short story writer can bring with it many satisfactions. There is the gift of creation, and the joy of doing something well done. If the world scorns you and rejects your work, there can be a deeper and more intense personal fulfillment. Betty-Lou will quit her job at the literary magazine after the old lech comes on to her for the umpteenth time. She will marry a dull fellow, have children, live reasonably unhappily, always dreaming of the young men she wanted in her own way but could never get on the right terms. Todd will make millions, then lose it all when he signs up a phony biography of Howard Hughes or Juanita Castro that is quickly exposed. Chance will have all the sex he wants but be found dead under mysterious circumstances on a dark pier near an abandoned warehouse. Rover's stamp will come out, but Rover will be made over into a cocker spaniel, as that's what the Focus Groups demanded, and her memory will outlive them all. The cheerleader-Governor will be nominated for Vice-President but have to step down once your short story is published, as it happens, in the most famous skin rag of them all, which is the market these days.

Writing today's short story can be a glorious adventure!

PART TWO

AIDS • Identity

AIDS

AIDS has influenced, irrevocably, how gay men live and think in the world. The disease not only casts a pall over simple, everyday actions, but also provides us with a new lens through which we view the world—whether we like it or not. AIDS has provided a measure by which we judge action, feeling, thought, and memory. The range of writing about AIDS spans genre and tone, politic and emotional fervor; AIDS has so crept into our collective subconscious that it manifests itself unprompted, unsolicited. We write about AIDS in an attempt to explain it to ourselves, to make sense of the senseless, to convey the complexity of our conflicted emotions, and to simply state the obvious: we are often hurt, confused, angry, and embattled. Writing about AIDS sometimes gives solace, but it is often simply to give witness. To say: this is what happened, this is what I feel, this is how I live now.

Jesse Green's "These Things" recounts the author's emotions while wearing the clothing left behind by a friend who has died. With pride, regret, and longing Green writes about how even the smallest choices—of gesture, of presentation—take on new meaning in a life that is bounded by AIDS. "These Things" illuminates the quiet moments of the AIDS epidemic, the places where silence is not quite enough, and where solitary contemplation leaves us more lonely than alone.

Green's journey of remembrance is echoed in Ron Caldwell's "Love With the Light On," a three-part essay that charts—in journal entry, a fiction, and eulogy—Caldwell's relationship with the late writer Allen Barnett. Caldwell and Barnett became friends in October 1990 when they met at the Lesbian and Gay Studies Conference at Harvard University and remained so until Barnett's death ten months later. Caldwell's juxtaposition of genre and form—alternately jarring, mysterious, and evocative—demonstrates how difficult it is to capture on paper the myriad realities of AIDS. By interweaving fact and fiction, reporting and imagination, Caldwell is able to give us some approximation of how AIDS intimately affects the life of the mind as well as the daily routine, the intensity of emotions as well as the tending of incipient, nearly unacknowledged feelings.

Caldwell's "Love with the Lights On" provides an introduction to reading Allen Barnett's "From A Reluctant Journal." Written in 1982, before Barnett's illness, "A Reluctant Journal" never mentions AIDS by name or even indicates that its author is concerned with the disease, yet it is impossible to read these entries, in retrospect, without thinking of the author's future. These ideas, notes for future short stories, expressions of emotions, musings on life are, along with his collection of short stories, *The Body and Its Dangers*, and a handful of reviews and essays, all we have left of Barnett's writing. Published here for the first time, they are a glimpse into his inner life, his creative process, and offer a silenced promise of what he might have written next. They stand as a fitting memorial to all of the writers whose possible future work has been cut short, denied us.

The loss of the gay artist brings us not only sorrow but anger. And, indeed, AIDS has instilled a sense of rage in many of us. We rage against the disease, against an uncaring government, against a society that would as quickly blame as help those affected by the illness. But John Weir's intensely personal and controversial essay, "Rage, Rage," moves us into another realm. Weir was the best friend, confidante, and main caretaker of novelist David Feinberg before and during his struggle with AIDS. Feinberg, whose penchant—genius—for anger was so beautifully wrought in his fiction, was a difficult friend and more so when he became ill. Weir writes about how Feinberg's anger finally destroyed (at least for a time) their friendship, and how Feinberg's inability to understand the feelings of those helping to care for him caused terrible hurt. Speaking ill—or even critically—of the dead has never been a particularly sanctioned custom, and Weir's insistence on holding David Feinberg to the same standards he holds his living friends, raises difficult and vital questions about the nature of gay male friendship and community in the age of AIDS. But Weir's piece is more than simply a personal account of a hard death of a difficult person, it is also a challenge to the AIDS activist movement (and, by extension, the gay movement as well) to think seriously about the political and personal uses of anger. Feinberg's anger, Weir claims, was in the end self-indulgent and unproductive. So too, the anger that fueled ACT UP, an organization to which both he and Feinberg belonged. Anger has always played an important role in gay politics—and with so much to be angry about, why not? But the rage engendered by AIDS is often not productive or even healthy. Weir's essay recall the words of Gombold, the comic/tragic hero of Joe Orton's novel, *Head to Toe*: "cleanse my heart, give me the ability to rage correctly." And his challenge in "Rage, Rage" is for us to find ways to "rage correctly" and retain our integrity, peace of mind, and vision of the future.

These Things
JESSE GREEN

A confession, Mark: When you died, last August, what I wanted most was your clothing. Others in attendance just wanted you back, but what good would that have been, in your condition? No, I coveted the leather jacket and the dozen pairs of pleated chinos (though they'd have needed taking up by several inches), the cashmere scarves, the ottery overcoat I'd seen so often, gleaming in street light, with you gleaming inside it. I wanted these things not as mementos to hang in the closet and remember you by but on their own merits, as merchandise. I just liked your taste. Ah, well, it wasn't to be: Your family, with its various upshooting bodies to clothe, swept in and swept up. I can't imagine your father sporting that leather jacket in tiny, provincial Beaver Falls, but that's what he wanted, so that's where it went. And what will your Christian nephews do with all those oversexed pleats and plackets, designed only to celebrate the body, as you did so well, both living and dying? I'd like to think those straight and narrow boys (if that's what they are) will be cloaking themselves in your tolerant spirit, but I don't know.

You made good money, and it was something of a mystery to your parents what you did with it; as you got sicker, the answer revealed itself. From your checkbook they learned how much you gave away. From your closets and boxes and drawers they learned how much you wore on your back. Your friends already knew this, of course. We had seen you daily in your finery, your *moderate* finery— for though you were a dandy, you were always a subtle one. That paradoxical effect didn't come cheap. It was achieved with tiny but expensive details: a whipstiched hem, a nubby weave, a slightly oversaturated color. Your family, though, mostly saw you sick, and among the greatest indignities you suffered as AIDS went about its methodical business was that you had ever fewer occasions on which to wear what you loved. You, of all people, forced to endure a hospital gown— polyester, yet. ("I wouldn't be caught dead in this!" you deadpanned.) We bought you proper pajamas, but even when you were home for a while your lovely things no longer became you. How could they? They were *not* you.

Still, the day we packed up your apartment, your parents said I should take a few things— *you would have wanted it that way*, they insisted. I palpated your sweaters like melons at market, weighing which ones were ripest with feeling. What should I take? Your 7 *Days* sweatshirt? No: too pilled to serve as a suitable reminder of those happy days at the magazine when we met. The plush socks you bought that August we spent— you, me, and John— in the crummy shack at Rehoboth Beach? (Socks? I don't *think* so.) Or what about one of your pullover shirts, still smelling of you: a little bit clean, a little bit not. But which one? The one with the zipper? The one with contrasting piqué sleeves? Characteristically, I chose first for John, who, characteristically, could not be there. Because I had spent so many sleepless nights since he and I broke up, John would get the plaid madras shorts—Black Watch plaid.

For myself I hesitated. I already had a closetful of clothes that reeked of loss. What had John *not* left me when he left me? Hat, tie, tuxedo vest, beach shirts, flannel nightshirts, winter coat, summer shirts, boxer shorts, embarrassing underwear from International Male, an old suit that kept not fitting either of us— all these he had given me, or just abandoned. And even what was solely mine was nevertheless infected with him: what I wore on our first date (which you, clever Mark, helped engineer), what he liked me in, what he liked me out of. These items comprised the exhibit hanging at the museum of my life, underwritten by love and titled *Indestructible Habits*. Sorting through your folded treasures, Mark, I wondered whether I could bear to introduce your relics into my collection. What would the real loss of you, my friend, do to the intangible loss of love that was the permanent subject of my show?

No one tells us how to let things end. Or we are told contradictory things. Save everything, but start anew. Throw out your ex's clothes, but bury the dead in their Sunday best. One of the most surreal conversations I've ever had was about dressing my grandfather, a few hours after his fatal stroke, for his date with eternity. "Which tie, do you think?" my father asked me, since I was the one who was thought to know the magic calculus by which things matched. "Stripes?" he ventured. "Navy blue?" I wondered why one had to dress him at all: He had never cared about clothes while alive and would surely have no use for them now. So I picked a tie I was absolutely certain no survivor could want. My father took it to the undertaker; for myself, I took a black pinstripe jacket, which, sixteen years and two linings later, I still wear often, though I didn't like its original owner. Apparently his clothes were better made than he was.

Perhaps that's what gay men find so compelling in fashion. Tenderized by gym-class beatings, or by the body's refusal to do what the world recommends, we have always understood (and then often denied) the primacy of flesh—and its weakness. Now AIDS has come to overstate the case. Can any of us doubt how quickly life unravels? But clothes live on, forever fabulous. AIDS is a lavish couturier, every day remaindering perfectly good collections at rock-bottom, everything-must-go prices. We might as well accept it; if death is to be the new skeleton in our closets, we have little choice but to make it feel at home. Which is why you loved the AIDS quilt, Mark, and even those bitty, flop-eared ribbons. Like the ancient Greeks, they made fate domestic if it must be inexorable: an act of drawing, spinning, and cutting the thread of life. We gay men, at our best, honor what is delicate in us, so that even in grief we refuse to harden completely.

Therefore I chose the tenderest thing left in your drawer, a polo shirt quintessentially you: long-sleeved, simply cut, but honeydew green and meltingly soft. I remember you wearing it, with jeans or chinos; how it domesticated and advertised you, all in one gesture. *I am safe*, it seemed to say, *so neat and reliable*. And yet I am surprising—this thought offered by the buttons that run from throat to heart, preserving, beneath their antique glass domes, tiny paintings of pink carnations. How lovely it is! Yet not as lovely as you were, whose eyes were brighter and more florid than any glass bouquet. Another friend tells me that when she wears the sweater she took that day she feels your arms embracing her still. But I have less imagination. Walking home with my prize in a Bloomingdale's bag, I already know your shirt will never bring you back, or even let me feel you near me, any more than John's boxers will substitute for his hands at my waist. Clothes can only do so much; when I wear your shirt on one of my first postmortem dates, it may look good, it may go well, but it does not make me more like you. It makes me more like *me*.

So be it; we cannot change our spots (or stripes)— let alone our Black Watch plaids. But that doesn't mean we inherit our dear ones' clothes in vain. "These things do not remember you, beloved," goes the Conrad Aiken poem, "And yet your touch upon them will not pass." He means that we give our relics meaning; neither the dead friend nor the lost lover is the source of the strange power they have to move us. John's boxers (which I wore at your memorial, Mark) do not preserve the man himself, but my love for him, which despite repeated washings has not begun to fade. These things we wear and fold and hold to our faces are not reminders of what we've lost but of what we've saved, if only for a time: ourselves. For better and worse, you are in me now, but you always were. The arms in your honeydew shirt are my own. And though all the ties and shorts and ribbons on earth will not give us back the things we mourn, they can remind us that we have loved and suffered, been passionate without hope of reward, felt large and sometimes imaginary things—that we have dared to be alive. So if we must bear the clothing of loss upon our shoulders, let us do so victoriously, without sanctimony: not as a shroud, but a mantle.

Love With the Light On
RON CALDWELL

Part 1:
Liminal Spaces (a Diary)

8/9/91

I'm at the hospital again now and Allen looks about the same as yesterday, though he's resting much more quietly. His old boyfriend's secretary just called and wants to send me something—I have no idea what. He's Luciano Pavarotti's manager and is known for pitching money at problems, though in my case I'm more of a solution, so maybe it will just be a card. Or perhaps the offer of a job answering fan mail? Probably just a card. Or a CD (compact disc, not certificate of deposit). Am I displaying my one-track-mindedness yet?

I've managed to amass another fairly large stack of parking tickets over the past week. The City Fathers must have a special place for me in their hearts. Irresponsible little soul that I am. My sense of priority is pitched keenly in favor of immediate gratification. Lately the feeling has been that I'd better park, and fast, or else

Allen might not be alive when I get to the hospital. I'd really better look into the possibility of re-registering my car. (At least I'm going to have to get a new inspection sticker—mine expired a year ago 8/31.) My final car payment is in October, and I'm very happy to have that little experiment in financial encumbrance at a close. When I buy my Volvo, I want to pay cash.

Allen's resting now after a few tense moments with the urinal. The staff has to measure his intake and output of fluids. He's extremely prolific on the output side, but it's very hard for him to go. As for diarrhea, he's been lucky the past couple of days, since the doctor prescribed a stronger medication. That was not only literally draining him almost like clockwork—every half-hour sometimes—it was also extremely stressful and took all his energy. He's had the oxygen going almost all week, but his blood gas level has remained stable and he hasn't had to have the flow increased. His doctor, who is very good for the most part, keeps telling Allen that he'll do certain things that he then forgets to pass on to the nursing staff. I've become very sensitive to his state without actually being able to do any good. When anyone asks me a question about how Allen's doing—any of the doctors or nurses—I find that I'm awfully inarticulate. I've no way of expressing most of the facts I've picked up. I know the difference between one state of a bodily discharge and the next, I know the whole spectrum of his coughs, but I can't explain the difference. They don't know how he wheezes when they're not around, can't see how much of his physical state is directly related to his psychological one. He always perks up when the doctor enters the room, but immediately sinks into deep physical discomfort and distress as soon as we're left alone. When someone else comes to visit (rarely, since he's asked me to tell them all not to come), he gets even more feeble. Sometimes I'm just a crutch, I'm sure, and probably not even very good to have around. He does less for himself than he could—and in the end that makes him weaker. If I suspected he were conscious of the way he manipulates me, I'd probably tell him to piss off. But he needs the crutch more than he needs the lesson. I have to risk that.

He has a friend named Kevin whose lover has AIDS, too. Mark (the lover) has been in the hospital with meningitis. Kevin came by to visit when I was staying over in co-op care. Since then, Mark has gotten much better and has gone home. Kevin still comes by once in a while and we've gotten to be friends. He's the one person who has a very clear understanding of the situation—they were in the same unit Allen's in now (and I'm in too, really)—and knows Allen well enough to understand his peculiar difficulties and difficult peculiarities. He came by to take me to the cafeteria for a birthday cup of coffee. I find myself going on for long stretches at a time, disgorging all of the medical and psychological information we amassed during the day. He's become a minor expert on all of the treatments for all of the various opportunistic infections, and he's lost so many friends that he's developed a real patience and strength that are nice to see. At least from this extraordinary odyssey I'm going to make some good friends, I think. Two of the nurses, who were friendly with Kevin and Mark, took me to lunch yesterday. The real world feels much less so when I leave the sixteenth floor. Strange. Someone tried to pick me up here yesterday, a married dentist from Hicksville. I laughed hysterically—like a hyena, I think. It's too absurd to think about.

The friendliest nurse is a young guy named James who was raised in Alabama in the Pentecostal Church and who has a slightly more than slight wiggle when he walks. He told me tonight that I was in an elaborate dream of his that took place on Fire Island. It's funny to have him explaining this all to me in tremendous detail. He's so animated and funny, and well on his way to being free of his Fundamentalist upbringing. There's no way you could work on this floor without getting over it. I'll have him over for dinner when we get out of here.

Allen's friends are another matter, and another odd part of this whole experience. Since I'm his eyes and ears, as well as his mouth, I have to speak to all of these people I've never met and talk to them about Allen in great detail. Then I have to gauge what they need from me, since most of them have some sort of unhappy feelings associated with Allen and his illness. When he dies, I'm going to have to take half the address book and make the calls, and it will be an exercise in psychotherapy and self-discipline if I can manage it. Janine, Allen's friend with the general power of attorney, will take his mother. I don't think I'm built to do anything that difficult. I can understand what his friends feel, but I can't imagine how hard it will be for her—no matter how awful she might be.

Although I'm talking to all these strangers (and really quite like most of them), I can't even tell Allen about most of my conversations with them. They have to be told things that will make them feel better at a time when he's pretty much indifferent to all of them. I have to say that he's mentioned them or that he specifically asked me to call. Then I have to improvise through years of not knowing them—or Allen—explain how it is that he can't or won't talk to them, and make them feel like he likes them—some of them at least—better than he ever actually did. Sometimes I can't even go back and tell him that I spoke with them at all. Tonight I talked with a woman named Karen whom Allen has had a grudge against ever since I've know him. For a man who is as much of a misogynist as he is, he certainly does know a lot of women. Something's happened with those relationships, though—he's begun to exclude them. Karen seems genuinely concerned about him and wants him to be told that, but I know that if I tell him he'll just sneer, say something rude about her, and start coughing. I can't tell him because I can't bear to see his response.

I suppose I'm a little afraid of him, and afraid of hurting him, too.

Today he sent me to fetch some information on an experimental drug that his doctor is supposed to start him on tonight (if he left the order!). I was so angry I walked all the way to the West Side and then sixteen blocks downtown in the pouring rain shouting under my breath. I haven't been able to do anything right today. And I was feeling rather sorry for myself because it is, after all, my birthday.

The problem with sick people is that they lose their decorum. Some people, of course, never have it and it's no surprise when they get sick. But other people, who hadn't been completely self-absorbed before, suddenly become so, and the whole world, or what is left of it for them, begins to revolve around them. Allen has lost, with his health, his feeling for pleasing other people. Somewhere he probably feels that it would take too much energy, that perhaps he only has enough spirit to make himself up for the doctors. It hurts, really, to feel that all of the power in my friendship with him—even though I'm the healthy one—rests with him, and that he isn't using it honorably. He is afraid and he's gathering himself together for this metaphorical battle he's fighting. Instead of fighting just the disease and continuing his love affair with the world, he's firing on everyone. Some of the volleys are hitting their mark.

I wish among the things I could do for him were to have the power and charm to entertain him. Most of the time I've spent with him has centered on his life and his illness and very little on me. So I have little to say to him. I'm often sitting here watching him breathe and think of little stories I might tell, but I stop short of saying anything. It is as if—and it is probably true that—nothing about me matters to him in the least, nothing that doesn't serve his purposes. This may be true of all friendships, ultimately, but it is rarely so obvious as when the field of common experience is so narrow and focused, and relegated to such a brief time. It's not so much that I care about talking about myself—it's that I want him to feel like he knows me, that I can be trusted, that the mistakes I make here are honest mistakes—that I'm not completely stupid.

"When you leave the room, could you tell me how long you'll be gone, because I panic," he just said. While the nurse was hooking up an IV feed to his Hickman catheter (the one that goes into his chest) I stepped out to call my answering machine. Now I can see even more clearly how closely we're linked in his mind, and don't know how to keep myself spiraling into his orbit. Of course I couldn't say anything that would both reassure him and release me. He knew how to get to me. All anyone would have seen on my face would have been "That Look" that tells all, the smirk that will free up the seats around me on the subway at rush hour. Allen's eyes were dilated for an exam this afternoon and I doubt if he could quite make it out. It is, in many ways, my only defensive strategy. I no longer have the fortitude to make a point by leaving. It won't teach him anything—it only frightens him more. Besides, that and most of my other tactics and tests are so subtle (if we're charitable to me—if we're realistic, we might call them "impossible"—that most people even in their moments of greatest sensitivity and concentration couldn't figure out how or why to please me in those circumstances. I'm like a Byzantine puzzle. Or perhaps I'm Waldo of the puzzle—only instead of my shoes missing it's a little something inside of me, something I know almost no one will see, but I keep trying to lead them to it anyway. It would spoil the whole enterprise, everything mysterious about me, if I were to be direct, and simply show them how vulnerable I am. How much I need to be loved and listened to. Allen's in no state to be tested that way. I have nothing to teach him.

My feelings for him don't run to pity, really. Or if they do, I have lost sight of what I used to think defined the pathetic. The awful things that have happened to his body have made me sad for him. The ways in which he has retreated and become critical might have been there before I knew him, before he was ill, even—I'm not sure. Judging from what his friends say about him, I doubt it.

Right now he has all this anguish about his relationship with his mother that I am most sympathetic with, but which causes in me no deep empathy. The only feeling that wells up inside me when I hear him speak of her is horror. Horror and fear that he might die without having figured out what they mean to each other. She occupies his thoughts too much to say that he is indifferent to her. She is for him a symbol of all that is wrong with the world and in it, and his life has been an exercise in escaping her—or if not her, the world she has come to represent to him. The faster and farther he has traveled, the more apparent is the tremendous influence she has wielded in his life. There is no forgiveness in his voice nor any compassion, and even when he pretends not to care his whole face assumes the position of misery. But I think his fury betrays him, and that he loves her more than he'll ever know. Maybe he loves her too much. That breaks my heart: he feels a pain worse than any I can imagine or am likely to endure, because I've always been sure of my mother's love, have no doubt I'll keep the memory of it long after she's started drooling in a bucket and calling me "Bubba," when I have no hair except what's on my back.

In a way his pain is worse than dying, but dying is all the more painful because of the uncertainty and distance. I can't imagine that I'd leave the planet with any huge regrets, really. I do have a wonderful life, as rich with friends and events and suffering and love, and you, that has worked out. Fate will, at the worst, balance things out.

"All that we are not stares back at what we are." One could think of this thing life as a chance to make the "what we are not" face resemble the "what we are" one, rather than the other way around. Instead of contorting the one we know into some garish semblance of a future we'll never have, based on a past that never was, would it, instead, be possible to shift one's expectations to the face we know? After the plastic surgery, of course. What a barrel of contradictions I am.

Which brings me to what races through my mind while I sit here.

I think a lot about love and about Love. The first occupies my thoughts almost all the time; the second has probably more to do with insecurity than anything else. Love with the capital "L" is what we're always reading about and watching in the movies, and which never comes to any of us for more than a few months at a time. It's been so often plunked down at my table that I'm suspicious of anyone who's wearing the apron that bears its name. I think maybe I don't believe in big-L Love anymore—it's gone out to pasture with the Devil, with the Tooth Fairy, with The Love-of-My-Life. Maybe I don't believe in it the way I don't believe in God. (I still believe in the little love—as something small, intense, particular, and ordinary.) I think these things are all a little less than the sum of their parts—all of the capital-lettered items. And that the minuscule ones are just what they seem to be, a conglomeration of conflicting feelings with a common name, *equal* to the sum of its parts. Little "l" love is personal and different for every object. It is just as appropriate to "love" a beautiful object as it is to love a husband, because there is no need to pretend that the things have anything in common. We're always trying to test other people's pronouncements of love—and some of them are, or seem to be, awfully screwy—but that almost always seems to miss the point. We're always asking why or how people could love what and whom they do, when we should probably be asking ourselves why the range of what we love is so limited. Then we could move on to appreciation. Life is so exclusionary, when it could be so much more inclusive.

We've just had another urinary event here, and now Allen's lying back and dozing again. His breaths are shallow and his body turned in an awkward position. For me it would be intolerable for sleeping. But his body is learning rapidly to accommodate its waning capacities. The way I sit and walk and lie would send Allen into distress that would probably finish him off completely. In fact, barring an unexpected trauma, the way that he will go out will be when he and his doctor decide to trick his body into "believing" that it needn't compensate anymore. When things get too bad, they'll start giving him morphine and he'll begin to relax. For a while he'll be pain-free. But pain is one of the ways our bodies adjust to various onslaughts. It keeps him sitting up so his lungs won't fill with fluid. It keeps him awake and alert—even though the vigilance has no value, the enemy is within. All the symptoms now are really his body's defenses gone haywire. How the morphine will work for/on Allen I can't be sure, but if things continue to progress the way they are now, it will make him feel like he is getting enough oxygen when he breathes the way he used to, the way his brain remembers. He'll feel numb and euphoric and then, overcome by the sensation and unaware of its falsity— of the disparity between what he feels and what is possible, he will lose the will to breathe. The contract between his mind and body— his *constitution*—will dissolve, and he will die. And for a moment, at least, it will be a huge relief. For him, I hope it will feel like forever.

Then we'll all—the rest of us—plod along, stupefied and unhappy, which is not the same as sad.

8/10

I spent the night, and only managed four or five hours' sleep. Allen was in a pretty dreadful mood this morning and was wielding his power over me. I had descended to the point that I was ready to have an argument with Allen and give him a few pointers on deathbed diplomacy, but thought better of it. He looked pretty good when I left, even given that he was throwing up a little. A lot, in fact. When I got back this afternoon with the stuff he requested, he was less alert than usual. He doesn't tell me when the doctors come or what they say if I've been out; he was prescribed Percoset by the on-duty physician, the first time he's had anything stronger than Tylenol. It's a rather drastic step, I think, since painkillers—

even the weaker ones—result in slightly arrested pulmonary function. I'm not sure how much he's taking now, but I came slightly unhinged when I heard the nurse mention the sedative. It was part of Allen's doctor's chat with him/us on Tuesday. For a while I sat clasping his hand when he dozed off, but I eventually couldn't bear it anymore. Every few minutes he has enough energy to try to force his eyes open, but is usually unsuccessful. He's in a fitful, drug-induced sleep right now. His blood pressure is still normal, though. Today's nurse is a Dane, with a certain cheerful coldness they're known for, and I can't get much out of her. I'm not sure whether this is the beginning of the end or not. If it were, I wish they'd all give me some hint. If it's not, I'd like very much to know that. When he moves now it is as if he were in suspended animation—"slow motion" is probably a better way to describe it.

There's a very handsome young guy named John in the next bed now who's fighting testicular cancer. He's probably about twenty-six, and has had some very good news on his blood count last week; he hopes this will be his last round of chemo. He's lost most of his hair, but he's a big, strapping fellow with a great body. He told me all about his treatment history, which sounds pretty grim. He didn't tell me whether or not he has any sex drive left, but he has managed to hang on to his girlfriend, who was here this afternoon to keep him company.

So it goes.

8/11

Allen has told the doctor he doesn't want to stay alive any longer. In a moment of great care and gentleness he asked me how I felt about that. Suddenly, the decision being made, he became very magnanimous. I started crying and told him that it was all right. We sat and stared into each other's eyes for a little while. The nurse will start an IV with a low dose of morphine, then she will increase it whenever he starts to show signs of discomfort or agitation.

Unfortunately, he'll probably sleep through most of the rest of his life.

He began to hallucinate, mildly. To imagine he was with friends now long dead. He talked about how much he was looking forward to seeing them. At one point he woke up and said to John that he had dreamed that all three of us were in Philadelphia having a very good time.

8/13

The days unfolded more slowly; nothing much to do. I feel like I'm losing my reason for being. One night I go to sleep in the solarium; someone comes to awaken me early in the morning. Allen is dying, really dying.

John is awake but quiet. Allen is wheezing steadily, in measured breaths. I talk to him—almost immediately I forget what I've said, but I know I haven't promised him anything that isn't true. I think I tell him that he will never be alone, that I will always be with him. I tell him that I love him. He squeezes my hand. We share the earphones and listen to pieces of the Verdi *Requiem*. Tears stream out of the corners of Allen's eyes. He stops breathing. A rush of deep colors moves up and down his face. There is another long, deep gasp. He is perfectly still; we are alone. I tell him again that I love him; I thank him for letting me in. He is no more.

Part 2:
Love With the Lights On

You wake up in the morning feeling all right, then it hits you that the roach motels have closed up for the summer and it's time to replace them with The Waldorf-Astoria model, because the roaches are bigger than the Roches; the sound they make is more threatening than harmony.

And you see the box with your friend's ashes in it sitting on the speaker that someone has inherited but not yet retrieved. Your life is on hold because no one has picked up their stuff. You won't be able to properly move into this half-legal place until that occurs, either. Everything is making the wrong kind of noise. You reach across the bathtub to pull the window down so you won't shock the nursing mother next door and half a pane of glass falls out into the airspace, leaving a perfect angle in the shape of a guillotine. The irony would be lost on anyone but you, and you have to huddle in the front of the shower to avoid flashing the tender matron behind her oscillating fan. Probably she would not notice, but it is likely that the landlord would be called in and the end of something wonderful would begin.

Today I got three letters from the surviving family of my friend whose remains remain on the speaker. They sent photographs from happier times, and misspelled my name on the envelope. "Ron Crawford" I have become. I have been my friend since he died and he has gotten a great deal more accomplished since he suffocated in the fluid that was filling up his lungs than he did for the few months before that. If people knew how much had to be done to erase them, legally, from the banalities of this planet they would be embarrassed and either take care of it all first or they would leave it to professionals. I feel I am the junior partner of a corporation headed by my dead friend. I can't make any executive decisions without him and he does not return my frequent phone calls.

He is lunching with Elvis and they are enjoying a good laugh at my expense.

It is not that there aren't certain advantages to surviving. There are. Beyond the obvious ones, there is the fact that one tends to get certain things that one never thought in a million years one would actually own. Think how useful it is having a Black and Decker vacuum cleaner that charges on the wall and comes with all its attachments. When something breaks, it's not the end of the world;

now I own two of just about everything a writer in New York in 1991 could want. There was a little money, as well—just a little, but it has been enough not to worry for a couple of months, until the IRS catches up with me.

If I told you that grieving on this level was mostly dissimulation, you might think that I am insensitive, or a callous boor who always wants something clever and contrary to say no matter how delicate the situation. And though you might be right about the latter, you would be sadly mistaken on the former count.

People keep turning up who haven't heard that my friend died; so I have to tell them. I have to start from the moment when he let go of my hand and go with that and drop whatever I happen to be doing and go through the whole thing with them again. I am not an actor playing the same role eight times a week, but I have done this little number about fifty times and it still isn't easy to leave behind. I can find a little humor in it, but then again I'm the closest person to the whole sick pageant and that's not good enough for the sentimental mother or the sister who never knew her brother or the name-dropping writer-friend who was in England when it happened. He called because I'd left messages on his answering machine and I told him as gently as I could and he told me that he had known, that he had felt it, that our friend had come to him in London. Being from a family of people who said they were raised right, I didn't tell him he was full of shit, nor did I ask what it was that our dear departed friend had said or how he manifested himself in his fly-by. But I thought, how utterly stupid to say something like that. If it had happened he would have called me back and told me. But it's like deja-vu. Hume said it is more likely that we are deceived than that something out of the ordinary course of events should happen. I believe that. I believe in it, even.

But you still get yourself in the situation of the downstairs neighbor going into paroxysms of tears on the fourth-floor landing. And then she says the same thing. Well, I think, why didn't he leave a to-do list when he dropped by the building. And, I hope he alerted/didn't alert the landlord, depending upon what he knows now that he's Over There. The landlord occupies a place somewhat like that. He's on Long Island, might have lost the mortgage on the apartment, and may never get the rent-strike money out of escrow. The place needs a paint job; my friend was partial to earthtones and I am partial to white. The place is full of house-dust mites trying to burrow into my lungs, irritating my throat, making me sleepy. The attempted cure last night was Robitussin with dextromethorphan. I slept until ten.

At which time I decided to go out to the post office and try to get a few things accomplished before being overwhelmed by the whole purple haze of it.

I'm trying to write a letter to the mother, who seems to want to adopt me. She thinks I sound much older than I am. What she doesn't yet and may never realize is that I am much older than I am. I'm not up for adoption, however. I have a perfectly difficult family to deal with as it is, and don't need or want any other people who are going to require Christmas cards and who have the ability to conjure up guilt, who practically have the need to do it. There is now a space where a mother's son had been. She needs to fill it for better and for worse, and I approximate the shape of the things she has lost. When one fits even as well as that, how can one not fall prey to comfort?

He would be appalled by it all, really, since the one thing he could always depend on from his mother was that she would embarrass him. That quality was inside him and had very little to do with her, even though she supplied a name and a location for his ambient, progressive misery. There is much talk of what he would have said or what he would have wanted. Maybe our culture has given birth to that sentiment and it has become nothing more than a complex figure of speech. He never would have abided by it in his own case. He never would have countenanced it, nor do I— since it diminishes him so much in our eyes. When he's dead all of a sudden he becomes so much more predictable than when he was alive.

The death itself was an astonishing process. A friend of mine says that he watched *Wuthering Heights* last night and laughed when Merle Oberon dies, watching the clouds and being held aloft by Olivier in the last moments. It is comedic. People, as far as I can tell, almost never die like that. Instead, it's a nasty business, worthy of scorn, and one you can hardly help but look away from. It is scandalously slow in coming when it is expected, not measured out in scenes within an act. Nor does it compress well for the small screen, either. The commercial one is waiting for, or the avuncular explanation by the man on PBS simply never comes. All the scene changes are administered either by people you know well or by people you never see, none of whom know each other. And the oddest thing of all: when my friend had died, he didn't get up offstage and walk anywhere else. That was that; it was over; nothing spiritual or lovely happened. The man was quite simply dead.

Maybe you don't believe me and, since I don't look anything like a seer, there is little chance I'll be able to convince you. This is not a holy text. I claim no inspiration for it, nothing but necessity, a heartless taskmaster one can never be sure is here in person. I don't believe in muses because they tend to read over one's shoulder and I find that bad manners all around, and bloody inconvenient when one is trying to be sincere or sexy. Muses are easily embarrassed by truth and shockingly prone to believing in falsehoods. The muses I have met rarely look offstage to see that the body refuses to abandon its lifelessness and be called back to the stage. The muse never stands as a beard at the publication party, nor does the muse intercede on one's behalf with the people who pay one vast amounts of money for movie rights.

You can rarely convince a muse that sex, not inspiration, is what is required.

I once had a lover who seemed, each time I told him a story or a fact, to respond as if it were something he already knew. For a while, I believed that this was, indeed, the case, but later discovered that he was posturing. It was probably a chemical thing. I had wanted very much to surprise him, but he conquered me in that posture, made the bargain of our romance perched that way, and that was it. The whole kit and caboodle could be reduced to that if one lacked imagination.

There have been many such misunderstandings, internal and external, and the possibilities for many more.

My friend whose lover is living/dying with/of AIDS and I end our phone conversations with "Platitude, platitude." "Ditto." Because that is what we can feel and what we no longer can bear to say.

One would have thought there would have been enough time, but of course, there wasn't. I never took him up to those lovely gardens he saw in *House Beautiful*, nor did he get to be my cicerone in Italy. In fact, we never really went out anywhere, as far as I can remember, except to a drag version of Camille in the West Village. The rest was dinner parties and restaurants in our neighborhood and a lot of sitting together in doctors offices and The Hospital, way the hell on the other side of town. It makes you appreciate how rich and corrupt this city used to be and might always remain. It is next to impossible to get to the East Side of Manhattan from the West Side in a decent period of time. It is marvelously complicated to get there, really, and very difficult to take a sick person there. It makes you wonder. Of course the Tammany Hall set didn't know about HIV-related disease. But if the best hospital for treating typhoid were on the East Side in 1910, it probably would have been a bitch to get there then, too.

There was the lesbian who had immigrated with her Hungarian family to Germany after her parents were released from concentration and labor camps. She was blond and blue-eyed and Jewish; of course the Germans thought she was Aryan. They put her on the cover of a youth magazine because she was so blond and so beautiful they loved looking at her and didn't know the difference. Most of these prejudices are skin-deep, we always said.

She doesn't talk very much about being a lesbian—still isn't out of the closet to her WASPish ex-boyfriend, the father of her child. When her lover, my friend, stays over, she has to sleep in the guest room. I try to imagine that and can't. The fear and anger and frustration of living up against an idea so strong baffles me. They are each beautiful and lovely together.

We go through life waiting for people to start feeling okay about themselves and they continue not to, and die nasty deaths disillusioned or deluded. Aggie will die that way, with Bergman's pain etched into her brow and her own body staring back at her asking why she didn't, why she couldn't find it in herself to give.

It probably isn't as if there aren't plenty of things to regret anyhow. And mostly when we're put in that position of thinking only about ourselves and our immediate physical needs, the past tends to blur and become less poignant. It would be a handy defense mechanism, but not one evolution would have had much use for. That is why it is so miserable to die, because it should be—otherwise we would jump joyfully at a tender age before reproducing. It would be a godsend to die happy when it was convenient, and God does not have enough faith in us to pass that on. God ceased to believe in us around the turn of the century, if not just before the beginning of recorded history.

I think I would know if God ever thought about us. I would send him a sign if he enquired. So we have made a pact for eternity not to disturb each other. I have even given up blaming him for the odd disaster.

You think you know somebody pretty well and then you begin to live with them, or they die, or you hear them talk about their parents. Or they fall in love with you.

He had begun to think both that his stories mattered and that they were no longer connected to him. Once he could formulate them, that would be enough. He believed that he could end with rejecting the things that caused him pain; no longer would it be necessary to examine them closely. Whether there was any truth in that remains to be seen. He did not escape. He didn't manage to protect himself from the obscure sadnesses.

I found among his things a couple of letters from his biological father to his mother. They are cramped metaphorical letters that could only have been written in the fifties, full of "honeys" and "sweeties" and completely devoid of any mention of sex. There are certainly letters written today with those attributes, but I don't think there would be any confusing them. The letters date from just after Allen must have been conceived. His mother probably had no idea she was pregnant yet. From these close scraps of a teenage romance come the beginnings of unhappiness that would last a whole man's life. Once reinvented and abstracted, he could never have found joy or comfort in his father's simple words. He would have wanted to read about the aching ambivalence that the young soldier felt for his girl. Or better yet, some confession of love for a fellow soldier. He would realize that the object of his mature romantic longings was male. He would try to explain that to her and find eloquence lurking in the truth.

In the cool September night on his bunk he would dream of her, would ache with the knowledge that he would have to tell her, or avoid telling her. The pain would increase, then diminish with the new object of his affections coming to mind. Another boy from the country, a thin, well-spoken young man who had grown up on a farm in Kentucky but had learned something true about himself, a way of being, some time earlier. By chance. And was able to project that fact to his acquaintances without frightening them away. The fact was merely a vague and unthreatening difference. That is the way it had manifested itself to him, not as a revelation of epic proportions (though it might easily have become that), but rather a warmth where others felt nothing. Males never hold each other in contempt for purely physical reasons, but he felt a positive pleasure in the company of his fellows. That was all. Later he knew that he had the capacity to love them. This, too, he found out almost by accident.

He never recorded his thoughts, exactly. And they were lost to posterity because of the ephemeral nature of telephone calls. He had tried to reveal the difference to her but came up lacking.

The boy was born in May of the next year. A normal first birth: labor a little longer than average. The baby was fat and red and healthy. The mother was thin and forlorn and depressed. Both cried too much.

Shortly before the baby was born the mother had begun to see a young insurance salesman who lived on the other side of town. He was an oily and slightly undependable fellow, but he was unfazed by her present condition, brought her yellow roses and Whitman Samplers on Saturday nights and dined her as best he could. They had not made love; she said she was in no mood. He had heard somewhere that it was dangerous to have intercourse with a woman in advanced pregnancy, so they avoided it. Neither minded very much.

She had been depressed, and it would not have taken a sensitive person to have seen that, but she herself did not know and neither did her new boyfriend. Introspection was not one of their strong suits. Sharing that lack was one of their strongest bonds. It mattered hardly at all that neither was philosophical. Neither was conventionally moral, either, and that suited them, as well, since she was in no condition to marry a respectable man and he had few prospects for marrying a woman as lovely as she who was not in distressed circumstances. It had been decided one day on the verandah that they would marry as soon as the baby was born and she had regained her figure. He had asked in serious and low tones for her mother's permission for the marriage, which was given readily enough with nothing more than a sigh and a nod. The bride who would be a mother soon was still a girl, not old enough to consent to her own marriage, so this gentle gesture arose as it did out of necessity.

They would live in a saltbox-sized house on the outskirts of a rural town. The suburb had been adopted in the middle of nowhere and for no apparent reason: plenty of cheap land and yet the young shunned the opportunity to lead lives with unobstructed views and opted, instead, for tract homes, sold by slick con men from the hot little cities springing up on trucking routes.

Had either of them been in the least bit cynical they might both have been spared six years of boredom and four not very bright children. They had begun having daughters after the son was born and had continued to have them, thinking that eventually another son would come and change the course of their lives, without knowing that is what they felt. It was another common thread that ran through them, hemmed them in, but was woven in such a way as to be invisible to them. They had children; they smoked; they ate dinner; he worked; and they remained faithful to each other because it had never occurred to either one of them not to be.

One element of culture, among many, that was conspicuously absent from their lives was a regular infusion of music of any kind. They had never gone dancing, partly because he felt awkward in his body and was uninterested in learning the new steps that did not require that he lead, partly because she was usually pregnant or nursing and had a hyperbolic, almost hysterical fear of something happening to one of her babies. This fear, coupled with their real and present lack of money turned any kind of entertainment into frivolity. Both had acute memories of the Depression, though she had been younger and had not been vanquished by it, as her mother and father had been.

She had been a pretty and vivacious girl and had turned into a woman of a certain beauty that remained girlish. When she had met her young soldier and was getting ready for her first real date with him, she had put on makeup, but when she had finished saw how much it aged her, drew back from the mirror and wiped her face clean. There might come a day when she would look younger with it, but that was sometime in the distant future.

With her son came the first responsibilities she had known. There had been grueling moments in her pregnancy where she felt the pressure of stares on her while she walked down the street, but so promising did the prospect of having the baby seem (and her mother, when once her consternation abated because of a cool day and good digestion, had divined with a strand of thread and a wedding ring that the baby would be a boy) it was worth the trouble. She planned to love her son with all her heart, and would.

Rosy as he was and good-natured, from early on he seemed to shun her affection. She was as lavish with it as she could be, never giving him the chance to cry long before she ran to his side and swooped him up into her arms. He would stop crying, but turn away just the same, or when he did look at her she felt as if he were doing it quizzically, some days quick to judge. She half-bragged, half-complained to her own mother and sometimes to the insurance salesman that her son was already having higher thoughts, that the life of the mind was more important to him than his mother's milk.

From his infancy he looked as if he were about to speak; when he did actually say his first word she forgot that there was a time when he had not spoken. He had not said "momma," but "book." And she heard this as some sort of revelation about his character. Then, though it was not something she had been fond of as a child, she felt compelled to read to him and borrowed books from the lending library. Even when there were daughters in the house requiring attention, she would barricade her son and herself in the laundry room and read to him alone, dreaming that someday he would read to her.

He brought home a television one day when all that was on were the fights. She could still remember the names of the boxers [wrestlers] that had inhabited the big box in the living room with the tiny screen. It was the envy of the neighborhood. How could they afford it, with all those kids, the neighbors would ask each other. The whole world had changed when that high-pitched whine could be heard from down the block. As soon as the department store manager turned the corner in his Packard he could hear a piercing sound, an electronic scream, that had not been there before. For the first few days he would wonder whether it were dangerous to his family's health, whether the X rays or gamma rays would do any damage to them, make the children look like some of the *Life* magazine pictures from the aftermath of Nagasaki. By the time he would have decided to check into it, his wife and children had banded together to convince him that they, too, must have a television because a mere insurance peddler with all of those children couldn't possibly be in any better position to afford such a thing.

You see, these might have been people I knew who lived next door, whose children rode the bus with me when I was a child. I was younger than they. The children were a little younger than my parents. They were the boys who would go off to a year's tour in Vietnam. My parents knew none of those people well. Somehow the whole affair seemed to pass them right by. They were busy trying to earn enough money to support us and had little time left for socializing. I wonder whether they thought about anything but supporting us, now that I think about it—whether the wider world ever impinged itself squarely on their lives. They never spoke about national politics unless it was my father posturing himself as a Nixon supporter in order to drive my maternal grandmother into a frenzy. There was more talk in kindergarten about politics than at home. For years my mother insisted that she had voted for JFK until in an idle moment I realized that he had been elected before she was twenty-one. She had dreamed she had had a piece of that pie and was too young to have claimed it. She remembered very well where she had been when she heard he had died.

My father was a long way from the Texas School Book Depository when it happened. I promise.

Part 3:
from A Eulogy for Allen Barnett delivered at
The Cathedral of St. John the Divine, September 19, 1991

I found when I started going through Allen's address book making calls that almost everyone in it had a singular, peculiar relationship with him in a social vacuum. Something on the order of 260 announcements went out, from Beverly Hills to Berlin, to men and women he knew and cared about, most of whom could easily have believed they were his closest friend. Those were only the ones who were still alive. I shudder to think of how many of the 300,000 people who have died from the effects of AIDS knew Allen. There wouldn't be room for them all here.

I am the person who spoke with many of you around the time of his death and told you a little about how he died. The common wisdom is that *I* took care of *him* in the final days of his illness, but the truth is much more complicated than that. In fact we took care of each other. Through him and with him I learned an immense amount about AIDS and his particular complications, about his life, about compassion, sensitivity, and about love in extreme circumstances. I have learned that death is not ghoulish nor is it poignant, but the end of hard, dull work whose only rewards are presence and closeness, and finally, consciousness of inevitability. If I am better off for having been so close to him then, *now* I feel his absence very acutely indeed.

Allen Barnett was a small guy with a bright smile, a lyrical, arresting voice, and what Robert Patrick said were "upside-down eyes."

His smile, as you can see from the photo on the program, was utterly intoxicating; he could and did use it to great effect a couple of hours before he died. His *sneer* (which I've also seen on a few occasions) was enough to curdle milk and inspire a little fear in me. Allen was a beautiful man—not in a conventional way—who had an ageless face and the most penetrating gaze I have ever had to meet.

Allen, who took pains to invent himself, was a moralist and an aesthete. He had an ever-changing, unrelenting aesthetic ideology: he believed, not so much in the goodness of beautiful things, but rather in the inherent beauty of goodness, excellence, clarity.

He had favorite everything and was a great repository for musical, literary, and visual advice. He had favorite recipes, and I had thought a month ago that the best tribute to him might have been to have gotten together here at the high altar and had a buffet of pasta with pignoli nuts, basil, garlic, sun-dried tomatoes and anchovies, with a side of escarole. Allen and I shared a lust for comfort, that most fleeting of middle-class values, and it broke my heart when in the hospital he had so much trouble finding a position he could relax in.

In his hospital room he was propped up looking at a dreadful laminated reproduction of a family of partridges, à la Currier and Ives. Then when his first roommate moved out and we switched to the window he was stuck with a sun-bleached Dufy marina-scape. In an effort to personalize his room a little I brought in the only thing I had mounted, an old film-noir poster showing a forlorn woman and a brooding man in evening clothes on a Paris rooftop. It stayed up a week, but a couple of days before he died he called me over and said, "Ron, honey, that picture of yours is beginning to depress me." He asked me to bring the etching that hung over his couch at home. It seems emblematic—that he hadn't lost his humanity, his taste, his sense that beauty mattered, and that the absence of it could take precedence over his physical struggle. It was one of his last requests that we gather here.

I was frankly exhausted by the demands of his illness and terrified of leaving him alone. When he had decided to start the morphine drip that would both soothe him and, possibly, sedate him to the point that he would no longer be able to speak, that might suppress his already labored breathing, he asked me how I felt about the decision. He gave me the chance to tell him. His hand, that I had held continuously and deliberately for so many hours, held my hand back with new strength. He knew I needed to know he cared for me. I still need to know that. He had strong, soft hands, and I miss them.

I met Allen through a mutual friend, Phil Gambone, who introduced us over breakfast in Cambridge, Massachusetts. Phil told me a little about Allen's book, about St. Martins' having nominated it for the Pulitzer. Allen smiled but said very little. We walked through Harvard Yard and Allen and I lagged behind and talked. I wish I could remember what we said. He impressed me immediately and, although I was always a little in awe of him (for one thing, he spoke in perfect, crystalline English sentences), I knew he was accessible to me. Within twenty-four hours I had read *The Body and Its Dangers* and I knew I was in the presence of a great writer as well. I called him when I had read it and we immediately became friends. He inscribed this in my copy later on: "Older writers told me that my life wouldn't change when my book came out. Well, I met you because of it and that should count for something. I write this with gratitude for that meeting, a cold morning in Cambridge before the coffee had kicked in. I woke up at the table and there you were. Thank you for managing your way into this journey. The book, after all, is only the sound of one hand clapping."

At first I would hardly have known he had other friends. Many of you and others who are not here have realized that he kept most of us in orbit around him and we seldom met each other through him. His apartment was furnished to accommodate the inhabitant and one very special guest, a combination I think he must have thought sacred. Whoever spent time with him could never have felt anything less than the absolute center of his formidable attention. This treatment I found to be a profound and generous act of love, and its absence a loss I can just bear because I have felt it. When you were alone with Allen you could not feel lonely, bored, or disengaged. His trust was palpable. He believed that indifference, contrary to poetic belief, was the worst we had to fear, and never allowed it near him.

He was passionate about his work and was patient and generous enough to share without condescension. He was sweet and difficult, honest and brilliantly conniving. His need for love was somehow more obvious than for others, and that was upsetting sometimes, refreshing at others. He was never cloying or pitiful. He was sharp and defiant and strong-willed and soft-hearted. We had plenty left to argue about, and I will wait a long time for anyone who will challenge me the way he did.

Please take your memories of Allen, of his immense complexity, into your hearts, minds, and souls and hold him close to you always. Be grateful that you knew him however well you knew him. Realize that he has left us great gifts. Take credit for having been chosen to be a part of his life. Hold within you his contrariness with his magnanimity, his wisdom with his innocence, his joy and sadness, courage and fear. Cut the platitudes—they are too crude to describe him. Never speak of what Allen *would* have done or what he would have wanted. Because the only thing we know for certain is that he *should* have been healthy, and that he *should* be alive right now to tell us, with style and grace, how we could possibly begin to register the loss of him.

from The Reluctant Journal
ALLEN BARNETT

Allen Barnett, author of The Body and Its Dangers, *died of AIDS-related causes on August 14, 1991, in Manhattan where he had lived for more then a decade.* The Body and Its Dangers, *released in 1990 to critical acclaim, was Barnett's only full-length published work. The following are excerpts from his unpublished journals.*

Provincetown, October 1982

A river, a warehouse, a parking lot: a bright-white truck that said, "Blue Sky Van." One could buy sandwiches and other truck food from its side window. The van was so pretty, as was the sky, the boats, the warehouse; one could imagine the food was actually appetizing.

This must be Bridgeport, he thought.

Now AOB had not been in Bridgeport, nor passed through it on the Amtrak to Boston in three years, but it was indeed Bridgeport. There was the Jai-Alai building just ahead.

How amusing! Bridgeport, he thought.

He was amused by the fact that he had guessed, looking up from his reading for the first time since leaving Penn Station.

He was then amused by his own self-amusement. Masturbation was called self-abuse. It should be called self-amusement. He was, however, beginning to find it less and less amusing, as the weeks went by.

A heavyset-ish woman across the aisle was/is wearing a small-print, houndstooth pantsuit. When she stands, the pattern across the ass waves like a Vasanly (?) painting. He doesn't like Vasanly an iota, but all this is amusing to him.

Seagulls on dirt hills to cover landfill trash. An ultra-modern, suburban grain tower? New Haven.

The colors of the day are lovely. He had thought over the past couple weeks that he might be going blind. Borges, nearly blind, sees yellow. There does seem to be an abundance of yellow leaves.

Memory: masturbation caused blindness. He had perfect vision until puberty, then the world became indistinct.

Two people behind him: a black man talking about his education at some good school. He can't talk worth a shit. The black, buzzy English is driving AOB mad; if only the train would start the noise may drown out the man's idiocy.

Sex and blindness: let's see; Oedipus pulls out his eyes when he discovers the truth. Extreme but effective: the stuff of great drama. A man's a man for that.

There are ways of keeping his mind off his married-man lover who he suspects of seeing still another on the side. Well, so what. The other night after sex he had discovered blood on his sheets. The lover was dressing, and AOB said, "Hmm," as if amused by something.

"What is it?"

"Oh, nothing… Hmm," he said again, feeling his own asshole and finding blood.

"What?"

"Oh, nothing."

The black man in the backseat is making slurs against Ricans. He wished the black man suddenly dead.

He doesn't have sex with hardly anyone because he is afraid of catching something, which would mean at least then he could not have sex with his married-man, who would then probably have sex with others and not get anything.

"I just ask that you be careful."

"Excuse me, I don't know your name, but before you stick your cock up my ass do you have a recent certificate of health?"

And recently his trick had only wanted to touch him.

"Do you want me to play with your tits or something while you jerk off?"

The black man: "We is talking about style and structure." He knows not of what he speaks. "Keep the knowledge flowing," he says. Then he looks out the window and says, "I see a horsey."

A VFW cemetery out the window.

So he ends up jerking off with the trick, with his married-man lover, and more often by himself because it amounts to the same thing, right? Of course he's going blind.

He should not drink more than one cup of coffee for he only gets upset lately.

He is going to the ocean. He is going to it at the attraction of any great body. He feels the desire in every part of his tissue, muscle, nerve, and body fluid. His best friend is coming, but later. For a while, it will be just him. He will write his book on the serenity and sensuousness of Dutch art. It will not make him famous, but accepted.

There were swans out the window...

Jury Duty; Day 2

I had spent the last of my 75-cent tokes yesterday and stood in line to buy the same old token at a new, startling price. It seems to me there was a rush the last time the fare went up to buy out tokens—to save, resulting in a shortage of tokens and the limiting of their sales. For all our huff and puff at the indignities of the fare increase, New Yorkers do seem to resign themselves quickly to their fates. Perhaps that is why we are—can be—so terribly rude to one another, or extraordinarily gracious.

The subway ride was crowded and rough. I see a handsome

man—husband of a woman who is a friend of a friend of mine. A distant relationship. One night I was in his apartment at a small party where the women outnumbered the men two to one, and there were three men, and me—one of them gay. It was a ribald evening, with the women dominating the conversation; only one of them married, one of them with a relationship on the rocks, and all the rest wanting a man. Yet the conversation centered around the worst common topics of the day—co-ops and why are men so stupid. The two other men took the ribbing of the women in good nature. I being the gay fellow would probably side with the women, for it is quite true that I, for the most part, find men, all of them, quite a stupid lot—with gay men having a slight edge over the rest. But this particular evening I was in the limbo middle field—not really one of the girls, for in their eyes I would have been one of their possibilities for romance if not for the fact that I'm gay, which I'm told by women friends, of whom I have many and am employed by several, that the fact of a man's gayness is just a rejection of them, a limiting of the field, an emptying of the woods.

Nor was I one of the men that night. The man I stood on the subway with this morning offered the other man a cigar, but not one to me. Whether or not this was a masculine jab, which it most probably was, or a real offer of a cigar, I do not know. I was not included in the offer and I did indeed want a cigar. But most of all startling about the evening was as we were leaving, wishing each other a happy new year and congratulating ourselves for the adult, reasonable, pleasant way we brought in the new year, this married man bent over and kissed my cheek. I floated home in a cloud. It was like a basketball game where the score is neck-to-neck and *my side* has the ball in the other court, but throws the ball madly and squarely into the basket from clear across the floor. That won the evening for me, this selfless peck.

Now I stand right next to the handsome man in the subway. It is midweek, Wednesday morning, and we don't speak. In a sense

I am bothered by this. Then I think, I am in no mood to speak to anyone. I doubt that he is either, therefore into our New York sphere, that little space we make for ourselves on the subway that stretches between our eyes and our paperbacks, or our eyes and the backs of our minds.

I read Annie Dillard on the subway. Yesterday, waiting for my name to be called for jury duty, I read the novel I had bought before lunchtime. Last night I found the Bantam edition of *Pilgrim at Tinker Creek*—two and a quarter. A bargain. I read Dillard because she gives rhetoric a good name. She is not afraid of rhetorical devices—alliteration, repetition, interior rhymes, metaphors. She reminds me again of my pleasure in reading. Sometimes she is feminine in a way I don't like—coy, cute, dumb-blonde, awestruck. But this is a sexist thing to say. She is sometimes this way because she goes for the big effect and something fails, in my mind. I think I love her all the more for this, because one sees fewer writers—men or women—going for this effect. I love her sense of wonder, her delight with her thought process. I also suspect that she grew up rich and had the privilege of her consciousness. Compare Dillard to Tillie Olsen and see what privilege does to focus. Fine talents both; however, both write with an attempt to understand—to know—while so few do. I myself find myself reading less and less because I feel constantly lectured. Opinions come so strong, so furious, so self-involved that I want to run from periodicals, especially those with a New York base. Even friends can be terrifying in this respect: at Christmas dinner, one friend, however usually pleasant, started to pontificate on the "ultimate failure of the Met's gala." Why do we live in such a critical age? "Ultimately" one wonders what difference the failure of the Met gala makes on anyone. The friend did not intend to be boring—to pontificate and lecture—and often suffers something of that outlandish criticism opera-lovers get when they want to listen to the Saturday Met broadcast while at an apartment-painting party where everyone else wants to listen to the disco station. My friend, however, did not realize at this moment that when one expounds critically about an area he basically enjoys, he excludes everyone from that enjoyment.

Exuberant love for something includes people, I believe, much the same way we are drawn to warm people and turned away by the cold. People who expound at *any* length at parties on the "ultimate failure" of say, the latest critic's favorite movie, or this or that, ultimately are bringing themselves to that same level of failure. To let the bad sink with the bad, we give such credence to our daily critics. I wonder if these people aren't getting paid too much.

I wonder why we city-dwellers are so always critical, analytical, serious, about the trivial. Is it our age? Is it our educations? Is this the way we were taught to enjoy our music, our books, our movies, our ice cream? Do we pay so much for it all that we expect to participate in its being to such an extent that we analyze it as we analyze ourselves?

An older man in my office gym told me that if I did not have chest hair or a moustache I would look like a sixteen-year-old athlete. When I told this to the man I was living with, he smiled at the thought, but I did nothing about it. In the shower, then, in the most tender and unself-conscious moment I have ever felt towards myself, I reached for the straight-edged razor, the lather brush, and cup, and beat up a lather in the cup, brushed my chest, and shaved my torso from breastplate to navel. The sun had passed the highest point in the sky and was just spreading an angle of light into the bathroom. I stood covered with water, catching the light. I felt generous towards the world in a way that did not totally obliterate me, but altered the balance... I did look sixteen, and more than a little handsome and even strong. I felt light and still and strong. And if everything were not completely right, it just might be.

Rage, Rage
JOHN WEIR

My friend David Feinberg, the novelist and essayist who died of AIDS last November, has been moralized as a kind of alternative North American martyr. He was not just homosexual, he was self-consciously "queer." His novel, *Eighty-Sixed*, was not just a brilliant monologue about male horniness, Jewish guilt, and AIDS anxiety, it was "transgressive." He was not merely a regular ACT UP member who was routinely arrested at demonstrations, he was "countercultural." He did not die, he was "killed by government neglect."

In short, David has emerged post-mortem as the kind of outsider who is sentimentalized by the left and demonized by the right. He is noted for being difficult because we expect difficulty from antagonists and sufferers. Mourners celebrate his jokiness, his irritability, his honesty about how much of his life he spent wanting, having, or not getting sex. If David was popular among heterosexual readers, I suspect it was in part because his writing satisfied certain preconceptions about homosexual men. Of course, gay men like to believe clichés about themselves, too.

David's writing is not clichéd. Rather, it is profoundly superficial. It works because it skirts so quickly and so hectically over the surface of things, accumulating so many details, fact upon fact, that it gives the effect of deep feeling. It has virtual depth. There is no comfort in his writing, only anxiety, humor, sentimentality, rage, and despair, as well as a lot of silliness. His genius was in being silly; he could make it feel like a meaningful connection. He was also an artful complainer. His last book, *Queer and Loathing: Rants and Raves of a Raging AIDS Clone*, which was published the week he died, is the least wisecracking, and the hardest to read of all his work because it is the most unmitigated by irony. He used irony to distance himself from pain, but irony failed him in the end, and all that was left was his devastating fear and rage.

He was my closest friend for the past five years. As death approached, I was asked, "How do you feel about David's dying?" and I would answer, "If AIDS doesn't kill him, I will." People would laugh as if I were making a kind of Feinbergian joke, as an homage to him. What I didn't say is that shortly before he died, I stopped liking him. I stopped liking him not just then, but always. It was retroactive. He was so mean to me and to all of his devoted friends, so relentlessly and mindlessly and destructively angry, that I forgot, for a long time, what I ever liked about him.

Yet he is being honored for his anger. Anger is the orthodoxy of the self-proclaimed AIDS activist community. It is the authority invested in the individual as well as the group. "Where is your anger?" people still ask, over and over, at ACT UP meetings, as if checking other people for I.D. Rage bestows authenticity. Anger is seen as wholly reliable because it is so intensely felt. The fundamental sentimentality of ACT UP is the belief that emotions always tell the truth. The group's miscalculation is that feelings alone, directly and powerfully expressed, can change things.

I am speaking now as someone who has lain across pavement in sub-zero temperature in February, my arm hooked to David's arm through steel tubing, blocking the entrance to Hoffman-LaRoche, a big pharmaceutical company in New Jersey. For three hours we chanted, "Arrest the real criminal," while the four local police officers who bothered to show up watched with bemused contempt. In Albany, in New Hampshire during primary season, in Washington, D.C., inside Grand Central Station, marching around through the financial district in Manhattan, I held David's hand, or clenched my fists with his and raised them high to shout, "We'll never be silent again." When I ran across the set of the "CBS Evening News" during the height of the Gulf war, chanting "Fight AIDS, not Arabs," I was doing it for David.

Like David, I thought that if I got angry enough, he would not have to die. I was wrong, and so was he. ACT UP was wrong. Anger is a useful strategy—so is foolishness—if it remains a strategy, and does not become a faith. David was angry for a living. Not only did it not keep him alive, it kept him from whatever comfort he might fleetingly have felt when he was dying. I learned a lot about anger, watching David die. The New Age premise that "finding your anger" is the key to health and strength turns out to be wishful thinking. Anger generates nothing but anger. It doesn't express truth, it glorifies ego.

The limitations of anger as a public cry to action were clear to me when I went with David last October to help him deliver what he called his "scathing diatribe" to ACT UP. He weighed 106 pounds that night, down from 150. He was three weeks from death. His body, which he was always careful to maintain in perfect shape, as if he might be called upon to use it as a weapon, had disintegrated. His skeleton showed everywhere. He clutched his trousers in an angry fist to keep them from sliding halfway down his thighs. Like King Lear back from the heath, he looked and sounded furious, raving, and crazy. There was, however, no catharsis in his rage. It was wasted on him, and it was wasted on the room.

There ought to be a sign hanging over New York's Gay and

Lesbian Community Center on Monday nights—ACT UP nights—
that says, "ABANDON HOPE, ALL WHO ENTER HERE."
The night David showed up, he was addressing an organization that
no longer exists. So much anger was spent by so many people so
quickly, to so little effect, that the residue of bitterness left most of
New York's AIDS activist community burned out. A lot of people
died. But many more were exhausted by the group's ineffectual
ethos of collective, unquestioned rage.

It isn't poetry that makes nothing happen, it's anger. I don't
remember much of David's speech. I remember he said "fuck" a lot.
Like many ACT UP members, he had an adolescent's faith in the
totemic power of the word "fuck." He also used the word "anger."
He was angry about dying. He was angry at everyone in the room,
and everyone who had ever attended a meeting, living or dead. It
was the kind of speech that has a long tradition in ACT UP, a
purging cry of rage, meant to renew activist fervor. I couldn't
listen. I thought the point was not that David wanted a cure for
AIDS, but that he wanted a cure for him. For the past five years,
he'd put all his faith and energy into a group that was supposed to
be a community. In the end, however, David didn't care that his
friends were dying, he cared that he was dying.

Many people in the room that night, and others who heard
about what went on there, feel he had a perfect right to his self-
interest. I don't. His death wasn't something that happened only
to him. I was losing something, too. So were a lot of people.
Apart from anger, one of the implicit faiths of ACT UP is selfishness. What ACT UP wants as a group is to provide an outlet
for the personal gratification of each individual soul. The HIV-
negative members want to be affirmed. The HIV-positive
members want to be cured. David's speech was not courageous or
inspiring, it was egotistical. What he finally said to the AIDS
activist community was, "This is about *me*. Nothing matters now
except saving *me*."

I would have done anything to help him, but finally what David wanted rescuing from wasn't AIDS. He hated AIDS, but more than that, he hated being human. Like a lot of AIDS activists, he thought that he alone was too special to die.

IDENTITY

The question of identity—any identity—is problematic in the twentieth century. In this post-structuralist, post-modern, deconstructed age, how does anyone "identify"—with anything?

In this context, gay and lesbian identity is both easier and harder. Easier because being outlawed because of one's sexual feelings and actions gives one an instant, ready-made, off-the-rack identity. But harder because such identities—being essentially prefabricated—are hardly exact, not form-fitting to individual lives. Even in our post-Stonewall culture there are many identities that gay men and lesbians can choose—homosexual, gay, queer, lesbian, lesbian-separatist, radical fairy, faggot, dyke, fem, drag queen, butch, top, bottom—but the array of choices is often more perplexing than satisfying. Which actually suits the best? Can one mix and match? Is it possible to have too many "choices" of identity? Aren't these very labels limiting how we each might grow and define ourselves?

Writing about the issue—the problem?—of identity has long been a gay concern, and the writers here address not the overarching question but speak on very specific, and often personal, issues. Charley Shively's "Malcolm X's Wild Side" uncovers, in some detail, the personal—homosexual—life of the great African-American visionary and leader. Shively's evidence is forthright and well presented, but the questions raised are not the predictable "Was Malcolm X gay?" but rather how personal identity is constructed around sexual activity, race, ethnicity, religious beliefs, and even history. "Malcolm X's Wild Side" is sure to stir controversy but this should not obscure the more profound questions Shively raises.

"Danny," by Rondo Mieczkowski, tells the story of an intense, long-standing relationship between two gay men who begin as lovers and, when that phase is over, continue as best friends. Mieczkowski charts the everyday happenings that make up any relationship and the cumulative effect is a saga of detail and affection, love and sustenance. But beneath its affirmative, calm exterior, "Danny" is really about how difficult it is for gay men to break through the traditional, and culturally mandated, identities of "tricks," "lovers," "friends," "ex-boyfriends," and "partners." Mieczkowski and Danny have to work hard at defining and redefining who they are and what they want to be to one another: personal and social identities overlap here; and gay men who are attempting to forge new types of relationships, of identities, have little to go on except their own desires and intuitions.

Inventing new models of relationships can only happen after we discover and come to terms with our sexuality. This is a constant problem facing young gay people. Gay teens have few role models in our society. Larry Gross's "You're the First Person I've Ever Told I'm Gay: Letters to a Fictional Gay Teen" is a startling look at how necessary, and vital, the need is for gay teen visibility. By examining the letters written by gay teenagers to Billy Douglas—a fictional teenaged gay character on the television soap opera *One Life to Live*—Gross explores the longing and the loneliness of gay youth. That the presentation of a single gay character—even a fictional one—could be so important and so moving to so many people is a testament to how much the isolation and heartache of the closet still exists in our culture that at times seems to be making such progress.

The omnipresent reality of the closet is at the center of Lawrence Mass's "Musical Closets: A Personal and Selective Documentary History of Outing and Coming Out in the Music World." Mass's essay is a long, complex, personal analysis/documentary of the author's attempts to "do the right thing" when dealing with closeted friends in the world of classical music. His purpose here is not simply to "out" closeted composers and critics but to examine, in detail, all of the ways in which sexual and personal identity interact with relationships, the manufacture of culture, and the interplay between the mainstream media and the world of politics. But his bottom line is what it means to tell the truth—about sex, about politics, about AIDS, about friends, and about what it means to be gay in a world that rewards the closet and punishes those who are openly gay. The essay is composed of two sections. The first is the original piece that Mass wrote several years ago and which was eventually rejected for publications after two initial acceptances; the second is a description of how those rejections played out and the ramifications for both the author's thinking and his relationships. There is much you may disagree with in Mass's essay— the author himself is constantly asking himself the same questions that may reel through the reader's head—but it is his unabating honesty with himself (and the same honesty he expects from others) that fuels the moral and narrative passions of "Musical Closets."

Unrestrained honesty also marks "I'm Going Out Like a Fucking Meteor," one of the final pieces written by Craig G. Harris before his death in 1991 at the age of thirty-three. Having struggled—in a racist and homophobic culture—with his self-acceptance as a black gay man Harris writes movingly of dealing with his new identity as a person with AIDS. Between the trips to the doctor, the small and large opportunistic infections, and the constant threat of public and private humiliations, Harris maintains a valiant struggle for dignity and self-respect. Any identity—especially an identity that is unwelcomed—is always in flux, and Harris manages with wit, anger, and a will to survive to integrate his new identity with his existing life. The terror of AIDS and of death permeates every line of "I'm Going Out Like a Fucking Meteor"—the fear is palpable—but Harris never gives up or surrenders to the inevitable. His identity as a person with AIDS never takes control of his life and to the end he rejoices in his bravery, individuality, and ability to survive.

Michael Lowenthal's "Saying Kaddish for Peter" is a story of how identity can be found in the most surprising of places. With its opening sentence, "There was an angel in my grandfather's obituary," Lowenthal tells of his discovery, as a teenager, of an uncle who had died at the age of twenty-one in a German concentration camp. As he struggles with his own coming out and attempts to make sense of his life, the image of his uncle Peter—whom he fantasizes was just like him in so many ways—gives Lowenthal the promise of hope in dealing with everyday life and its attendant problems. Like a magical apparition, or a guardian angel, Peter helps give the author the ability to explore his own identity in a world that too often feels heartless, cruel, and confusing.

Malcolm X's Wild Side
CHARLEY SHIVELY

In life and in death Malcolm X (1925–1965) symbolizes uncompromising, revolutionary integrity. Actor and director Ossie Davis in his 1965 eulogy called Malcolm "our manhood, our living black manhood…. our own black shining prince." So much emphasis on "black manhood" can imply a reproach to queers and women. The masculine thrust of Martin Luther King, Stokely Carmichael, Eldridge Cleaver or Huey Newton defined a new African-American. This manhood excluded lisping and obscured the role played by women and queers in making the revolution. Carmichael as leader of the Student Non-Violent Coordinating Committee said that "the only position for women in SNCC is prone."

"Manhood," so framed, leaves no place for Malcolm's wild side; it obliterates every testament of his gay activity. Spike Lee in his film *Malcolm X* (1992) invents scenes to distance his hero from any queerness. Malcolm's wild side, however, demonstrates a greater man than his image makers would allow. Sexual relations with men strengthened him. Liberated from the specter of homosexuality (which drives so many straight men), Malcolm X offered his whole body without reservation to all who would join him.

While the wild side has been ignored, clues and clear indications remain. Bruce Perry, *Malcolm, The Life of a Man Who Changed Black America* (1991) and Clayborne Carson's edition of *Malcolm X, The FBI File* (1991) present quite specific evidence. I have myself examined Malcolm's prison files and spoke with queers who knew him as a hustler in Boston. Since Perry's book appeared, the Massachusetts Commissioner of Corrections has blotted out all the names and addresses of Malcolm's contacts and has restricted researchers' access to the dossier. Only after two letters, many phone calls, and an interview, did I obtain access to the file. The research director was concerned about my "focus" and suggested that the files would "contribute nothing of value" to my investigation. One file contains a desperate plea, "Do Not Destroy." Malcolm's draft records have already been obliterated; his letters and other unpublished writings cannot be quoted; doubtless those, too, will be sanitized to remove any hint of homosexual love. For instance, he worried that the poems he wrote in prison might seem too "effeminate."

The "correctional" files which survive are certainly contaminated since the examiners intended to discipline and punish Malcolm— to correct his blackness no less than his queerness. One shrink complained, "Subject is reported to be a shrewd and cunning individual." Nonetheless, other sources corroborate his homosexual activity and document relationships to johns and other queers. And the FBI files indicate how they tried to use homosexuality both to discredit him and at the same time to stir up trouble with prominent African-American homosexuals such as Bayard Rustin or James Baldwin. But Malcolm, Baldwin, and Rustin learned to work around such provocation.

On entering the Massachusetts prison system in 1946 when he was twenty years old, Malcolm gave his occupation as "Show business." During his assessment, he answered that he had started using marijuana at the age of seventeen by "associating with people in the theatrical world" as he attended "occasional parties." His stage name was "Rhythm Red" and he also performed under the name "Jack Carlton" in New York's "Lobster Pond." Of course, then and now "the theatrical world" was a code name for deviant sexuality. Even in his *Autobiography*, Malcolm bragged about waking "up a white actor I knew who lived in the Howard Hotel on Forty-fifth Street, off Sixth Avenue.... I got some opium from that fellow." Who would give up opium at that hour without getting some love in return? Malcolm's favorite singer was Lady Day and his favorite song her "You Don't Know What Love Is" ... "until you face each dawn with sleepless eyes." Lady Day has long been a gay icon; as late as the 70s, the Atlantic House, a gay bar in Provincetown had only Billie Holiday numbers on its juke box.

To the neo-Freudian shrinks who examined him, Malcolm had the typical markings of a "homosexual." His father, a black nationalist Garveyite preacher, persecuted by white supremacists, was crushed to death under a streetcar in Michigan. ("Suicide" according to the coroner.) His mother, whom he loved dearly, broke under the strains of widowhood, racism, and the Great Depression. She was forced into a mental hospital in 1939. Only fourteen years old, Malcolm then had to depend on the "kindness of strangers" to survive.

The stories of his early years in Michigan portray a sensitive, "sissy" child. With a neighboring tomboy, he played house; Betty Jean played husband and he played wife. Malcolm and a boyfriend romped in the woods with another boy, who had a big cock. Malcolm liked to watch the stud jerk off; Robert also gave blow jobs. Some of the boys called Malcolm "Sissy" (he loathed sports, but enjoyed dancing). They also called him "Madame Harpy," because he was reported going in drag. The nickname "Harpy" never bothered him so much as the name "Red" (he had reddish hair), which he disliked. Unlike the teenagers who dreamed of being firemen, policemen, or soldiers, Malcolm wanted to be a lawyer. His guidance counselor told him, "That's no realistic goal for a nigger."

After being bounced around between foster homes and a juvenile detention center, Malcolm left Michigan when he was fifteen and joined his half-sister Ella Little in Boston. After the boy woke up one morning with milk coming out of his nipples, she rushed him to the doctor, who reassured them that "endocrinological factors" were to blame.

Malcolm rapidly entered the famous fast lane during his late teen years. He wore a "zoot suit," conked his hair, bounced around from job to job and from city to city; he worked on the railroads, which facilitated his movements. In these years Malcolm hated "romance without finance," and spread the story among his Michigan friends and later in his *Autobiography* that he was busy pimping women.

There is evidence that he worked the gentlemen more than the ladies. Toward the end of 1942 he moved to Flint, Michigan, for a couple of months. There he lived with a drag queen called "Miss Jones" or "Willie Mae." In the same year he contracted a case of clap. Back in New York City, Malcolm introduced Michigan home boys to the Harlem YMCA, where they met the Reverend Witherspoon, who blew them (one at a time) and in return paid their rent for a week along with a chicken dinner. When the boys joked about needing a chicken dinner, they were talking about more than mashed potatoes.

These were the years when Harlem was in vogue, and when the Second World War led to a lot of men coming out under fire. James Baldwin himself left the ministry in 1942. Only ten months older than Malcolm, Baldwin took up with a Harlem gangster lover about the same time Malcolm was working Small's Paradise. If their paths crossed then, neither mentioned it later, but they shared the same relaxed milieu where drugs, drink, dancing, music, and sex were easy. That world, however, suffered the continuous presence of police surveillance. Eventually the tension between police and residents erupted into one of many Harlem uprisings in August 1943. Part of the discontent was the demand of the United States for African-American servicemen to go into a segregated army. The disorders in Harlem and the police crackdowns made the place less enticing for customers; downtown trade dropped off and uptown regulars often drifted away. Baldwin (with a hardship exemption from the army) took a job in New Jersey. Malcolm registered for the draft after he turned eighteen. In October 1943, Selective Service classified him IV-F for psychiatric reasons: "Psychopathic personality[;] inadequate, sexual perversion." In the *Autobiography*, Malcolm said he "never bothered to ask why I was rejected."

Happy to escape the army, Malcolm returned to Boston, He soon got caught stealing his aunt's fur coat; she prosecuted; he got a three-month suspended sentence and returned to Michigan. Here his adventures turned mainly on the wild side. He tried to rob a drag queen with whom he was sleeping but she clobbered him and he was scarred for life as he hurt himself trying to escape her anger. Soon he was living with a heavyweight queer named Jimmy Williams. Malcolm robbed Williams but the gay network tracked Malcolm down. He begged forgiveness and quickly went to Detroit where he robbed another queer (Douglas Hayes) and was this time arrested. With bail and a postponed trial, Malcolm then returned to Jimmy Williams, who welcomed him back with open arms. A foreman at the Capital Bedding Company, Jimmy found Malcolm a job working under him making mattresses but the midwest bed business soon bored Malcolm and he went east again.

Back in Boston he organized a gang of three Armenian women and two other black men. One of the women set him up in a room near Harvard University, where they fucked while her husband was off to war. His lesbian friends had taught him the importance of making sure a woman came when she was having sex. The *Autobiography* describes the gang's burglary and sexual exploits as they worked the Boston suburbs of Belmont (headquarters of the John Birch Society), Newton, Arlington, Brookline (birthplace of John F. Kennedy, present home of Michael Dukakis) and Milton (birthplace of George Bush).

Meanwhile, Malcolm was working the johns in Boston; he had studied closely how to respond to the desires of other men. In the *Autobiography*, he identifies with the women prostitutes; they taught him how to satisfy men. The words he puts in their mouths could be his own: "After most men passed their virile twenties, they went to bed mainly to satisfy their egos, and because a lot of women don't understand it that way, they damage and wreck a man's ego."

Malcolm's sessions with William Paul Lennon on Beacon Hill followed his own advice. And the relationship between the two men typifies some of the dynamics between Boston's Irish and African-American communities. According to Michael Bronski (author of *Culture Clash*), each dreams of the other beating them to death as they jerk off. Lennon described Malcolm as a "butler" doing "general housework." According to one member of the B&E gang, "Lennon paid Malcolm to disrobe him, place him on his bed, sprinkle him with talcum powder, and massage him until he reached climax." (Perry, 83) Likewise, Malcolm helped recruit other handsome African-American youths to play the game. They, of course, robbed Lennon, but that seems only to have endeared them to him. Lennon's Beacon Hill apartment was only a fuck joint; he lived more comfortably in Sandwich, Massachusetts, on Cape Cod with his elderly mother.

Malcolm and his comrade Jarvis greatly exaggerated Lennon's wealth and social position. Lennon's father worked in Pawtucket, Rhode Island. Born there in 1888, Lennon attended the working-class St. Mary's parochial school. He never married, never joined the army, never worked much and lived after 1934 with his mother on Cape Cod. When he died in 1964, seventy-six years old, he was buried in Pawtucket's St. Mary's Cemetery. Doubtless, if he could have been interviewed for *The Advocate*, William Lennon would have exaggerated Malcolm's wildness just as Jarvis exaggerated Lennon's being a Boston Brahmin. After Lennon's death in October, Malcolm followed him four months later in February 1965.

Spike Lee's *Malcolm X* plays strange games with the wild thing. Malcolm's relations with Lennon are sanitized even further than in the *Autobiography*, where only Rudy (who is more Italian than African) goes to bed with the john (off screen). In the movie, Spike Lee invents a scene where Malcolm humiliates the bisexual (and half-Italian) Rudy by making him quiver in a Russian roulette episode where Malcolm wants to be the gang leader. In the *Autobiography*, Malcolm fired three blank shots into his own head; in the movie, he fires two into his head, then two into Rudy's head. Rudy in fiction quivers; in real life he was "built like Jersey Joe Walcott."

In the movie, when the boys go to rob Lennon, Malcolm jimmies a lock on a historic Beacon Hill mansion facing onto the Boston Common; wimpy Rudy waits in the car. Malcolm and his buddy Jarvis take their shoes off and climb the stairs into the elegantly furnished bedroom. Here the john is fast asleep and in bed with a bearded young white man. Malcolm even takes a big diamond ring from the queer's finger without waking him or his lover up. In Harvard Square, the audience gasped at this scene; in Boston's Park Square, many applauded. The latter movie house was just beside Jacques, a favorite of black transvestites.

Unlike Spike Lee, Bruce Perry uncovers many homosexual facts of Malcolm's life, but he fails to understand the wild side either of Lennon or of Malcolm. Without other evidence, he claims that Malcolm's homosexuality "was sporadic." Perry's evidence is understandably sporadic, but does it follow that Malcolm's practice was sporadic? Malcolm in his initial prison interview called Lennon one of the only men in the world "interested" in him. Malcolm's father and Lennon were born about the same time and Lennon "was old enough to be the gentle, loving father Malcolm had never had."

Perry's psychologizing implies that our sexuality is something pathological, loathsome, and in need of explanation. Nonetheless, he recognizes that Malcolm X's homosexuality formed an integral part of his life. Perry writes that:

> Malcolm's income-producing homosexual activity....constituted a key link in a chain of events that included the absence of appropriate male role models; tyrannical females at home and school; the excessive demands that had been made on him; the fact that there was no one to teach him how to meet those demands; his fear of combat...his unsatisfying sexual experiences; and his inability to support himself or to make his way in a competitive, bigoted world. Perhaps that is why he asserted, years later, that a man's "greatest urge" is the need to feel masculine. (p.83)

In 1946, Malcolm Little's life of sex, drugs, and jazz ended as he entered the Charlestown Prison in Boston; he served a long sentence for breaking and entering charges. The women in his gang claimed they had been forced to rob houses. They turned state's evidence in return for reduced sentences. Because they were seen as white, Malcolm's sentence was unusually harsh and he did not leave prison until 1952. There he converted to the Nation of Islam.

A curtain of silence falls over his relationship to the homosexual among his fellow prisoners. Malcolm Jarvis, who was a member of his gang and went to prison with him, recalled his saying that "One should carry one's brains in one's head, not between one's legs." He worried that his writing poems might be considered effeminate. While in prison, Malcolm told Jarvis that life incorporated an interchange of opposites: love/hate; black/white;

morality/criminality; generosity/selfishness; self-deprivation/greed; loyalty/treachery; submissiveness/tyranny; sensitivity/ toughness; homosexuality/heterosexuality; timidity/courage. Significant in its absence is the duality of man/woman and equally significant Malcolm's inclusion of homosexuality/heterosexuality as one of the great dualisms of the universe. Every other of the dualities have been documented in accounts of Malcolm's prison time but a veil of censorship covers sex behind bars.

Here Spike Lee makes a daring leap in suggesting homosexual overtones in Malcolm's relations with an older man in prison. The *Autobiography* calls the man "Bimbi." Perry identifies him as John Elton Bembry; Spike Lee calls him "Baines." In Spike Lee's version, Mr. B gives Malcolm nutmeg: Denzel Washington (who plays Malcolm) wears a very discreet white towel; Mr. B is fully clothed. Spike Lee conflates Mr. B first with those who converted Malcolm to Islam and then with the leader in the Nation of Islam who turned Elijah Muhammad against Malcolm. This conflation provides dramatic point only from the underlying homosexual subtext. Two men alone in the shower: one offers gifts; the other accepts. They become lovers, but later the young beauty is betrayed by the older man to whom he had given his life and ass.

Malcolm's homosexual activities in prison are not unlike those of Jews in the concentration camps who survived because they served their Nazi guards. Malcolm left prison with a bleeding asshole. While he was in prison, his rectum was so injured that he required medical attention ("hemorrhoid operation"). For a young man, still in his 20s, hemorrhoids are relatively rare. Getting fucked too soon after the operation, "Stitches pulled loose, a cyst developed."

The prison sexuality was more than "situational." Immediately upon leaving prison, Malcolm headed for the gay streets of Boston. "The first stop I made was a Turkish bath," he wrote in his *Autobiography*. "I got some of that physical feeling of prison-taint steamed off me." The only Turkish facility at the time was known as "Our Lady of Vapors" (Lundin Baths), located just behind the Trailways bus station and beside a gay bar known then as "12 Carver Street" and in the Seventies as "The Ramrod Room." (Now relocated in the Fenway.)

In the *Autobiography*, Malcolm explained that the loathsome details were not to titillate readers but to awaken them to the truth of Islam. He believed that "the full story is the best way" to show how someone "sunk to the very bottom of the American white man's society" could still find "Allah and the religion of Islam…" Detailing homosexual loves and lusts could have provided even greater proof of how far down he had gone and then of how far he could rise with Allah. There are two possibilities: one that he never gave up his homosexual pleasures but pursued them discreetly in prison, among his friends, and in Moslem lands. Alternatively, he may have indeed given up cocks for Allah.

The best evidence of the first suggestion is that Malcolm maintained a relationship with his beloved "Bimbi," until his death. When Bimbi got out of prison, the older man rented a room near where Malcolm was living with his family. Malcolm saw him regularly and turned to him to discuss the most difficult crises in his life as a Muslim. Bimbi noticed when Malcolm was mad, when sad, when worried, and when happy (after visiting his mother in Michigan).

Once released from prison Malcolm quickly rose to be second only to Elijah Muhammad inside the Nation of Islam. He expanded the temples, organized the newspaper, publicized the group. Mike Wallace's CBS special on the Nation of Islam made Malcolm an overnight celebrity. While he advanced far beyond his spiritual father, Malcolm dearly loved Elijah Muhammad, but he hated the man's heterosexuality, which was a major cause of his split from the Nation. Malcolm's preaching against adultery exceeded the standard Islamic denunciations. He himself had little interest and some repugnance for any heterosexuality. Indeed he may have been pressured into marriage by his position as the leading minister and possible heir apparent. Malcolm's wife bore him four children. But he was the first to acknowledge how little time they spent together. Once split from the Nation of Islam, Malcolm traveled to Africa and received Islamic teachings in Egypt and Arabia. He rallied the nations of Africa to support UN intervention against the U.S. mistreatment of African-Americans. He organized the Organization of African-American Unity. The Nation of Islam (including a man recruited by Malcolm, Louis Farrakhan) called for his death. Farrakhan himself had been a calypso singer and violin player; Malcolm had personally recruited him from the theater world. With CIA, FBI, and perhaps New York City police complicity, Malcolm X was gunned down February 21,1965, while addressing his followers in Harlem's Audubon Auditorium.

Malcolm X's relationships with well-known African-American homosexuals such as Bayard Rustin and James Baldwin are instructive. The FBI tried to stir up trouble on the homosexual issue as they spread reports that Malcolm had said that Rustin was "nothing but a homosexual." (FBI File, 253) But the two nonetheless remained on cordial terms. And James Baldwin and Malcolm (if they hadn't run into each other during their wild days in Harlem during the Forties) became fast friends later. Malcolm may have helped Baldwin obtain an interview with Elijah Muhammad; and Baldwin in turn helped set up a meeting between himself, Malcolm, and Martin Luther King, Jr.—a meeting scheduled for two days after Malcolm's assassination.

They said the revolution would not be televised, but Malcolm's memory has become big business. His *Autobiography*, published shortly after his assassination, sold over two and a half million copies in paperback; and it has again returned to the best-seller lists. James Baldwin attempted a screenplay on the life of Malcolm X for Columbia Pictures, but the film never appeared. James Baldwin invented fictional heterosexual scenes to provide a cover for the real yin/yang mixture of gay/straight. Spike Lee is so scared of any wild taint that he has refused all interviews with gay reporters (black or white).

Village Voice columnist Stanley Crouch explains the difficult position of black queers: "homosexuality is a form of identity so interwoven with exploitation and oppression that very few black Americans would connect it with liberation, regardless of the eloquence of its champions." Black homosexuality "reinforces the white man's superior image of himself while allowing white women with racial sexual fantasies the freedom to play them out right in front of their husbands." In *Notes of a Hanging Judge* (1990), Crouch denounces as faggots Alain Locke, Countee Cullen, Langston Hughes, Richard Bruce Nugent, "Jelly Roll Morton's mentor Tony Jackson, Duke Ellington's co-composer Billy Strayhorn," Ma Rainey, Bessie Smith, Billie Holiday, Cecil Taylor, "and a closeted gaggle of others." Biographer Arnold Rampersad, however, denies Langston Hughes' wild side because "the evidence suggests a more complicated sexual nature." Having kept Langston Hughes clean, Rampersad took on the task of keeping Arthur Ashe straight as he redacted the tennis player's life as he died of AIDS.

The pressure against African-American writers and artists not to display any homosexuality remains strong. But the feeling of queerness remains greater: we are everywhere, we are in everyone, nowhere are we free. Bringing Malcolm out liberates him from the closet of dead heroes. Gay filmmaker Marlon Riggs responded in an interview: "To censor ourselves says to me that it's better to have a lie that might mobilize people into some form of community—an artificial community—rather than to engage in real soul searching about our identities. I think if one can come through that fire, one is forged through something much more enduring than a fabricated myth."

Malcolm's wild side should discredit him only with the Don't Ask

Don't Tell Crowd. He was shot down on the eve of his meeting with Martin Luther King, Jr. who himself was shot down on the first anniversary of his denunciation of the Vietnam war. As Marlon Riggs reflected, "Yes, Malcolm's death connected to our own personal death, as well as to that of our communities and our brothers who are killing each other and are being killed by outside forces."

There is no hopeful spin on Malcolm's Death. Himself fallen too soon to AIDS, Riggs mused that "No matter what we do—whether we're sexually repressed or sexually promiscuous, whether we assert our identities or police them—the end result is always death." Clarence Thomas on the Supreme Court is no more consolation to those who loved Malcolm than closeted gays on the same court. Riggs's great film, however, offers a great hope: "Black men loving black men is the Revolutionary Act." The tragedy of Malcolm was not just that he was killed, everyone dies sometime, but that his death is so seductive. Riggs fears that "In a society that demands our assimilation and erasure, death seems like an apt metaphor for the condition of our lives." (Marlon Riggs, "Sexuality, Television, and Death," *Malcolm X in Our Own Image* [1992])

Note on nomenclature: His birth certificate and other official records read "Malcolm Little" but in the Nation of Islam surnames inherited from slavery were dropped and replaced with an "X" until a real name could be identified. Malcolm took the name "El-Hajj Malik El-Shabazz" when he went to Africa, and his wife and children use Shabazz for their last name. Here, "Malcolm X" has been most commonly used. Likewise, Malcolm X pioneered the use of "Afro-American" in place of "negro;" the Black Power movement preferred "black;" and some now prefer "African-American." The use of "black" and "African-American" here intends to respect the memory of Malcolm X and those who admire him.

Danny
RONDO MIECZKOWSKI

I met Danny shortly after 2:00 A.M. one June morning in 1981 on the "Meat Rack" in front of Provincetown Town Hall. During the day that series of park benches served as rest stations for weary bus tourists, weighed down with postcards and fudge, who flocked to this Cape Cod resort town. After dark, and especially after the bars let out, it became the gay posing, performance, and pick-up spot.

I sat on one of the benches watching the show. A trio of drag queens sang their covers of tea-dance disco hits. Guys walked by either singly or in gossiping packs. Attempts at trysts for the night were being made all around the Meat Rack. Too shy, I feigned disinterest in most of the passing bodies, or else averted my eyes away from the ones who really did prick my fancy. The tangy, salty decay of Provincetown Harbor's low tide only a few yards away drifted over this scattered crowd.

I turned as a tall silhouette of a man approached me. I couldn't make out his face; light haloed his head as the streetlight glare passed through his curly hair. As he walked closer I saw he sported a grin the envy of any angel or devil.

My hair snaked over the back of my collar in that year's tail-style. Danny gave my hair a tug, "I like your tail."

"I like yours, too," I pulled his, tight and curly like a pig's.

"Want to go fuck in front of a fireplace?" he said.

In my cruising encounters up to then, people had asked me many things, but never that, and never so bluntly. I quickly agreed.

He introduced himself, "I'm Danny." As we headed down the street, Danny put his arm around me and I reciprocated. He felt warm against the ocean air. I imagined the fireplace Danny promised, little realizing the sexual fire of our initial meeting would transform into a hearth we would build a home around.

I come out of Polish stock from the glacial plains of the Midwest. My home life in Toledo, Ohio, was erratic—silences and nervous calms punctuated by unpredictable eruptions. I hid from the furies of my mother and father by shielding myself behind books, encyclopedias, comics. Reading was my port in the emotional storms that would explode between my parents.

Sometimes they would fight over money, the only time they spoke in Polish. Most of the time I could never decipher the reasons for their rages.

I hid behind walls of paper. And embraced religion and spirituality. Ethereal, intellectual things became more real to me than my confusing family. I took the Christian gospels to heart and identified with the teenage martyrs. The nuns could always count on me to sell the most candy and bring in baggies filled with pennies to save the pagan babies from starvation. I wanted to help people, but it was difficult when I was called upon to simply speak for myself, and not return the catechism saws.

My near-pathological shyness generally rendered me mute in the dating realm when I attended college at Michigan State University.

I imagined the hotbed of San Francisco—where men were men and men were available—would thaw my shyness. My use, then abuse, of alcohol, kept the walls up. Pain couldn't touch you through a barrier. But then, neither could love.

Because quick, anonymous sex was always available in San Francisco, I still didn't learn how to act in a relationship, much less date. Although guys said they were interested in me as "husband material," I wasn't enticed by these proposals.

Some friends at the restaurant I worked at in San Francisco were heading to Provincetown for the summer and asked if I wanted to come along. I knew the town contained a literary scene and an arts center, along with Patti Page's, "sand dunes/ and salt sea air." I wanted a change. San Francisco wasn't enough. Years later I discovered I was the one lacking.

Danny talks to people about anything, anytime, anywhere. Whether it's the usefulness of Greek translations of the Bible, which micro-sprinkler is best for hillsides, or verbal foreplay in a bar, Danny loves to talk.

I'm sure his Italian upbringing encouraged this trait. I've spent holidays and celebrations with twelve members of his family around one table. Afterward my ears hurt from their joyful racket. I had always equated noise with anger. I didn't know you could be both loud and happy.

Danny's steady chatter slowly chipped away at my defensive walls. I had to respond to his questions about my life, his comments on the passing scene. I couldn't get away anymore with hiding behind a book.

Right from the beginning we shared things with each other. Including hepatitis. Danny passed it on to me our first summer, which effectively put an end to the waiter career that was going to sustain my writing endeavors.

Thousands of miles from my last home and without money, I asked Danny for a loan to help pay my exorbitant summer resort town rent. When he cheerfully gave me the cash, a voice in my head declared, "You two are going to be together for a long, long time." I didn't believe the voice. Although a nice guy, Danny was not the love of my life.

He seemed a little weird. When I met him he painted the nail on the pinky of his left hand black. Possessed of an amazing knowledge of the Bible, Danny had recently left his position as an apostle-minister in a small born-again religion.

After uprooting himself from his native Southern California to attend college in Connecticut, Danny was "blown out" by the desperate state of things in 1970/71. Kent State and Vietnam were proof of a corrupt world. Danny expanded his consciousness through acid, and was ready to advance to the next step, and shoot up pure LSD.

A hippie buddy-crush of Danny's, Gary, became involved in a fundamentalist cult, whose leader claimed to be God. Danny went off to rescue Gary, but instead found he liked the extended, Christian communal life the group's members practiced. Danny became a cult member too. When his homosexual behavior kept popping up, he was ordered to marry his female best friend in hopes the union would keep his homosexuality under control.

A year before I met Danny, he left the cult, cursed by his God. Danny had applied the teachings he had learned over the past ten years to his own life and found that since he truly loved men, he had to live honestly.

In Provincetown, Danny was easing back into the world, sorting through true teachings spouted by a false prophet. In spite of his bizarre ten-year Connecticut cult experience, Danny appeared almost always happy, inquisitive, and horny.

From the start our relationship was never monogamous. I did just move from San Francisco where whoredom ruled the politically correct realm. Danny would have fit in better there than me. Danny is a pig.

Whether peeking in the men's bathroom windows of North Hollywood biker bars at age sixteen, or in later years getting involved in a bondage scene with a coffin or videotaping orgies, Danny's life has always been tumescent with sex. Danny doesn't look like a model, and we both have bellies that never seem to go away completely. But as a friend once said of Danny, "He exudes sex, he reeks of it."

At first I didn't have a problem with Danny's lust for lust. We would have three-ways or pair up with another couple and that worked out fine. But when Danny would bring someone home when I was out, or have an assignation at someone else's home or hotel room, I would feel jealousy breeze through me. I tried to suppress it, but after half a year together, I found I could generate the same emotional storms that racked my childhood. In my alcoholic blackouts, Danny tells me, I picked fights with him about his sleeping around. I only have jagged recollections of our shouting back and forth, broken glass, slammed doors.

It became clear one Halloween that my parents were stuck inside of me. If I ever wanted to get beyond my family legacy, I somehow had to melt this internal iceberg that the heat of sex couldn't shrink and alcohol only preserved.

During our second autumn together, the restaurant where I waited tables in Provincetown prepared to throw its annual Halloween costume bash. The staff, required to wear costumes, were forbidden to do "drag." My way around this restriction was to dress as a transvestite, not as a drag queen.

I had lived in San Francisco with a bunch of tough drag queens, and managed to learn a few things about fashion. Danny was a virgin to drag. One bored winter evening, I finally managed to coerce Danny into this little orange shift with a rhinestone collar and my white pumps from Lane Bryant. We added balloons for earrings, a ratty wig, and black lipstick. I created a monster! Danny wouldn't get out of the dress! I had to dissuade him from the idea of walking to the corner while a foot of snow blanketed the ground and the temperature hovered in the teens.

Although not much help clothes-wise, Danny had skills as a graphic designer and was carefully applying my makeup that Halloween afternoon. I shaved off my beard and mustache for the occasion (last time I razored my face clean I was a punk rock groupie in San Francisco). A wig tightly grasped my head and my lips slashed a bright scarlet when Danny gasped.

"My God, you look just like your mother, only forty years younger." He held the blush brush in mid-air.

"I do not!" I yelled, annoyed. I had to get to the restaurant, and I was running late.

I whirled around to face the mirror and my heart froze. I saw my mother, younger than I remembered her in the flesh. I matched her face in the twin photographs of her and my dad that topped the living room television set in Toledo, Ohio. The photo was taken a few years after their marriage. I had my mother's same lovely skin, and the same bitter, judgmental curl to her lips, "No, nothing is ever good enough for me." I trembled. This mother inside me could leap out at any time.

That night, in spite of all the glitter and insanity: a band playing swing, Barry Manilow and polkas; escaped lobsters causing turmoil in the kitchen; and the momentary diversion of my having to tactfully fend off the attentions of a wealthy regular customer— a lesbian besotted not only with me but with Scotch—I could feel great chunks of the shell around my heart slough away.

Here I was, trying to live a different life from my parents, but it was a sham. My present home life was turning into a bad rerun of my parents' lives. Memories flowed through me: my father drunk, head bobbing at the dinner table; my mother screaming in the yard; shouts; accusations.

Wasn't I also keeping Danny in the cold, judging him not by what I thought were my standards, but my mother's? I hadn't even created my standards yet.

Once, Danny and I argued over how to do the dishes. He favored washing in the order of glasses, silverware, plates. I insisted on plates, glasses, silverware, defending my family's pattern for no other reason than its familiarity.

I had depended on my intellect for salvation, nurtured by my childhood escape into reading, and it had failed me. I didn't even know what I was doing until I saw my mother's face glare back at me through the veil of my makeup.

I'd like to say things changed immediately after seeing my mother/my self in the Halloween mirror. But I continued drinking that autumn, into the winter, churning over the lover relationship I thought I deserved out of my gay life. I wanted to move out, to get away from Danny. However, stuck in the winter on Cape Cod, dribbles of unemployment checks barely keeping us in groceries, there was no way to escape.

One rare sober winter afternoon I realized Danny's choice to sleep around with other people was *his* choice. Over our early months together I remembered he enjoyed a spiritual experience when he made love with another man. He joined with them in an ecstatic ritual; he described melting, fusing with the other person during sex. Doing it often did not mean he didn't take it seriously. And doing it at all, without me, didn't mean he loved me less.

I started tallying all the positive things about Danny: how he trusted me to return the money I had borrowed; the way he sang Janis Joplin songs at full volume; the wonderful pastas and casseroles he would create on our budget to brighten the long winter—compared to the monotonous meat-potatoes-salad routine of my upbringing.

The clincher was remembering how he did my laundry for me when I fell ill. Money can be plentiful, anyone can sing along, and there's always take-out, but only someone who really cares about you will wash and dry your clothes.

Why give up this life we were creating because I insisted he sleep only with me? His friendship was too valuable to throw away for my schoolboy ideal of a lover.

We didn't sleep together anymore. I got help and stopped drinking. I didn't have sex with anyone for four years—too busy trying to discover who I was. Danny's companionship and attention at home made it possible for me to start to believe in a future.

Part of living with someone is working out money. From the start, Danny and I shared our finances. The car is in both our names, and it's a chore to untangle who owes what on whose credit cards. Danny pays one third of my daily *Los Angeles Times* and I contribute toward his subscription to *Sunset: The Magazine of Western Living*. Neither of us fears getting ripped off by the other—which I can't say is true for people we have dated since.

When I met Danny I couldn't tell the difference between a Chrysler and a Ford. I had never owned a car before. Danny, who fantasizes some day owning a 1959 Chevy El Camino, has tried to educate me about automobiles. I can pick out an old Barracuda or Mustang, but models from the early 1970s all blur together in my mind.

In Provincetown, Danny introduced me to Miss Belle, a 1970 Chevy Impala Custom with a black vinyl roof he bought from a couple of gearheads in Connecticut for $225—all he could afford after his wife in the religious cult divorced him when he declared his homosexuality.

Miss Belle was the first car I ever felt was even partly mine. She had "personality." Her yellow sides were dented, windshield pitted by the blowing sand at Herring Cove Beach parking lot where we drove to watch winter sunsets. The floor (but not the frame, yet) under the driver's feet had rusted away and driving too fast through a puddle would splash water through the wooden boards we had covering the holes. Her fenders were held on by graying and fraying duct tape.

But she was ours. Danny describes her better than I can: "With a 4 Barrel, 350 Small Block turbo-hydromatic 'tranny,' she had *big* balls."

"I'm taking Miss Belle to the A&P," I'd say. Or Danny would remind me, "Miss Belle needs a case of oil if we're gonna make it to Boston." I wanted to keep her when we moved from Provincetown to Los Angeles in the fall of 1987. Danny doubted whether Miss Belle, with a quarter of a million miles on her, could survive the cross-country trip. We ended up selling her for a dollar to a lesbian rock-and-roll band who could haul their drums and equipment in Miss Belle's spacious trunk and backseat.

Danny snapped a picture of me hugging Miss Belle's fender, saying good-bye. As the dykes drove away, I began sobbing. Danny laughed while he held me. Only an old wreck of a car, it marked my time with Danny, our years in Provincetown, and an unknown future in California.

Danny and I love to celebrate holidays, but at Christmas/Solstice we go all out, starting with the design of our holiday cards several months in advance. They have evolved from our first year of twenty hand-painted cards depicting the orange-and-scarlet bittersweet berries that perked up the Cape's dull winter landscape, through the "whale years" (one year our card featured two whales kissing under mistletoe, another year they sprouted reindeer antlers) to our latest Christmas card of our faces replacing the serene countenances of Raphael's ubiquitous pair of angels.

Danny's cult forbade the celebration of Christmas, a "pagan" holiday; they claimed biblical injunctions in the Book of Jeremiah against decorating trees. I remember some years my parents announcing off-handedly, without warning or explanation, that this year we aren't going to have a tree.

Is it any wonder Danny and I now get the biggest goddamn tree we can fit under our nine-foot apartment ceiling? Each year we trek down to the railroad yards in downtown Los Angeles and wander among the tree dealers. The trees are delivered in boxcars, pine needles sometimes still dressed with snow. We haggle over its price, tie it to the roof of our Honda, and head home for a Laurel and Hardy comedy act getting it into the house.

A few days later we throw our annual Christmas tree party. Danny and I are in the kitchen for days beforehand. I make a version of a date nut cake recipe Danny received from his Nanny in Nebraska. Danny bakes Italian breads: pizza dough lined with thin slices of mortadella, prosciutto, cappicolla, provolone, broccoli, and basil. The dough is rolled up, brushed with garlic and olive oil, then baked. When sliced, the breads display an aromatic pinwheel pattern. I buy pounds of shrimp; it's just not a perfect party to me unless there's an unending bowl of icy, crunchy shrimp. Every year I make Polish pecan cookies: little balls of vanilla-scented dough caked with powdered sugar. My mom gave me the recipe; her mother carried it with her when she left Poland.

Danny strings colored Christmas lights on the porch and over a thousand on the tree (after about three years I managed to wean Danny from his insistence on only white and amber lights for the tree), while I clean and prepare hot spiced cider. Christmas music blares on our stereo (Peggy Lee, Beach Boys, Mannheim Steamroller, Bing Crosby, The Roches, Chanticleer), occasionally punctuated by obscenities as we accidentally electrocute, burn, or stab ourselves in our preparations.

Our friends start arriving about 7:30 in the evening to help decorate the tree. People bring ornaments they've made or bought. We save them and put them on the tree year after year: a tin mermaid, a revolving ballerina in a glass ball, one year half a dozen people brought nutcrackers, a bagel shellacked green and red, a skeleton with red rhinestone eyes. A friend who sculpts in metal fashioned a little wire man holding his little wire penis. There are lots of other ornaments, talismans for our friends here and gone.

Folks from my writers' groups, Danny's jack-off clubs, co-workers, neighbors, current boyfriends, ex-boyfriends, and boyfriends-to-be, as well as uninvited guests (one year four very lost people from Iceland appeared at our door) mingle and trim the tree. If they haven't brought their own ornament, they dip into our accumulated wealth of black glass balls, feathery birds, or plastic fruits spray-painted silver, and fill up our Noble Fir's branches.

After our well-fed friends depart, Danny and I collapse in the early morning darkness, gazing at the shimmering tree. We listen to slow holiday music. The windows stay open even if it's chilly, Los Angeles jasmine mixing with our tree's pine aroma. I drift back to our first Christmas in Provincetown.

We splurged for a tree—a twelve-foot Balsam—but had no money left to buy food. I hadn't saved any money from summer due to hepatitis, and Danny's unemployment check had gone for the rent. Some freezer-burned pork chops and canned pea soup filled the menu for Christmas dinner. I was still waiting for a disability check (in an alcoholic blackout I fell and broke my leg the day before Thanksgiving). Our Christmas would have made Scrooge cry. But our first Christmas tree did look pretty, with red bows we tied from yarn someone had thrown away, all white and amber lights. All the Portuguese ladies loved it as it shone over the neighborhood through our second story apartment window.

On Christmas Eve, the magic started to happen. In the morning a friend dropped by, carrying a twelve-pound turkey as a gift. Then in the afternoon *two* of my disability checks arrived in the mail. We drove like crazy to the bank to cash them and then sped to the supermarket and bought stuffing fixings, and food, food, food. I even bought both kinds of olives offered by our little A&P. Back home we got on the phone and invited friends who had even less than we did to come over and share the bounty. Someone baked a pie, a neighbor brought a can of mixed nuts and a carton of whipping cream. We prepped, cooked, and laughed till late. First thing Christmas morning, the turkey went in the oven and we spent the day feasting and telling stories—our little impromptu family—finally passing out after the best Christmas dinner ever.

How have we stayed together for so many years? On a certain level I don't know. Danny still feels as comfortable as an old pair of 501s. I'm not obligated to impress him and he doesn't have to fulfill my expectations. We are there to help one another. Once, when a co-worker pulled a knife on Danny and freaked him out (but didn't hurt him), I bought him a pink stuffed piggy to make him feel better. His co-workers are envious when I send him extravagant floral arrangements for his birthday and Valentine's Day.

He designs me little cards and calendars and silly dog drawings on his MacIntosh computer. If I read something in the newspaper or in a magazine I'll save it for Danny and give it to him. He records programs for me on his VCR.

Danny is always in my thoughts. I think of him throughout the day, wherever I am, whatever I'm doing, "Oh, Danny would like this," or, "Danny should be here now." I thought of him when I went to Europe for a month. "Gosh, I wish Danny could taste this pastry." I spent two rolls of film taking shots of the underside of the Eiffel Tower because of Danny's fascination with architectural forms. I always want to do things for him.

When I returned from Europe, he had criss-crossed my bedroom with pink crepe streamers, a big paper tropical fish. A sign said, "Welcome Back, BABS," (our favorite nickname for each other).

If we go to the store we'll bring back a favorite treat for the other. I'll get three-bean salad (which I despise) for Danny. When he wakes me up in the morning he'll ring the glass wind chimes at my door and sing-song, "Wake up, Babs, wake up."

I would much rather read a magazine than paint walls. For a bookshelf, cinder blocks and wooden planks are just fine. My childhood experience never led me to explore the idea of a comfortable, convenient home life.

Danny showed me there were lots of things to do to make a place "homey," pulling out his tool boxes and do-it-yourself magazines. He's hung specially-constructed earthquake-resistant shelves for my books, and created this amazing cabinet in our dining room that transforms into a guest bed. He's still reworking our apartment building's garden into quite a neighborhood showcase. Elephant ears shade fountains and clumps of lush impatiens and begonias. Amazingly, I enjoy all these homey things, now that I have someone to make a home with. A "home"—a sanctuary, a nest, is something I never could imagine as a child.

There is nothing I enjoy more than when we get home after work, take off our clothes (we don't wear clothes at home), eat dinner (baked potatoes for me, hot dogs for Danny, and there has to be something for dessert), and laugh while we watch reruns on the cable Cartoon Network.

People tell us we're more like lovers than the lovers they know. I don't miss having sex with Danny (he and I have sex with other people, sometimes we end up making love to the same person, but at different times—Los Angeles is smaller than you might think!). In fact, although I still adore his naturally curly hair (even now that it has advanced to mostly silver, a fact he blames on me, although I credit him for my receding hairline and expanding bald spot), I never even think about having sex with Danny.

I'm not worried about Danny (or me) finding a boyfriend and

leaving. When, and if, it occurs, we'll work it out. Although I would bet the other guy would probably move in with us.

That did happen one summer with one of Danny's longest-lasting boyfriends, Jean-Louis. A tall, dark-haired Quebecois with gold-rimmed eyeglass, Jean-Louis was part of the illegal-alien labor force that fueled Provincetown's summer resort machine. Jean-Louis loved to wander the dunes and woods of the lower Cape. He and I became best fishing buddies.

Jean-Louis and I would get up before dawn to cast for bluefish or bottom-fish for flounder while Danny only wanted us to shut up and get out of the house so he could get back to sleep. In spring, Jean-Louis and I brought home big buckets of inky squid. Some to deep fry now, others to freeze for bait later in the year. Danny screamed when, half-asleep, he would walk into the kitchen and see them staring at him from the sink.

Before we left Provincetown for Los Angeles, we drove up to Montreal to see Jean-Louis for the last time. Although always thin, Jean-Louis's physique had been wasted by AIDS to that of a death-camp prisoner. He could barely shuffle from his room at his sister's house to the bathroom down the hall. While staying there we heard him cry out in the night for morphine to kill the pain. Danny and I wept, for Jean-Louis, and for ourselves.

Danny and I have both tested positive for the HIV virus but as of this writing, neither of us has any opportunistic infections. But the world is an unpredictable place; by the time you read this one or both of us could be gone.

However, I do live in Los Angeles; a drive-by shooting, urban unrest, floods, fires or the always predicted, unpredictable, "Big One" earthquake could put me away. I try to live each day fully, consciously—something I rarely achieve.

As you might imagine, Danny and I are very leery of any who set themselves up as spiritual teachers. Danny's negative cult experiences and my disillusionment with the empty rhetoric of the Catholic church and other organizations kept us far away from religion, although we still stayed up for hours discussing the meaning of Bible passages and spiritual philosophies.

In the past few years we have both found a guru, Ma Jaya Bhagavati. Born a Jew in Brooklyn, she is now a Hindu who loves Jesus Christ.

Ma works mostly with people affected by HIV/AIDS. What we like about her is her humor and simplicity. She cares about you, not who you might or should be. This was in contrast to other non-western teachers I investigated who didn't want to deal with my homosexuality, "We teach celibacy," they'd say. "So your sexual orientation doesn't matter at all."

I have seen Ma conduct union ceremonies to sanctify the love of lesbian and gay couples, and embrace and publicly celebrate the accomplishments of transsexuals. Looking into Ma's face, I don't see my mother's judgmental scowl, or even my own face. I see an inspiration for me to try to practice the religious ideals of my youth: feeding the hungry, caring for the sick; ideals I could not find in the everyday practice of most religions.

Danny met Ma a year after I did, a week after finding out he tested HIV positive. When he told Ma about his recent test results, she questioned him on his calmness. Where was the anger, the fear? Danny said, to my surprise, that watching me live with the knowledge of being HIV positive for the past few years gave him hope.

During this plague constantly carrying off friends and lovers I often felt helpless. I wanted to know, just once, I would make a difference—to enable someone to live a little longer, a little easier. Without knowing it, I had repaid Danny (not that he asked for repayment) for helping me find a way to strive through my alcoholism. By being the person he helped me to become, I helped the man I love most. Instead of thinking he'll only be around for a couple years, Danny is now a little daunted by feeling he could be around a long time.

One day Ma said to Danny and me, "You know, you two really love each other, yet you're so separate." And that pretty much describes our relationship. I'm never going to lure Danny on a weekend fishing trip, and he's never going to entice me to attend an auto show. Our love for each other isn't diminished by our differences.

There's no one else I would rather sit with on a park bench—like the one on which we met in Provincetown—and enjoy a cool summer evening. To sit with each other, quietly, in the night air, while the future rushes too quickly toward us.

That would be heaven.

You're the First Person I've Ever Told:
Letters to a Fictional Gay Teen
LARRY GROSS

August 31, 1992

Dear Ryan,

First of all, I want to thank you for the courage you have shown playing the part of a homosexual teenager. Especially in this day and age when discrimination and violence against gays is on the rise.

As you act on *One Life to Live* as a gay teenager, I also act. I act as a straight, normal twenty-one-year-old. It has become routine to act like the perfect son or brother. You are the first person I have ever told, and may be the last, that I am gay. I don't think I will ever be able to tell anyone the truth. Had not your portrayal and this story-line of a gay teen hit me so deeply, I probably would not be telling you. Your character is so realistic and you do such a great job portraying how gay teens really feel.

Recently, I saw phone numbers for gay youth in *Soap Opera Weekly* magazine. For those who are troubled about their sexuality. I honestly don't feel I have enough courage to call any of these places. For some reason, I think somehow someone will find out.

If my family or friends find out, I'm afraid they wouldn't look at me the same or would never love me as much as they do now.

I feel that way because of things I hear my family say about homosexuals. Until recently, I would laugh at jokes about gays or would pretend to dislike the way they were. I cannot and will not do that anymore. Now I just stay silent and try to ignore things that are said about gays and even AIDS itself. I overheard my father say that faggots started AIDS and normal people like Magic Johnson have to suffer for what gays have done. Well, do you think I could ever tell him that I am one of those who he thinks have caused normal people to suffer and die from AIDS? It's something I could never foresee.

I know this is just your job and I'm sorry for throwing all of my problems at you like this. I certainly don't expect you to solve any of them but it feels good just to tell someone... Thank you for your time.

In the summer of 1992 the daytime TV serial *One Life To Live* (*OLTL*) began what was to be the longest and most complex television narrative ever to deal with a lesbian or gay character. Billy Douglas is a high school student who had recently moved to Llanview (the fictional small town outside Philadelphia where *OLTL* takes place) and become a star athlete and class president. When Billy confides, first to his best friends and then to his minister, that he is gay, he sets off a series of plot twists that differ from the usual soap opera complications in that they expose homophobia and AIDS-phobia among the residents of Llanview and thus offer the characters—and the audience—an opportunity to address topics that daytime serials, along with the rest of U.S. mass media, have generally preferred to ignore.[1]

The plotline featuring Billy Douglas was the dominant thread of *OLTL* from July through early September 1992, after which Billy appeared less frequently until he left Llanview for Yale the following spring. Billy Douglas was played by a young actor named Ryan Phillippe, in his first professional role, and he found himself at the center of a great deal of media and audience attention. He received an unusually large amount of mail even for a good-looking young soap opera actor. Even more unusual was the fact that so many of the hundreds of letters he received during the months that he appeared on *OLTL* came from young men, most of whom identified themselves as gay—in one interview Phillippe reported getting two thousand letters, adding that "a good 45 percent... from homosexual teenagers" (Mallinger, 1993: 14).

Many of the young gay men—and several of the older men—wrote that they were particularly moved by and grateful for Ryan's sensitive portrayal of an experience much like their own, being isolated and vulnerable in a society that would prefer not to know they existed.

While it is not difficult to imagine that an African-American, Asian-American, or Latino actor would get letters from teenagers who identify with and appreciate their representation of an underrepresented group on the public media stage, it seems inconceivable that they would receive letters like the one quoted above, let alone similar letters from adults:

Dear Ryan:

Your performance has been "right on." I am a happily married, successful father of two teenagers (one, your age, equally good-looking as you)...

You see, I lived the character you are playing, and still live it, although in the "closet." I've never been a victim of homophobia, because no one knows I'm a life-long, born-that-way homosexual, comfortable with who I am, but not comfortable with living as a gay person. Still your character has created an empathy in me, because I can relate so well to your character.

You are doing a service to millions of people, whether you know it or not, just by bringing the subject to a mass audience. Keep up the good work.

Sorry, I can't sign this letter.

When Ryan Phillippe was offered the role of Billy Douglas, the seventeen-year-old actor was just graduating from New Castle (Delaware) Baptist high school and it was his first real professional acting role—"The most dramatic scene I did before this was a Nintendo commercial" (quoted in Harris, 1992). Despite his qualms about the nature of the role he was to play, the young actor approached the role and the unexpected visibility it brought with remarkable maturity. In the initial flurry of press attention Phillippe was, as he later acknowledged, somewhat too eager to establish that he himself is heterosexual.

> I did want people to know that I was straight. It was an immature act, but what more can you expect from a seventeen-year-old who has not really been out in the world a whole lot? But then I got to the point soon after that, where I thought, "You know, that's really not the issue"… My sexual orientation is not necessarily all that important. And if I'm not asked, I won't say, "Hey, you have to print that I'm straight." But if it comes out, there shouldn't be any reason why I should hide it and there shouldn't be any reason why a homosexual person should hide it. (quoted in Mallinger, 1993)

The producers helped Phillippe and other cast members prepare by having them meet with Richard Isay, a gay psychiatrist who works with gay teens, and he was also given books such as Aaron Fricke's memoir of growing up gay (1981). But his real education began when the letters started pouring in.

> The most research for me probably came from my fan mail, because a good 45 percent was from homosexual teenagers. Siblings of these teenagers or these teenagers themselves would write in to me, and it was incredibly touching. I'd get some letters with kids telling me, literally, that they were going to commit suicide if they didn't get the right answers by the end of the summer, and did I have any help? They were wrestling with the decision on whether to

come out or not and if it's wrong; that's where most of my research came from.

Answering many of these letters was a more demanding and sensitive task for Phillippe than it typically is for soap opera actors, although he also received a lot of the standard letters from teenaged girls, asking for his photograph and often hoping for more.[2] Letters from gay teenagers—and some quite a bit older—required more than the usual signed photograph.

> I had to be very tactful. I couldn't write anything that would sway a kid either way, because of course that's not my place. But I wrote back, and I would send some hotline numbers. And I took one of the letters in particular that really was disturbing in terms of suicidal tendencies to a psychiatrist for the show, and he kind of wrote a form letter for me to send which helped a lot.

Ryan Phillippe provided me with access to the letters he received, and I examined a sample of 150 letters written between June and November 1992.[3] As noted already, the letters came disproportionately from male viewers and, as Ryan said in the interview quoted above, 66 of the 150 writers (44%) identified themselves as gay men under the age of 25. Overall, 103 of the letters came from men and 46 from women (one letter came from the members of an organization of gay and lesbian youth in New Jersey).

Somewhat surprisingly, there were literally no negative or hostile letters received by Phillippe or the show's producers in response to the gay teenager or the other elements of the plotline focusing on homophobia and AIDS-phobia.[4] It was only later, in December of 1992, when Billy Douglas, who was by then playing a much smaller role on *OLTL*, met and began a friendship with another gay youth, that the program began to receive negative letters. The relationship between Billy and his friend was never developed, however, by the time Billy "left for Yale" and thus the viewers—and the producers—were spared the question of whether soap opera's first gay teenagers would be allowed to kiss.

A few of the letters from young women were obviously stimulated by the specifics of Billy Douglas's situation in addition to Ryan Phillippe's attractiveness as a young soap actor. One Milwaukee eighteen-year-old wrote, "I guess I'm interested in this story because my brother is gay. He just told our family about a year ago and I can honestly say it's been the hardest year of my life." A fifteen-year-old girl from New Jersey wrote that "this storyline has held some special meaning for me. It's helped me sort out some of my feelings about homosexuality. You see, my mother 'came out of the closet' four years ago, and while I willingly accepted the fact that she was a lesbian, I never quite understood it."[5] A college junior from Memphis wrote about her parents' divorce, when her mother "told me that my father was a homosexual," and her eventual decision to live with her father:

> When your character, Billy Douglas, stood up and told his family and friends that he was gay, my heart leapt out for his bravery and I lost touch of reality, wanting to hug him for being who he was and no longer pretending. It was the same feeling I got when my dad told me he was living with someone, and that someone was a man.

The relatively few letters from older women included some standard fan letters (one enthusiastic California fan predicted that Phillippe would become "the Cary Grant of the Nineties—the ultimate figure of grace and style") as well as several from writers who had a more personal response. One woman identified herself as a thirty-nine-year-old lesbian and told how she tried to use the *OLTL* plotline to tell her father about the "sad hatred of prejudice and bigotry." His response was to exclaim, "Don't tell me they still have that faggot storyline going," and walk away. "This is a subject we have always been unable to discuss." A group of four women in northern California who did not identify as lesbians sent identical letters to Phillippe and to the producers, congratulating them on their wonderful contribution to the education of their viewers, and the courage that has "put you into the very special category of people who can really make a difference in the social and spiritual growth of the human race."

The letters from male viewers, not surprisingly, were quite personal, whether the writer identified himself as gay or straight. While many of the letters from gay male viewers simply congratulated Phillippe on his acting and thanked him for being a role model for gay youth, a very large number included deeply personal and often emotional accounts of their own experiences. Like the twenty-one-year-old whose letter opened this paper, many of the younger (and even some of the older) gay correspondents wrote that they have never told anyone that they are gay:

> It's like everything you say on the show is related to what I was feeling this past year! The only difference between your character Billy and myself is that I haven't told anyone that I am gay. I think like maybe I should wait awhile because my friends would not be cool about it at all. When I go to college this fall, maybe I'll join the Gay Students Group but I have to be careful that my friends don't find out!... Ryan, you are the only person who knows I'm gay. This letter was difficult to write and I hope I did the right thing by sharing my secret with you.

Some of the gay teens writing to Phillippe went further than merely revealing a secret they had never told anyone else, trying to develop a relationship with the actor who was playing a role that carried such emotional power for them:

> I know that you probably get sick and tired of this, but I think that I may be bisexual... I don't have any close friends, you're the first

person I've ever talked to this way. I'm scared. I'm sixteen and I feel all alone. Can you help me? Maybe you could come to Nebraska for a week sometime so that I'd have someone to talk to. I could show you around here (maybe some farms and surrounding cities)... I can't wait for your help when you write back. Thank you for listening to me. I already feel as if you're a real good friend. I have opened up like never before. I trust you with my secret.

But even beyond these forays into para-social interaction (Horton & Wohl, 1956), reaching out for a friendship with someone they feel they know and identify with, some of the gay teens were writing out of a frightening despair. One Kentucky sixteen-year-old wrote on First Baptist Church stationary:

Ryan, what I'm about to tell you is something very hard for me to tell anybody. Ryan, I'm gay BUT I don't want to be. Ryan, the only person in this world I can relate to is your character Billy Douglas. Ryan, I'm so scared. I don't know what to do and I'm afraid of what I might do. You, God, and I are the only ones that know! Ryan, PLEASE help! I need someone to talk to... You are the only one that I am telling. I need to talk to someone one-on-one, or (I hate to say it) but I'm afraid that I may come to the point where I may (I hope not!) but, I may kill myself... Please call me soon (please very soon).

And some of the stories they told confirm that feelings such as these cannot be dismissed as adolescent self-dramatization:

I'm almost seventeen. I've got a girlfriend but I've been hiding my true feelings, especially since what happened last March. Last August I met a new friend at school. His name was Derek. By Thanksgiving, we had become really good friends. He told me he was gay. I was afraid to tell him how I felt, at first. Before Christmas I told him. For the next couple of months, we talked about the difficulty of living gay in a straight world. Then one day, he said he was going to tell his father and mother that he was gay. I told him to do whatever he wanted, but he'd better not mention my name or I'd never speak to him again. He told his father he was gay. His father beat the shit out of him. Then Derek took his father's gun, drove out to the country and killed himself. I miss him so much.

Older gay men wrote less emotional letters, though many recalled experiences similar to those Billy Douglas was encountering, and some were inspired by Billy's courage:

You and Billy have been an inspiration to me this summer. I am twenty-eight, gay, and still in a painful closet, but I want to get out of it. I am tired of hiding. I have thought about coming out for a while now, but Billy's story has hastened my desire.

Others, like the father of two teenagers quoted earlier, recount more moving life stories:

I am fifty-five years old, and have kept my sexual preference (gay) a secret, except for a few very close friends, all my life. I have stepped on land mines through high school, college, the army, for two years as a bank official, anti-poverty worker, and college professor. Have I been successful? Yes. Has my life been a torture chamber of lies and deceit? Yes... Ryan, your performance as Billy makes me so proud. I cry every time you face a new crisis, but the tears are cathartic. I know it must seem impossible to you that a youngster such as yourself can do so much to help a fifty-five-year-old, but you have made me proud of who I am, for the first time in my life.

Some of the most interesting letters came from young men who identified as straight (though, in some cases, it was hard not to wonder whether the writer might not yet come out to himself). A large proportion of these writers seemed especially moved by the relationship between Billy Douglas and his best friend, Joey Buchanan. On the program, Billy first tells his close female friend,

Alana, that he is gay, and she is consistently supportive. But when he later tells his "best friend" Joey the response is less heartening. Joey has a hard time accepting the news and dealing with his friend's sexuality.[6] Eventually, as Billy encounters hostility from others in the community, Joey comes around and supports his friend. There seem to be many Joeys among the viewers of *OLTL*.

> I'm attached to this storyline because a friend of mine came to me with his secret of homosexuality a few months ago. Like Billy, his parents would probably freak and do God knows what. However, also like Billy's friend Joey, for whom I see myself as, I was very uncomfortable. It is upsetting for me to see what Billy feels and experiences and then relate it to my friend.

Some of the Joey Buchanans didn't come around as quickly as the fictional version:

> I am a little confused as how to begin this letter since I have never written to a soap before or a soap actor for that matter... I am twenty-two years of age... I have to admit something to you, one of the reasons why your character struck a chord in me was because the events going on in the show happened quite similarly to me. I had a good friend who confided in me that he was gay. I, like Joey, did not take it very well. I was seventeen at the time and anyone who even talked, walked, or acted gay was instantly an outcast... Unfortunately, it took an accident that almost cost him his life that made me see more clearly. One night, after a school dance, he was being picked on and he was beat up in the parking lot. Next day FAGGOT was painted all over his locker and I think that pushed him over the edge. A few days later he didn't come to school, we all thought he was hiding at home ashamed of himself but the reality was that he had tried to commit suicide. He, fortunately, did not die, but he did transfer to another school. I cried for I really never got a chance to say how sorry I was... Now, you're probably asking yourself what does this guy want? Actually a response of some kind

or other just so I know someone received it. Hell, we may even become pen pals.

And some of the Billy Douglases were not as lucky:

> My best friend, whose name ironically was also Billy, told me in May that he was gay. I got pretty upset with him. After all of these years of being friends, why was he just now telling me? I never suspected it and when he told me, it caught me off guard. I said some things that I probably should not have, well, I know I should not have said them. Billy was telling me his deepest secret, and all I could do was act like a jerk. Billy tried to tell his parents, but they are super conservative. Both of our families live in the X Country Club, which is filled with conservative families…. Billy's father was a Representative in the state House of Representatives, and any flaw in his family life could hurt his chance for re-election…. On June 6, two weeks after Billy told me he was gay, he was acting real strange. He was crying and he asked me to hold on to his class ring. He told me he was all right though. I know that I should not have believed him, but I did. We were graduating from high school that evening. He told me he would see me that night around seven. At eight o'clock right before graduation started I left because Billy was not there and I knew something was wrong. When I got to Billy's house, I knew what was wrong. There were police cars everywhere in Billy's yard. His mother told me—Billy was dead. He killed himself with his father's gun. I never had a chance to tell him that it didn't matter if he was gay. He was still my best friend and I loved him. That is something I can never change… He was my best friend for eleven years. I miss him. You could not tell that Billy was gay just by looking at him. He was never a sissy. He played football and baseball, and he was great with kids. I hope your role in *OLTL* makes a difference in people like Billy's life.

There were relatively few letters from older men who identified as straight, and most of these recounted similar experiences with friends or relatives who were gay, including one man whose younger brother committed suicide at seventeen. Some writers were older Joey Buchanans:

> This is the first letter I have ever written to an actor but after watching your character these past few weeks I felt I had to. I am a farmer here in Illinois and watched *One Life to Live* occasionally. I happened to catch the show in which your character told Joey he was gay. Since that day I have been taping your show... Please let me explain why I am so interested in your character. Shortly after I graduated from high school a friend of mine from church, who was a couple years younger than myself, told me he was gay. I am sorry to say that I did not handle it very well and I lost a good friend because of it. Watching your character has helped me to understand what he was going through back then.

And some, still struggling with the hostility of family members towards their gay children and siblings, found the *OLTL* plotline a help in dealing with an issue too many families prefer to repress:

> In the past I had distorted views of homosexuals basically because I was angry and disappointed with my family situation. You see it was almost ten years ago that my older brother revealed to the family that he in fact was gay. From that day forward the entire family was ripped apart. There was separation, isolation and plenty of anger... My father watches *OLTL*, but it's hard for him to watch your storyline. We encourage him to, especially me because I want him to know what it was like for his young son and what it is like now. Your storyline is far from being a solution to the rift in my family but in so many ways it provides us all with a start.

How to think about, understand the nature of the relationships these writers feel that they have with Ryan Phillippe, an actor they have seen in a single role and, possibly, in TV and magazine interviews; or is it with Billy Douglas, the troubled but courageous gay teenager, who reminds them of themselves or of a friend or relative?

Certainly, some of the writers seem to confuse the fictional character with the actor, addressing letters to Billy or, even while writing to Ryan, seeming to treat Billy and his family as real people:

> Like you, I am also having the difficult time in dealing with the fact that I'm gay. My parents are not as (freaked out) as your parents are—but they're not far from it... Sometimes I wish that we could have been friends... As for me, if things don't get better soon—I feel like things will never work out. I truly hate being gay. I would rather be dead then disappoint my parents, friends, by them finding out that I'm gay. All this hiding is very tiring. Take care. [signed] Confused

But most seem well aware that Ryan Phillippe is an actor and Billy Douglas is a character.[7] When the writers veer across the line into the territory of para-social interaction it seems mostly to be young women hoping for a more personal relationship with an attractive media figure,[8] but not always. Many of the letters from young men, mostly gay-identified but some as well who identify as straight, are explicitly or implicitly reaching out for some form of relationship beyond the one-way channels of TV-viewing and letter-writing:

> Many people, like me, are still afraid to come out... I myself am a gay teen who had no one to talk to and thought about suicide constantly... All I ask is that maybe we could be friends. (18 year old)

> I'm 19 years old and I live in XX, Colorado, and I'm gay. This is the first time I have ever told someone that.... Some of my closest friends say prejudiced things about gays and it hurts me very deeply because I am pretty sure they would have nothing to do with me if they knew about me. I hope that you aren't like that in real life; I'm

pretty sure that you aren't but one never really knows… If it's alright with you maybe we could write each other every so often? I would really like that!!

Let me tell you that you are the most courageous young person that I've ever seen. I know that I would never have the courage to play a homosexual teenager because I would be worried about what my friends and family would be thinking about me…. I'm 17 and I can't really relate to Billy Douglas' position because I'm not gay and none of my friends are gay, but I'm sure it's present in our age group…. I know a lot of people write to you and share some of their deepest secrets, but I can't do that because I don't even know you, though I wish I did…. I know you live way up there in Delaware or New York and I live way down here in Florida, but I really wish I could get to know you and talk to you more. I guess I've taken up enough of your time, but just one more thing. I'm sure you have hundreds of friends up where you live, but if you ever need anybody to talk to, that doesn't really know you (I know this sounds funny, but hang in there!) but wishes he did, and is willing to lend an ear to a friend, give me a call any time (call collect).

Even some of the adult male writers gave clear evidence of wanting to move beyond the confines of fan-letter writing and signed photographs:

Times have changed a great deal since I was a young man of your age. I wasn't 'found out' till my freshman year in college. My parents and I didn't have any conflict or even discussion. When I was asked to leave the seminary, they sent me to a psychiatrist who confirmed that I had latent homosexual tendencies… Know this. You would be welcome here—no commitments, sexual or otherwise, if in your real life situation you needed a home. One rule—no drugs.

I am writing to you because of the storyline that your character, Billy, is involved in. What a challenge for you!… About ten years ago I had a brother who was your age, seventeen, when he told me he was gay. He was very troubled by this and to make a long story short, about 6 months later, he killed himself because he couldn't come to grips with his feelings for other guys. You remind me of him a lot... Please, if you could find the time, write to me and give me your thoughts on this very sensitive issue. I'm giving you my address and even my phone number, in case you might even see fit to call me.

Why do these writers, both isolated and fearful gay teens and adults haunted by memories of unhappy friends and siblings, feel that a young actor (known to be straight) portraying a confused and troubled youth, is an appropriate target for their confessions, their overtures, and their pleas for help? Back in the 1950s, when Horton and Wohl first labeled the phenomenon of para-social interaction, within a psychiatric framework (though the issue of "unrealistic" audience response to media celebrities is as old as the fact of media celebrity), they defined such responses as pathological only when they are a "substitute for autonomous social participation, when [they proceed] in absolute defiance of objective reality" (op.cit., p. 200). As Joli Jensen summarized their view:

These extreme forms of fandom, they claim, are mostly characteristic of the socially isolated, the socially inept, the aged and invalid, the timid and rejected. For these and similarly deprived groups, para-social interaction is an attempt by the socially excluded (and thus psychologically needy) to compensate for the absence of "authentic" relationships in their lives. (1992, p. 17)

Apparently it is the case that in the 1990s many teenagers and even adults who are confronting the choice between the stifling agony of the closet and the possibility—even certainty—of familial and societal rejection are living in pathological circumstances and do not have the option of authentic relationships with anyone who can help them deal with their emotional crises. Thus an inexperienced but sincere young heterosexual actor can find himself playing not only role model but also confessor and phantom friend to people in great pain and need.

Notes

1. As recently as January of 1991, eighteen months before "The Accusation" appeared on *OLTL*, an article in *Soap Opera Weekly* explained "Why Daytime Isn't Gaytime," concluding that "homosexuals seem forever doomed to reside in the daytime's dark and lonely off-screen closet, deprived of light by narrow-mindedness and bigotry, kept there by ignorance and intolerance" (LeCuyer, 1991: 22). The article may have been excessively pessimistic about the willingness of a soap's producers and network to introduce a gay character, but it was accurate on another score: the difficulty of having a regular character turn out gay. A writer for *OLTL* is quoted, "It's difficult to maintain a homosexual character as a hero over a period of time"—certainly true as long as such a character is not permitted to engage in numerous romantic couplings with other characters. As *OLTL* head writer Michael Malone explained at a University of Pennsylvania symposium in 1993, they decided to introduce a new character—Billy Douglas—to be the centerpiece of "The Accusation" because they didn't want to have a regular long-term teenage character turn out to be gay.

2. e.g., a 14 year-old Virginia girl wrote: "When I saw you on TV, I started realizing that I wanted to do work on soap operas. I have always wanted to work with you and Chris McKenna. You both seem like nice guys. I'm free and I was wondering what you look for in a girl... I love you and Chris. Tell him that I love him, too. Don't tell him that I love you more."

3. This is an appropriate point for me to acknowledge the assistance and cooperation of Ryan Phillippe and his family, of Michael Malone, head writer (and now producer) of *OLTL*, and my colleague Joan DeJean, who had better write the full story of *OLTL*.

4. One of the 150 letters I examined did come from a "nut," but a friendly one, who recounted his experience when, "as a cute blond-blue-eyed little boy of six, seemingly innocent and immature, I met Albert Einstein in Princeton, NJ—he talked about the wonders of science—I talked about the wonders of God. At the end of the meeting, we agreed that the world would never set itself as a utopia unless people were willing to accept the sovereignty of God in human affairs. Proving that God exists...was the challenge I accepted at age 6." The correspondent wrote again (10/92), this time focusing on his knowledge of Bill Clinton's true identity (Zlotny Dvorak) and the question, "Is he a traitor or a patriot?" Unfortunately the writer seems not to know why Clinton/Dvorak "has never disclosed his Russian heritage? What's he hiding from people? Why is he such a pal to Russian gay community? Will Clinton sell America to highest bidder?"

5. Interestingly, this teenager recounts that she is "very active with gay and lesbian organizations," has written, marched, "spoken on panels about being a child of a lesbian," and joined in creating a "group for teens of gay and lesbian families," and yet she also writes that "I haven't confided in any of my friends that my mother is gay."

6. To the credit of the writers, they completely avoided the tired sitcom cliché in which a character comes out as gay to a straight friend who is immediately worried that the gay character will "come on" to him, and is then insulted when told that his friend is "not attracted" to him.

7. The one writer who addressed a letter to Billy was a straight adult who seems to be somewhat retarded: Hi Billy. Still watching *One Life to Live* glad that Joey still your friend. I would. I also wouldn't take it hard like Joey. When I first moved here, 11 years old, 1981, and went to Omaha public schools, lot of people thought I was gay. My ex sister in law was one of those people. It used to upset me, no more, none her business. It my life I would have to live it... Take a lot of work to be a soap star. I always dream to be a soap star, make more buddy's on a soap. Billy hope think work out for you wish they stop picking on you. Wish I could help ya... Hope I hear from you, stay in touch Buddy. Well Billy, would like a picture pal. Want to know more about you in real life. Best wishes Billy Okay.

8. A Texas girl wrote, "I hope this doesn't sound forward, but do you have a girlfriend? I'm sorry I shouldn't have asked that, anyway if you do she has nothing to worry about, because I'm too ugly... Do you think it would be alright if we write to each other and get to know each other?" There were many, many similar comments and questions from young women.

Musical Closets:
A Personal and Selective Documentary History of Outing and Coming Out in the Music World
LAWRENCE D. MASS

Dedicated to Michaelangelo Signorile

"Musical Closets" is in two parts. The first contains the body of the essay as it was originally written for Queering The Pitch. *In the few instances where footnotes have been updated, that material has been placed in italics. The second part is an epilogue that tells of the controversies surrounding the essay—its eleventh-hour rejection by the editors and publishers of* Queering The Pitch, *followed by the same acceptance-then-last-minute-rejection sequence for publication in the* Harvard Gay and Lesbian Review. *The current epilogue (an earlier version was to have accompanied the essay in* HGLR *) updates several of the histories being followed in "Musical Closets." "Musical Closets" is reprinted here with the generous permission of Cassell, which will retain first publication rights and which will feature it in my forthcoming collection,* Musical Closets: Homosexuality, Judaism, Music, and Opera.

Ever since the U.S. Supreme Court's decision in *Bowers v Hardwick* that homosexuals do not have the right to be consensually intimate in the privacy of their own bedrooms, the story has circulated that a clerk who was very close to one of the deciding justices was a closeted gay person. In another anecdote, Justice Powell, the swing vote, was said to have admitted that if he had known any gay men or lesbians, his decision might have been different. In her remarkable book, *Epistemology of the Closet*, Eve Sedgwick uses the example of the closeted clerk to demonstrate just how clearly, directly, and profoundly the act of coming out turns the personal into the political. The basis of her discussion is a comparison of the Bowers v Hardwick circumstance with the biblical story of Esther, the ethnically closeted queen who saved her people from genocide by risking her life to come out as a Jew to her husband, King Ahasuerus. (1)

To give today's "closet cases," as they are popularly designated, fair consideration, we must grant that despite striking similarities, there are differences between coming out as an ethnic person and coming out as gay or lesbian, even when the ethnicity, like Judaism, may be in many respects as covert as same-sex preference. As Sedgwick puts it:

> The suggested closeted Supreme Court clerk who struggled with the possibility of a self-revelation that might perceptibly strengthen gay sisters and brothers, but would radically endanger at least the foreseen course of her or his own life, would have an imagination filled with possibilities beyond those foreseen by Esther in her moment of risk. It is these possibilities that mark the distinctive structures of the epistemology of the closet. (2)

Sedgwick then proceeds to delineate a range of such possibilities, all of which reveal distinctions between the effects of a gay identity and those of an ethnic or religious identity. Notwithstanding these differences, the similarities between Esther and the Supreme Court clerk are so obvious they may serve as the foundation, without further elaboration, of the documentary which follows. In the arts, as in politics, there have been countless instances where the closetedness of individuals in positions of influence has obscured important aspects of the truth, if not the serving of justice on the scale of Bowers v Hardwick. From my own experience in the worlds of music and opera, I wish to discuss examples which I believe to be illustrative of this predicament. Some names will be named and some will be outed. But as I told William M. Hoffman—the playwright and co-creator of *The Ghosts of Versailles*, a close friend with whom I discussed the ethics of outing in the early 1990s, when the phenomenon acquired its name and became nationally controversial—the bottom line for me in the outing debate, as in the debate about coming out, is one simple, five-letter word: truth.

The truth is more important than a public person's right to privacy. Often enough, the truth turns out to be a matter of public record that has no discernible impact on an artist's creativity— e.g., details of birth, residences, education, marriages, children, divorces, affairs, illnesses, etc. Likewise often enough, however, the revelation of an artist's sexual orientation, ethnicity, religious or political affiliations will be of some interest or pertinence. This is especially so when sexual preferences, ethnicities, or politics exist in circumstances of marked intolerance. One wants to know, for example, about the ethnicity and politics of World War II era artists and critics. I would propose that learning that a contemporary American artist or critic is homosexual or homophobic is of comparable interest and importance to learning that a European artist or critic in the 1930s was Jewish or fascist (e.g., the Nazi collaborator Lucien Rebatet was among France's foremost music critics). In any event, it is inconsistent for critics, historians and other scholars to be rigorous about the recording and consideration of all matters of public record, including the details of extramarital affairs, for living as well as deceased artists who are heterosexual but not for those who are homosexual. Finally, there is the irony of Bowers v Hardwick, which showed up the fiction of the right to privacy in the United States. Hence, when gay men are dying of AIDS and the gay community faces the fiercest onslaught of prejudice and hatred since the McCarthy era, it can no longer be maintained by artists, writers, and musicians that a homosexual identity is irrelevant to their professional activity, certainly not now that the private has been judged officially to impinge on the public.

At the start of the game known as musical chairs, there's a chair for each player. Music is played and abruptly stopped as the participants walk around in a circle, in the center of which are the chairs. As the game progresses, a chair is removed each time the music starts. When the music stops, the players must scramble to claim the remaining seats. Those left standing are eliminated from the game. As in musical chairs, the outing of some persons will cumulatively limit the closet space left to scramble back to as discussion progresses. If it achieves nothing else, "Musical Closets" will have served a valuable purpose, meanwhile documenting some significant truth of gay and lesbian life in the arts for a generation that will hopefully perceive this discussion to be as quaint a vestige of its time as musical chairs is of the 1950s.

The reader is advised that "Musical Closets" is written in the form of a documentary—hence the substantial quotations from letters and texts—and is meant to be appreciated as history. So even where arguments are not entirely persuasive and/or there is discomfort with viewpoints, there may be value in their preservation as documentary of their time and place.

In the mid-to-late 1970s I shared a rich friendship with two of the country's leading music critics, Richard Dyer of the *Boston Globe* and Peter G. Davis, formerly of the *New York Times* and currently with *New York*. In the early 1980s we grew apart. Time had passed, I moved from Boston to New York, and we each went on to new friendships and new lives. But some of our estrangement had to do with my developing gay consciousness and activism; with my determination, as a start, to come out to my family and colleagues in medicine. Dick and Peter were gay and led gay lives, even professionally to the extent that they didn't take "beards" to parties or performances. Certainly everyone who knew them personally must have suspected, at some level of consciousness, that they were gay, but they were not otherwise out to their families, colleagues, or readers, except as it might be gleaned between the lines—e.g., in a piece on the Liberace-esque organist, Virgil Fox, Dick made reference to "an important pink rug." A somewhat less covert indicator of the writer's sexual preference were his periodic reviews of gay literature—e.g., of J. R. Ackerly's *My Father and Myself*. In those days, such clues were known as "hairpins."

Like Dick, Peter faced considerable homophobia from his colleagues. In those years, Peter was not alone among *Times* employees in likening the paper, under the dictatorship of (then) notoriously homophobic editor-in-chief A. M. Rosenthal, to the K.G.B. Peter correctly sensed that his prospects for advancement were limited by his being "a bachelor," something he was actually told by a senior editor. As Michelangelo Signorile points out in his feature on the *Times* for the *Advocate*, people were terrified to come out at the *Times* under Rosenthal, and no one did. (3) But that time has passed and Peter still hasn't come out, neither in Signorile's history of gay people at the *Times* nor in any other capacity. (3a) The last time I had lunch with Peter, nearly a decade ago, he likened his years at the *Times* to "an affair with a beautiful woman."

The issue of coming out was important, even (and especially) back in those days when so few did, but more disturbing and a source of growing friction among us (between Peter and me, and Dick and me) were the evasions, distortions, and omissions that were taking place in public discussions, in mainstream media columns such as theirs, that skirted the subject of homosexuality when it was pertinent to understanding. The last straw for a budding liberationist like myself was an interview with Peter Pears, conducted by Stephen Greco, that was published in the *Advocate* following Britten's death, in which the composer's homosexuality was discussed with unprecedented specificity. (4) When I brought the piece to their attention, Dick and Peter showed little interest. They did not agree with me that the *Advocate* piece warranted a follow-up news story. And there was obviously no interest on their parts for what I had really hoped for: a more searching interview with Pears and/or a feature discussing emerging gay perspectives in music, especially opera, during this time—our time—of gay liberation. What I regarded as their indifference and failure to respond to this development was a marker of the distance we'd grown apart. Eventually, I expressed my indignation in a piece for the gay press called "Confessions of an Opera Queen":

> Diva-worship may be the most conspicuous connection between opera and homosexuality, but it is by no means the only one. As they have in most art forms, homosexuals have made staggering contributions to opera—as composers, impresarios, directors and singers. Unfortunately, one reads almost nothing about those contributions [in a gay context]. It's no secret that many of this country's leading music critics are gay, but they don't want the public and certainly not their bosses to know what everybody already knows. So they take elaborate pains to minimize, rationalize, homogenize, or otherwise avoid the subject, regardless of its absolute interest or relevance.
>
> Take the case of Benjamin Britten, a gay man and one of history's greatest opera composers. During the Seventies, the decade of gay liberation, much of what was written about Mr. Britten by American music critics emphasized the "universality" of the composer's themes while conveniently ignoring the importance of homosexuality in the expression of those themes.

> Several years ago, the *Advocate* published an interview with Britten's lover, Peter Pears, in which the composer's homosexuality was (finally!) explicitly discussed. What many of us had long suspected but virtually never read was confirmed by Pears. Homosexuality, homophobia, intergenerational sex, and sadomasochism were, it turns out, conscious preoccupations of the composer in the writing of such masterpieces as *Peter Grimes*, *Billy Budd* and, of course, *Death in Venice*. (5)

I was particularly upset with Peter, whose reluctance to deal with gay issues, to say nothing of coming out, didn't change when he became music critic of *New York*, a job I helped him get. *New York*, under editor-in-chief Edward Kosner, was seriously homophobic, almost as bad as the *Times* under Rosenthal. When I interceded on Peter's behalf with *New York*'s film critic David Denby, who was among those aiding Kosner to find a successor to *New York*'s music critic Alan Rich and who enlisted me in his efforts to snare Dyer (who didn't want the job), I naively hoped that despite his conservatism, Peter would become part of a revolution of gay consciousness at the magazine. That did not turn out to be the case. On the contrary, here's what happened. Three years into Peter's tenure at *New York*, nothing had changed. Three years into an epidemic that was decimating his own people, Peter still had not touched the subject of homosexuality in any of his columns and the magazine was as homophobic as ever. Then, on March 18, 1985, *New York* published a piece by theater critic John Simon that sent seismic shockwaves throughout the gay and theater communities. Reviewing P. J. Barry's play, *The Octette Bridge Club*, here's what Simon had to say:

> ...In other words, the sisters are first cutely condescended to as silly but lovable hypocrites, then lampooned as ludicrous jerks from a typically homosexual, misogynist point of view...Altogether this is a play manifestly destined to become a perennial favorite in gay

bars, there to be performed by all-male casts. Why having come from the Actors Theater of Louisville…did it even bother to detour to Broadway? I suppose because it knew it could pander successfully to the trashiest and most benighted sensibilities in the audience. As my readers know, I have nothing against honest work by homosexuals, but this is faggot nonsense.(6)

Believe it or not, this wasn't the worst of Simon's invective. During the same time frame, he was overheard making imprecations about gays in the theater, according to Liz Smith. In her *Daily News* column she reported him as saying, "Homosexuals in the theater! My God, I can't wait until AIDS gets all of them!" The producers of *The Octette Bridge Club*, she wrote, noted that "at the performance Simon attended, he talked out loud throughout, saying things like 'Look at all these faggots laughing!'" (7) This was a shining moment for Smith, who, like Leonard Bernstein, often went to bat for gay and lesbian people and causes (she is a leading spokesperson and, indirectly, perhaps the leading fundraiser for AIDS) while remaining in the closet herself. (8)

The scandal was huge. It provoked responses and counter-responses in many publications. Smith kept up her attacks and the *Village Voice* published an "R.I.P." on Simon by Don Shewey. (9) Ned Rorem, on the other hand, did an interview with Simon for the *New York Native* in an effort to save the reputation of the man he still acknowledged as a friend. Preceding the interview, they attended Larry Kramer's play, *The Normal Heart*, together. (10)

I failed then as I fail today to understand why Rorem, whom I counted as a friend, should be so well-disposed towards Simon, who graduated from his debate with Rorem to become the film critic of William F. Buckley's ultraconservative *National Review*. Judging from the following highlights of the *Native* interview, and especially from the concluding remarks, Rorem isn't quite sure either.

Rorem: ...It occurred to me this morning that we first met already fifteen years ago...In the years since then, we've had a staunch acquaintanceship. I certainly have admired your tenacity. You're among the best-informed critics in the world...

Rorem: ...I've never found you, tête-à-tête, to be homophobic. Of course, I don't know what you say about me behind my back...

Simon: ...It was something I said in anger. I said, "Don't you sometimes wish that all the faggots in the theater"—or "fags" or "homosexuals," I don't know which, and it does make a difference, incidentally, to me, which of those three words I might have used—"would get AIDS and die, and we'd be rid of them, and we could go on from there." Now, obviously this is not something I believe...

Simon: ...I do think homosexuality is a form of sickness...

Simon: ...the blacks, at one point, wanted to be "colored," so then there were people who were polite and called them "colored"; then they wanted to be Negro," so one called them "Negro"; then they wanted to be "black"; there's no telling that they won't change to "Afro-American," or who knows what else.

Simon: ...And I think that two groups have devalued sex more than anybody else: one is the macho, yahoo, male brutes who have invented prostitution...and the other group...what I would have called "faggots," and what I might still call "faggots" between you and me, even if not in *New York* magazine, who will have eight sexual encounters during one night...

Rorem: John, I've not been out to nail you here, really not. I've wanted to see what makes you tick. I haven't quite seen. Though probably if we learned what makes our friends tick, we'd grow less interested in them. [end of interview] (11)

My own response to Simon's review of *The Octette Bridge Club* was an enraged letter to Kosner, hand-delivered the day it was written to the *New York* office. A copy was also sent to Denby. In the letter, I noted that although *New York* had praised me for my "excellent articles" on the AIDS epidemic, I had stopped reading the magazine because of its homophobia. "As I recently told my former friend (and your current music critic) Peter G. Davis, a spinelessly closeted homosexual," I wrote, "I don't read that greasy, sleazy thing."

Needless to say, they did not print my letter in *New York*, but they printed a number of others, including one from *New York* critics and writers Peter G. Davis, David Denby, Rhoda Koenig, Kay Larson, John Leonard, and Tobi Tobias criticizing Simon for his column.

...We believe it is a critic's job to examine stereotypes—the lazy catchphrases of people who prefer not to think—rather than create them, use them thoughtlessly, and encourage others to use them. (12)

Around the same time, I received a letter from Denby, reprimanding me for my characterization of Peter, for trying to haul him out of the closet, and urging me to send a second letter correcting the first.

I did send a second letter—to Kosner, with copies to Denby and others—in which I responded to Denby's charges and spelled out my first, primitive thoughts about what would eventually become known as outing, and my position on it, as it has remained over the years:

...I admit that my letter was a very angry response to the explosions of homophobic prejudice that were published...Viscerally, I seized that moment to express my disappointment in another of *New York*'s arts critics, Peter G. Davis.

Peter and I were close friends throughout the 1970s. In the early years of this friendship there seemed to be little conflict between my evolving gay identity and Peter's inviolable neutrality (like Switzerland) in all things "political." As an admirer of Peter's otherwise formidable commitment to objectivity and fairness, to what I used to call "the truth," I believed that Peter, like all music critics, had an obligation to devote more serious (i.e., written) attention to the burgeoning phenomena of gay artists, gay themes, and gay issues in the worlds of music and opera. It never happened. With the spectacular exception of Ned Rorem and a few obligatory crumbs about Benjamin Britten and Tchaikovsky, this subject continues to be almost completely ignored outside the gay press.

Since a significant number of this country's leading music critics were and are in fact gay, it seems "spinelessly closeted," as I said in my letter, for these writers not to have dealt more openly, honestly, and regularly with a subject whose time had arrived a decade earlier; a subject whose pertinence—-nothing more or less than the truth— should transcend the sexual orientation of the individual critic, his or her readership, or the publication for which she or he writes. (For your reference, more specific complaints about what I'll call Musical Closets are contained in the enclosed piece, "Confessions of an Opera Queen.")

I apologize for hauling Peter out of the closet, as you put it, but I daresay that if Peter had really been out of the closet (not stridently but publicly) as the music critic of *New York*, John Simon's paranoid blabber and the editor's complicity in it might never have happened. That is, it seems most unlikely that Simon and Kosner would want to suggest that the music critic of *New York* is writing from "a typically homosexual, misogynist point of view."

Finally, I wish to apologize for singling out Peter to bear the brunt of an attack that is aimed not simply at (the vast majority of) critics, gay and nongay, but at those legions of men and women, gay and nongay, whose sense of privacy, decorum, and good taste (i.e., whose careers) seem to be more important than the truth.

I heard nothing further from Denby, but several days later I received a letter from Kosner acknowledging and apologizing for what happened. The letter noted that *New York* had published a letter critical of Simon, signed by the magazine's other leading critics and writers, as well as a "regretful" statement by Simon. But in fact, Simon was equivocal and lukewarm in his apology, as so many of his remarks in his *Native* interview Rorem indicated:

Rorem: How do you account for this hue and cry, because the people who have hued and cried aren't all stupid, including your five or six colleagues [*New York*] who signed the letter—

   Simon: Well, I think my five or six colleagues here have proved pretty stupid, actually. (13)

Kosner's letter contained nothing about Davis and it would be some years before *New York*, as a principal target of the outing movement, would finally become discernably less homophobic, more affirmative and responsible in its coverage of issues and events of concern to gay men and lesbians. Although there is still no major writer or editor at *New York* who is openly gay or lesbian (who has publicly affirmed his or her sexual orientation), in contrast to the situation at the *New York Times* (13a), and although Simon has continued to make snidely homophobic, racist, sexist, and anti-Semitic remarks (certainly, the case cannot be made that he has changed), the climate is ripe for movement in that direction, a readiness I believe the outing of Davis affirmatively influenced.

If Davis had let it be known that he was gay, it is less likely that *New York* would have permitted Simon's pejorative generalizations, replete with hate words, to appear under its auspices. I believe this observation is valid, notwithstanding that the *New York Post* during the mid-1980s was as rabidly homophobic as the Nazi propaganda newspapers were anti-Semitic, despite the presence on the *Post*'s staff of openly gay reporter Joe Nicholson, and notwithstanding the knowledge that many known Jews on the staff at *New York* did not prevent Simon's cunningly anti-Semitic slur against the Jewish actor Mandy Patinkin, who as Leontes in Joseph Papp's 1989 Public Theater production of *The Winter's Tale* he described as looking "rather like a caricature in the notorious Nazi publication *Der Stuermer*." (14) What they would have prevented was the use of an anti-Semitic epithet like "kike." In the same vein, if there were openly gay staff at *New York*, it seems less likely that

Simon would have used or would have been allowed to use the word "faggot." It's a little like the situation with Assistant Secretary of Defense Pete Williams, who was finally outed by Michelangelo Signorile in the *Advocate* in 1991. Like Davis, Williams still hasn't publicly acknowledged his homosexuality and the military still hasn't changed its homophobic policies, but the outing of Williams was justified, many of us believe, in the interests of affirmatively influencing readiness for change.

Similarly, if P.J. Barry, author of *The Octette Bridge Club*, had been openly gay, that might have mitigated Simon's attack. Some of its special savagery seems to derive from the pleasure of outing a playwright who is trying at some level to hide in the closet. As Sedgwick puts it in *Epistemology of the Closet*: "The glass closet can license insult. ('I'd never have said those things if I'd known you were gay!'—yeah, sure)…" (15) It's impossible, by contrast, to imagine Simon writing offensively about anything, no matter how tacky or inferior, by Harvey Fierstein, for whom Simon has so often expressed great respect.

It's true that Davis wrote a program note for a Gay Men's Health Crisis benefit, although a more dispassionate response would be hard to imagine, and that he periodically acknowledged the epidemic (perhaps five or sex sentences total in more than a decade) in his column, but it wasn't until 1992 that Davis for the first time explicitly wrote about anyone's sexual orientation. Of course it wasn't his own. It was Schubert's. Reviewing the 1992 Schubertiade at the YMHA in New York, which had received the imprimatur of several of New York's leading heterosexual critics, here's what he had to say:

> Most people…were eagerly anticipating Susan McClary's talk, *"Schubert's Sexuality and His Music,"* which enlarged on musicologist Maynard Solomon's persuasive argument that the composer, as the program booklet primly put it, "was part of a subculture of men

who engaged in male-male sexual activity." In other words, Schubert was—gasp!—gay. But then, so were many other great composers, a hush-hush subject that is only now receiving serious attention. I'm not sure I buy McClary's contention that Schubert's gayness is somehow reflected in the Unfinished Symphony, but the speculation alone airs a complex and once-forbidden topic that can now be more openly discussed... (16)

"In reality," as I wrote in my survey of the critics' responses to the Schubertiade panel in *N.Y.Q.*:

> the subject of gayness in music has not been nearly so much forbidden as ignored, especially during the last ten years, and by no critic more conspicuously during that time frame than Peter G. Davis (When was the last time Davis wrote anything other than a performance review or star profile?) (17)

With the exception of the aforementioned program note, a review of Joan Peyser's biography of Leonard Bernstein, and rare, terse acknowledgments of the epidemic, Davis in fact wrote nothing in his pieces for the mainstream public about gay experience or concerns during the entire decade of the 1980s. Apart from his signing that letter of protest against Simon which all the other critics at *New York* also signed, at no discernible level did he lobby for the change he acknowledged in his review of the Schubertiade to be finally taking place. On the other hand, he contributed to homophobia at *New York* on a number of occasions with references to people being "effete" and/or "sissies."

Consider the following examples. In his review of the at-one-time openly gay director Franco Zeffirelli's admittedly ugly, soulless new production of *Don Giovanni* for the Met, Davis characterized Dawn Upshaw's Zerlina as "another potentially superb interpretation that might have come to life in less effete surroundings." (18) "Effete" re-emerged from Davis's psyche again during the same time period in comments on a new *Salome* at the Met: "...the irrelevant cross-culture crowds of effetes..." (19) Reviewing the Met's revival of *Parsifal*, Davis wrote: "Worst of all, Levine's slow-motion performance has paradoxically taken on a mannered, even prissy delicacy that makes the opera appear positively coy..." (20) More recently: "A song like 'Order No. 2 to the Army of the Artists' (1929) almost makes Bert Brecht and Kurt Weill sound like sissies." (21) To insiders who know that Davis, Zeffirelli, and Levine are gay, such remarks could be interpreted as coy. To the majority of readers who don't have access to that information, however, the use of such epithets confirm and encourage homophobic prejudices. It's one thing for a gay activist like Larry Kramer to rail at his gay brothers for being "sissies" and "faggots," but quite another when those hate-words are being used by a John Simon or anyone else not known to be gay or lesbian. So much for Davis's contention, in the letter he signed with the other writers at *New York*, regretting Simon's use of pejorative language and noting that "it's a critic's job to examine stereotypes...rather than to create them, use them thoughtlessly and encourage others to use them."

Like James Levine, director of the Metropolitan Opera, Christopher Keene, director of the New York City Opera, is said to be gay, but even the most basic information about the private life of this gifted conductor and champion of American and contemporary opera—information one would expect from any introductory feature on an artist on the occasion of that artist's appointment to an important new post (e.g., John Rockwell's Sunday *New York Times Magazine* cover story on Kurt Masur, when Masur became director of the New York Philharmonic, included background information about Mr. Masur, his wife, and family)—was cleverly obscured by Davis in his profile on Keene for *New York* at the start of Keene's first season as the new head of the NYCO. Instead, there was a single mention of Keene's two teenage sons with no other reference to domestic partnerships or circumstances, past or present. (22)

It was finally in the context of a hostile review of Joan Peyser's *Bernstein* that Davis may have been attempting to show his hand as a gay liberationist, when he asked:

> What gives Peyser the right to drag an entire generation of unde-clared gay musicians and composers out of the closet? Gratuitous homophobic comments abound. The plain-tomboy-chases-hand-some-cowboy scenario of the Agnes De Mille-Aaron Copland ballet, Rodeo, we are told for no good reason, "appropriated Copland's own sex life"—a remark so evil that one begins to wonder about the author's problems. (23)

It's true that Peyser's book is profoundly homophobic, and how wonderfully surprising and contemporary of Davis to have pointed that out, but he completely misses the historical importance of her work. Does he really think it's better for "an entire generation of undeclared gay musicians and composers" to remain in the closet, even if that is their preference? Is mendacity on such a scale ethical? Did it ever occur to him that her homophobia would have had no impact at all if her subjects hadn't so aggressively endeavored to obscure the facts of their lives to such extreme degrees, even when the risks had diminished? Davis's misgivings were of course shared by most homosexual musicians of renown—e.g., Copland, Bernstein, Virgil Thomson (A few exceptions, heroic and respected but less-known composers, such as David Diamond and Lou Harrison, come to mind)—and the general moratorium on maintaining "discretion" on composers' homosexuality was still being maintained by a broad range of critics. As Larry Gross notes in *The Contested Closet*, his encyclopedic discussion of the ethics and politics of outing, John Rockwell's lengthy obituary on Aaron Copland in the *New York Times* respected the composer's wishes and did not mention his homosexuality, notwithstanding Joan Peyser's having opened the door to more candid discussion of Bernstein's homosexuality at the time of his death several months earlier. (24) In this section, Gross further explores the complicity of critics, gossip columnists, and other writers in obscuring the facts of a celebrity's homosexuality. For his penultimate example, he selects Glenn Plaskin's obfuscations (as alleged by Michelangelo Signorile in *Outweek*) about Calvin Klein in the *New York Daily News* at the time of Klein's announcement of his intention to marry. (25) As Gross also notes, Plaskin, a gay man who championed openness about homosexuality (at least at the time of his interview with *Christopher Street* on the occasion of the publication of his biography of Vladimir Horowitz), but who is currently a gossip columnist for a mainstream daily, is best known for having outed the pianist in his book. (25a)

What gives anyone the right to drag an entire generation of undeclared gay musicians and composers out of the closet? As noted by Gross, lesbian writer Victoria Brownworth turned the ethical question around:

> every gay man and lesbian woman who "passes" (and tries to) oppresses me further and reaps the benefits of my activism while hiding the strength of our numbers from the people to whom those numbers would make a difference...Is it ethical to stay in the closet, pass for straight, assume the mantle of heterosexual privilege and enjoy its benefits while those who are openly gay suffer the oppression of their minority status? (26)

While Brownworth succinctly and successfully establishes the ethical context for outing, there is, I maintain, the even more important justification of fact, whether it should prove to be an incidental detail of public record or a key factor in creativity and interpretation.

The question of outing does not merely arouse the ire of the closeted. Even some of those in the music profession who have allowed their sexuality to become common knowledge have been notably hostile to it. This came out in my interview with our "official queer," as Ned Rorem described himself (before *queer* became politically correct parlance and before John Corigliano began to succeed him in that office). "I will not, and neither will Lou Harrison, compromise my friends, especially those of an older generation (those happy few!) who have their own perfectly decent set of standards. If I've done so in the past, I regret it." (27) On this account I was obliged to make statements rather than to ask questions in my desire to get some facts on record. Consider the following exchange.

> *Mass:* Terry McEwen [former director of the San Francisco Opera] is widely known in the gay community to be gay, though he has never been openly so in interviews. Respecting that opera was McEwen's business and that he was a professional, I think it says something about the minority status of gay people in the music world that he was the officially closeted homosexual director of the opera company of the city with the world's largest (proportionately) and most politically progressive gay community and audience during the era of gay liberation and the AIDS crisis. For New York, I think similar observations could be made about such leading musical figures as Stephen Sondheim.
>
> We touched on McEwen's tenure as director of the SFO and the issue of new commissions. To some extent, we've been exploring the status of opera in America. How would you contrast the state of opera in America with that in Europe?
>
> *Rorem:* Almost without exception, opera in Europe has been written by what we call experimental composers... (28)

Rorem wouldn't touch the subject of McEwen or Sondheim, even though McEwen had made preposterous generalizations about gays in an interview with the *Advocate:*

You know Giuseppe di Stefano said that if it weren't for gay people there would be no art. There's certainly a correlation between San Francisco being an opera-mad town and having the largest gay population in the world. But it is not a gay art form and not a lot of gay people are involved in it—at least onstage. They [the gay people who are involved] tend to be the fanatic admirers. (29)

I had already responded to McEwen's statement, pointing out that:

McEwen, who said nothing in this or any other interview about his own sexual orientation, is one of our era's more notorious diva worshipers. In the *Advocate* interview, in fact, he talks about little else. What he seems to be saying about the relationship between opera and gay people is this: gay diva fans are offensively conspicuous. Otherwise, homosexuality is not a distinction we want or need to make in the world of opera. Not, one might add, as long as diva worshipers continue to be in charge of that world. (30)

In the same article, I cited other instances of how pertinent gay perspectives were being obscured by closetedness and homophobia:

Two years ago, the Paris Opera presented one of this generation's most important musical events: the world premiere of the complete version of Alban Berg's *Lulu*. When *Lulu* arrived at the Metropolitan Opera the following season, *Opera News* featured a cover-story interview with Evelyn Lear, a famous Lulu of a preceding generation. In the new Met production, Miss Lear was singing not Lulu, but the role of a lesbian, the Countess Geschwitz. Even after a decade of gay liberation, however, neither Miss Lear nor the editorial staff of *Opera News* (nor, for that matter, any of the music critics) could bring themselves to acknowledge the simple fact that Geschwitz is the first openly gay character in history to enter the international operatic repertoire. (31)

Six years later, when I sought commiseration from Rorem (who never composed anything explicitly gay until he was 65) for my disappointment that the music critics had failed to place the world premiere of the complete (three act) *Lulu* in the context of today's feminist and gay liberation movements, here's what happened:

Mass: Do you think gay liberationists like myself are misguided in regarding the Countess Geschwitz, the first explicitly lesbian, homosexual, and feminist to enter the international repertoire, as a source of gay and feminist pride…?

Rorem: …We can put motivations into Berg's works, and we might even be correct on one level, although he may have been quite unaware of what we think he was thinking. One can write doctorates about *Lulu* until the cows come home. The Countess can be interpreted in many different ways, unsympathetically as well as sympathetically. Finally, she is only what the music tells us she is.

Mass: You must think, then, that I was likewise misguided in expecting our music critics to have said something about why the Countess might be especially interesting to today's opera-going public, with its large numbers of gay and lesbian persons, during this era of gay liberation struggles and AIDS. Incidentally, George Perle [the composer and Berg authority], who has characterized lesbian sex as "naughty," wrote me that he knows of no criticism, neither at the time of the writing and premiere of Lulu nor today, that engaged this question, period. I don't think he sees the pertinence of the Countess to today's audience and to our time as any more worthy of comment than you or Peter G. Davis do.

Rorem: …I think you're asking [critics] to discuss something that's not pertinent in a review. It might be in a Sunday article.

Mass: In a little review in the *New York Times* of *Albert Herring*, Donal Henahan, of all people, suggested that perhaps Britten identified with the character as a homosexual and that it's possible to see the opera as a kind of "coming out" story. That's the kind of timely, pertinent observation…we almost never get in mainstream music writing, even when the critic is gay.

Rorem: But Henahan's point had to do directly with Britten and the opera. With *Lulu,* you're asking critics to talk about social issues in their performance reviews.

Mass: When the social issues are pertinent and interesting, yes, that's precisely what I'm asking them to do! (32)

My dialectic with Ned, rich and frustrating, was inevitably about group bonding and identity. Ned had often made the point, in interviews, in his diaries, and in conversations with and letters to me, that being gay was no more interesting or pertinent, no more worthy of comment or analysis, than being heterosexual. In *The Nantucket Diary of Ned Rorem: 1973-1985,* his engagement of our debate revealed earnest struggle and courage as well as generational differences:

The so like-able, and to an extent intelligent, Larry Mass, unable to see the forest for the trees, keeps writing me about what he feels to be the responsibility of the gay composer. Yes, at this point I am indeed attracted by the thought of a "gay libretto" (whatever that might be), but I'm more strongly drawn to a pacifist libretto. I am as much a Quaker as a gay, and man's inhumanity and identity and poetry are expressed as much through common conflict on our fatal globe as through sexual conflict. Perhaps an opera on a debarred hero? Oscar Wilde? Even Alexander the Great...?

Larry Mass responds docilely to my ultimatum about discontinuing our, to me, fruitless exchange on gay music, with: "On Thursday Arnie and I are going to see [sic] the NYC Gay Men's Chorus, which will feature music by Barber, Bernstein, Copland, Gershwin, Porter, and Rorem. Nowhere, not in the program notes, certainly not in the mainstream press, but probably not even in the gay press or in Ned Rorem's diaries, however, will one read that all of these composers were/are homosexual, or any analysis of what that might mean."

Larry can't stop. Perhaps pink triangles could be placed by appropriate names in the program (although I never knew that

Gershwin was homosexual). Doesn't Larry worry about Jewish composers? What has Bernstein's and Copland's (and, yes, Gershwin's) Jewishness to do with their music?...What would a program note say about, for example, Poulenc? "Poulenc, rumored to be gay (although he sired a daughter upon whom he doted), wrote his mass in…" Or Copland? "Copland, rumored to be gay, was also Jewish, but wrote goyish music all his life, being the first to celebrate cowboys." To dignify Larry's obsessions here is sadistic. Maybe I'll eat my words one day. (33)

The answer to Ned's first question is a resounding affirmative. Stimulated by my evolving awareness of sexual identity, I naturally have pondered the issue of the Jewishness of Jewish composers. What I've discovered, moreover, is that it is almost as closeted as the sexuality of homosexual composers, and in similar ways. Greatest culpability for this, I believe, rests with Richard Wagner, the composer whom the lovers of European classical music relish finding excuses to adore. Owing to Wagner, principally, and the racist and nationalist attitudes everyone knows he propounded— most notoriously in his anti-Semitic tract, "Jewry in Music," among many other political writings, and metaphorically in his *Nibelung* tetralogy, *Die Meistersinger*, among other operas—the earnest desire was born after World War II to minimize if not completely repress awareness of the Wagner problem, a movement that was central to the greater process of attempting to establish nonpolitical status for music in a world of post-Holocaust chaos, wherein any significance that might be granted to the Jewishness of Jewish composers would be effaced. (34) For an example of the internalization of anti-Semitism resulting from this, one has only to turn to Eric Gordon's biography of Marc Blitzstein to reveal a case both combined with and paralleling internalized homophobia. "Blitzstein rarely thought about his Jewishness," Gordon observes, "and took no pains to explore Jewish themes in his work. He knew almost nothing of Jewish history…" (35) "Rather like Ned Rorem's frequent assertions," I concluded in my review of Gordon's book, "ongoing today, that homosexuality has nothing to do with art and music, Blitzstein's rare observations about Judaism and music were negative and defensive…" (36) As for Ned's second question—what would programs say about the gayness or reputed gayness of composers such as Copland and Poulenc?—if you take the facetiousness out, what he wrote isn't a bad start (though "true to form," as my life-partner Arnie Kantrowitz observed after reading these *Nantucket Diary* comments, "Rorem doesn't know there *were* Jewish cowboys"). I not only agree with Ned's devil's advocate point about the pertinence of Copland's Jewishness to his art, I suspect that, as with Blitzstein, it probably can't be disentangled from the pertinence of the great American composer's homosexuality. (36a)

The closeting of Lulu's lover, the Countess Geschwitz, in that cover-story issue of *Opera News* Ned and I were arguing about, was not a coincidence. It was in every way consistent with the policies and practices of *Opera News* editor-in-chief Robert Jacobson. Jacobson, well-known in the gay community, would attend performances wearing his trademark mink coat, arm-in-arm with his lover. And he solicited pieces by officially queer Ned Rorem. He even went so far as to do an interview for the Advocate in which he discussed homosexuality and the importance of coming out, suggesting that Bernstein and Levine had become more open about themselves, while slyly failing to come out himself. (37) In fact, throughout his tenure at *Opera News*, there was never an editorial or feature on gay people and opera, or even on AIDS, which he died of and which was not mentioned, just as his sexual orientation was not mentioned, in his obituary in *Opera News*, which likewise didn't mention that he was survived by his life partner. By contrast, Jacobson's close friend and colleague, Matthew Epstein, the impresario with whom he worked on several AIDS benefits, had clearly come out in a similar interview for the *Advocate* during the same time frame. More recently, Epstein was the subject of a feature interview with music critic Tim Page for *Newsday*, in which he (Epstein) came out as a PWA. (38)

The complicated case of someone like Jacobson, who wears his identity on his sleeve, who encourages openness about homosexuality for others and in other publications but refuses to explicitly, publicly, acknowledge it about himself and who eschews explicit discussion of homosexual identity in his own copy, helps to explain another phenomenon of musical closets: it is heterosexual critics more often than homosexual ones who initiate the exploration and discussion of gay issues in music. Thus it was Tim Page, as a music critic (The *New York Times*, *Newsday*) and radio host who was the first critic to approach the gay press about responding to the epidemic, calling upon me to advise him about putting together a radio memorial retrospective and tribute to musicians who had died of AIDS. (39) Likewise it was Joseph Horowitz, Donal Henahan, and Edward Rothstein who wrote the first articles in the mainstream press about Schubert's homosexuality. Why was it Page, Henahan, and Horowitz who took the initiative rather than Peter G. Davis or Andrew Porter? Porter, for example, was notably dismissive about the important 1992 Schubertiade (organized and chaired by Horowitz), an event that, for whatever reasons, he didn't even attend: "Another topic for discussion at the symposium was Schubert's homosexuality," Porter wrote in his *New Yorker* column. "This is now being treated as 'news'; it has long been apparent just below the surface of Schubert's letters and diaries and the memoirs of his friends, which have been in print for decades." (40) All very well, as I observed in my review, "but why does it turn out to be Horowitz and Rothstein (and even Donal Henahan), rather than Porter and Davis, who are at least willing to try to deal with the issues at some length, to make them a principal subject of discussion, no matter how tardily or uncomfortably (or, in the case of Henahan, homophobically)?" (41) The domination of the discourse on homosexuality in music by heterosexuals does of course betray homophobia in the profession, but leaves us with no option but to thank someone like Joseph Horowitz "for his leadership in taking the largest step to date in opening up the subject of Schubert's homosexuality to the mainstream public, even if, as in days of olde, [his] was a public forum on homosexuality that failed to include any gay or lesbian visibility." (42)

The darkness within the closet is such that its inhabitants can't see even obvious inconsistencies in their thinking. Witness the case of John Ardoin, music critic of the *Dallas Morning News* and author of *The Callas Legacy*. In the mid-1980s I wrote to ask him questions about the telecast of the Bayreuth Centennial production of the *Ring* cycle, for which he had written the intermission features. The other matter I had asked Ardoin about had to do with Callas. It's intriguing that several of her closest involvements were with gay men who were outspokenly socialist, like Pier Paolo Pasolini and Luchino Visconti. Some deeper exploration of these associations, I implied, would be of interest to those of us who are trying to understand the phenomenon of Maria Callas in broader sociocultural perspective.

His response was skeptical. He noted that Callas was not unique in her associations with homosexual men and that her rare remarks about homosexuality had been pejorative. Perhaps, he proposed, this stemmed from her infatuation with Visconti and her shock on learning he was homosexual. But Ardoin also wondered if she had ever come face-to-face with questions about homosexuality. Did Ardoin, a gay man and one of Callas's closest friends, ever attempt to discuss the subject of sexual preference—his own or anyone else's—with her? The only association he knew of with a homosexual that she went into with her eyes fully open and completely aware of the fact, he believed, was with Pasolini. He saw the two of them together, he went on to explain, but she and others told him it was a sort of brother-sister relationship and that she felt very close to him as a human being, much as she did with the late Lawrence Kelly [the gay impressario and companion of Ardoin, under whose auspices Callas made her American debut and sang some of her most memorable performances in Chicago and Dallas]. But to see any broader "sociopolitical" meaning in all of this, Ardoin concluded, would be to belabor the point.

A subtler characteristic of musical closets is the degree to which some composers or artists who are already officially out may wish, on certain days and over certain issues, to slide ever-so-gently back into that comforting space. Witness my experience with William M. Hoffman and John Corigliano, who reluctantly agreed to an interview with me for *Opera Monthly* that also would be for my collection of interviews on homosexuality and music. I submitted my questions in advance and agreed, in writing, that those dealing with homosexuality could be expurgated if they so wished (and they did so wish) from the text for Opera Monthly.

Bill, for whom I have the highest regard, and I had been engaged in friendly and informal disagreement for years about the whole business of homosexuality and art. Like Ned Rorem, Bill was openly gay when the risks were greater, and is a source of community pride for his diverse achievements, especially his contributions to gay theater, culminating in his play *As Is*, the first commercially successful play to deal with AIDS. But also like Ned, Bill didn't want himself or his art to be "pigeonholed" as "gay." (43)

My position, as I had continually and sometimes acrimoniously argued with Ned over it, was that it was important to be affirmative rather than defensive about one's minority status with regard to one's art. Unlike Rorem, Hoffman, and James Purdy, Edmund White is proud to be known as a "gay writer," even though he's also an American writer, an outstanding writer, and a writer who should be judged first and foremost as a writer, period. Why should the affirmation of an artist's minority status imply compromise of artistic integrity?

Bill's position on outing was likewise conservative and he seemed genuinely distressed by its first major bid for public attention—Michelangelo Signorile's exposé of Malcolm Forbes in *Outweek*. (44) At the personal level, perhaps Bill feared, not unreasonably or unsympathetically, that an outing reign of terror could reach the Met and sabotage their wonderful opera (and anyone who has experienced *The Ghosts of Versailles* cannot fail to empathize with the work's profound mistrust of mob psychology, if not revolution altogether). Bill, working with closeted colleagues, could not be expected to be comfortable with some of the outing rhetoric that was proliferating in 1990: e.g., "when we talk about outing, what are we really talking about? We're talking about exposing the collaborators." (45) After John officially came out in a cover story in the *Advocate* (46), however, Bill seemed less defensive and anxious.

I was consistently on the opposite side of the outing debate, citing my bottom-line-importance-of-truth position: if a public figure were Jewish, divorced, had a mistress, or had AIDS, you'd want to know. You'd likewise want to know if he or she were gay or lesbian, especially if you're a historian or other scholar.

The truth issue, I continue to believe, supercedes all others, including the importance of having gay and lesbian role models (46a), and even the most potent of the other arguments in favor of outing, as captured by Michael Bronski:

> And for the straight world, outing represents a fearful loss of power because the straight world—maybe even more than the gay world—knows the power of the closet and the enormous possibilities of social control that the closet can wield…Outing is—for straight people—a direct, uncompromised challenge to their insistence on controlling our lives. (47)

But what about the potentially terrible costs of outing persons against their will? As Fran Leibowitz put it, when asked her opinion about outing (after she had been outed by Signorile in *Outweek*), "To me this is a bunch of Jews lining up other Jews to go to a concentration camp" (48), an analogy that would have special resonance for Bill, whose family was almost entirely murdered by the Germans in the Holocaust. (Anyone who thinks *The Ghosts of Versailles* is "too sentimental" or who otherwise doubts the sincerity of its politics or nonpolitics should re-experience the work with this knowledge of the author's background.) But as Gross points out, "the analogy to Jews and concentration camps is also used by the proponents of outing, who see powerful closeted gays as analogous to the assimilated Jews who never believed that they would be touched by the crude anti-Semitism of the ghetto dwellers." Gross suggests that gay liberationists might well respond to such people by citing Hannah Arendt's 1968 account of her experiences as a Jew in Germany:

> I cannot gloss over the fact that for many years I considered the only adequate reply to the question, who are you? to be: a Jew. That answer alone took into account the reality of persecution...The statement: I am a man—I would have considered as nothing but a grotesque and dangerous evasion of reality. (49)

Again, a turning point for Bill was John's official (media) coming out in a cover story for the *Advocate* on the occasion of the world premiere of John's First Symphony, which was about and dedicated to persons with AIDS. But the *Advocate* is a gay and lesbian community publication. At the time of my interview with him, John had yet to come out in a mainstream publication, even though press coverage of his First Symphony implied that he was gay. Would acknowledging his homosexuality have been inappropriate for *Opera Monthly*?

When we got to the questions about homosexuality in our interview, John asked me to stop the tape. He (suddenly?) didn't want
to answer the questions at all, even though I was led to believe
that he'd agreed to do so. At that point I threatened to cancel the
interview altogether. John's point was this: He had nothing to hide
about his homosexuality and was not opposed to discussing it
where it might have pertinence—e.g., with regard to the First
Symphony, or if he were being interviewed for a gay publication like
the *Advocate*. But *Opera Monthly* (the staff of which is mostly gay)
was a *mainstream* publication (as if gay men don't make up a huge
proportion of any opera public or readership, as if questions of
sexual orientation can't be of interest, pertinence, or value to a
mainstream readership) and the subject of our interview was the
opera which, he and Bill were insistent, had nothing to do with
homosexuality. After I reassured John that I would honor our
agreement not to include any of the gay content in the *Opera
Monthly* piece, we resumed our discussion. "Why should I trust
you?" John asked me off the record. Years ago, he explained, Robert
Jacobson had published, without his permission, John's suggestion that a certain leading composer was gay and that it had gotten
him (John) into a lot of trouble. John then answered the few questions I was allowed and had time to ask about this subject (e.g., I
wanted to know how Bill and John felt their early relationship had
influenced their collaborations over the years.)

In fairness, it should be noted that there were two other factors
in John's anxiety. First and foremost, he was in the midst of breaking up with his lover of thirty years. I didn't have to ask whether to
delete my question about *their* relationship, which was simply this:
"Would you care to tell us about your life-partner?" In a subsequent telephone conversation, John seemed genuinely disconcerted
by the breakup and declined to participate in the editing of the
interview, which Bill helped me complete. The second factor was
that the *Opera Monthly* piece would be the first in-depth interview

with Corigliano and Hoffman about the opera to appear in antic-ipation of the premiere. As prepared for *Opera Monthly*, the inter-view was published without any of the gay content and designated (at my insistence) as "specially abridged." At my further insistence, however, there was also a statement, for which I did not ask for the interviewees' approval, that the complete text would eventually appear in a forthcoming collection, *Homosexuality and Music: An Introduction to Gay and Lesbian Persons, Themes, and Issues in Music*. (50)

Two months later *New York* ran a feature on Corigliano by Peter G. Davis, with as much space devoted to his First Symphony as to the opera. In John's logic, his being gay was more pertinent and appropriate for discussion here, and he acknowledged breaking up with his "companion" of thirty years and mentioned something about the theoretical advantages a "gay sensibility" might have for the writing of a work about AIDS. Needless to say, however, there was no direct discussion, no *affirmation*, of being gay. (51)

The idea of *affirming* one's gayness, especially if one is being asked to do so outside the gay press, just isn't very popular, I guess. My most recent encounter with this reality came when I spoke to Peter Kazaras about doing an interview in the same format as those with Rorem, Hoffman, and Corigliano, jointly for the collec-tion on homosexuality and music, and for *Opera Monthly* (in a "specially abridged" version, if he so wished and as had been the case with the others). I told him I would like to be able to make the point, to state for the record, that he is the first openly gay singer in the history of the Metropolitan Opera. Kazaras didn't formally decline the project, though he didn't mention it when I ran into him at a GMHC benefit some months later, or with any of the mailings I've received from the AIDS thrift shop he volunteers at. More recently, as we watched the television premiere of *The Ghosts of Versailles* (in which Kazaras, as Count Almaviva, sings some of the opera's most transcendent music), snuggled together on Bill

Hoffman's living room couch, he said he was continuing to think about our proposed project, and would get back to me on it.

Meanwhile, last year, baritone Sanford Sylvan became the first singer of international stature to affirm his homosexuality in the mainstream press, in a piece by openly gay music writer K. Robert Schwarz for the *New York Times* at the time of the American premiere of John Adams's opera *Klinghoffer*. Sylvan came out in discussing the depth of personal meaning of the Whitman texts John Adams had set for him, the ones Jamie James found more convincingly set by Adams than by Rorem. (52)

In 1991 Ed Iwanicki, director of group publishing at Viking-Penguin, asked me to blurb a novel they were publishing that explored the worlds of gay people, AIDS, and opera. Knowing of my intersecting work and interests in these areas, he thought I'd be a good choice and he was right. Here's the blurb I gave them for *The Uncle From Rome* by Joseph Caldwell:

> Not since Terrence McNally's *The Lisbon Traviata* has there been such a passionate record of love and opera in the age of AIDS. In this drama giocoso about an American comprimario tenor who dreams of greatness, whose lover died of AIDS and who suddenly finds himself at the center of a blood-feuding Neapolitan family, Joseph Caldwell has fashioned a parable of humanity that transcends its genre to achieve operatic grandeur.
>
> — Lawrence D. Mass,
> co-founder, Gay Men's Health Crisis
> associate editor, *Opera Monthly*

Caldwell sent me an affectionate letter, saying how much he appreciated and loved my comments. Then, several weeks prepublication, I got a letter from him attempting to explain his discomfort with references to AIDS and saying how sorry he was about not clearing text changes with me. I didn't know what he was talking about, so I called Ed Iwanicki, who told me Caldwell had decided he didn't want any explicit references to AIDS or homosexuality in any of the promotional material! Ed said he, Ed, had to fight tooth and nail to keep a single mention of AIDS in the description on the inner cover of the dust jacket. Their revision of my blurb, which I reluctantly allowed them to use, is/was as follows:

> Joseph Caldwell has fashioned a parable of humanity that tran-
> scends its genre to achieve operatic grandeur. (52a)

The quote identified me as associate editor of *Opera Monthly* but not as a co-founder of Gay Men's Health Crisis.

The broader impact of the closet comes out when one examines the writing of closeted critics for consciousness in parallel areas of social and political concern—racism, sexism, and anti-Semitism. Being both gay and Jewish has been an advantage for me in notic-ing how these various areas of consciousness intertwine, and my most recent writing engages this subject at considerable length, compar-ing critical indifference to gay phenomena and perspectives with that toward the ongoing political fallout from Wagner's anti-Semitism. What the music critics keep insisting is that Wagner's politics, like Benjamin Britten's homosexuality, are so irrelevant to a full appre-ciation of the timelessness and universality of the composer's achievements that they don't merit anything more than passing mention. (53) The same approach extends to parallel questions of ethnicity. Thus, in Peter G. Davis's profile on Kathleen Battle for *New York*, there was no discussion of race or racism. (54) This is like-wise the case with Richard Dyer's profile of Shirley Verrett for *Opera News*. (55) Here, as with Davis's interaction with Battle, deconstruction of the text revealed a closeted gay man conversing with a (racially) closeted black woman. The same circumstance exists in Erick Neher's interview with Eugene Perry for *Opera*

Monthly. (56) On the other hand, perhaps Battle, Verrett, and Perry wanted to speak about racism but weren't given the chance by interviewers who presumed that racism was no more a factor in the lives and careers of these artists than homosexuality was in theirs. This was clearly the case when Jessye Norman was interviewed by Charlie Rose for WNET. When asked point blank if she had experienced racism in her career, she responded that indeed she had, and often. Rather than probing her response, however, the otherwise socially conscious but voluble Rose abruptly changed the subject. (57) As John La Chiusa, the librettist for Anthony Davis's *Tania* (based on the story of Patty Hearst), put it in K. Robert Schwarz's piece on the new opera in the *New York Times*:

> What's relevant in this story for women, for blacks, for gays, is that identity is defined by your experience. But when you negate your experiences, what kind of identity do you have? Either we find a peaceful coexistence with our experiences, or we shove them back into the closet, where they'll become a nightmare that we'll be dealing with for the rest of our lives. (58)

We're back where we began, with Eve Sedgwick's comparison of the closet in contemporary gay and lesbian life with that of ethnically threatened persons in history. Today, as in the past, moral and ethical choices involve breaking decorum and taking risks. The political is always, initially and at a very fundamental level, personal. It's still the same old story.

Part 2:
Epilogue: The Controversy Surrounding
the Publication of "Musical Closets"

In 1991 I was invited by musicologists Philip Brett and Elizabeth Wood to be a contributor to their book, *Queering The Pitch*, for

Routledge. As anticipated, it would become the first collection on homosexuality and music in the academic literature. "Musical Closets" is the piece I submitted.

Though we'd never met, I had interviewed Philip by correspondence for *Christopher Street* (this interview was subsequently published in the second volume of my *Dialogues of the Sexual Revolution*) (59), and I had become friends with Liz through our participation in the Center for Lesbian and Gay Studies (CLAGS) at the City University of New York. Liz and Philip had been leading figures in the establishment of the Gay and Lesbian Study Group of the American Musicological Society, and its newsletter, to which I became a contributor with a piece called "Musical Quilts," about compositions inspired by the Great Quilt of the Names Project. (60)

"Musical Closets" was controversial from its inception, and it says something about the courage and political convictions of Brett and Wood that they stuck with the piece to the extent that they did, at least on paper and in their communications with me. If I at any point became suspicious of Liz's occasional cryptic comments that the essay might fit better in a different anthology, I was reassured by our mutual hard work through three drafts over several months. Editors don't expend that kind of time and effort on pieces they don't plan to use, do they? Despite our diligence, however, at the eleventh hour, I was told that the Routledge editor, Bill Germano, would not sanction its inclusion in the collection; not, I was told, unless I were willing to rewrite the piece in such a way that those who are outed would not be. That would not be possible, Liz had to agree with me, without eviscerating it, and so we were at loggerheads.

I spoke with Germano, whose principal reservations seemed to be fear of litigation, the personal nature of my work, and the implicit militancy of its politics. Without anger or condescension, I tried to get him to see something I thought very germane, something he might not have considered: that the outing controversy isn't where it was in 1988, when most editors and publishers set or reset their policies on this matter; that what had been outsider and street politics by people who were widely regarded as trouble-makers and radicals ("people with earrings," as Michelangelo Signorile might say)—e.g., Larry Kramer and Signorile (to whom "Musical Closets" is dedicated)—were now mainstream, as were their leading advocates. Clearly, Signorile's became the leading voice of the outing movement, just as Kramer's became the leading voice of the AIDS movement. More recently, Signorile had become a featured columnist for the world's leading gay and lesbian publication, the *Advocate*, and had published one of the most historically and politically important pieces ever written about the gay movement—"Out at the *New York Times*."(61) Meanwhile, there were now two new books on outing from distinguished presses. (62) I tried to get Germano to see that, not so unlike the AIDS epidemic in its earliest days (though the comparison is otherwise inappropriate), the phenomenon of outing isn't going away, and eschewing it will not make it do so.

Germano indicated a willingness to consider these arguments with his colleagues, and to hear from other observers. At my request, Larry Gross and Martin Duberman both read "Musical Closets" and sent their opinions, in writing, to Germano.

The following excerpts are from their letters:

...Journalism isn't the only domain tainted by the lies and evasions of collusive closet construction. History and criticism—as taught in schools and published in books and periodicals—are equally culpable. Larry Mass's account of some notable examples from the world of music performs an important service for all who are open to the truth about a significant segment of our culture. The world of classical music, like Hollywood and the Catholic church, is both filled with gay people and pervaded by the musty odor of closeted souls.

Light and air will only be beneficial to all of us, including the denizens of the closet themselves (the year after he was outed by the "page scandals" Gerry Studds told a gay paper that he felt "better than I've ever felt in my life")....

—Larry Gross (63)

...It seems to me there are two questions at issue: the quality of the essay and its appropriateness in this particular volume. I think the essay itself is absolutely first-rate. Learned and yet written in accessible prose, it is infused with a delicate moral sensibility; Mass has clearly thought long and hard about what he has decided to write and the tone is one of sorrowful regret—there is no hint in it of self-righteousness or of paying off old scores.

...The piece seems to me of a distinction to grace any volume, but especially a pioneering anthology on the subject of music and homosexuality. I can understand—abstractly—why you might be fearful of lawsuits. But practically, I would think there is next to no chance, realistically, of such a suit or suits. For one thing, Mass has indisputably told the truth—and truth continues to be the best defense (in court and out)...I hear no one these days objecting any longer to naming names when the well-being of the gay community and the larger interests of truth are at stake. In my view, Mass has done us all a decided service—and my hope is that you, too, will reach a similar conclusion and restore the essay to its rightful place in the volume.

—Martin Duberman (64)

Approximately one week later, I received the following letter from Mr. Germano, who had additionally received a letter, arguing in favor of including the essay, from Philip Brett, who sent me a copy. (I was never apprised of any such letter from Wood.)

Thank you for your patience while we mulled over the issues raised by your essay. I've given this careful consideration, and have appreciated not only the thoughtfulness of Liz Wood and Philip Brett, with whom I have discussed the matter, but that of Larry Gross and Marty Duberman.

Although it is not an easy conclusion, I've decided that the piece needs to appear in a publication other than this book. I respect the position you argue so forcefully in your paper, but I believe that the essay ultimately complements neither the specific volume as to tone, nor Routledge's publishing program as to strategy. You've asked me to rethink the position I am taking here on outing. I still don't see it as part of Routledge's brief, nor the best way we here can contribute to gay and lesbian studies, or to academic inquiry in general.

I understand this is as difficult for you as it is for us here, and that it is certainly an uncomfortable decision for the editors of the volume who are, of course, your colleagues. But I ask you to see that absent your essay the volume will be stronger because more coherent, and thus more likely to be treated seriously by the musicologists who are its audience.

I regret any embarrassment this decision may cause either to yourself or to any of our mutual friends, but I'm convinced this is the best path for the book.

—William Germano (65)

Although Routledge declined to publish "Musical Closets," at Liz Wood's suggestion, the conciliatory gesture was made to reprint my interview with Ned Rorem in *Queering The Pitch*. Meanwhile, media and film mogul David Geffen, who had been outed by Michelangelo Signorile in a number of pieces over several years, has more recently been acknowledged in an *Advocate* cover story for his enormous financial and leadership contributions to the gay community—mostly the former and mostly within the last year—culminating in his being named the *Advocate*'s "Man of The Year." Notwithstanding Geffen's stated reasons for coming out—mostly having to do with the AIDS epidemic—and his denunciations of both Signorile and Kramer in the interview, it's crystal clear that outing is what catapulted Geffen to his current openness and involvement. Consider the following statements by Geffen from the interview:

> So many friends of mine have already died and so many more are infected that whether I want to be a public figure or not, I am a public figure. Along with that comes a certain amount of responsibility, and so I felt that it would be wrong of me not to come out.
>
> The one thing I know about being open about being gay, for me, is that it's very empowering. In Alcoholics Anonymous they say, "You're as sick as your secrets." I think that when you feel you need to have secrets, it's hard to feel good about yourself, and I think part of growing up is being able to feel good about yourself. (66)

As was the case with Gerry Studds, outing is one of the best things that ever happened to Geffen, and one of the better things to have happened to the gay community.

In early 1993, *Lambda Book Report* presented the Routledge controversy. "The most controversial part of Mass's essay," it noted, "is his outing of *New York* critic Peter Davis, which includes a withering analysis of Davis's use of terms like 'effete' and 'sissy'" in reviews of operas staged by gay men." (67) In a subsequent review of a production of Virgil Thomson's *Four Saints in Three Acts*, Davis wrote what was, so far as I can glean, the first unequivocally gay-affirmative, as opposed to gay-neutral, statement of his career (albeit in parentheses): "...(Thomson and Stein, be it remembered, were gay Americans adjusting to early-twentieth-century mores, and their joint work has yet to be properly appreciated in that context)." (68) As was the case with Studds and Geffen, the outing of Peter G. Davis is doubtless a good thing—for Davis, for the gay community, for truth. Unlike Studds and Geffen, however, Davis has yet to come out himself. As a gay man coaching rehearsals of *The Mother of Us All* (the other Thomson/Stein collaboration) at Harvard College in the 1950s, did Davis know that Stein and

Thomson were gay and ponder implications? In the absence of Davis's willingness to probe the pertinence of his own life experience to his perspectives, one must extend Davis's parenthetical affirmation to include Davis himself.

In the August 30, 1993, issue of *New York*, Davis wrote a review of Humphrey Carpenter's biography of Benjamin Britten and of Barbara Heyman's biography of Aaron Copland that contained an unprecedented affirmation of the importance of homosexuality in the lives and works of these composers, and in which he came very close to coming out himself, recalling a homophobic incident involving a famous opera singer he declined to name. (69)

In mid-August 1994, I submitted "Musical Closets," as it exists above (through footnote 69 at the end of the preceding paragraph) to Richard Schneider, Jr., for consideration for the *Harvard Gay and Lesbian Review*, an ideal venue in terms of the Harvard backgrounds of Peter G. Davis, Richard Dyer, and myself. A week or so later Schneider called to say that he not only liked it but wanted to run it as the lead story of his next issue (Fall 1994), which would be devoted to the subject of censorship and would include a number of pieces that had been banned in various circumstances. The only problem, he said, was its length, so we edited it down by approximately two-fifths, which involved a lot of work on both our parts, and notwithstanding the concern we shared that editing it would interfere with our stated intention of presenting the chapter that Routledge had rejected. As finally "typeset" (for desktop publishing) and ready to go to press, the lead story was indeed "Musical Closets," above which was a banner headline, "The Missing Chapter from *Queering The Pitch*." At the top of the page, above a listing of other featured writers in the issue, was another headline: "The Banned." Boxed within the piece on page 2 was an "Author's Note": "…The original work has been revised for this publication due to its length, but none of the most controversial material has been omitted (original text available on request)." (70)

So far as I knew, the piece was being printed, when I received a call from Schneider saying there had been a last-minute snag. A senior advisor to the *HGLR*, he confided, had suddenly voiced strenuous objections. (They hadn't been voiced earlier, Schneider claimed, because the advisor had been away on vacation and hadn't had a chance to really consider the piece.) Though another reader had admired the essay, Schneider said, the advisor had characterized it as nothing more than "a vendetta" and "a rant." In fact, he had given Schneider an ultimatum: if the piece were published, he would resign from advisorship and ask that his name be removed from the masthead of the journal. The advisor, Richard told me in confidence, was Warren Goldfarb, acting chair of Harvard's Department of Philosophy. "Was he a personal friend of Richard Dyer?" (who had held a guest chair at Harvard in the mid-1980s), I inquired. Schneider said he knew of no such connection.

Although Schneider never formally rejected "Musical Closets," and although we've engaged in cordial communications since (Schneider asked me to review a biography of Nureyev; I declined), neither of us has attempted to initiate further discussion of the essay.

In place of my essay in that fall issue of *HGLR*, Schneider ran the short introduction to my book, *Confessions of a Jewish Wagnerite: Being Gay and Jewish in America*, which was being published by Cassell (see 76); but the headline feature was by Richard Mohr. Entitled "The Politics of Dignity," it sat incongruously under the banner Schneider retained at the top that read "The Banned." Inside, Schneider's hastily revised editorial on this subject did not mention "Musical Closets." When I wrote Mohr a note about what had happened, together with before-and-after copies of the two cover pages of *HGLR*, there was no response, though he had responded to earlier mailings about the last-minute rejection of "Musical Closets" from *Queering The Pitch* by condemning

Routledge. At that time, however, he had also criticized me for allowing them to use the Rorem interview. He had responded similarly to an earlier revelation about my experience with Viking, criticizing my capitulation to Caldwell's demand to sanitize my blurb for *The Uncle From Rome*. Mohr was correct, of course. Ideally (as in his confrontations with Columbia University Press over the use of "pornographic" photos for his book, *Gay Ideas*?) I should have been uncompromising. But his tone of smug moral superiority rang dissonant against his silence in light of the developments with *HGLR*, though it should probably be mentioned here that *Confessions of a Jewish Wagnerite* raises serious questions about Mohr's intoxication with Wagner and *Parsifal* in the essay that dominates his book, *Gay Ideas: Outing and Other Controversies*. (70a)

"Musical Closets" was subsequently rejected by the *Village Voice* (respectfully and supportively by Richard Goldstein, who urged me to contact Micah Sifry at the *Nation*), the *Nation* (very condescendingly by Andrew Kopkind), and the *Journal of Homosexuality*.

When *Queering the Pitch* was published, it was reviewed by Eric Gordon (in *Lambda Book Report*),whose biography of Mark Blitzstein I had reviewed for the *Journal of Homosexuality*. Citing its failure to come to grips with the nearly complete absence of homosexual and Jewish consciousness and subject matter in the composer's works, in deference to the composer's party-line socialism, I had noted additionally that Russian-Jewish American "Gordon," the likewise politically-correct socialist to whom I had now become a rival reviewer (of books on "serious music" for *LBR*), had failed to identify himself as either gay or Jewish in his introduction to *Mark The Music*. Despite its serious criticism, however, the review was respectful and affirmed Gordon's achievement to such an extent that Gordon himself later went on record with his belief that it was the most substantial and intelligent of the reviews his book had received. (See 72a) If that were genuinely his belief, it seemed strange that in his review of *Queering The*

Pitch, entitled "Perfect Pitch," Gordon did not mention my contribution or acknowledge any of the controversy that had taken place. When I wrote to ask him why he had completely ignored the "Musical Closets" controversy in his review, he wrote me back that he was aware of "the Peter Davis article" but that his space was limited and the controversy had already been written about in *LBR*. (71) Subsequently, he wrote a wildly supercilious review of my book, *Confessions of a Jewish Wagnerite* (72). In fact it was the most insufficient and unintelligent review of my book to date. It was, as several people have suggested, impossible to believe that he actually read it. Gordon's review engendered further back-and-forth over my accusations, as published in *LBR*, of breaching of journalistic ethics and conflict of interest on Gordon's part; e.g., as Gordon himself noted in his review, the book contains a critical reference to him. (72a) Indeed, when *LBR* editor Jim Marks read my first letter to the editor, explaining that I had previously reviewed Gordon's book, he wrote me a letter of apology:

> Thanks for your letter to the editor about Eric's review, although I wish I'd been clever enough, or informed enough, so that you wouldn't have needed to write it. As you know, our assignment sheet asks reviewers to notify us of any potential conflicts of interest... (72b)

The back-and-forth in the letters column of LBR included a letter from Martin Duberman questioning Gordon's "brittle, ungenerous review."

Confessions of a Jewish Wagnerite, which contained a good deal of personal reminiscence and commentary not covered in "Musical Closets" about music critics and writers, was published by Cassell in November of 1994 and reviewed in the March 18 issue of *Opera News* by K. Robert Schwarz, a feature writer for the *New York Times* and an occasional contributor to *Out*. In the course of the review, Schwarz—to whom his friend and admirer Eric Gordon had once introduced me—came out as a gay Jew and drew the following conclusion:

> And I agree with what I take to be Mass's central thesis: that the distinction between silence and self-hatred is narrow indeed. Ultimately, *Confessions* is an angry refusal to participate in a conspiracy of silence—about being gay in the age of AIDS, about being Jewish in an age of increasing anti-Semitism, and about being a Wagnerite in the shadow of the Holocaust. *Confessions* may be a messy conflation of autobiography, political manifesto, and operatic histrionics, but the questions it poses are bold, risky and rarely asked in print. I for one admire the author's courage. (73)

In the spring of 1995, *Confessions of a Jewish Wagnerite* became a Lambda Literary Award finalist in the category of biography/auto-biography.

Two issues of *Opera News* later, Bill Hoffman, who had provided a strong blurb for *Confessions*, which makes reference to my friendship with Hoffman, accused the critics of homophobia and resentment—that the huge popularity of *The Ghosts of Versailles* had been in spite of the critics—in their unfriendly, suspicious, and ungenerous responses to *Ghosts*—in an interview with Schwarz. (74) A week later, Peter G. Davis wrote the following with regard to the New York premiere of *Harvey Milk*, which coincided with the Met's revival of *The Ghosts of Versailles*:

> In the interests of political correctness, and for those who must know where everyone is coming from, I preface this discussion with a statement of orientation, even if it "outs" no one: The librettist (Michael Korie) is gay; the composer (Stewart Wallace) is straight, and the author of the following comments (yours truly) writes from a gay perspective." (75)

Now, you can't get any closer to actually coming out than that, can you? In his discussion of *Ghosts* in the latter half of this review, Davis indirectly responded to Hoffman's allegations as follows:

> As a rule, nothing is simpler than disposing of a Met ticket, but no one who had already seen *Ghosts* cared to sit through it again, and the friend I finally persuaded to come found the opera tiresome and cheap and left after Act 1.

If I'm not mistaken, the "friend" Davis was referring to was his life-partner, Scott Parris, to whom Davis has never made reference in all his years of writing and fifteen years of that relationship. Which again points to the issue of how gay, and for that matter Jewish, closetedness is served by the fierce "neutrality" and depersonalization, the "objectivity," we've come to value as the highest standard of criticism. If one were to confront a Peter G. Davis regarding his never having mentioned his life-partner, he'd probably respond that not only is it inappropriate to an objective review, but no other critics discuss such personal matters—lovers, wives, families—in their columns either. While this is not entirely true—as noted elsewhere in this essay, heterosexual critics do mention their families from time to time—there is real truth to it. The standards are such that it *is* highly unusual for critics to get personal—to talk *directly* about themselves, their lives, their families, their politics, their beliefs. The standards are, in fact, tailor-made for gays and Jews who want to remain in the closet. How those standards got to be this way and to such an extent, is the subject of "Confessions About Confessions" (the introduction to *Confessions of a Jewish Wagnerite*) (76), and a principal concern of *Musical Closets: Homosexuality, Judaism, Music, and Opera.* (77)

In the Arts and Leisure section of the Sunday *New York Times* (August 27, 1995), Christopher Keene was revealed to be a gay man, terminally ill with AIDS. (78) On the opening night of the

1995 New York City Opera (NYCO) season, Keene made a pre-performance announcement to the audience. The eagerly-awaited new production of Paul Hindemith's rarely performed master-piece *Mathis der Mahler* that everyone had come together for was in trouble. The lead singer had laryngitis and would act the role on stage. Another baritone would sing the part from the pit. Keene could not have been more charming or articulate in his presenta-tion, which included a raucously funny tale of a similar mishap-penstance at the NYCO a few seasons earlier. But there was something else striking about Keene's appearance that evening. His illness looked to be very far along. (In fact, he dropped out of subsequent performances.) In his review, Davis gave Keene and the NYCO his highest praise. And, of course, he adored the opera, which is indeed a fascinating and beautiful work that happens to be all about artistic creativity and responsibility. Its viewpoint, that artists are overridingly responsible to their creativity rather than to any politics or causes, could not be more in synch with Davis's. With regard to its immersion in these subjects, Davis noted the opera's affinity with Pfitzner's *Palestrina* and Wagner's *Die Meistersinger*.

But just as Davis found nothing to say about the fact that all three composers were varyingly involved in politically questionable or reprehensible politics, rendered irrelevant and excused in the much greater interest of the *heilige kunst* they were serving, not a word was said about Keene's health or circumstances. (79) That subject having already been publicly discussed in James Oestreich's *Times* feature a few weeks earlier, I found myself feeling that Davis had done the right thing. No further word was necessary. By contrast, during precisely the same time frame, there was a feeling of some-thing missing from the frenzy of press activity in anticipation of the return to America, for the first time in twenty-six years, of Paul Bowles, who was eighty-four and was to attend a festival of his music at Lincoln Center. As a number of writers have pointed out,

Bowles's inscrutability has been a real part of his appeal, but that characteristic seemed inflated and questionable by the absence of any discussion of Bowles's sexuality—its role in his life and works, and his participation in the gay subcultures of his generations—in any of the press coverage of the festival (as was the case in the recent documentary film about Bowles by Regina Weinrich); neither in the otherwise splendid pieces by K. Robert Schwarz that appeared in *Opera News* (80) and the *New York Times* (81); nor, more predictably, in Peter G. Davis's review of the festival. (82)

During the intermission of the first concert of the Paul Bowles Festival at Alice Tully Hall (September 19, 1995), I went outside for "a breath of fresh air," which, as Robert Hilferty, my date that evening, points out, is paradoxical now that smoking has been banned from all public spaces and all the smokers go outside, where one is immediately enveloped by the resultant smog. (Hilferty made the controversial film *Stop the Church*. His current project is another documentary, entitled *Babbitt: Portrait of a Serial Composer*.) But out I went, where the first person I ran into was James Holmes, the organist, choir director, and composer who is Ned Rorem's life-partner of decades. He was by himself, having a cigarette. The last time we had conversed, Ned had recently had prostate surgery and was having a tough time. Eager to talk, Jim dropped the (unsolicited) bombshell I'd been suspecting, ever since Ned first told me, a year earlier, that Jim had been diagnosed with lymphoma: He's positive. I didn't feel comfortable asking Jim questions at such a moment. I deferred to his need to speak. When the moment was finally right for me to say something, instead of questions I spoke from my heart, telling him of my own circumstances—that I hadn't gotten a test result in four years. (My last test, in 1990, was negative. In 1992 I was retested but couldn't face getting the results.)

Now, what do I do with this information? Do I keep it to myself? Tell Ned? Does Ned know? Turns out, Ned does know. He called me a week later for a second opinion re Jim's medical circumstances and plans. Tell Rob Schwarz? *Not* put it here? Am I doubly treacherous—as a physician as well as a friend—to even contemplate making this information public? (As with my beloved Bill Hoffman and his partnership with John Corigliano, who am I to breach these privileged and cherished friendships, to intrude on some of the closest and most important relationships in all of musical culture?) Are these little shards of *heilige* "truth" really *that* important? Do they amount to anything more than gossip? And how much of "Musical Closets" *is* just grievance settling—primarily against Peter G. Davis, over an extremely close and rewarding friendship gone sour; for the great crimes of his caring more about the sanctity of art and his own career than the politics of the moment, and his success in achieving the dream I had to give up: of being able to earn my living with my writing? On the other hand, what would Ned—who I dearly love and revere and who is perhaps premiere among mentors who have tried to capture something of the complexity of how our arts interact with our subcultures—have done if he were I and the information were about someone else? And if I have this unquestionably pertinent if not all-important information and decide, in the interests of confidence and friendship and decorum and decency, to keep it to myself, does this mean I'm doing what "Musical Closets" has been accusing nearly everyone else of doing? In the final analysis, shouldn't I just do the right thing?

Keene died on October 8, 1995. In the *New York Times* obituary by James Oestreich, the cause of death was listed as "lymphoma arising from AIDS." "In a recent conversation," Oestreich noted, "Keene revealed that he had tested positive for HIV... more than a decade ago. Yet he insisted that his illness was not related to AIDS and he spoke avidly of his plans for the coming years." Two years ago, Oestreich then recalled, Keene had been admitted to the Betty Ford Center for alcoholism. At that time, the press published reports of his having had "a nervous breakdown" and of his admission to the

Betty Ford Center for treatment of alcoholism, but the public was not informed of what Keene more recently acknowledged to be the fuller range of precipitating factors: "...we lost so many friends and colleagues, close and professional, and the company seemed to be going under. [That's as much as the public was told then.] My health was in doubt, and it was a time when I couldn't go on." Among those being lost, according to Oestreich, was Thomas Forsyth, Mr. Keene's "longtime companion, who was dying of AIDS..." Keene will be long-remembered and revered by serious opera lovers for his commitment to the rarely performed, fiendishly difficult, offbeat, and contemporary. In fact, his loss is overwhelming. Probably no other figure of this generation has done as much to open the closet door of operatic obscurity. But Keene's wizardry wasn't limited to the artistic. At his finest, he was also an administrator of the first rank. In fact, as Keene himself told Oestreich, which the obituary quoted for its single callout, "a lot of the changes I'm proudest of are totally invisible." (83)

Notes

1) Sedgwick, Eve Kosofsky, *Epistemology of The Closet*, University of California Press, 1990, pp. 74-90.

2) *Ibid*, p. 78

3) Signorile, Michelangelo, "Out at the *New York Times*," *The Advocate*, Part 1—issue 602, 5/5/92, pp. 34-42; Part 2—issue 603, 5/19/92, pp. 38-42.

3a) Though Davis was not in Signorile's feature, "Out at the *Times*," he did, on my recommendation, speak to Ed Alwood regarding this experience for Alwood's forthcoming study of gay men, lesbians, and the media (Straight News, Columbia University Press, series editors Larry Gross and Lilian Faderman)

4) Greco, Stephen, Interview with Peter Pears, the *Advocate*, 7/12/79, pp. 36-37.

5) Mass, Lawrence, "Confessions of an Opera Queen," *Christopher Street*, 10/82, pp. 26-27.

6) Simon, John, *New York*, 3/18/85, pp. 69, 72.

7) Smith, Liz, "AIDS Comment is…Simply Simon," the *New York Daily News*, 3/17/85, p. 10.

8) Notwithstanding all her good works on behalf of gay and lesbian anti-discrimination and AIDS, Smith has been criticized in the gay press for her participation in "innings," the phenomenon of respecting and perpetuating the closetedness of prominent persons she knew to be gay or lesbian. (Gross, Larry, "The Contested Closet: The Ethics and Politics of Outing," *Cultural Studies in Mass Communication*, vol. 8, 1991, p. 369; see also *Contested Closets: The Politics and Ethics of Outing* (to be published by the University of Minnesota Press, 1993).)

9) Shewey, Don, "R.I.P.," the *Village Voice*, 3/26/85, p. 101

10) Rorem, Ned, "The Real John Simon," the *New York Native*, 5/5-19/85, pp. 22-27.

11) *Ibid*, pp. 22, 22, 23, 23, 24, 26, 27.

12) Letters to the Editor, *New York*, 4/1/85, pp. 6-8.

13) Rorem, *op. cit.*, pp. 22, 26.

13a) See (3) and the epilogue for updating of this statement.

14) One reviewer of the event noted that Colleen Dewhurst, at that time president of Actors Equity, Papp, and Hazel Dukes of the NAACP were just a few of the many who called for Simon's dismissal at that time. (Breindel, Eric, "The Mean-Spirited Critic," the *New York Post*, 4/20/89, p. 27.) As with the earlier scandal, there were news stories and editorials. Once again I wrote Kosner, reminding him of the earlier fracas. There was no response this time, though Kosner did write a letter that was quoted in the *Daily News* defending Simon. (O'Haire, Patricia, "Publisher Kosner Backs What Simon Says," New York *Daily News*, 4/10/89, p.37.) So far as I know, Simon never apologized or otherwise responded to his critics, except to continue his special brand of sadistic baiting based upon ethnic, physical, sexual, or generational vulnerabilities. E.g.,

in his review of *Kurt Weill: Composer in a Divided World* by Ronald Taylor for the *New York Times* (Book Review, 12/13/92, pp. 15-16), Simon relishes his opportunity to explore the composer's troubled relationship to his Jewishness, just as he had relished the opportunity to trumpet Franz Werfel's Jewish-associated travails and internalized anti-Semitism in an earlier *Times* review. To Taylor's description of Weill as "a European composer who was a Jew, not a Jewish composer," Simon asks: "Who or what is a 'Jewish composer'? Darius Milhaud? Ernest Bloch? Leonard Bernstein?" Simon then proceeds to quote anti-Semitic statements Weill made, citing his "profound contempt for these Jewish circles," as the Jewish composer put it in a letter to his mother, and worse: "Never will a Jew write a work like the 'Moonlight' Sonata." Instead of empathizing with the anti-Semitism that created this environment, however, Simon is delighted to agree with Weill's blaming of the Jews for the failure of his opera, *Die Burgschaft*. "The blame lies at least as much with the wishy-washy, spineless attitude of the liberals," Weill observed; liberals, Simon hastens to add, "who, then as now, included a great many Jews" (the latter quote is Simon's).

More recently, Simon concluded of the unabashedly ethnic musical *Hello Muddah, Hello Fadduh!*: "You don't have to be Jewish to enjoy *Hello Muddah, Hello Fadduh!*; all you need is extremely poor taste...Call this pig swill 'foddah' at best." *New York*, 1/11/93, pp. 53-54. [Since 1994, Simon's pieces have been more minority-sensitive. Whether this development is genuine or tactical remains to be seen.]

15) Sedgwick, *op. cit.*, p. 80.

16) Davis, Peter G., *New York*, 2/17/92, p. 59.

17) Mass, "Was Schubert Queer?", *NYQ*, 5/3/92, p. 44.

18) Davis, *New York*, 4/9/90, p. 95.

19) Davis, *New York*, 12/3/90, p. 178.

20) Davis, *New York*, 3/30/91, p. 79.

21) Davis, *New York*, 5/4/92, p. 83

22) Davis, *New York*, 7/30/90, pp. 34-36.
Whether Keene's closetedness within Davis's profile was at Keene's request or Davis's decision or by mutual agreement is a matter for conjecture.

23) Davis, *New York*, 6/1/87, pp. 93-94.

24) Gross, *op. cit.* (see Note 8), p. 364.

25) Gross, *op. cit.*, p. 365.

25a) Gross, *op. cit.* (prepublication manuscript—draft of July 2, 1992—of *The Contested Closet: The Politics and Ethics of Outing* for the University of Minnesota Press), pp. 37-38. Plaskin is no longer writing for the *Daily News*.

26) Brownworth, Victoria, "Campus queer query," *Outweek*,
5/16/90, pp. 48-49, as quoted in Gross, p. 379.

27) Mass, "Homosexuality and Music III: A Conversation with Ned Rorem," *Homosexuality as Behavior and Identity: Dialogues of the Sexual Revolution, Volume II*, Harrington Park Press, 1990, p. 103.

28) Mass, *Ibid*, p. 88.

29) The San Francisco Opera's New Impressario: Terry McEwen, the *Advocate*, issue 343, May 17, 1982, p. 48.

30, 31) Mass, "Confessions of an Opera Queen," *Ibid*, p. 27.

32) Mass, "Homosexuality and Music III," pp. 95-96.

33) Rorem, *The Nantucket Diary of Ned Rorem: 1973-1985*, North Point Press, 1987, pp. 576, 578.

34) Mass, "Mark the Music" (book review), *Journal of Homosexuality*, vol. 21, no. 3, 1991, p. 132.

35) Gordon, Eric, *Mark The Music: The Life and Work of Marc Blitzstein*, St. Martin's Press, 1989, p. 506.

36) Mass, "Mark The Music" p. 134.

36a) The block of text from the last line of 412 through the end of line 7, page 415, was excerpted from this text for the introduction to my interview with Ned Rorem, as published in *Queering The Pitch*.

37) Heymont, George, interview with Robert Jacobson, the *Advocate*, 8/85.

38) Page, Tim, "The Improbable Impresario," *New York Newsday*, 2/2/92, pp. 6, 7, 20.

39) Unable to participate in the program myself, I referred Page to Bruce-Michael Gelbert, music critic of the *New York Native*, with whom Page presented, on 7/27/87 on WNYC radio, a program called "The Impact of AIDS on Music."

40) Porter, Andrew, music column, the *New Yorker*, 2/10/92, p. 78.

41) Mass, "Was Schubert Queer?", prepublication manuscript.

42) Mass, " 'Was Schubert Queer?' ", *NYQ*, 5/3/92, p. 44.

43) As Rorem stated it most succinctly and recently in a letter to the *New York Times* complaining about Jamie James's review of his Whitman settings, "I am not, as Mr. James would have it, 'a gay composer,' but a composer." (Rorem, Ned, Letters to the Editor, the *New York Times*, 3/15/92) Rorem was responding to Mr. James's observation that "interestingly, it is not Mr. Rorem, a gay composer, but Mr. Adams who dares to emphasize explicitly the poet's homosexuality, and thus implicitly his work's connections with the AIDS epidemic, by concluding with the line, 'Many a soldier's kiss dwells on these bearded lips.'" (James, Jamie, "Two Americans Converge on Whitman," the *New York Times*, 3/1/92, section H, p. 32) Teasingly, Ned had called to ask if *I*, who have been arguing the very points James made, would write a letter in his defense to the *Times*! Needless to say, I declined.

44) Signorile, "The Other Side of Malcolm," *Outweek*, 3/18/90, pp 40-45.

45) Brownworth, *op. cit.*, p. 48.

46) Krishman, Cindy, "A Score to Unsettle," the *Advocate*, 5/22/90, pp. 32-36.

46a) Although it is an otherwise inapt analogy, there is a parallel in the argument about the importance of role models for persons who are gay and lesbian, and those who are struggling with HIV infection. In an editorial in the *New England Journal of Medicine* (vol. 327, no. 19, 11/5/92, p.1389), Gellert et al. note the considerable benefits that have accrued to persons with AIDS as a result of the public "Disclosure of AIDS in Celebrities":

"In a society as fragmented along lines of race, culture, age, and socioeconomic class as the United States, the recognition and love of pop-culture celebrities are rare unifying features that represent an opportunity to overcome barriers to communication...Disclosure by celebrities may also serve to promote nondiscrimination...In weighing the good of the many against that of individuals...physicians should actively but supportively encourage HIV-positive celebrities to disclose their status..."

47) Bronski, Michael, "Outing: The Power of the Closet," *Gay Community News*, 6/3/90, p. 11.

48) Lewin, R. "A Few Minutes With Fractious Fran," the *Advocate*, 7/3/90, p. 63.

49) Gross, *op. cit.*, p. 377.

50) Mass, an interview with John Corigliano and William M. Hoffman, *Opera Monthly*, 11/91, pp. 5—12.

Homosexuality and Music was the original working title of my book *Musical Closets*, which is being published by Cassell and which will feature the essay "Musical Closets."

51) Davis, "The Big Score," *New York*, 12/9/91, pp. 59-67.

52) Schwarz, K. Robert, "Sylvan Gives Voice to America," the *New York Times*, 7/21/91, section H, p. 21.

In the spring of 1995, Sanford Sylvan, who is Jewish as well as gay and who had read and admired Confessions of a Jewish Wagnerite, agreed to be interviewed by me for Opera Monthly and for Musical Closets. Several months later, he informed me that he had changed his mind. Deeply immersed in the artistically refined and fragile song and concert repertoire, he felt it just wasn't the right project for him at that time. We agreed to leave the door open for the future.

52a) Caldwell, Joseph, *The Uncle From Rome*, Viking/Penguin, 1992.

Note: For the paperback edition, the quote was changed to read: "A passionate record of love and opera in the age of AIDS—Lawrence Mass, associate editor, *Opera Monthly*."

53) As discussed in Mass, "Confessions of a Jewish Wagnerite" (essay), *Christopher Street*, issue 98, 1985, pp. 21-31.

54) Davis, *New York*, 9/16/85, p. 66.

55) Dyer, Richard, profile of Shirley Verrett, *Opera News*, 2/17/90, pp. 8-12, 52.

56) Neher, Erick, An Interview with Eugene Perry, *Opera Monthly*, 1/92.

57) The Charlie Rose Show, "A Talk With Jessye Norman," WNET TV, 4/10/92.

58) Schwarz, "A Composer Between Two Worlds," *New York Times*, Arts and Leisure, 6/7/92, p. 30.

59) Brett, Philip, "Homosexuality and Music: A Conversation with Philip Brett, *Homosexuality as Behavior and Identity: Dialogues of The Sexual Revolution, Volume II*, 1990, pp. 36-54.

60) Mass, Lawrence, "Musical Quilts," GLSG Newsletter, vol. II, No. 2, 10/92, pp. 11-13.

61) Signorile, Michelangelo, "Out at the *New York Times*."

62) The two books are:
Gross, Larry, *The Contested Closet*, see Additional References
Mohr, Richard, *Gay Ideas*, see Additional References

63) Gross, Larry, letter to William Germano, 11/12/92.

64) Duberman, Martin, letter to William Germano, 11/14/92.

65) Germano, William, letter to Lawrence Mass, 11/23/92.

66) Lemon, Brendan, "Man of The Year: David Geffen," *Advocate*, issue 619, 12/29/92, pp. 35-40.

67) Marks, Jim, "A Look Inside: Check It out," *Lambda Book Report*, vol. 3, #9, Mar/Apr 1993, p. 40.

68) Davis, *New York*, 5/17/93, p. 82.

69) Davis, *New York*, 8/30/93, pp. 141-2.

70) Mass, "Musical Closets: A Personal and Selective History of Outing and Coming Out in the Music World," *Harvard Gay and Lesbian Review*, Volume I, Number 4, Fall 1994, pp. 1-8.

70a) Mohr, Richard, *Gay Ideas: Outing and Other Controversies*, Beacon Press, 1992.

71) Gordon, Eric, "Perfect Pitch," *Lambda Book Report*, (March/April 1994), pp. 27-28.

72) Gordon, Eric, review, "Confessions of a Jewish Wagnerite," *Lambda Book Report*, volume 4, #7 (November, 1994), pp. 43-44.

72a) Letters to the editor, *Lambda Book Report*, vol 4, no. 8, January-February 95, page 5; LBR, vol. 4, no. 10, May-June 1995, p. 6

72b) Marks, Jim, letter to Lawrence Mass, October 26, 1994.

73) Schwarz, K. Robert, review of "Confessions of a Jewish Wagnerite" in *Opera News*, March 18, 1995, page 47.

74) Schwarz, K. Robert, "Ghostbusters," *Opera News*, April 15, 1995, pp. 12-13, 44.

75) Davis, *New York*, April 25, 1995, pp. 70-71.

76) Mass, Lawrence D., introduction to *Confessions of a Jewish Wagnerite: Being Gay and Jewish in America*, Cassell, 1994, pp. ix-xii.

77) Mass, Lawrence D., *Musical Closets: Homosexuality, Judaism, Music and Opera*, Cassell, scheduled for publication in 1997.

78) Oestreich, James, "The Job is Undoable, and That is the Easy Part," a profile of Christopher Keene, Arts and Leisure (section 2), *New York Times*, August 27, 1995, pp. 1, 23.

79) Davis, *New York*, 9/25/95, pp. 114-115.

80) Schwarz, K. Robert, "Incidental Music," *Opera News*, September 1995, pp. 28-29, 69.

81) Schwarz, K. Robert, "A Composer Long Ago, An American Far Away," *New York Times*, 9/17/95, pp. 27-28.

82) Davis, *New York*, Oct. 19, 1995, pp. 94-95.

83) Oestreich, James, "Christopher Keene is Dead; Head of City Opera was 48," *New York Times*, p. A18.

Additional References:

Goldstein, Richard, "The Art of Outing: When Is It Right to Name Gay Names?", *Village Voice*, 5/1/90, pp 33-37.

Moon, Michael, "Flaming Closets," *October*, issue 51, winter 1989, pp. 19-54.

Rotello, Gabriel, on the Tactics of Outing, *Outweek*, pp. 52-53.

I'm Going Out Like a Fucking Meteor
CRAIG G. HARRIS

I want to live the rest of my life, however long or short, with as much sweetness as I can decently manage, loving all the people I love, and doing as much as I can of the work I still have to do. I am going to write fire until it comes out of my ears, my eyes, my noseholes—everywhere. Until it's every breath I breathe. I'm going to go out like a fucking meteor!

—Audre Lorde

It is a beautifully warm Monday afternoon and I wake with good spirits to receive a telephone call from a former colleague in Washington, D.C. We talk about my current situation, I crack jokes in the face of adversity, and we laugh hilariously like old times. After a few minutes, she tells me that someone is waiting outside her office, that she must run but had just wanted to holler at me for a second. She tells me that I haven't changed a bit and that she loves me. She'll keep in touch.

I remember that today is the last day I can remit my rent check without penalty of a 5 percent late fee. I find my checkbook and cringe as I write the check. When I signed the lease almost two years ago, I knew full well that the rent was outrageous. But now, my hand shakes a little more nervously each month as I sign the check.

I take the check to the management office on my way to the corner *bodega*. I notice that somehow I have only one dollar bill in my wallet and realize I must stop at the automatic teller machine before I can buy milk, juice, and butter for breakfast. Two twenties are ejaculated from the machine along with a receipt. The record indicates that the current balance of my checking account is only four dollars more than the amount of the check I have just given to my property management. That doesn't worry me as much as the fact that my savings account is at a zero balance, and pay day isn't until Friday.

I head to the *bodega*. I buy a pint of half-and-half, a can of papaya nectar, and a pack of cigarettes. I hand the Arab woman behind the counter a twenty-dollar bill. She packs my groceries and hands me six dollars change. I stare at the change in my hand, thinking that if I could really get around like I used to, I could have gotten a better bargain at Balducci's. Small matter. This place is grossly overpriced, but it is convenient.

By the time I return to my complex, the mail has been delivered. Despite appearances, my life has become so solitary that I am forced to look forward to this daily ritual. As I lock the box and peruse the envelopes, I am overjoyed to find that today's assortment contains two reimbursement checks from Blue Cross/Blue Shield.

I return to my apartment, pour my first cup of coffee, and sit with a cigarette to open the good news. The checks total three hundred and twenty-five dollars—an amount I have already paid my therapist and hematologist. This will carry me through the remainder of the week. I open the next envelope, which is a three hundred and eighty dollar bill from my radiology oncologist. After reading every word on the bill three times, I conclude that these fees cannot be billed directly to my insurance carrier as I had been led to believe. I must remit payment and then submit a claim for reimbursement. The worst of it is that this bill only covers the cost of two radiology treatments and I receive four treatments per week. I lose my appetite and decide to skip breakfast, though I know quite well that my body is in desperate need of the vitamins and nutrients, calories and bulk. It is six hours later when I read the bill for a fourth time and realize that it can be directly submitted to Blue Cross/Blue Shield. By this time, however, I have missed two meals and spent the day in a depressed mood.

I could bitch and complain. I could become depressed and withdrawn.

But what good would either do? So I sit and contemplate my situation. I am one of the lucky ones. No matter how unfortunate my situation may seem, I know that I am a "privileged nigger." I know this because not only have I worked every day of my life, but for the last seven years I have worked in various positions in HIV prevention and service delivery. I have a good job. I have health insurance coverage. I have access to the most updated medical information and a stellar medical team. In no way could I compare my case to Evelyn, a former client.

I met Evelyn shortly after returning to New York in the spring of 1988 to assume the position of executive director of the Minority Task Force on AIDS. Evelyn had been diagnosed with Lupus in addition to HIV disease. Her drug habit was one she had great difficulty shaking. She was only somewhat literate, and dependent on social services as her man had left her to marry another woman. She had a five-year-old son, but couldn't depend on the father for child care because his wife was afraid that the young boy would infect her infant. Bureaucratic systems both baffled and intimidated Evelyn.

Through Evelyn I gained my first real insights into the horrors of the American health care and social services systems. It is not that I was totally naive until this time. Like most progressive activists, I had a conceptual handle on such injustices, but had really never encountered them first hand. I had that opportunity the day that Evelyn came into my office sobbing, interrupting my work on a grant proposal which, if approved, would allow the Task Force to increase its over-stressed staff of two. Evelyn explained to me that she had no money, her food stamps had been cut off, and no one at the local welfare office could explain why.

I called the welfare office, explained my position and politely requested to speak with a manager. That request was initially denied by the most surly public servant I have ever encountered. She told me that Evelyn's food stamps had been discontinued because she was "too stupid" to know how to fill out the forms. I informed her that I would be happy to send someone to the office to pick up the forms. I would then complete the forms for Evelyn and have them returned by the close of business. The clerk told me that they didn't operate that way. That I couldn't push through the process, and that Evelyn would have to make an appointment later in the month to pick up the forms.

I realized it was now time for me to demonstrate my trilingual roots (I am fluent in Anglo, Afro, and Homo). "Look girlfriend," I told her, "I run this muthafuckin' agency and I would strongly suggest that you go find someone in a comparable position at yours quick, fast, and in a hurry, because you're dancing on my last damn nerve and your office is only nine blocks from mine. I will not hesitate to jump into a gypsy cab and before you can blink, suck your teeth, roll your eyes and head, I'll be whipping your ass all up and down 125th Street." Within moments, a supervisor was on the line and the situation was corrected. Nonetheless, when I returned home that evening I cried at the day's events knowing that there were a lot more Evelyns out there and, more often than not, they do not have advocates for their cause.

On January 29, 1991, my hematologist informed me of my diagnosis of pulmonary Kaposi's sarcoma. He compassionately explained to me that I would probably have to undergo aggressive chemotherapy treatments for several months. When I complained, he explained that the most recent studies from San Francisco indicated that, left untreated, the average post-diagnosis life expectancy of someone with my condition was three months. He ordered blood to be drawn, X rays, and a Gallium scan. On the way home, I stopped at a liquor store and purchased a bottle of Haig & Haig Pinch Scotch. I also stopped at Li-Lac Chocolates and purchased a pound of champagne truffles.

Back at my apartment, I poured myself a drink, and placed a half-dozen of the chocolates on a china dish. I surveyed my mail, paid bills, renewed my subscription to *OUT/LOOK*, and proceeded to conduct my personal business. I played back my telephone messages and copied the numbers of callers onto a message pad. I had received a call from my friend Lauri, with whom I co-chair the African-American Alumnae/i of Vassar College.

Positioned with my Scotch, chocolate, cigarettes, and my Vassar file, I returned the call. Lauri and I discussed pending business, divided up assignments, and made lists of the items we would fax to each other the next day from our offices. With all business efficiently taken care of, the conversation became more social.

"So, how are you doing anyway?"

"Okay, I guess. But my doctor diagnosed me with AIDS today. Pulmonary Kaposi's sarcoma, more specifically."

"What? And you let me go on like that about business? Why didn't you stop me?"

"Well, you know, the shit has to get done and life does go on—"

After I finished talking with Lauri, I started to make a few of the perceived obligatory calls to inform people of my condition. The first call was to George. George and I have worked together with these issues for numerous years. I suppose that's why I expected him to react to the news in a very enlightened, professional manner (whatever that might be). George listened to the details and then asked me what I was doing. I explained to him that I was having cocktails and eating chocolate. He told me that I was in denial.

"No, I'm not in denial. I just told you I'm drinking Scotch, eating chocolates, and I have AIDS. That's not denial, George."

I firmly believe that every individual has the right to select a support group which works for them. Mine, for the moment, happened to consist of Benson & Hedges menthol lights, twelve-year-old whisky, and expensive confections. Without them I don't know how I would have made it through that first night. With them I managed to call my brother, some cousins, and assorted friends realizing that each time, I'd have to assist them in dealing with their issues before they could assist me in dealing with mine. Disclosure is a very tedious task.

After completing the calls, I turned on the television set hoping to find something other than coverage of the war in the Middle East which our country had entered into thirteen days earlier. I had no idea that I would find President George Bush delivering his State of the Union Address. It seemed as though he talked forever about the wonderful job the troops were doing in Kuwait. He insisted upon referring to Saddam Hussein only by his first name, which he consistently mispronounced. He tried to assure us that adding to the devastation in the Persian Gulf was what made the United States a great country—the greatest!

President Bush dedicated only a short portion of his speech to domestic issues. Somehow he managed to work AIDS, illiteracy, and homelessness into one sentence and indicated that the government really couldn't solve these problems. He did not, however, make the logical leap proposing combined efforts on the part of government, private industry, philanthropic societies, etc. Wizard political electrician that he is, Bush suggested that U.S. citizens become a thousand points of light to tackle these dark, despairing, social ills, and recommended that each American visit a person with AIDS.

I was too plucked to even get angry. I just turned off the set thinking to myself, "Darling, the last thing I need right now is company. What I could really use is the assurance that you are doing everything within your means to ensure that Anthony Fauci and his buddies at NIH [National Institutes of Health] are getting all the perks they desire. I don't care what it takes, keep that bucka-roo happy and hovering over a petri dish!"

Feces, or the lack thereof, figure prominently in my life these days. Like many other individuals infected with H1V, shit has become a friend, a confidant, a significant other, an adversary, an enemy, and a nemesis. It is rarely a source of pleasure. Recently, it has had an almost liquid consistency which burns vehemently upon exit—leaving my rectum with a sensation similar to those occasions when I attempted to accommodate suitors who were larger than life.

The rotation of chemotherapy drugs (Doxorubicin, Bleomycin, and Vincristine) which I receive weekly may be the cause of the unrelenting constipation or uncontrollable diarrhea. I must sched-ule events according to these side-effects with little advance warn-ing. On several occasions, I have had to forego parties or dates to go dancing because my bowels were so incredibly constipated that it caused severe pains in my abdomen and back, making it difficult to walk or even stand for an extended period of time. At other times, warnings of upcoming diarrhea have caused me to resched-ule appointments, calling ahead to say that I'd be late. On these occasions, I have sat on the toilet with a book, counting time by the quarter hour and carefully investigating anything that lands in the lavender water so that I will be able to report it to my physicians.

Yes, my shit has become something I study. My shit has become an anticipated activity. My shit has become a topic I have had to learn to become comfortable discussing with my service providers. My shit is no longer a private matter. In fact, my shit, at times, has gone quite public.

A few weeks ago, after a relaxing weekend, I spent Monday morning and afternoon at the computer and taking care of other business from my home office. I organized all my files and computer discs with the intent of stopping at my office between my 6:30 cobalt radiation treatment and my 8:30 appointment with my ther-apist. Preparing to go to the city, I showered and dressed in a

Senegalese suit I had taken out of the cleaners over the weekend. I looked into the mirror and found it to be one of those days when I felt somewhat good about the way I looked, despite minimal weight loss and skin imperfections. As I boarded the PATH train at about 5:45, I thought to myself that my timing, so far, was pretty good. I was pleased at the thought that I had completed a great deal at home and should have just enough time for printing, xeroxing, and transmittals between appointments.

Between the Pavonia/Newport, and Christopher Street Stations, I felt a churning and heard a bubbling in my abdomen. First, I thought it was just a case of gas. That happens quite frequently. Then I panicked, remembering that as often as not, it is impossible to distinguish gas from pending defecation until after the fact. Then it happened. I felt the mass of shit filling the scant space between my hips and cotton briefs–a feeling of outrageous discomfort, not particularly because of the tactile sensation, but rather because of the social awkwardness.

Situations such as this really challenge one's problem-solving abilities. I exited the train station at Christopher Street, then thought that this was a poor choice because of the potential number of friends and associates I might bump into in that area. Thoughts flashed quickly, what ifs, and how tos. I stepped out of myself in order to address myself in the second person.

"Take a taxi home —You can't take a taxi to go New Jersey, you only have two dollars in your wallet—Get to a bank machine—No, don't use the one at Sheridan Square, you'll definitely be spotted there—Use the Chase on Eighth at Twelfth, no one is ever around there—Check yourself, is it showing through?—Okay, honey, you're at the bank, it's gonna be okay—No, no, take out more money—Yeah, eighty dollars is good, that will get you out of this one—Now, find a nice restaurant that will let you use their men's room—Clean up—Hide the soiled briefs in paper towels before you place them in the trash can—Find a discount store on Fourteenth

Street so you can get yourself a new pair of underwear and a wash-cloth—Okay, so they didn't sell washcloths, you got the under-wear, you're gonna be okay—Call your radiology technician and see if she'll wait—She won't wait? Oh well—Take a taxi to your office, it's late enough that almost everyone is gone—Sit on one hip in the taxi, and tip well—Smile really friendly at your office's secu-rity guard, they'll never suspect anything—Beeline it to the men's room—Take your time to wash up more thoroughly—Change into the clean underwear—There, that's better—Now, go salvage the rest of your evening, honey, 'cause you haven't seen the worst of it."

I went to my desk, printed from my computer files, xeroxed, addressed envelopes, read my mail, etc. I completed all the tasks I had planned. Then I took a taxi to my therapist's. I didn't tell about the incident. We spent the hour discussing other issues. After all, with how many people do I have to sit and chat casually about my shit?

During my second visit to my hematologist, he prescribed a number of medications. Aside from the antiviral, Retrovir, I was instructed to purchase Myambutol tablets, Zovirax capsules, and a five-day supply of Vepesid oral chemotherapy capsules. I went to a nearby pharmacist who had been recommended by my physician, hoping that he would assign the costs to my insurance carrier.

When I presented the prescriptions to the pharmacist and asked about assignment, he explained to me that he couldn't do this with Blue Cross/Blue Shield, but that there shouldn't be a problem. If necessary, I could write a check. Thinking to myself that I don't possess any major credit cards, carry a New York State driver's license but live in New Jersey, and have no identification which bears any reasonable resemblance to my current blond bombshell look, I figured there could be a problem if the acceptance of my check were to be based on any of these qualifiers.

The pharmacist packaged the drugs and used an electric

calculator to tally the costs. When he reached the balance, he looked up at me with a smile and said, "Mr. Harris, that will be $1,329.55. Oh, and you can post-date the check."

"THIRTEEN HUNDRED AND TWENTY-NINE DOLLARS! AND I CAN POST-DATE THE CHECK? UNTIL WHEN?"

I picked my chin up from the counter and nervously wrote the check. The lack of identification wasn't a problem. The pharmacist explained to me that he didn't have to see any ID because he was fully aware that my doctor didn't see "riff-raff." But what if I was one of the many who received medical attention in a clinic or emergency room? What if I didn't have health insurance coverage which would reimburse me eventually? Thirteen hundred dollars for four prescriptions. And I knew that this was only the beginning. There would be lots more drugs to be bought.

I told this story to a friend who suggested that I might be eligible for free AZT under the ADAP program. I explained that only New York State residents are eligible for this program and that New Jersey has nothing similar. It was around this time that I realized that while I have worked for the Gay Men's Health Crisis, the world's oldest and largest AIDS education, advocacy, and service provider for over two years, I was not eligible to become a client because GMHC only services residents of the five boroughs of New York City.

Access becomes a relative issue. I am thankful for the privileges I have. I resent the fact that these are not readily available to the bulk of people of color dealing with HIV disease. I am angry that because of the differences in the manner in which local municipalities and state health agencies set health policies, I am cut off from certain benefits as a result of the county of my residence. And sure, there are times when I can beat the system, but the real solution will only come when the system is destroyed, demolished!

I suppose that my romantic and sexual involvements have not diminished considerably over the past few years. It's difficult to assess this situation, however, as HIV has totally warped our perspectives on sexuality—both individually and collectively.

Without a clear understanding of safer-sex guidelines, so many have adopted the practice of celibacy (which frequently manifests itself in drunken or drug-induced forays of unsafe sex that are lamented the morning after) or the limiting of sexual partners on the basis of medical membership in my "Church." Despite increasing rates of HIV infection and venereal diseases, it seems that no one is having sex, or at least they're not talking about it. I, for one, couldn't prove them wrong.

I was able to successfully dissolve a lover relationship during the winter of 1988. During the three years that followed, I spent a great deal of time contemplating what went wrong, and why the relationship lasted much longer than it should have. I've concluded that at age thirty, I was determined to settle down, and that I had enough false confidence in myself to have believed that I could make that union work. But the obstacles of fear of intimacy, co-dependence, lack of commitment, political differences, and poor communication were too much to overcome.

The question I have asked myself most about that relationship is why I tolerated so much so long. My basic rule is: one strike, you're out, and preferably far, far away. The answer I have come up with is laziness.

It is a real chore to acquire and maintain a loving, working relationship during the age of AIDS. Fear of HIV and its related problems have entered every recess of our consciousness, constructing even more barriers than those which already existed for gay men of African descent. The stamina to keep searching, to keep trying, is very difficult to muster. More frequently, I am inclined to agree with the lyrics of an old Mary Clayton tune, "Love me or let me be lonely."

Entering into a conversation with each new sexual partner regarding one's personal interpretation of safer sex and sexual boundaries is a very emotionally loaded situation. In it, one usually uncovers one's personal sexual history, political viewpoints, medical knowledge, fantasies, and fears. Of course, I contend that communication need not take the form of conversation, and in certain situations (baths, tearooms, parks) such chatter would be totally inappropriate. In many anonymous sexual situations, actions speak much louder. But in dating situations, the silence around such issues is noticeably deliberate.

Since my diagnosis, I have shared details of my health with two men whom I am attracted to. The initial news of my illness and subsequent updates have been met with compassion and consideration. Both of these men have been a major part of my support system, offering varying levels of affection. I have not had sex with either of them. At least I don't think I have. One of the strange things about this era is that we interpret sex very differently now, and do not always reach a consensus. The lines become fuzzy and we never know if we have crossed them. Was this a sexual act? Was anyone penetrated? Did anyone have an orgasm? Are we having fun yet?

No. I'm not having fun. Six months of unintentional celibacy is not fun. But rather than push harder to solidify either of my two existing relationships (neither of these men is looking for what I am looking for within a relationship), or to seek other suitors, I try to satisfy myself with video lovers who don't ask questions, shy away from the intricate details of my body's malfunctions, or tell me during intimate moments that they are really having difficulty dealing with my "terminal illness."

This approach is not without its merits. When I become fatigued in the middle of the act, I can always push a pause button on the remote and resume activity with a second wind at any time. I do not have to fear exposing my body and its multiple lesions. I do not have to listen to any arguments about why I decided not to take my medication this morning. I do not have to explain why the soreness of my rectal tissue will not allow penetration.

On the other hand, I haven't been held tightly in bed in four months. I haven't been allowed to curl up with my back against another's chest and feel his arms around me. I haven't been awakened by a light kiss on my eyelashes. I have not shared a bath or received a message from someone who cares from more than a professional perspective. My sex life has been sanitized far beyond the impact of the intrusion of latex props.

I do not at all feel lonely. There are always enough telephone interruptions, cards, and even occasional floral arrangements sent by friends. My family has been there for me constantly, offering support, money, transportation, and hands to hold for support during medical procedures. My many friends are good to me. But I still feel alone.

I feel alone on Friday nights when I want to celebrate making it through the seven medical appointments of the week. I feel alone on Monday evenings when I stop at a flower stand on the way from my therapist. I feel alone when I am particularly pleased with a new poem or essay I have just finished, but there is no one I can immediately turn to share these words with. I feel alone most when I realize that through the years I have become strong. I have become stronger than would be necessary if I had a shoulder to sob on, arms that reassured me, lips that passed on a reason to live.

I'm not waiting for a cure. I'm not looking for a miracle. I am not resisting the inevitable. I will die. I will die much sooner than I would like to accept, and there is little I can do about this fact. Kubler-Ross can call that acceptance if she wants, but in doing so, I believe she minimizes one's will to fight. It is precisely because I know I will die that I work even more diligently for the causes I believe in.

It is within this framework that I make decisions about my medical care. It is within this framework that I have made decisions to increase my activities or lessen my involvement in certain organizations. It is within this framework that I continue to plan and conduct HIV prevention programs for African-American gay men. It is this philosophy which has caused me to renew work on a manuscript of poetry and fiction which was begun over two years ago.

It is all about the quality of life I have found. My quality of life is a control issue. I refuse to be controlled by a daily regimen of oral medications and radiation therapy, controlled by weekly chemotherapy treatments, controlled by the increasing number of side-effects, fatigue or depression, medical bills or reimbursement checks. I refuse to be controlled by limitations imposed upon me by my race/ethnicity, class, sexual orientation, and health.

I have made a commitment to relinquish control only as a last resort. I want to live the rest of my life with an energy that ignites and irritates, burns and bubbles, soothes and inspires until it bursts from this atmosphere, dissipating into the cosmos.

Saying Kaddish for Peter
MICHAEL LOWENTHAL

There was an angel in my grandfather's obituary. He was there, crouched between the lines of the *Boston Globe* clipping my father had sent, waiting for me to discover him.

Reading this utterly public recounting of my grandfather's life seemed a violation of his trust, when in the privacy of our home so little had ever been told. My father's father was a storyteller, but his tales were Talmudic, intellectual word games, never anything about his own life. He and my grandmother had escaped Hitler's Germany miraculously late, and they refused to speak about their lives before America.

Although almost all of the obituary's facts were news to me, most fit snugly within the image I had of my Papa Eric, a formidable, white-goateed rabbi with a severe accent. But one brief, chillingly matter-of-fact paragraph stunned me to a halt: "Rabbi Lowenthal and his wife, Suzanne (Moos), fled to New York in July 1939, escaping the Nazi purge of the Jews. However, a son, Peter, from an earlier marriage, was a victim of the Holocaust."

A son? Peter? Why had nobody ever told me about this man? The fact of the earlier marriage had been alluded to vaguely but never discussed, even when a daughter from that marriage visited one holiday. But nobody had ever mentioned Peter.

I was midway through my fifteenth year. Like most boys that age, I was struggling with raging hormones, but there was the confusing twist that my crushes were on other boys. Since my parents' divorce four years earlier I had been living with my mother and sister, a life nearly devoid of older male figures. I yearned for a big brother or uncle, someone I could trust with my secret.

Now, with a single line of the newspaper's cold black type, I was in one staggering instant granted and then deprived of an Uncle Peter.

I asked a few tentative questions about this mystery relative, but nobody in my family wanted to talk. The person who would know the most—even though Peter was not her son—was my grandmother. But her own father had been killed at Theresienstadt, and I couldn't ask her to dredge up those painful memories.

So, knowing nothing more than the single sentence in the *Boston Globe*, I developed my own stories about Uncle Peter.

From the start I felt a strange, visceral connection to this gift of a relative. Sometimes a child will be born with red hair or green eyes, some trait exhibited by neither parent, and it will only be an uncle or cousin with the same features who proves that the new child is one of the tribe. Peter as I conjured him in the following years was precisely such a genetic match. Like identical twins separated at birth and then reunited as adults on *Unsolved Mysteries*, a miraculously revived Peter and I would discover amazing similarities: we both drove 1978 Volkswagens, we were both jazz trumpet players, we parted our hair on the same side. In my most private moments I was sure that he, too, was gay.

I never told anybody about my feelings for Peter, embarrassed by what might be taken as desperate wish-fulfillment. I distrusted the feelings myself; they seemed too easy, the convenient fantasies of a lonely teenager. But in synagogue, when we recited the mourner's Kaddish, I always said it for him. I would see him sitting on the edge of the bimah, dangling his legs awkwardly as if embarrassed that I would call his name.

Then at this year's seder, the tenth Passover since my grandfather's death, I learned that in his final months, Papa Eric had recorded a cassette of his memories. I asked for a copy of the tape, and when my grandmother gave me one on my next visit I rushed home to listen. I was eager to glean any details I could about my grandfather's sketchy biography. My secret, desperate hope was that he would say something about Peter.

I pressed play and suddenly the room was filled with the gravelly, cigar-stained sound that had haunted my dreams for a decade. In his painfully direct manner, still mixing Germanisms into his stiff English after forty-five years in America, Papa Eric recounts his devout childhood and his studies at university. He explains his rejection of Orthodox Judaism, choosing to become a merchant instead of a rabbi like his father and grandfather before him.

Fifteen minutes into the monologue, I knew I was getting close. Papa Eric tells of marrying his first wife, then of going to Palestine during the depression of the 1920s. Finally, the payoff: "My former wife arrived…giving birth to our son Peter, born in Tel Aviv, February 17, 1924."

I moved to the tape recorder, slid the volume control up to high. There is a sentence about the baby boy's circumcision. Then, with no particular emotion: "On April 9, 1924, we returned to Berlin with our son Peter, who died in Bergen-Belsen concentration camp on March 13, 1945." Without so much as a pause, Papa Eric resumes his account of the Hebrew-character typewriters, flower-pot lamps, and mother-of-pearl jewelry he sold back in Germany.

This is all, I thought? A first-born son, reduced to a couple of dates?

I continued to listen to my grandfather's memories but with only half an ear, distracted by my disappointment. He recounts more of his merchant's life and eventually comes to the sudden death of his father, one of the most prominent Orthodox rabbis in Germany. Papa Eric says that he loved his father and knew it was the old man's "deep sorrow that I had alienated myself from the Jewish tradition."

He describes the large funeral and then sitting shivah, the traditional week-long mourning vigil in the dead man's house. "On about the fourth day," he says, "our son Peter led me into the study."

Subtracting dates in my head, I determined that Peter would have been only four years old. I pictured a tiny dark-haired boy in late 1920s European garb.

"On the huge table he had spread opened books from the bookshelves and told me, 'Study them!' That was like a voice from heaven. At that moment I decided to become a rabbi myself."

I stopped the tape, rewound, and listened again, memorizing instantly the cadence of the sentences and the sound of Papa Eric saying "heaven," a word he never once uttered in my presence.

My grandfather was probably the most anti-mystical person I've ever met. One of my clearest memories is of him at the head of the seder table, quizzing us grandkids on the Pythagorean theorem as if this geometric formula were the Eleventh Commandment. Yet here was his confession of a profound spiritual conversion—and the direct catalyst was Peter.

I have listened to Papa Eric's cassette over and over in the past few months. Strangely, each time I hear the story of Peter and the books—the only account I have of an actual event from his life—he becomes less and less real to me. Did a four-year-old's commandment really change the course of my grandfather's life? Did the actual Peter bear any resemblance to my fantasy uncle sitting before me in synagogue?

But Peter has never been about reality, he has been about possibility: The possibility of a merchant becoming a rabbi, the possibility of a confused gay teenager having somebody to turn to.

I am already three years older than Peter was ever allowed to be. Yet I still think of him as my protecting uncle, my benevolent guardian angel. I know that he waits for me in all the unexpected places.

CONTRIBUTORS

Bill Andriette joined the North American Man-Boy Love Association when he was fifteen, and broke into gay publishing with an essay in *One Teenager in Ten: Writing by Gay and Lesbian Youth* (Alyson Publications). Fifteen years later, he is editor of the *NAMBLA Bulletin* and works at the *Guide*, a Boston-based gay monthly. His writings on sex and censorship have appeared, among other places, in *Gayme*, *Steam*, *Gay Community News*, *Playboy*, and *Newsday*.

Allen Barnett's work appeared in the *New Yorker*, *Men on Men 2*, *Christopher Street*, the *Advocate*, and *Poets and Writers*. *The Body and Its Dangers and Other Stories* (St. Martin's Press), his first short story collection, was nominated for two Lambda Literary Awards and received a special citation from the Ernest Hemingway Foundation. He died of complications from AIDS on August 14, 1991.

Bruce Bawer is the author of five books of literary and film criticism, of a collection of poetry, *Coast to Coast* (Story Line Press) in 1993, and of *A Place at the Table: The Gay Individual in American Society* (Poseidon Press). A former director of the National Book Critics Circle, he has reviewed books for the *New York Times Book Review*, the *Washington Post Book World*, and the *Wall Street Journal*; has contributed essays to the *New Criterion*, the *American Scholar*, the *Hudson Review*, the *Nation*, and *Newsweek*; and has published poems in *Paris Review* and *Poetry*. He lives in New York City with his partner, Chris Davenport.

Ron Caldwell, a native of Texas, is a graduate of Rice University and the M.A. program in Creative Writing at Boston University. Some of the publications in which his verse, fiction, interviews, and reviews have appeared or are forthcoming are *Defining Moments* (an anthology of gay writers' coming out stories edited by Patrick Merla), *Turnstile*, the *Harvard Gay & Lesbian Review*, *RFD*, *Christopher Street*, the *GMHC Volunteer*, the *Gay Review*, *GCN*, *Guys*, and *Bay Windows*. In the fall of 1993 he was a Writing Fellow at ART/OMI—Ledig House in Ghent, New York. He lives in New York City, volunteers as an intake clinician at GMHC, teaches creative writing at Marymount Manhattan College, and works as a freelance editor.

Lawrence Chua is a writer living in New York. His writing has been published in numerous anthologies as well as the *Village Voice*, *Rolling Stone*, *Vibe*, *the Nation*, *Artforum*, *Out*, and *A Gathering of the Tribes*. He is the recipient of a 1995 Fellowship from the New York Foundation for the Arts and is a founding member of the black broadcast collective, Radio Bandung.

Larry Gross, professor of communications at the University of Pennsylvania and Co-chair of the Philadelphia Lesbian and Gay task Force, is the author of *Contested Closets: The Politics and Ethics* *of Outing* (University of Minnesota Press) and *Lesbians, Gay Men and the Media* (forthcoming from Chelsea House). He is also the editor of the Columbia University Press's Between Men/Between Women Book Series in lesbian and gay studies.

Jesse Green is a journalist and fiction writer. His much-praised first novel, *O Beautiful* (Ballantine Books) was published in 1992; his short fiction has appeared in *Mademoiselle, Mississippi Review, The American Voice* and in the 1994 anthology *Waves*. His articles for such publications as the *New York Times Magazine, Premiere, Philadelphia, GQ, Out, Mirabella* and *7 Days* have been honored with several National Magazine Award nominations and, in 1994, with the National Lesbian and Gay Journalists Association's first Crossroads Prize for excellence in journalism. He has also created, with novelist Meg Wolitzer, popular word-game columns for *7 Days, Connoisseur, Town & Country* and, currently, *Civilization*; a collection of their most diabolical efforts was published as *Nutcrackers* by Grove Weidenfeld in 1991. Born in Philadelphia, graduated from Yale University in 1980, Green now lives in New York City, where he is at work on a second novel.

Craig G. Harris was an Afrocentric griot, community health educator, AIDS activist, and staff member of Gay Men's Health Crisis, who died on November 26, 1991, at St. Luke's Hospital of HIV-related complications. He was thirty-three years old. Mr. Harris's articles, essays, and poetry have appeared in a variety of publications, including the *Advocate*, the *New York Native, OutWeek*, and *Art & Understanding*, and in the following anthologies: *The Road Before Us* (Galliens Press), *Tongues Untied* (Gay Men's Press), and *Brother to Brother* (Alyson Publications).

Craig Hickman, a native of Milwaukee, Wisconsin, received a bachelor's degree in government from Harvard University in 1990.

He is an AIDS education and diversity consultant. His articles, essays and poems have appeared in the *Boston Phoenix*, *Bay Windows*, the *Harvard Gay and Lesbian Review*, and *Gents, Bad Boys, and Barbarians* (Alyson Publications) and his own collection of poetry and prose, *Rituals* (Parfait de Cocoa Press). He has won numerous awards for his poetry and stories including the Gertrude Johnson Williams literary award from *Ebony* magazine. He has toured his critically acclaimed solo performance piece *skin & ornaments*, *Through the Fire* with Brothers de Jour, and appears in the feature film *Never Met Picasso*. He worked on the film adaptation of Leslie Feinberg's award-winning novel *Stone Butch Blues*, and is currently writing a new performance piece. He lives in Cambridge, Massachusetts.

Christopher J. Hogan hails from Iowa but now lives and works in Boston. His video reviews regularly appear in the *Guide* and *Drummer*, and his poetry has appeared in the *AEEF Newsletter*. He hopes someday to be a professional bon vivant and raconteur.

Tony Kushner is the author of *Angels in America, Part One: Millennium Approaches* and *Part Two: Perestroika* for which he received two Tony Awards for best play on Broadway and the Pulitzer Prize for Drama. His other plays include an adaptation of Corneille's *The Illusion*, *A Bright Room Called Day*, and *Slaves! (Thinking About the Longstanding Problems of Virtue and Happiness)*. He lives in New York.

Michael Lassell is the author of two award-winning collections of poetry: *Poems for Lost and Un-lost Boys* (Amelia, 1985) and *Decade Dance* (Alyson, 1990). He is the author of *The Hard Way* (A Richard Kasak Book, 1995), a collection of poetry, fiction and nonfiction; and the editor of *The Name of Love: Classic Gay Love Poems* (St. Martin's Press, 1995) and *Eros in Boystown: Contemporary Gay Poetry* (Crown Publishing, 1996). His work has appeared in numerous anthologies, including *Gay & Lesbian Poetry in Our Time* (St. Martin's Press,

1988), *Men on Men 3* (Dutton, 1990), *Hometowns: Gay Men Write About Where They Belong* (Dutton, 1991), *Flesh and the Word* (Dutton, 1992), *New Worlds of Literature* (W.W. Norton, 1994), *Looking for Mr. Preston* (A Richard Kasak Book, 1995), and *The Badboy Book of Erotic Poetry* (Masquerade, 1995). His writing has appeared in scores of literary journals from *Fag Rag* and *The Portable Lower East Side* to *Kansas Quarterly* and *City Lights Review*, and in such publications as the *New York Times*, the *Los Angeles Times*, *L.A. Weekly*, *Interview*, *Mirabella*, *Dance Magazine*, *Metropolitan Home*, *Out*, the *Advocate*, and *Frontiers*. He holds degrees from Colgate University, California Institute of the Arts, and the Yale School of Drama.

Michael Lowenthal was born in 1969, grew up near Washington, D.C., and graduated from Dartmouth College. His short stories and essays appear in more than ten books, including *Men on Men 5: Best New Gay Fiction* (Penguin/Plume), *Wrestling with the Angel* (Riverhead), *Sister and Brother* (Harper San Francisco), *Best American Erotica 1994* (Touchstone), and the three books he completed for the late John Preston: *Friends and Lovers: Gay Men Write About the Families They Create* (Dutton), *Flesh and the Word 3* (Penguin/Plume*)*, and *Winter's Light: Reflections of a Yankee Queer* (University Press of New England). His writing has also been published in numerous periodicals including the *Advocate*, *Genre*, the *James White Review*, *Lambda Book Report*, and the *Boston Phoenix*. He lives in Boston.

Lawrence D. Mass, M.D., is a co-founder of Gay Men's Health Crisis and the author of the first five editions of the GMHC publication *Medical Answers About AIDS*, and of *Dialogues of the Sexual Revolution: Homosexuality and Sexuality, Volume I*, and *Dialogues of The Sexual Revolution: Homosexuality as Behavior and Identity, Volume II* (Haworth Press/Harrington Park Press). He is on the editorial board of the *Journal of Homosexuality* and was an associate editor of *Opera Monthly*. His essays and interviews have appeared in anthologies, including *S & M: Studies in Sadomasochism*, *The Christopher Street Reader* and *Queering the Pitch*. Dr. Mass is a medical director of Greenwich House's substance abuse treatment programs in New York City, where he lives with his life-partner, gay activist and writer Arnie Kantrowitz. His most recent book, *Confessions of a Jewish Wagnerite: Being Gay and Jewish in America* (Cassell), was a 1994 Lambda Literary Award finalist in the category of biography/autobiography. Mass is currently working on two books for Cassell, an anthology on Larry Kramer and *Musical Closets*: *Homosexuality, Judaism, Music and Opera*, from which "Musical Closets" is excerpted here.

Vestal McIntyre was born and raised in Nampa, Idaho. He graduated from Tufts University in 1994. His fiction has appeared in *Christopher Street*, and "Naming the Addiction" was first published in *Wrestling with the Angel: Faith and Religion in the Lives of Gay Men* (Riverhead). He currently lives in Brooklyn, New York.

Rondo Mieczkowski's writing appeared in the *Los Angeles Times Sunday Magazine*, the *Advocate*, *Lambda Book Report*, *LA Weekly*, and *Bay Windows*. He edited *Sunday at Seven: Choice Words From a Different Light's Gay Writers Series* (Alamo Square). He is compiling an anthology, *Make Me Scream: Humorous Writings About Life With HIV/AIDS*. He founded the "Me & HIV" reading series at Being Alive in L.A. "Leather Jacket Love Story," his gay romantic comedy screenplay is in development. He and Danny Barillaro celebrated fifteen years of friendship on June 9, 1996. Congratulations can be sent to P.O. Box 29478, Los Angeles CA 90029-0478.

John Mitzel was born in 1948 in Lakewood, Ohio. Over the past quarter century, he has been a contributing writer to Boston's *Gay Community News*, *Fag Rag* and many other publications. He has been a columnist for various gay periodicals since 1975; his column has appeared in the *Guide* since 1986. A book of short stories was published in 1977; he has also published a short biography of John Horne Burns. His work has appeared in numerous anthologies. His latest collection of short stories, *Last Gleamings*, is published by Glad Day Books.

John Preston was born in 1945 in Medfield, Massachusetts, and lived for many years in Portland, Maine. He was active in the gay rights movement and was an editor of *The Advocate*. He wrote extensively for the gay press and his novel, *Mr. Benson*, first published in *Drummer* Magazine is now considered a classic. He is the author of more then twenty-five other books including the Alex Kane books, an adventure series for gay teens, *Franny, Queen of Provincetown*, *The Arena*, *My Life as a Pornographer*, and the anthologies *Hometowns*, *A Member of the Family*, *Friends and Lovers*, and the Flesh and the Word series. John Preston died of complications from AIDS in 1994. A posthumous collection of autobiographical essays, *Winter's Light: Reflections of a Yankee Queer* was published in 1995.

Charley Shively is a member of Boston's *Fag Rag* collective and author of two books on Walt Whitman: *Calamus Lovers* (Gay Sunshine Press) and *Drum Beats* (Gay Sunshine Press).

Andrew Sullivan is the editor of the *New Republic* and the author of *Virtually Normal: An Argument About Homosexuality* (Alfred A. Knopf).

Scott Tucker is a queer artist and writer, a health care activist, and a democratic socialist. His pamphlet, *Fighting Words: An Open Letter to Queers and Radicals* was recently published by Cassell, and South End Press will soon publish *Our Right to the World*, a collection of his essays.

John Weir is the author of *The Irreversible Decline of Edie Socket* which won a Lambda Book Award for Best Gay Debut in 1990. He lives in New York and has written for *Outweek*, *Details*, and the *Advocate*.

Reed Woodhouse has lived in what remains of Boston's gay ghetto, the South End, for sixteen years. During that time he has taught English literature at Wellesley, Boston College and Massachusetts Institute of Technology, coached singers at Boston and New England Conservatories, conducted operas in Atlanta and Des Moines, and written personal essays and reviews for a variety of journals and books including *Boston Magazine*, the *Harvard Gay and Lesbian Review*, *Bay Windows*, *In Newsweekly*, John Preston's *Hometowns: Gay Men Write About Where They Belong*, and Emmanuel Nelson's *Contemporary Gay American Novelists*. The essay in this anthology forms the basis of his forthcoming book, *Five Houses of Gay Fiction*, to be published in 1996 by the University of Massachusetts Press.

Credits continued from page iv:

MASQUERADE

MARCO VASSI
THE STONED APOCALYPSE
$5.95/401-1/mass market
"Marco Vassi is our champion sexual energist."—VLS

During his lifetime, Marco Vassi was hailed as America's premier erotic writer and most worthy successor to Henry Miller. His work was praised by writers as diverse as Gore Vidal and Norman Mailer, and his reputation was worldwide. *The Stoned Apocalypse* is Vassi's autobiography; chronicling a cross-country trip on America's erotic byways, it offers a rare glimpse of a generation's sexual imagination.

ROBIN WILDE
TABITHA'S TEASE
$5.95/387-2
When poor Robin arrives at The Valentine Academy, he finds himself subject to the tortuous teasing of Tabitha—the Academy's most notoriously domineering co-ed. But Tabitha is pledge-mistress of a secret sorority dedicated to enslaving young men. Robin finds himself the utterly helpless (and wildly excited) captive of Tabitha & Company's weird desires!

ERICA BRONTE
PIRATE'S SLAVE
$5.95/376-7
Lovely young Erica is stranded in a country where lust knows no bounds. Desperate to escape, she finds herself trading her firm, luscious body to any and all men willing and able to help her. Her adventure has its ups and downs, ins and outs—all to the undeniable pleasure of lusty Erica!

CHARLES G. WOOD
HELLFIRE
$5.95/358-9
"[Wood] betrays a photographer's eye for tableau and telling detail in his evocation of the larger-than-life figures of the late-'70s to mid-'80s sexual demimonde."
—David Aaron Clark

A vicious murderer is running amok in New York's sexual underground—and Nick O'Shay, a virile detective with the NYPD, plunges deep into the case. He soon becomes embroiled in an elusive world of fleshly extremes, hunting a madman seeking to purge America with fire and blood sacrifices. A thrilling mystery set in New York's infamous sexual underground.

CLAIRE BAEDER, EDITOR
LA DOMME: A DOMINATRIX ANTHOLOGY
$5.95/366-X
A steamy smorgasbord of female domination! Erotic literature has long been filled with heartstopping portraits of domineering women, and now the most memorable have been brought together in one beautifully brutal volume. A thrilling collection—and a must for all fans of true Woman Power.

TINY ALICE
THE GEEK
$5.95/341-4
"An adventure novel told by a sex-bent male mini-pygmy. This is an accomplishment of which anybody may be proud."—Philip José Farmer

A notorious cult classic. *The Geek* is told from the point of view of a chicken, who reports on the various perversities he witnesses as part of a traveling carnival. When a gang of renegade lesbians kidnaps Chicken and his geek, all hell breaks loose. A strange tale, filled with outrageous erotic oddities, that finally returns to print after years of infamy.

CHARISSE VAN DER LYN
SEX ON THE NET
$5.95/399-6
Electrifying erotica from one of the Internet's hottest and most widely read authors. Encounters of all kinds—straight, lesbian, dominant/submissive and all sorts of extreme passions—are explored in thrilling detail.

AKBAR DEL PIOMBO
SKIRTS
$4.95/115-2
Randy Mr. Edward Champdick enters high society—and a whole lot more—in his quest for ultimate satisfaction. For it seems that once Mr. Champdick rises to the occasion, nothing can bring him down.
A CRUMBLING FAÇADE
$4.95/3043-1
The return of that incorrigible rogue, Henry Pike, who continues his pursuit of sex, fair or otherwise, in the most elegant homes of the most debauched aristocrats.

MASQUERADE

STANLEY CARTEN
NAUGHTY MESSAGE
$5.95/333-3
Wesley Arthur discovers a lascivious message on his answering machine and becomes obsessed with tracking down the woman behind the seductive voice. His search takes him through strip clubs, sex parlors and no-tell motels—and finally to his randy reward....

DAVID AARON CLARK
THE MARQUIS DE SADE'S JULIETTE
$4.95/240-X
The Marquis de Sade's infamous Juliette returns—and emerges as the most perverse and destructive nightstalker modern New York will ever know.

Praise for David Aaron Clark:
"David Aaron Clark has delved into one of the most sensationalistically taboo aspects of eros, sadomasochism, and produced a novel of unmistakable literary imagination and artistic value."
—Carlo McCormick, *Paper*

ANONYMOUS
NADIA
$5.95/267-1
Follow the delicious but neglected Nadia as she works to wring every drop of pleasure out of life—despite an unhappy marriage. A classic title providing a peek into the secret sexual lives of another time and place.
THE ROMANCES OF BLANCHE LA MARE
$4.95/101-2
When Blanche loses her husband, it becomes clear she'll need a job. She sets her sights on the stage—and soon encounters a cast of lecherous characters intent on making her path to sucksess as hard as possible!

NIGEL McPARR
THE STORY OF A VICTORIAN MAID
$5.95/241-8
What were the Victorians really like? Chances are, no one believes they were as stuffy as their Queen, but who would have imagined such unbridled libertines! Follow her from exploit to smutty exploit!

BREN FLEMMING
CHARLY'S GAME
$4.95/221-3
A rich woman's gullible daughter has run off with one of the toughest leather dykes in town—and sexy P.I. Charly is hired to lure the girl back. One by one, wise and wicked women ensnare one another in their lusty nets!

TITIAN BERESFORD
THE WICKED HAND
$5.95/343-0
With an Introduction by *Leg Show*'s Dian Hanson. A collection of fetishistic tales featuring the absolute subjugation of men by lovely, domineering women.
CINDERELLA
$6.50/500-X
Beresford triumphs again with this intoxicating tale, filled with castle dungeons and tightly corseted ladies-in-waiting, naughty viscounts and impossibly cruel masturbatrixes—nearly every conceivable method of erotic torture is explored and described in lush, vivid detail.
NINA FOXTON
$5.95/443-7
An aristocrat finds herself bored by run-of-the-mill amusements for "ladies of good breeding." Instead of taking tea with proper gentlemen, naughty Nina "milks" them of their most private essences. No man ever says "No" to Nina!

P. N. DEDEAUX
THE NOTHING THINGS
$5.95/404-6
Beta Beta Rho—highly exclusive and widely honored—has taken on a new group of pledges. The five women will be put through the most grueling of ordeals, and punished severely for any shortcomings—much to everyone's delight!
TENDER BUNS
$5.95/396-1
In a fashionable Canadian suburb, Marc Merlin indulges his yen for punishment with an assortment of the town's most desirable and willing women. Things come to a rousing climax at a party planned to cater to just those whims Marc is most able to satisfy....

LYN DAVENPORT

DOVER ISLAND
$5.95/384-8
Dr. David Kelly has planted the seeds of his dream— a Corporal Punishment Resort. Soon, many people from varied walks of life descend upon this isolated retreat, intent on fulfilling their every desire. Including Marcy Harris, the perfect partner for the lustful Doctor....

THE GUARDIAN
$5.95/371-6
Felicia grew up under the tutelage of the lash—and she learned her lessons well. Sir Rodney Wentworth has long searched for a woman capable of fulfilling his cruel desires, and after learning of Felicia's talents, sends for her. Felicia discovers that the "position" offered her is delightfully different than anything she could have expected!

LIZBETH DUSSEAU

TRINKETS
$4.95/246-9
"Her bottom danced on the air, pert and fully round. It would take punishment well, he thought." A luscious woman submits to an artist's every whim—becoming the sexual trinket he had always desired.

ANTHONY BOBARZYNSKI

STASI SLUT
$4.95/3050-4
Adina lives in East Germany, where she meets a group of ruthless and corrupt STASI agents who use her for their own perverse gratification—until she uses her talents and attractions in a final bid for total freedom!

JOCELYN JOYCE

PRIVATE LIVES
$4.95/309-0
The lecherous habits of the illustrious make for a sizzling tale of French erotic life. A widow has a craving for a young busboy; he's sleeping with a rich businessman's wife; her husband is minding his sex business elsewhere! Scandalous sexual entanglements run throughout this tale of upper crust lust!

CAROUSEL
$4.95/3051-2
A young American woman leaves her husband when she discovers he is having an affair with their maid. She then becomes the sexual plaything of a circle of Parisian voluptuaries.

THE WILD HEART
$4.95/3007-5
A luxury hotel is the setting for this artful web of sex, desire, and love. A newlywed sees sex as a duty, while her hungry husband tries to awaken her to its tender joys. A Parisian entertains wealthy guests for the love of money. Each episode provides a new variation in this lusty Grand Hotel!

SARAH JACKSON

SANCTUARY
$5.95/318-X
Sanctuary explores both the unspeakable debauchery of court life and the unimaginable privations of monastic solitude, leading the voracious and the virtuous on a collision course that brings history to throbbing life.

LOUISE BELHAVEL

FRAGRANT ABUSES
$4.95/88-2
The saga of Clara and Iris continues as the now-experienced girls enjoy themselves with a new circle of worldly friends whose imaginations match their own. Perversity follows the lusty ladies around the globe!

SARA H. FRENCH

MASTER OF TIMBERLAND
$5.95/327-9
A tale of sexual slavery at the ultimate paradise resort. One of our bestselling titles, this trek to Timberland has ignited passions the world over—and stands poised to become one of modern erotica's legendary tales.

RETURN TO TIMBERLAND
$5.95/257-4
Another pulse-pounding trip to Timberland—the world's most frenzied sexual resort! Prepare for a vacation filled with delicious decadence, as each and every visitor is serviced by unimaginably talented submissives. The raunchiest camp-out ever!

AMARANTHA KNIGHT

THE DARKER PASSIONS: THE PICTURE OF DORIAN GRAY
$6.50/342-2
In this latest installment in the Darker Passions series, Amarantha Knight takes on Oscar Wilde, resulting in a fabulously decadent tale of highly personal changes. One young man finds his most secret desires laid bare by a portrait far more revealing than he could have imagined....

CHINESE JUSTICE AND OTHER STORIES
$4.95/153-5
The story of the excruciating pleasures and delicious punishments inflicted on foreigners under the leaders of the Boxer Rebellion. Each foreign woman is brought before the authorities and grilled. Scandalous deeds!

CAPTIVE MAIDENS
$5.95/440-2
Three beautiful young women find themselves powerless against the debauched landowners of 1824 England. They are banished to a sexual slave colony, and corrupted by every imaginable perversion. Soon, they come to crave the treatment of their unrelenting captors.

SLAVE ISLAND
$5.95/441-0
A leisure cruise is waylaid, finding itself in the domain of Lord Henry Philbrock, a sadistic genius. The ship's passengers are kidnapped and spirited to his island prison, where the women are trained to accommodate the most bizarre sexual cravings of the rich, the famous, the pampered and the perverted. An incredible bestseller.

MARY LOVE
MASTERING MARY SUE
$5.95/351-1
Mary Sue is a rich nymphomaniac whose husband is determined to declare her mentally incompetent and gain control of her fortune. He brings her to a castle where, to Mary Sue's delight, she is unleashed for a veritable sex-fest!

THE BEST OF MARY LOVE
$4.95/3099-7
Mary Love leaves no coupling untried and no extreme unexplored in these scandalous selections from *Mastering Mary Sue, Ecstasy on Fire, Vice Park Place, Wanda,* and *Naughtier at Night.*

JOHN NORMAN
TARNSMAN OF GOR
$6.95/486-0
This legendary—and controversial—series returns! *Tarnsman* finds Tarl Cabot transported to Counter-Earth, better known as Gor. He must quickly accustom himself to the ways of this world, including the caste system which exalts some as Priest-Kings or Warriors, and debases others as slaves. The first volume of this million-selling series.

OUTLAW OF GOR
$6.95/487-9
Volume Two. Tarl Cabot returns to Gor, where he might reclaim both his woman and his role of Warrior. But upon arriving, he discovers that his name, his city and the names of those he loves have become unspeakable. In his absence, Cabot has become an outlaw, and must discover his new purpose on this strange planet, where danger stalks the outcast, and even simple answers have their price....

PRIEST-KINGS OF GOR
$6.95/488-7
Volume Three. Tarl Cabot, brave Tarnsman of Gor, searches for the truth about his lovely wife Talena. Does she live, or was she destroyed by the mysterious, all-powerful Priest-Kings? Cabot is determined to find out— even while knowing that no one who has approached the mountain stronghold of the Priest-Kings has ever returned alive....

RACHEL PEREZ
ODD WOMEN
$4.95/123-3
These women are sexy, smart, tough—some even say odd. But who cares, when their combined ass-ets are so sweet! An assortment of Sapphic sirens proves once and for all that comely ladies come best in pairs.

AFFINITIES
$4.95/113-6
"Kelsy had a liking for cool upper-class blondes, the long-legged girls who came into the city looking for breathless ecstasies...." A scorching tale of lesbian libidos unleashed, from a writer more than capable of exploring every nuance of female passion in vivid detail.

SYDNEY ST. JAMES
RIVE GAUCHE
$5.95/317-1
The Latin Quarter, Paris, circa 1920. Expatriate bohemians couple with abandon—before eventually abandoning their ambitions amidst the intoxicating temptations waiting to be indulged in every bedroom.

GARDEN OF DELIGHT
$4.95/3058-X
Follow an innocent but insatiably curious young woman's journey from the furtive, forbidden joys of dormitory life to the unabashed carnality of the wild world. A coming of age story unlike any other!

MASQUERADE

MARCUS VAN HELLER

TERROR
$5.95/247-7
Another shocking exploration of lust by the author of the ever-popular *Adam & Eve*. Set in Paris during the Algerian War, *Terror* explores the place of sexual passion in a world drunk on violence.

ALEXANDER TROCCHI

THONGS
$4.95/217-5
"...In Spain, life is cheap, from that glittering tragedy in the bullring to the quick thrust of the stiletto in a narrow street in a Barcelona slum. No, this death would not have called for further comment had it not been for one striking fact. The naked woman had met her end in a way he had never seen before—a way that had enormous sexual significance. My God, she had been..." Trocchi's acclaimed classic returns.

HELEN AND DESIRE
$4.95/3093-8
Helen Seferis' flight from the oppressive village of her birth became a sexual tour of a harsh world. From brothels in Sydney to harems in Algiers, Helen chronicles her adventures fully in her diary. Each encounter is examined in the scorching and uncensored diary of the sensual Helen!

DON WINSLOW

SECRETS OF CHEATEM MANOR
$6.50/434-8
Edward returns to his late father's estate, to find it being run by the majestic Lady Amanda. Edward can hardly believe his luck—Lady Amanda is assisted by her two beautiful, lonely daughters, Catherine and Prudence. What the randy young man soon comes to realize is the love of discipline that all three beauties share.

KATERINA IN CHARGE
$5.95/409-7
When invited to a country retreat by a mysterious couple, the two randy young ladies can hardly resist! But do they have any idea what they're in for? Whatever the case, the imperious Katerina will make her desires known very soon—and demand that they be fulfilled...

THE MANY PLEASURES OF IRONWOOD
$5.95/310-4
Seven lovely young women are employed by The Ironwood Sportsmen's Club A small and exclusive club with seven carefully selected sexual connoisseurs, Ironwood is dedicated to the relentless pursuit of sensual pleasure.

CLAIRE'S GIRLS
$5.95/442-9
You knew when she walked by that she was something special. She was one of Claire's girls, a woman carefully dressed and groomed to fill a role, to capture a look, to fit an image crafted by the sophisticated proprietress of an exclusive escort agency. High-class whores blow the roof off!

N. WHALLEN

TAU'TEVU
$6.50/426-7
In a mysterious land, the statuesque and beautiful Vivian learns to subject herself to the hand of a mysterious man. He systematically helps her prove her own strength, and brings to life in her an unimagined sensual fire. But who is this man, who goes only by the name of Orpheo?

COMPLIANCE
$5.95/356-2
Fourteen stories exploring the pleasures of release. Characters from all walks of life learn to trust in the skills of others, only to experience the thrilling liberation of submission. Here are the joys to be found in some of the most forbidden sexual practices around....

THE MASQUERADE READERS

A MASQUERADE READER
$4.95/84-X
A sizzling sampler. Strict lessons are learned at the hand of *The English Governess*. Scandalous confessions are found in *The Diary of an Angel*, and the story of a woman whose desires drove her to the ultimate sacrifice in *Thongs* completes the collection.

RHINOCEROS

GARY BOWEN

DIARY OF A VAMPIRE
$6.95/331-7
"Gifted with a darkly sensual vision and a fresh voice, [Bowen] is a writer to watch out for."　—Cecilia Tan

The chilling, arousing, and ultimately moving memoirs of an undead—but all too human—soul. Bowen's Rafael, a red-blooded male with an insatiable hunger for the same, is the perfect antidote to the effete malcontents haunting bookstores today. *Diary of a Vampire* marks the emergence of a bold and brilliant vision, firmly rooted in past and present.

LAURA ANTONIOU, EDITOR

NO OTHER TRIBUTE
$6.95/294-9
A collection sure to challenge Political Correctness in a way few have before, with tales of women kept in bondage to their lovers by their deepest passions. Love pushes these women beyond acceptable limits, rendering them helpless to deny anything to the men and women they adore. A volume dedicated to all Slaves of Desire.

SOME WOMEN
$6.95/300-7
Over forty essays written by women actively involved in consensual dominance and submission. Professional mistresses, lifestyle leatherdykes, whipmakers, titleholders—women from every conceivable walk of life lay bare their true feelings about explosive issues.

BY HER SUBDUED
$6.95/281-7
These tales all involve women in control—of their lives, their loves, their men. So much in control that they can remorselessly break rules to become powerful goddesses of the men who sacrifice all to worship at their feet.

RENÉ MAIZEROY

FLESHLY ATTRACTIONS
$6.95/299-X
Lucien was the son of the wantonly beautiful actress, Marie-Rose Hardanges. When she decides to let a "friend" introduce her son to the pleasures of love, Marie-Rose could not have foretold the excesses that would lead to her own ruin and that of her cherished son.

JEAN STINE

THRILL CITY
$6.95/411-9
Thrill City is the seat of the world's increasing depravity, and Jean Stine's classic novel transports you there with a vivid style you'd be hard pressed to ignore. No writer is better suited to describe the unspeakable extremes of this modern Babylon.

SEASON OF THE WITCH
$6.95/268-X
"A future in which it is technically possible to transfer the total mind...of a rapist killer into the brain dead but physically living body of his female victim. Remarkable for intense psychological technique. There is eroticism but it is necessary to mark the differences between the sexes and the subtle altering of a man into a woman."
　　　　　　　　—*The Science Fiction Critic*

JOHN WARREN

THE TORQUEMADA KILLER
$6.95/367-8
Detective Eva Hernandez has finally gotten her first "big case": a string of vicious murders taking place within New York's SM community. Piece by piece, Eva assembles the evidence, revealing a picture of a world misunderstood and under attack—and gradually comes to understand her own place within it. A heart-stopping thriller, as well as an insider's look at the contemporary politics of "the scene"—and those threatened by it.

THE LOVING DOMINANT
$6.95/218-3
Everything you need to know about an infamous sexual variation—and an unspoken type of love. Mentor—a longtime player in scene—guides readers through this world and reveals the too-often hidden basis of the D/S relationship: care, trust and love.

GRANT ANTREWS

MY DARLING DOMINATRIX
$6.95/447-X
When a man and a woman fall in love, it's supposed to be simple, uncomplicated, easy—unless that woman happens to be a dominatrix. Curiosity gives way to unblushing desire in this story of one man's awakening to the joys of willing slavery.

MASQUERADE DIRECT

RHINOCEROS

LAURA ANTONIOU WRITING AS "SARA ADAMSON"

THE TRAINER
$6.95/249-3
The Marketplace—the ultimate underground sexual realm includes not only willing slaves, but the exquisite trainers who take submissives firmly in hand. And now these mentors divulge the desires that led them to become the ultimate figures of authority.

THE SLAVE
$6.95/173-X
This second volume in the "Marketplace" trilogy further elaborates the world of slaves and masters. One talented submissive longs to join the ranks of those who have proven themselves worthy of entry into the Marketplace. But the delicious price is staggeringly high....

THE MARKETPLACE
$6.95/3096-2
"Merchandise does not come easily to the Marketplace.... They haunt the clubs and the organizations.... Some are so ripe that they intimidate the poseurs, the weekend sadists and the furtive dilettantes who are so endemic to that world. And they never stop asking where we may be found...."

DAVID AARON CLARK

SISTER RADIANCE
$6.95/215-9
A chronicle of obsession—rife with Clark's trademark vivisections of contemporary desires, sacred and profane. The vicissitudes of lust and romance are examined against a backdrop of urban decay and shallow fashionability in this testament to the allure of the forbidden.

THE WET FOREVER
$6.95/117-9
The story of Janus and Madchen—a small-time hood and a beautiful sex worker on the run from one of the most dangerous men they have ever known—*The Wet Forever* examines themes of loyalty, sacrifice, redemption and obsession amidst Manhattan's sex parlors and underground S/M clubs. Its combination of sex and suspense led Terence Sellers to proclaim it "evocative and poetic."

ALICE JOANOU

BLACK TONGUE
$6.95/258-2
"Joanou has created a series of sumptuous, brooding, dark visions of sexual obsession, and is undoubtedly a name to look out for in the future."
—*Redeemer*

Exploring lust at its most florid and unsparing, *Black Tongue* is a trove of baroque fantasies—each redolent of forbidden passions. Joanou creates some of erotica's most mesmerizing and unforgettable characters.

TOURNIQUET
$6.95/3060-1
A heady collection of stories and effusions from the pen of one our most dazzling young writers. Strange tales abound, from the story of the mysterious and cruel Cybele, to an encounter with the sadistic entertainment of a bizarre after-hours cafe. A complex and riveting series of meditations on desire.

CANNIBAL FLOWER
$4.95/72-6
The provocative debut volume from this acclaimed writer. "She is waiting in her darkened bedroom, as she has waited throughout history, to seduce the men who are foolish enough to be blinded by her irresistible charms.... She is the goddess of sexuality, and *Cannibal Flower* is her haunting siren song."
—Michael Perkins

MICHAEL PERKINS

EVIL COMPANIONS
$6.95/3067-9
Set in New York City during the tumultuous waning years of the Sixties, *Evil Companions* has been hailed as "a frightening classic." A young couple explores the nether reaches of the erotic unconscious in a shocking confrontation with the extremes of passion. With a new introduction by science fiction legend Samuel R. Delany.

THE SECRET RECORD: MODERN EROTIC LITERATURE
$6.95/3039-3
Michael Perkins surveys the field with authority and unique insight. Updated and revised to include the latest trends, tastes, and developments in this misunderstood and maligned genre.

DIRECT

RHINOCEROS

AN ANTHOLOGY OF CLASSIC ANONYMOUS EROTIC WRITING
$6.95/140-3
Michael Perkins has collected the very best passages from the world's erotic writing. "Anonymous" is one of the most infamous bylines in publishing history —and these steamy excerpts show why! An incredible smorgasbord of forbidden delights culled from some of the most famous titles in the history of erotic literature.

LIESEL KULIG
LOVE IN WARTIME
$6.95/3044-X
Madeleine knew that the handsome SS officer was a dangerous man, but she was just a cabaret singer in Nazi-occupied Paris, trying to survive in a perilous time. When Josef fell in love with her, he discovered that a beautiful and amoral woman can sometimes be wildly dangerous.

HELEN HENLEY
ENTER WITH TRUMPETS
$6.95/197-7
Helen Henley was told that women just don't write about sex—much less the taboos she was so interested in exploring. So Henley did it alone, flying in the face of "tradition," by writing this touching tale of arousal and devotion in one couple's kinky relationship.

SOPHIE GALLEYMORE BIRD
MANEATER
$6.95/103-9
Through a bizarre act of creation, a man attains the "perfect" lover—by all appearances a beautiful, sensuous woman, but in reality something far darker. Once brought to life she will accept no mate, seeking instead the prey that will sate her hunger for vengeance. A biting take on the war of the sexes, this debut goes for the jugular of the "perfect woman" myth.

TUPPY OWENS
SENSATIONS
$6.95/3081-4
Tuppy Owens tells the unexpurgated story of the making of Sensations—the first big-budget sex flick. Originally commissioned to appear in book form after the release of the film in 1975, Sensations is finally released under Masquerade's stylish Rhinoceros imprint.

PHILIP JOSÉ FARMER
FLESH
$6.95/303-1
Space Commander Stagg explored the galaxies for 800 years. Upon his return, the hero Stagg, hoped to be afforded a hero's welcome. Once home, he is made the centerpiece of an incredible public ritual—one that will repeatedly take him to the heights of ecstasy, and inexorably drag him toward the depths of hell.

A FEAST UNKNOWN
$6.95/276-0
"Sprawling, brawling, shocking, suspenseful, hilarious..."
—Theodore Sturgeon

Farmer's supreme anti-hero returns. "I was conceived and born in 1888." Slowly, Lord Grandrith—armed with the belief that he is the son of Jack the Ripper—tells the story of his remarkable and unbridled life. His story begins with his discovery of the secret of immortality—and progresses to encompass the furthest extremes of human behavior. A classic of speculative erotica.

THE IMAGE OF THE BEAST
$6.95/166-7
Herald Childe has seen Hell, glimpsed its horror in an act of sexual mutilation. Childe must now find and destroy an inhuman predator through the streets of a polluted and decadent Los Angeles of the future. One clue after another leads Childe to an inescapable realization about the nature of sex and evil....

DANIEL VIAN
ILLUSIONS
$6.95/3074-1
Two tales of danger and desire in Berlin on the eve of WWII. From private homes to lurid cafés, passion is exposed in stark contrast to the brutal violence of the time. Two sexy tales examining a remarkably decadent age.

SAMUEL R. DELANY
EQUINOX
$6.95/157-8
The Scorpion has sailed the seas in a quest for every possible pleasure. Her crew is a collection of the young, the twisted, the insatiable. A drifter comes into their midst and is taken on a fantastic journey to the darkest, most dangerous sexual extremes—until he is finally a victim to their boundless appetites.

DIRECT

RHINOCEROS

THE MAD MAN
$8.99/408-9

"Reads like a pornographic reflection of Peter Ackroyd's *Chatterton* or A. S. Byatt's *Possession*.... Delany develops an insightful dichotomy between [his protagonist]'s two worlds: the one of cerebral philosophy and dry academia, the other of heedless, 'impersonal' obsessive sexual extremism. When these worlds finally collide...the novel achieves a surprisingly satisfying resolution...."
—*Publishers Weekly*

"This new novel by Samuel R. Delany not only expands the parameters of what he has given us in the past, but fuses together two seemingly disparate genres of writing and comes up with something which is not comparable to any existing text of which I am aware.... What Delany has done here is take the ideas of Marquis de Sade one step further, by filtering extreme and obsessive sexual behavior through the sieve of post-modern experience...."
—*Lambda Book Report*

"A fundamentally serious book that keeps open the possibility of a liberation which does not ignore the body, and which makes the world a more hospitable place for the erotic, and especially the homoerotic, life."
—*Harvard Gay & Lesbian Review*

"This powerful, unique, and distinctive book is not for the squeamish but is a very satisfying read for someone who wants to be challenged."
—*Our Own*

For his thesis, graduate student John Marr researches the life and work of the brilliant Timothy Hasler: a philosopher whose career was cut tragically short over a decade earlier. On another front, Marr finds himself increasingly drawn toward more shocking, depraved sexual entanglements with the homeless men of his neighborhood, until it begins to seem that Hasler's death might hold some key to his own life as a gay man in the age of AIDS.

ANDREI CODRESCU
THE REPENTANCE OF LORRAINE
$6.95/329-5
"One of our most prodigiously talented and magical writers."
—*NYT Book Review*

By the acclaimed author of *The Hole in the Flag* and *The Blood Countess*. An aspiring writer, a professor's wife, a secretary, gold anklets, Maoists, Roman harlots—and more—swirl through this spicy tale of a harried quest for a mythic artifact. Written when the author was a young man, this lusty yarn was inspired by the heady days of the Sixties.

LEOPOLD VON SACHER-MASOCH
VENUS IN FURS
$6.95/3089-X
This classic 19th century novel is the first uncompromising exploration of the dominant/submissive relationship in literature. The alliance of Severin and Wanda epitomizes Sacher-Masoch's obsession with a cruel, controlling goddess and the urges that drive the man held in her thrall. Also included are the letters exchanged between Sacher-Masoch and Emilie Mataja—an aspiring writer he sought as the avatar of his forbidden desires.

DIRECT

BADBOY

COME QUICKLY: FOR BOYS ON THE GO
$6.50/413-5

The pace of daily life is no reason a guy has to forgo a little carnal pleasure whenever the mood strikes him. Here are over sixty of the hottest fantasies around—all designed to get you going in less time than it takes to dial 976. Julian Anthony Guerra, the editor behind the phenomenally popular *Men at Work* and *Badboy Fantasies*, has put together this volume especially for you—a modern man on a modern schedule, who still appreciates a little old-fashioned action.

MATT TOWNSEND
SOLIDLY BUILT
$6.50/416-X

The tale of the tumultuous relationship between Jeff, a young photographer, and Mark, the butch electrician hired to wire Jeff's new home. For Jeff, it's love at first sight; Mark, however, has more than a few hang-ups. Soon, both are forced to reevaluate their outlooks, and are assisted by a variety of hot men....

JOHN PRESTON
MR. BENSON
$4.95/3041-5

A classic erotic novel from a time when there was no limit to what a man could dream of doing.... Jamie is an aimless young man lucky enough to encounter Mr. Benson. He is soon led down the path of erotic enlightenment, learning to accept this man as his master. From an opulent penthouse to the infamous Mineshaft, Jamie's incredible adventures never fail to excite—especially when the going gets rough!

TALES FROM THE DARK LORD
$5.95/323-6

A new collection of twelve stunning works from the man *Lambda Book Report* called "the Dark Lord of gay erotica." The relentless ritual of lust and surrender is explored in all its manifestations in this heart-stopping triumph of authority and vision from the Dark Lord!

TALES FROM THE DARK LORD II
$4.95/176-4

The second volume of acclaimed eroticist John Preston's masterful short stories. Also includes an interview with the author, and an explicit screenplay written for pornstar Scott O'Hara. An explosive collection from one of erotic publishing's most fertile imaginations.

THE ARENA
$4.95/3083-0

There is a place on the edge of fantasy where every desire is indulged with abandon. Men go there to unleash beasts, to let demons roam free, to abolish all limits. At the center of each tale are the men who serve there, who offer themselves for the consummation of any passion, whose own bottomless urges compel their endless subservience.

THE HEIR•THE KING
$4.95/3048-2

The ground-breaking novel *The Heir*, written in the lyric voice of the ancient myths, tells the story of a world where slaves and masters create a new sexual society. This edition also includes a completely original work, *The King*, the story of a soldier who discovers his monarch's most secret desires. Available only from Badboy.

THE MISSION OF ALEX KANE
SWEET DREAMS
$4.95/3062-8

Volume One. It's the triumphant return of gay action hero Alex Kane! In *Sweet Dreams*, Alex travels to Boston where he takes on a street gang that stalks gay teenagers. Mighty Alex Kane wreaks a fierce and terrible vengeance on those who prey on gay people everywhere!

GOLDEN YEARS
$4.95/3069-5

Volume Two. When evil threatens the plans of a group of older gay men, Kane's got the muscle to take it head on. Along the way, he wins the support—and very specialized attentions—of a cowboy plucked right out of the Old West. But Kane and the Cowboy have a surprise waiting for them....

DEADLY LIES
$4.95/3076-8

Volume Three. Politics is a dirty business and the dirt becomes deadly when a political smear campaign targets gay men. Who better to clean things up than Alex Kane! Alex comes to protect the dreams, and lives, of gay men imperiled by lies.

STOLEN MOMENTS
$4.95/3098-9

Volume Four. Houston's evolving gay community is victimized by a malicious newspaper editor who is more than willing to sacrifice gays on the altar of circulation. He never counted on Alex Kane, fearless defender of gay dreams and desires.

DIRECT

BADBOY

HOT BAUDS
$5.95/285-X
The author of *Fantasy Board* and *The Initiation of PB 500* combed cyberspace for the hottest fantasies of the world's horniest hackers. From bulletin boards called Studs, The Mine Shaft, Back Door and the like, Stone has assembled the first collection of the raunchy erotica so many gay men cruise the Information Superhighway for.

FANTASY BOARD
$4.95/212-4
The author of the scalding sci-fi adventures of PB 500 explores the more foreseeable future—through the intertwined lives (and private parts) of a collection of randy computer hackers. On the Lambda Gate BBS, every hot and horny male is in search of a little virtual satisfaction. Luckily, no man brave enough to post here leaves without being thoroughly gratified.

THE CITADEL
$4.95/198-5
The sequel to *The Initiation of PB 500*. Having proven himself worthy of his stunning master, Micah—now known only as '500'—will face new challenges and hardships after his entry into the forbidding Citadel. Only his master knows what awaits—and whether Micah will again distinguish himself as the perfect instrument of pleasure....

RITUALS
$4.95/168-3
Via a computer bulletin board, a young man finds himself drawn into a series of sexual rites that transform him into the willing slave of a mysterious stranger. Gradually, all vestiges of his former life are thrown off, and he learns to live for his Master's touch.... A high-tech tale of ultimate surrender.

THE INITIATION OF PB 500
$4.95/141-1
An interstellar accident strands a young stud on an alien planet. He is a stranger on their planet, unschooled in their language, and ignorant of their customs. But this man, Micah—now known only by his number—will soon be trained in every last detail of erotic personal service. And, once nurtured and transformed into the perfect physical specimen, he must begin proving himself worthy of the master who has chosen him....

JOHN ROWBERRY
LEWD CONDUCT
$4.95/3091-1
Flesh-and-blood men vie for power, pleasure and surrender in each of these feverish stories, and no one walks away from his steamy encounter unsated. Rowberry's men are unafraid to push the limits of civilized behavior in search of the elusive and empowering conquest.

ROBERT BAHR
SEX SHOW
$4.95/225-6
Luscious dancing boys. Brazen, explicit acts. Unending stimulation. Take a seat, and get very comfortable, because the curtain's going up on a show no discriminating appetite can afford to miss.

JASON FURY
THE ROPE ABOVE, THE BED BELOW
$4.95/269-8
The irresistible Jason Fury returns—and if you thought his earlier adventures were hot, this volume will blow you away! Once again, our built, blond hero finds himself in the oddest—and most compromising—positions.

ERIC'S BODY
$4.95/151-9
Meet Jason Fury—blond, blue-eyed and up for anything. Fury's sexiest tales are collected in book form for the first time. Follow the irresistible Jason through sexual adventures unlike any you have ever read....

"BIG" BILL JACKSON
EIGHTH WONDER
$4.95/200-0
From the bright lights and back rooms of New York to the open fields and sweaty bods of a small Southern town, "Big" Bill always manages to cause a scene, and the more actors he can involve, the better! And he's got more than enough for everyone, and turns nobody down....

DIRECT

BADBOY

LARS EIGHNER

WHISPERED IN THE DARK
$5.95/286-8
A volume demonstrating Eighner's unique combination of strengths: poetic descriptive power, an unfailing ear for dialogue, and a finely tuned feeling for the nuances of male passion.

AMERICAN PRELUDE
$4.95/170-5
Eighner is widely recognized as one of our best, most exciting gay writers. He is also one of gay erotica's true masters—and *American Prelude* shows why. Wonderfully written, blisteringly hot tales of all-American lust.

B.M.O.C.
$4.95/3077-6
In a college town known as "the Athens of the Southwest," studs of every stripe are up all night—studying, naturally. In *B.M.O.C.*, Eighner includes the very best of his short stories, sure to appeal to the collegian in every man.

DAVID LAURENTS, EDITOR

SOUTHERN COMFORT
$6.50/466-6
Another collection of today's most provocative gay writing. The tales here focus on the American South—and reflect not only Southern literary tradition, but the many contributions the region has made to the iconography of the American Male..

**WANDERLUST:
HOMOEROTIC TALES OF TRAVEL**
$5.95/395-3
Gay men have always had a special interest in travel—and not only for the scenic vistas. *Wanderlust* celebrates the freedom of the open road, and the allure of men who stray from the beaten path....

THE BADBOY BOOK OF EROTIC POETRY
$5.95/382-1
Erotic poetry has long been the problem child of the literary world—highly creative and provocative, but somehow too frank to be "literature." Both learned and stimulating, this volume restores eros to its rightful place of honor in contemporary gay writing.

AARON TRAVIS

IN THE BLOOD
$5.95/283-3
Early stories that laid the groundwork for later masterpieces. Among the many rewarding rarities included in this volume: "In the Blood"—a heart-pounding descent into sexual vampirism, written with the furious erotic power that has distinguished Travis' work from the beginning.

THE FLESH FABLES
$4.95/243-4
One of Travis' best collections, finally rereleased. *The Flesh Fables* includes "Blue Light," his most famous story, as well as other masterpieces that established him as the erotic writer to watch. And watch carefully, because Travis always buries a surprise beneath his scorching detail....

SLAVES OF THE EMPIRE
$4.95/3054-7
The return of an undisputed classic from this master of the erotic genre.

"*Slaves of the Empire* is a wonderful mythic tale.... Explores the timeless questions of light and dark in male sexuality. Travis has shown himself expert in manipulating the most primal themes and images. The locale may be the ancient world, but these are the slaves and masters of our time...."
—John Preston

BOB VICKERY

SKIN DEEP
$4.95/265-5
So many varied beauties no one will go away unsatisfied. No tantalizing morsel of manflesh is overlooked—or left unexplored! Beauty may be only skin deep, but a handful of beautiful skin is a tempting proposition.

JR

FRENCH QUARTER NIGHTS
$5.95/337-6
A randy roundup of this author's most popular tales. *French Quarter Nights* is filled with sensual snapshots of the many places where men get down and dirty—from the steamy French Quarter to the steam room at the old Everard baths.

BUY ANY 4 BOOKS & CHOOSE 1 ADDITIONAL BOOK, OF EQUAL OR LESSER VALUE, AS YOUR FREE GIFT

DIRECT

BADBOY

ALL-STUD
$4.95/104-7
This classic, sex-soaked tale takes place under the watchful eye of Number Ten: an omniscient figure who has decreed unabashed promiscuity as the law of his all-male land. One stud, however, takes it upon himself to challenge the social order, daring to fall in love.

1 900 745-HUNG

Hardcore phone action for real men. A scorching assembly of studs is waiting for your call—and eager to give you the headtrip of your life! Totally live, guaranteed one-on-one encounters. (Must be over 18.) No credit card needed. $3.98 per minute.

LARRY TOWNSEND
LEATHER AD: M
$5.95/380-5
The first of this two-part classic. John's curious about what goes on between the leatherclad men he's fantasized about. He takes out a personal ad, and starts a journey of self-discovery that will leave no part of his life unchanged.
LEATHER AD: S
$5.95/407-0
The second half of Townsend's acclaimed tale of lust through the personals—this time told from a Top's perspective. A simple ad generates many responses, and one man finds himself in the enviable position of putting these studly applicants through their paces.....
BEWARE THE GOD WHO SMILES
$5.95/321-X
Two lusty young Americans are transported to ancient Egypt—where they are embroiled in regional warfare and taken as slaves by marauding barbarians. The key to escape from this brutal bondage lies in their own rampant libidos, and urges as old as time itself.
MIND MASTER
$4.95/209-4
Who better to explore the territory of erotic dominance than an author who helped define the genre—and knows that ultimate mastery always transcends the physical.

THE CONSTRUCTION WORKER
$5.95/298-1
A young, hung construction worker is sent to a building project in Central America, where he finds that man-to-man sex is the accepted norm. The young stud quickly fits right in—until he senses that beneath the constant sexual shenanigans there moves an almost supernatural force. A superhot mystery.
2069 TRILOGY
(This one-volume collection only $6.95)244-2
For the first time, Larry Townsend's early science-fiction trilogy appears in one massive volume! Set in a future world, the 2069 Trilogy includes the tight plotting and shameless male sexual pleasure that established him as one of gay erotica's first masters.
THE LONG LEATHER CORD
$4.95/201-9
Chuck's stepfather never lacks money or clandestine male visitors with whom he enacts intense sexual rituals. As Chuck comes to terms with his own desires, he begins to unravel the mystery behind his stepfather's secret life.
MAN SWORD
$4.95/188-8
The tres gai tale of France's King Henri III. Unimaginably spoiled by his mother—the infamous Catherine de Medici—Henri is groomed from a young age to assume the throne of France. Along the way, he encounters enough sexual schemers and randy politicos to alter one's picture of history forever!
THE FAUSTUS CONTRACT
$4.95/167-5
Two attractive young men desperately need $1000. Will do anything. Travel OK. Danger OK. Call anytime... Two cocky young hustlers get more than they bargained for in this story of lust and its discontents.
THE GAY ADVENTURES OF CAPTAIN GOOSE
$4.95/169-1
The hot and tender young Jerome Gander is sentenced to serve aboard the H.M.S. Faerigold—a ship manned by the most hardened, unrepentant criminals. In no time, Gander becomes well-versed in the ways of men at sea, and the Faerigold becomes the most notorious ship of its day.

HITTING HOME
$4.95/222-1
One of our newest Badboys weighs in with a scorching collection of stories. Titillating and compelling, the stories in *Hitting Home* make a strong case for there being only one thing on a man's mind.

TORSTEN BARRING
PRISONERS OF TORQUEMADA
$5.95/252-3
Another punishing volume sure to push you over the edge. How cruel is the "therapy" practiced at Casa Torquemada? Barring is just the writer to evoke such steamy sexual malevolence.
SHADOWMAN
$4.95/178-0
From spoiled Southern aristocrats to randy youths sowing wild oats at the local picture show, Barring's imagination works overtime in these vignettes of homolust—past, present and future.
PETER THORNWELL
$4.95/149-7
Follow the exploits of Peter Thornwell as he goes from misspent youth to scandalous stardom, all thanks to an insatiable libido and love for the lash. Peter and his sex-crazed sidekicks find themselves pursued by merciless men from all walks of life in this torrid take on Horatio Alger.
THE SWITCH
$4.95/3061-X
Sometimes a man needs a good whipping, and *The Switch* certainly makes a case! Laced with images of men "in too-tight Levi's, with the faces of angels... and the bodies of devils." Packed with hot studs and unrelenting passions.

BERT McKENZIE
FRINGE BENEFITS
$5.95/354-6
From the pen of a widely published short story writer comes a volume of highly immodest tales. Not afraid of getting down and dirty, McKenzie produces some of today's most visceral sextales. Learn the real benefits of working long and hard....

SONNY FORD
REUNION IN FLORENCE
$4.95/3070-9
Captured by Turks, Adrian and Tristan will do anything to save their heads. When Tristan is threatened by a Sultan's jealousy, Adrian begins his quest for the only man alive who can replace Tristan as the object of the Sultan's lust.

ROGER HARMAN
FIRST PERSON
$4.95/179-9
A highly personal collection. Each story takes the form of a confessional—told by men who've got plenty to confess! From the "first time ever" to firsts of different kinds.

J.A. GUERRA
SLOW BURN
$4.95/3042-3
Welcome to the Body Shoppe, where men's lives cross in the pursuit of muscle. Torsos get lean and hard, pecs widen, and stomachs ripple in these sexy stories of the power and perils of physical perfection.

SEAN MARTIN
SCRAPBOOK
$4.95/224-8
Imagine a book filled with only the best, most vivid remembrances...a book brimming with every hot, sexy encounter its pages can hold... Now you need only open up *Scrapbook* to know that such a volume really exists....

CARO SOLES & STAN TAL, EDITORS
BIZARRE DREAMS
$4.95/187-X
An anthology of stirring voices dedicated to exploring the dark side of human fantasy. *Bizarre Dreams* brings together the most talented practitioners of "dark fantasy," the most forbidden sexual realm of all.

CHRISTOPHER MORGAN
THE SPORTSMEN
$5.95/385-6
Here are enough tales of carnal grand slams, sexy interceptions and highly personal bests to satisfy the hungers of the most ardent sports fan. Editor Christopher Morgan has gathered those writers who know just the type of guys that make up every red-blooded male's starting line-up....

DIRECT

BADBOY

MUSCLE BOUND
$4.95/3028-8
In the New York City bodybuilding scene, country boy Tommy joins forces with sexy Will Rodriguez in a battle of wits and biceps at the hottest gym in town, where the weak are bound and crushed by iron-pumping gods.

DAVE KINNICK

SORRY I ASKED
$4.95/3090-3
Unexpurgated interviews with gay porn's rank and file. Get personal with the men behind (and under) the "stars," and discover the hot truth about the porn business.

MICHAEL LOWENTHAL, ED.

THE BADBOY EROTIC LIBRARY VOLUME I
$4.95/190-X
Excerpts from *A Secret Life, Imre, Sins of the Cities of the Plain, Teleny* and others demonstrate the uncanny gift for portraying sex between men that led to many of these titles being banned upon publication.

THE BADBOY EROTIC LIBRARY VOLUME II
$4.95/211-6
This time, selections are taken from *Mike and Me* and *Muscle Bound, Men at Work, Badboy Fantasies,* and *Slowburn.*

ERIC BOYD

MIKE AND ME
$5.95/419-4
Mike joined the gym squad to bulk up on muscle. Little did he know he'd be turning on every sexy muscle jock in Minnesota! Hard bodies collide in a series of workouts designed to generate a whole lot more than rips and cuts.

MIKE AND THE MARINES
$5.95/347-3
Mike takes on America's most elite corps of studs—running into more than a few good men! Join in on the never-ending sexual escapades of this singularly lustful platoon!

ANONYMOUS

A SECRET LIFE
$4.95/3017-2
Meet Master Charles: only eighteen, and quite innocent, until his arrival at the Sir Percival's Royal Academy, where the daily lessons are supplemented with a crash course in pure, sweet sexual heat!

SINS OF THE CITIES OF THE PLAIN
$5.95/322-8
ndulge yourself in the scorching memoirs of young man-about-town Jack Saul. With his shocking dalliances with the lords and "ladies" of British high society, Jack's positively sinful escapades grow wilder with every chapter!

IMRE
$4.95/3019-9
What dark secrets, what fiery passions lay hidden behind strikingly beautiful Lieutenant Imre's emerald eyes? An extraordinary lost classic of fantasy, obsession, gay erotic desire, and romance in a small European town on the eve of WWI.

THE SCARLET PANSY
$4.95/189-6
A white-hot gay camp classic. The story of Randall Etrange, travelling the world in search of true love. Along the way, he engages one and all, as his journey becomes a sexual odyssey of truly epic proportions.

TELENY
$4.95/3020-2
Often attributed to Oscar Wilde, *Teleny* tells the story of one young man of independent means. He dedicates himself to a succession of pleasures, but instead finds love and tragedy when he becomes embroiled in a mysterious cult devoted to fulfilling only the very darkest of fantasies.

PAT CALIFIA

THE SEXPERT
$4.95/3034-2
The sophisticated gay man knows that he can turn to one authority for answers to virtually any question on the subjects of intimacy and sexual performance. Straight from the pages of *Advocate Men* comes The Sexpert, responding to real-life sexual concerns with uncanny wisdom and a razor wit.

HARD CANDY

PATRICK MOORE

IOWA
$6.95/423-2
"Moore is the Tennessee Williams of the nineties—profound intimacy freed in a compelling narrative."
—Karen Finley

"Patrick Moore has...taken the classic story of the Midwest American boyhood and he's done it fresh and shiny and relevant to our time. Iowa is full of terrific characters etched in acid-sharp prose, soaked through with just enough ambivalence to make it thoroughly romantic."—Felice Picano

A stunning novel about one gay man's journey into adulthood, and the roads that bring him home again. From the author of the highly praised *This Every Night*.

STAN LEVENTHAL

BARBIE IN BONDAGE
$6.95/415-1
Widely regarded as one of the most refreshing, interpreters of big city gay life, Leventhal here provides a series of explorations of love and desire between men. Uncompromising, but gentle and generous, *Barbie in Bondage* is a fitting tribute to the late author's unique talents.

SKYDIVING ON CHRISTOPHER STREET
$6.95/287-6
"Positively addictive." —Dennis Cooper

Aside from a hateful job, a hateful apartment, a hateful world and an increasingly hateful lover, life seems, well, all right for the protagonist of Stan Leventhal's latest novel. Having already lost most of his friends to AIDS, how could things get any worse? But things soon do, and he's forced to endure much more....

WALTER R. HOLLAND

THE MARCH
$6.95/429-1
A moving testament to the power of friendship during even the worst of times. Beginning on a hot summer night in 1980, *The March* revolves around a circle of young gay men, and the many others their lives touch. Over time, each character changes in unexpected ways; lives and loves come together and fall apart, as society itself is horribly altered by the onslaught of AIDS.

RED JORDAN AROBATEAU

LUCY AND MICKEY
$6.95/311-2
The story of Mickey—an uncompromising butch—and her long affair with Lucy, the femme she loves.A raw tale of pre-Stonewall lesbian life.

"A necessary reminder to all who blissfully—some may say ignorantly—ride the wave of lesbian chic into the mainstream." —Heather Findlay

DIRTY PICTURES
$5.95/345-7
"Red Jordan Arobateau is the Thomas Wolfe of lesbian literature... Arobateau's work overflows with vitality and pulsing life. She's a natural—raw talent that is seething, passionate, hard, remarkable."
—Lillian Faderman, editor of *Chloe Plus Olivia*

Dirty Pictures is the story of a lonely butch tending bar—and the femme she finally calls her own.

LARS EIGHNER

GAY COSMOS
$6.95/236-1
A title sure to appeal not only to Eighner's gay fans, but the many converts who first encountered his moving nonfiction work. Praised by the press, *Gay Cosmos* is an important contribution to the burgeoning area of Gay and Lesbian Studies—and sure to provoke many readers.

DONALD VINING

A GAY DIARY: 1933-1946
$8.95/451-8
Donald Vining's *Diary* portrays a long-vanished age and the lifestyle of a gay generation all too frequently forgotten. A touching and revealing volume documenting the surprisingly vibrant culture that existed decades before Stonewal.

"*A Gay Diary* is, unquestionably, the richest historical document of gay male life in the United States that I have ever encountered.... It chronicles a whole life in which homosexuality is but one part and an ever-changing part at that. And, it illuminates a critical period in gay male American history." —Body Politic

HARD CANDY

FELICE PICANO

AMBIDEXTROUS
$6.95/275-2

"Deftly evokes those placid Eisenhower years of bicycles, boners, and book reports. Makes us remember what it feels like to be a child..."

—*The Advocate*

"Compelling and engrossing... will conjure up memories of everyone's adolescence, straight or gay."

—*Out!*

Picano's "memoir in the form of a novel" tells all: home life, school face-offs, the ingenuousness of his first sexual steps. Soon, he's had his first gay fling—and is on his way to becoming the widely praised writer he is today.

MEN WHO LOVED ME
$6.95/274-4

"Zesty... spiked with adventure and romance.... a distinguished and humorous portrait of a vanished age."

—*Publishers Weekly*

"A stunner... captures the free-wheeling spirit of an era."

—*The Advocate*

"Rich, engaging, engrossing... a ravishingly exotic romance."

—*New York Native*

In 1966, Picano abandoned New York, determined to find true love in Europe. When the older and wiser Picano returns to New York at last, he plunges into the city's thriving gay community—experiencing the frenzy and heartbreak that came to define Greenwich Village society in the 1970s.

THE LURE
$6.95/398-8

"The subject matter, plus the authenticity of Picano's research are, combined, explosive. Felice Picano is one hell of a writer."

—Stephen King

After witnessing a brutal murder, Noel is recruited by the police, to assist as a lure for the killer. Undercover, he moves deep into the freneticism of Manhattan's gay high-life—where he gradually becomes aware of the darker forces at work in his life. In addition to the mystery behind his mission, he begins to recognize changes...in himself...

WILLIAM TALSMAN

THE GAUDY IMAGE
$6.95/263-9

"To read *The Gaudy Image* now...it is to see first-hand the very issues of identity and positionality with which gay men were struggling in the decades before Stonewall. For what Talsman is dealing with...is the very question of how we conceive ourselves gay."

—from the introduction by Michael Bronski

Email us!
MasqBks@aol.com

ROSEBUD

THE ROSEBUD READER
$5.95/319-8
Rosebud has contributed greatly to the burgeoning genre of lesbian erotica—to the point that authors like Lindsay Welsh, Aarona Griffin and Valentina Cilescu are among the hottest and most closely watched names in lesbian and gay publishing. Here are the finest moments from Rosebud's contemporary classics.

RED JORDAN AROBATEAU
BOYS NIGHT OUT
$6.50/463-1
A *Red*-hot volume of short fiction from this lesbian literary sensation. As always, Arobateau takes a good hard look at the lives of everyday women, noting well the struggles and triumphs each woman experiences. Never one to shrink from the less-than-chic truth, Red Jordan Arobateau has carved herself a niche as the foremost chronicler of working class dyke life.

ALISON TYLER
DARK ROOM: AN ONLINE ADVENTURE
$6.50/455-0
Dani, a successful photographer, can't bring herself to face the death of her lover, Kate. An ambitious journalist, Kate was found mysteriously murdered, leaving her lover with only fond memories of a too-brief relationship. Determined to keep the memory of her lover alive, Dani goes online under Kate's screen alias—and begins to uncover the truth behind the crime that has torn her world apart.

BLUE SKY SIDEWAYS & OTHER STORIES
$6.50/394-5
A variety of women, and their many breathtaking experiences with lovers, friends—and even the occasional sexy stranger. From blossoming young beauties to fearless vixens, Tyler finds the sexy pleasures of everyday life.

DIAL "L" FOR LOVELESS
$5.95/386-4
Meet Katrina Loveless—a private eye talented enough to give Sam Spade a run for his money. In her first case, Katrina investigates a murder implicating a host of society's darlings—including wealthy Tessa and Baxter Saint Claire, and the lovely, tantalizing, infamous Geneva twins. Loveless untangles the mess—while working herself into a variety of highly compromising knots with the many lovelies who cross her path!

THE VIRGIN
$5.95/379-1
Veronica answers a personal ad in the "Women Seeking Women" category—and discovers a whole sensual world she never knew existed! And she never dreamed she'd be prized as a virgin all over again, by someone who would deflower her with a passion no man could ever show....

THE BLUE ROSE
$5.95/335-X
The tale of a modern sorority—fashioned after a Victorian girls' school. Ignited to the heights of passion by erotic tales of the Victorian age, a group of lusty young women are encouraged to act out their forbidden fantasies—all under the tutelage of Mistresses Emily and Justine!

K. T. BUTLER
TOOLS OF THE TRADE
$5.95/420-8
A sparkling mix of lesbian erotica and humor. An encounter with ice cream, cappuccino and chocolate cake; an affair with a complete stranger; a pair of faulty handcuffs; and love on a drafting table. Seventeen tales.

LOVECHILD
GAG
$5.95/369-4
From New York's poetry scene comes this explosive volume of work from one of the bravest, most cutting young writers you'll ever encounter. The poems in *Gag* take on American hypocrisy with uncommon energy, and announce Lovechild as a writer of unforgettable rage.

ELIZABETH OLIVER
THE SM MURDER: MURDER AT ROMAN HILL
$5.95/353-8
Intrepid lesbian P.I.s Leslie Patrick and Robin Penny take on a really hot case: the murder of the notorious Felicia Roman. The circumstances of the crime lead the pair on an excursion through the leatherdyke underground, where motives—and desires—run deep.

PAGAN DREAMS
$5.95/295-7
Cassidy and Samantha plan a vacation at a secluded bed-and-breakfast, hoping for a little personal time alone. Their hostess, however, has different plans. The lovers are plunged into a world of dungeons and pagan rites, as Anastasia steals Samantha for her own.

ROSEBUD

SUSAN ANDERS

CITY OF WOMEN
$5.95/375-9
Stories dedicated to women and the passions that draw them together. Designed strictly for the sensual pleasure of women, these tales are set to ignite flames of passion from coast to coast.

PINK CHAMPAGNE
$5.95/282-5
Tasty, torrid tales of butch/femme couplings. Tough as nails or soft as silk, these women seek out their antitheses, intent on working out the details of their own personal theory of difference.

LAURA ANTONIOU, EDITOR

LEATHERWOMEN
$4.95/3095-4
These fantasies, from the pens of new or emerging authors, break every rule imposed on women's fantasies. The hottest stories from some of today's newest and most outrageous writers make this an unforgettable exploration of the female libido.

LEATHERWOMEN II
$4.95/229-9
Laura Antoniou turns an editor's discerning eye to the writings of women on the edge—resulting in a collection sure to ignite libidinal flames. Leave taboos behind, because these Leatherwomen know no limits....

AARONA GRIFFIN

PASSAGE AND OTHER STORIES
$4.95/3057-1
An S/M romance. Lovely Nina is frightened by her lesbian passions, until she finds herself infatuated with a woman she spots at a local café. One night Nina follows her, and finds herself enmeshed in an endless maze leading to a world where women test the edges of sexuality and power.

VALENTINA CILESCU

MY LADY'S PLEASURE:
WOMAN WITH A MAID VOLUME I
$5.95/412-7
Dr. Claudia Dungarrow, a lovely, powerful, but mysterious figure at St. Matilda's College, attempts to seduce virginal Elizabeth Stanbridge, she sets off a chain of events that eventually ruins her career. Claudia vows revenge—and makes her foes pay deliciously....

THE ROSEBUD SUTRA
$4.95/242-6
"Women are hardly ever known in their true light, though they may love others, or become indifferent towards them, may give them delight, or abandon them, or may extract from them all the wealth that they possess." One woman learns to use these secrets in a quest for pleasure with a succession of lady loves....

THE HAVEN
$4.95/165-9
J craves domination, and her perverse appetites lead her to the Haven: the isolated sanctuary Ros and Annie call home. Soon J forces her way into the couple's world, bringing unspeakable lust and cruelty into their lives.

MISTRESS MINE
$5.95/445-3
Sophia Cranleigh sits in prison, accused of authoring the "obscene" *Mistress Mine*. What she has done, however, is merely chronicle the events of her life—to the outrage of many. For Sophia has led no ordinary life, but has slaved and suffered—deliciously—under the hand of the notorious Mistress Malin.

LINDSAY WELSH

SECOND SIGHT
$6.50/507-7
The debut of Dana Steele—lesbian superhero! During an attack by a gang of homophobic youths, Dana is thrown onto subway tracks—touching the deadly third rail. Finding herself endowed with superhuman powers, Dana devotes them to the protection of her lesbian sisters, no matter how daunting the danger they face. With the help of her lover Astrid, Dana stands poised to a legend in her own time.

NASTY PERSUASIONS
$6.50/436-4

A hot peek into the behind-the-scenes operations of Rough Trade—one of the world's most famous lesbian clubs. Join Slash, Ramone, Cherry and many others as they bring one another to the height of torturous ecstasy—all in the name of keeping Rough Trade the premier name in sexy entertainment for women.

MILITARY SECRETS
$5.95/397-X

Colonel Candice Sproule heads a highly specialized boot camp. Assisted by three dominatrix sergeants, Col. Sproule takes on the talented submissives sent to her by secret military contacts. Then comes Jesse—whose pleasure in being served matches the Colonel's own. This new recruit sets off fireworks in the barracks—and beyond....

ROMANTIC ENCOUNTERS
$5.95/359-7

Beautiful Julie, the most powerful editor of romance novels in the industry, spends her days igniting women's passions through books—and her nights fulfilling those needs with a variety of lovers. Finally, through a sizzling series of coincidences, Julie's two worlds come together explosively!

THE BEST OF LINDSAY WELSH
$5.95/368-6

A collection of this popular writer's best work. This author was one of Rosebud's early bestsellers, and remains highly popular. A sampler set to introduce some of the hottest lesbian erotica to a wider audience.

NECESSARY EVIL
$5.95/277-9

What's a girl to do? When her Mistress proves too systematic, too by-the-book, one lovely submissive takes the ultimate chance—choosing and creating a Mistress who'll fulfill her heart's desire. Little did she know how difficult it would be—and, in the end, rewarding....

A VICTORIAN ROMANCE
$5.95/365-1

Lust-letters from the road. A young Englishwoman realizes her dream—a trip abroad under the guidance of her eccentric maiden aunt. Soon, the young but blossoming Elaine comes to discover her own sexual talents, as a hot-blooded Parisian named Madelaine takes her Sapphic education in hand.

A CIRCLE OF FRIENDS
$4.95/250-7

The story of a remarkable group of women. The women pair off to explore all the possibilities of lesbian passion, until finally it seems that there is nothing—and no one—they have not dabbled in.

BAD HABITS
$5.95/446-1

What does one do with a poorly trained slave? Break her of her bad habits, of course! The story of the ultimate finishing school, Bad Habits was an immediate favorite with women nationwide. "Talk about passing the wet test!... If you like hot, lesbian erotica, run—don't walk—and pick up a copy of *Bad Habits*."

—*Lambda Book Report*

ANNABELLE BARKER
MOROCCO
$4.95/148-9

A luscious young woman stands to inherit a fortune—if she can only withstand the ministrations of her cruel guardian until her twentieth birthday. With two months left, Lila makes a bold bid for freedom, only to find that liberty has its own excruciating and delicious price....

A.L. REINE
DISTANT LOVE & OTHER STORIES
$4.95/3056-3

In the title story, Leah Michaels and her lover, Ranelle, have had four years of blissful, smoldering passion together. When Ranelle is out of town, Leah records an audio "Valentine:" a cassette filled with erotic reminiscences....

A RICHARD KASAK BOOK

MICHAEL FORD, EDITOR
ONCE UPON A TIME:
EROTIC FAIRY TALES FOR WOMEN
$12.95/449-6

How relevant to contemporary lesbians are the lessons of these age-old tales? The contributors to *Once Upon a Time*—some of the biggest names in contemporary lesbian literature—retell their favorite fairy tales, adding their own surprising—and sexy—twists. *Once Upon a Time* is sure to be one of contemporary lesbian literature's classic collections. Includes work by Dorothy Allison, Red Jordan Arobateau, and many of today's most provocative writers.

HAPPILY EVER AFTER:
EROTIC FAIRY TALES FOR MEN
$12.95/450-X

A hefty volume of bedtime stories Mother Goose never thought to write down. Adapting some of childhood's most beloved tales for the adult gay reader, the contributors to *Happily Ever After* dig up the subtext of these hitherto "innocent" diversions—adding some surprises of their own along the way. Includes stories by Larry Townsend, Michael Lassell, Bruce Benderson, Mark Thompson and others.

MICHAEL BRONSKI, EDITOR
TAKING LIBERTIES: GAY MEN'S ESSAYS
ON POLITICS, CULTURE AND SEX
$12.95/456-9

"*Taking Liberties* offers undeniable proof of a heady, sophisticated, diverse new culture of gay intellectual debate. I cannot recommend it too highly."
—Christopher Bram

Taking Liberties brings together some of the most divergent views on the state of contemporary gay male culture published in recent years. Michael Bronski here presents some of the community's foremost essayists who weigh in on such slippery topics as outing, masculine identity, pornography, the pedophile controversy, community definition, political strategy—and much more.

FLASHPOINT: GAY MALE SEXUAL WRITING
$12.95/424-0

A collection of the most provocative testaments to gay eros. Michael Bronski presents over twenty of the genre's best writers, exploring areas such as Enlightenment, True Life Adventures and more. Sure to be one of the most talked about and influential volumes ever dedicated to the exploration of gay sexuality.

SHAR REDNOUR, EDITOR
VIRGIN TERRITORY
$12.95/457-7

Writing by women about their first-time erotic experiences with other women. From the longings and ecstasies of awakening dykes to the sometimes awkward pleasures of sexual experimentation on the edge, each of these true stories reveals a different, radical perspective on one of the most traditional subjects around: virginity.

HEATHER FINDLAY, EDITOR
A MOVEMENT OF EROS:
25 YEARS OF LESBIAN EROTICA
$12.95/421-6

One of the most scintillating overviews of lesbian erotic writing ever published. Heather Findlay has assembled a roster of stellar talents, each represented by their best work. Tracing the course of the genre from its pre-Stonewall roots to its current renaissance, Findlay examines each piece, placing it within the context of lesbian community and politics.

LARRY TOWNSEND
ASK LARRY
$12.95/289-2

Starting just before the onslaught of AIDS, Townsend wrote the "Leather Notebook" column for *Drummer* magazine. Now, readers can avail themselves of Townsend's collected wisdom, as well as the author's contemporary commentary—a careful consideration of the way life has changed in the AIDS era. From Daddies to dog collars, and belts to bruises, *Ask Larry* is an essential volume for any man worth his leathers.

CHARLES HENRI FORD & PARKER TYLER
THE YOUNG AND EVIL
$12.95/431-3
"*The Young and Evil* creates [its] generation as *This Side of Paradise* by Fitzgerald created his generation."
—Gertrude Stein

Originally published in 1933, *The Young and Evil* was an immediate sensation due to its unprecedented portrayal of young gay artists living in New York's notorious Greenwich Village. From flamboyant drag balls to squalid bohemian flats, these characters followed love and art wherever it led them—with a frankness that had the novel banned.

MICHAEL LASSELL
THE HARD WAY
$12.95/231-0
"Lassell is a master of the necessary word. In an age of tepid and whining verse, his bawdy and bittersweet songs are like a plunge in cold champagne." —Paul Monette

The first collection of renowned gay writer Michael Lassell's poetry, fiction and essays. A compendium of a remarkable writer's work.

AMARANTHA KNIGHT, EDITOR
LOVE BITES
$12.95/234-5
A volume of tales dedicated to legend's sexiest demon—the Vampire. Not only the finest collection of erotic horror available—but a virtual who's who of promising new talent. A must for fans of both the horror and erotic genres.

RANDY TUROFF, EDITOR
LESBIAN WORDS: STATE OF THE ART
$10.95/340-6
"This is a terrific book that should be on every thinking lesbian's bookshelf."
—Nisa Donnelly

One of the widest assortments of lesbian nonfiction writing in one revealing volume. Dorothy Allison, Jewelle Gomez, Judy Grahn, Eileen Myles, Robin Podolsky and many others are represented by some of their best work, looking at not only the current fashionability the media has brought to the lesbian "image," but important considerations of the lesbian past via historical inquiry and personal recollections.

MICHAEL ROWE
WRITING BELOW THE BELT:
CONVERSATIONS WITH EROTIC AUTHORS
$19.95/363-5
"An in-depth and enlightening tour of society's love/hate relationship with sex, morality, and censorship."
—James White Review

Journalist Michael Rowe interviewed the best erotic writers and presents the collected wisdom in *Writing Below the Belt*. Rowe speaks frankly with cult favorites such as Pat Califia, crossover success stories like John Preston, and up-and-comers Michael Lowenthal and Will Leber. A volume dedicated to chronicling the insights of some of this overlooked genre's most renowned practitioners.

FELICE PICANO
DRYLAND'S END
$12.95/279-5
The science fiction debut of the highly acclaimed author of *Men Who Loved Me* and *Like People in History*. Set five thousand years in the future, *Dryland's End* takes place in a fabulous techno-empire ruled by intelligent, powerful women. While the Matriarchy has ruled for over two thousand years and altered human language, thought and society, it is now unraveling. Military rivalries, religious fanaticism and economic competition threaten to destroy the mighty empire.

RUSS KICK
OUTPOSTS:
A CATALOG OF RARE AND DISTURBING
ALTERNATIVE INFORMATION
$18.95/0202-8
A huge, authoritative guide to some of the most bizarre publications available today! Rather than simply summarize the plethora of opinions crowding the American scene, Kick has tracked down and compiled reviews of work penned by political extremists, conspiracy theorists, hallucinogenic pathfinders, sexual explorers, and others. Each review is followed by ordering information for the many readers sure to want these publications for themselves.

ORDERING IS EASY!

MC/VISA orders can be placed by calling our toll-free number

PHONE 800-375-2356 / FAX 212 986-7355

or mail this coupon to:

MASQUERADE DIRECT

DEPT. BMRK86   **801 2ND AVE., NY, NY 10017**

BUY ANY FOUR BOOKS AND CHOOSE ONE ADDITIONAL BOOK, OF EQUAL OR LESSER VALUE, AS YOUR FREE GIFT.

QTY.	TITLE	NO.	PRICE
			FREE
			FREE

WE NEVER SELL, GIVE OR TRADE ANY CUSTOMER'S NAME.

BMRK86

SUBTOTAL _____

POSTAGE and HANDLING _____

TOTAL _____

In the U.S., please add $1.50 for the first book and 75¢ for each additional book; in Canada, add $2.00 for the first book and $1.25 for each additional book. Foreign countries: add $4.00 for the first book and $2.00 for each additional book. No C.O.D. orders. Please make all checks payable to Masquerade Books. Payable in U.S. currency only. New York state residents add 8.25% sales tax. Please allow 4-6 weeks for delivery.

NAME _____

ADDRESS _____

CITY _____ STATE _____ ZIP _____

TEL ( ) _____

PAYMENT: ☐ CHECK ☐ MONEY ORDER ☐ VISA ☐ MC

CARD NO. _____ EXP. DATE _____